BRIEF LIFE

Brief Life

COMPILED, EDITED, AND ARRANGED BY
KEVIN MARC FOURNIER

ENFIELD
&WIZENTY

Enfield & Wizenty
(an imprint of Great Plains Publications)
320 Rosedale Ave
Winnipeg, MB R3L 1L8
www.greatplains.mb.ca

Great Plains Publications gratefully acknowledges the financial support provided for its publishing program by the Government of Canada through the Canada Book Fund; the Canada Council for the Arts; the Province of Manitoba through the Book Publishing Tax Credit and the Book Publisher Marketing Assistance Program; and the Manitoba Arts Council.

Design & Typography by Relish New Brand Experience
Printed in Canada by Friesens

Library and Archives Canada Cataloguing in Publication

Title: A brief life : a novel / Kevin Marc Fournier.
Names: Fournier, Kevin Marc, 1974- author.
Identifiers: Canadiana (print) 20220244553 | Canadiana (ebook) 2022024457X |
    ISBN 9781773370811 (softcover) | ISBN 9781773370828 (ebook)
Subjects: LCGFT: Novels.
Classification: LCC PS8611.O874 B75 2022 | DDC C813/.6—dc23

ENVIRONMENTAL BENEFITS STATEMENT

Great Plains Publications saved the following resources by printing the pages of this book on chlorine free paper made with 100% post-consumer waste.

TREES	WATER	ENERGY	SOLID WASTE	GREENHOUSE GASES
10	830	4	36	4,470
FULLY GROWN	GALLONS	MILLION BTUs	POUNDS	POUNDS

Environmental impact estimates were made using the Environmental Paper Network Paper Calculator 4.0. For more information visit www.papercalculator.org

Canadä

FSC
www.fsc.org
MIX
Paper from
responsible sources
FSC® C016245

for Sarah, as always

PEOPLE WHO DREAM WHEN THEY SLEEP AT NIGHT know of a special kind of happiness which the world of the day holds not, a placid ecstasy, and ease of heart, that are like honey on the tongue. They also know that the real glory of dreams lies in their atmosphere of unlimited freedom. It is not the freedom of the dictator, who enforces his own will on the world, but the freedom of the artist, who has no will, who is free of will. The pleasure of the true dreamer does not lie in the substance of the dream, but in this: that there things happen without interference from his side, and altogether outside his control.—Isak Dinesen, *Out of Africa*

foreword

IN A BETTER WORLD, all books would only ever be published posthumously. In a perfect world, there might be no books written at all. Fortunately, the world is far from perfect; unfortunately, it isn't getting better.

Before sunrise the city is cool, fresh, and quiet, the stars revolve slowly across the sky, and all things seem attainable. Then you dress, wash, and eat your breakfast, and before long it is noon. Then you realize how quickly time passes. The day slips by like water in a stream, and the days slip by like water in the river. Weeks pass and years have passed; the sun, stars, and moon revolve in their dependable circuits, but the winds come and go as they please, the clouds form and scatter and form again, and we don't know what shape they'll take from one minute to the next. All that we know is that time passes, and all the time there is a continual change going on. Some change has taken place even since I began to write this sentence.

What delights me is the company and conversation of my family and friends. We do not wish to injure anyone, or make the world conform to our demands, and therefore our conversation is of no consequence to anyone else. But life scatters friends like the winds scatter clouds; preserving those conversations would be like trying to carry water in your bare hands. Children grow old, parents grow older; friends move away, or fall silent; the happiest days pass fastest. In the summers sometimes I sit by the lake and watch the waves lap peacefully at the sand, each wave fleeting and unique.

I have written and rewritten this *Brief Life* just for my own pleasure in the early mornings before the sun rises, before my family is awake. All of it is true, except for the parts I made up, which is most of them, or the other parts that I have changed, which is the rest of them. I have written down the story as it occurred to me, and even more I have rewritten it over and over again, for then I could enjoy the ephemeral but pleasant illusion that time is not forever escaping me. Life passes fast, but writing goes slow.

I set out in the beginning to record a brief life of Addy Mack; with a different approach and a little more effort, I could have written it out on a rolling paper. But what is the use of telling Addy's story, how could you understand it, if you don't understand the stories of the people and places who mattered to her life? And what is the use of telling *their* stories, if you don't also understand the stories of the people who mattered to *them*? And there is no end of telling stories, there is no end of things in the heart.

Someone may ask, "Why are you publishing this book, when you aren't even dead yet?" To which I reply (1) having written the damn thing, I might as well try to do something with it; (2) because at some point if I didn't send it away, I could only spoil it more with my endless tinkering; and (3) because it is just a hodgepodge of nonsense anyway, and cannot make me famous or even shame me.

I shall be glad and grateful if a few of my friends and family will read it and be entertained. Perhaps old friends, friends who have scattered like clouds, friends I no longer know how to talk to, will happen across it, and be reminded of old conversations and long-ago adventures, and smile for a while. Also everything anyone does will be posthumous eventually anyway, so why worry about it?

a

Brief Life

of

Adelaide

Mack

Table of Contents

prologue

THIS HAPPENED TO ADELAIDE MACK when she took the Greyhound bus from Montreal to Winnipeg for Nora and Davey's wedding. Nora was the oldest, closest friend of Addy's mother, Casey; more than that, Nora had always been like a second and surrogate mother to Addy herself, and Nora's children Jack and Natalie had been like Addy's brother and sister.

Addy was sixteen at the time, but they almost wouldn't sell her a ticket because they said she looked twelve, and where the hell were her parents? And even after she showed them all her ID they didn't want to do it, they said it was probably fake or her older sister's ID or something, and they made noises about calling the police, calling child protective services. She ended up having to ask a stranger at the bus station to pose as a parent and buy the ticket for her, and he charged her twenty bucks to do it.

The trip takes about thirty-six hours, two nights and a day. The first night was pretty rough. They left Montreal at nine p.m. and it was absolutely packed, she couldn't even get a window seat. All the way to Ottawa she had to sit next to this greasy old guy in his thirties who absolutely reeked of booze, it was practically coming out his pores. He kept asking her sly and creepy questions about why a "pretty young thing" like her was travelling alone, and wasn't she scared, and how far was she headed? An aluminum button, black with red letters, was pinned to the breast of his blue denim jacket and said, "Evil Steve." He kept offering her a drink out of his coke bottle that he had obviously spiked with something, vodka or rubbing alcohol or something, you could smell it every time he unscrewed the cap. He was so creepy he even asked her a question about her old surgical scar, which meant he must have been peering down her shirt to see it.

Luckily they had to get out and transfer buses in Ottawa at midnight, with forty minutes of standing around waiting. She managed to slip away from Evil Steve in the station, and he didn't get on the next bus, thank God; but from there to North Bay she had to sit next to a man with flabby hairless arms who had the disconcerting habit of sleeping with his eyes half open, snoring in fits. He wouldn't let her put on the overhead light so she couldn't read or write in her notebook, and she couldn't see anything out the window except an occasional smear of passing lights, and the minutes crept by with agonizing slowness. In North Bay she got one of her nosebleeds and had to ride all the way to Sudbury with a twist of toilet paper hanging from one nostril. But that was okay, because it kept anyone from wanting to sit next to her, even though the bus was still pretty full.

They had breakfast in Sudbury, where they had to transfer buses again. Addy had a chocolate bar and two extra-large cups of coffee for breakfast. She went for a bit of a walk, but there was nothing to see except the highway, and muddy fields, and occasional mounds of grey and brown half-melted snow, and a flat grey industrial haze hanging over everything.

That day's trip was much better. They passed through nothing but small towns; the biggest was Sault Ste Marie, where they stopped for lunch. There were a ton of little stops, in towns that all rather looked the same, and Addy got off the bus at every single one of those stops to stretch her legs and look around.

Making their way around the north shore of Lake Superior, the landscape was beautiful, all jagged looming rock face and tall skinny pines, bent and swaying. The bus was only half full now, she had a window seat and no one next to her, and she passed the time by writing in her notebook about the people on the bus with her, making up names for them and inventing little stories about their lives. For food she ate nothing but squashed warm granola bars and small stale raisins from a baggy in her backpack; she had decided she'd better not spend her rapidly dwindling cash on anything but hot coffee, which was expensive as hell at most of the stops. In Schreiber, out of sheer boredom, she bummed a cigarette off a woman with a puffy green jacket and henna-red hair beneath a green trucker's cap. The woman was very kind, told her how she was going to visit her grandkids in Thunder Bay, and Addy's legs almost buckled under her: the cigarette made her so dizzy and lightheaded she saw spots in front of her eyes. It tasted disgusting, it tasted like somebody's ass, and it gave her gas pains all the way to Nipigon, so that was interesting.

They got to Thunder Bay at about ten-thirty the second evening and had almost an hour's layover. Addy was starving, but she'd run out of supplies and was very nearly out of money. She finally decided to spend the last of her cash on a plastic-wrapped sandwich bun—turkey breast, wilted lettuce, and highly suspect mayonnaise—and almost instantly regretted it. Then she went and stood outside in the dark and the drizzling rain until it was time to reboard.

She was so tired she found she had been staring at an old poster on a telephone pole for several minutes before she even realized she was reading it. It was a grainy and poorly printed snapshot of a young woman standing beside what looked like those big gates at North Bay, and trying to smile. The young woman was wearing a green and plastic poncho with the hood pulled back, and she had stringy long black hair, bleached in streaks, and her face was puffy and smeared, her eyes sunk deep and hollow. Underneath the photo it said:

Tanya Akiwenzie
Last seen on the Greyhound bus
between Nipigon and Thunder Bay

Below that were some dates, a few phone numbers, and a small sad final plea: "Come home Tanya, we miss you very much."

Something about the girl's face on the poster stuck uncomfortably in Addy's head, she couldn't say why. Maybe it was something about the sad brave way the girl was trying to smile, or maybe it was just because Addy was so overtired.

They had to stop and get off again at Dryden at two-thirty in the damn morning—which was really three-thirty, because they'd gained an hour just west of Thunder Bay—anyway, it was the middle of the night, and they had to all get off and just sit there for half an hour while the bus got cleaned and refuelled. Of course nothing was open, there were a couple of dusty vending machines but Addy had no money left at all. Everyone was exhausted, strung out, huddled, and cold. Dryden smelled like burnt plastic and old piss. Addy bummed another cigarette, which tasted even worse than the first and made her cough so hard she almost threw up, and then she sat outside on the cold hard bench, hands in the pocket of her hoodie, half in and half out of sleep.

As she sat there, Addy suddenly heard a snatch of conversation going on, sounding very close beside her. There was a young man's voice, all loud and agitated, and he was saying, "She was sitting right beside me, she *could*n't have got off the bus." And the other voice, an older man's voice, was trying to calm him down, soothe him, and saying they would do everything they could.

Addy looked around to see who was speaking—only there was absolutely no one there, no one anywhere near her, and now the voices faded away. Except for one lone woman in a blue jumpsuit who was carrying cleaning supplies off the bus, there was just simply no one, everyone else was inside the station, sleeping, keeping warm. She decided she must have nodded off and dreamed it; or maybe she had been hallucinating, that would be cool. She'd always heard that if you go without sleep for long enough you'll start to hallucinate, but it had never actually happened to her before.

Back on the bus and moving again, Addy took her notebook out and turned it to a blank page, but she found she was too tired to write anything; she stared out the window at black nothing and faint reflections, and then she pressed her forehead against the window because it felt cool, and then she fell asleep.

She woke up, abruptly, about an hour, maybe an hour and a half later. Glancing down at the notebook on her lap, she saw that someone had written something on the page. Or maybe she had written something in her sleep; her pen was still propped loosely in her hand. The handwriting didn't look all that different from her own, either, except that the whole sentence was written backwards: all the letters and words were exactly reversed. It said, quite simply: *Help me.*

Now Addy really did feel sick, her stomach lurched, beads of clammy sweat sprung out on her hands and forehead, and she could feel the vomit at the back of her mouth. She got up and made her way quickly and carefully to the back of the bus, unsteady on her feet, past the rows of sleeping passengers, and locked herself into the little washroom.

She kneeled down at the toilet, leaned over, and threw up. It was probably lucky she'd eaten so little and had nothing much in her to vomit; but after the sandwich came up she dry-heaved a bit, and then kept kneeling there a while, forcing herself to breathe slowly. Now that she had thrown up, she felt a lot better. It must have been the mayonnaise on that damn sandwich. She was still leaning over the toilet bowl when three drops of thin bright blood dropped from her nose, plip plip plip. "Goddammit," she said. It was just one thing after another, this trip. She stood up carefully as the bus swayed and lurched along the narrow highway, grabbed a handful of toilet paper, and turned around to look in the mirror.

Except that she didn't see herself looking back out of the mirror—she saw the girl from that missing poster, looking thinner and paler than she had in the photo but the same girl without a doubt, tears in her eyes, her hands moving against the surface of the glass. And the girl could see Addy too, that was certain; she mouthed some words, but no sound came out.

Addy leapt away from the mirror, hitting the back of her knee against the toilet bowl and falling awkwardly down as the bus lurched again. It hurt like a bugger. She thought she might have even screamed, but no one came running, no one knocked on the door or asked if she was all right, so she must not have. She was terrified to look in the mirror again, but somehow she felt impelled to; and very slowly, very hesitantly, she stood up again and looked.

The girl was still in there, but now she was sitting away from the mirror, hunched on the floor beside the toilet, her face in her hands, silently crying. Addy lifted her hand and tapped gently on the glass with her knuckle. The girl didn't seem to hear her, so she was going to try again, a little louder, when she realized that in the mirror, the door to the bathroom was sitting half open.

She turned quickly to look at the real door behind her. It was still closed, the latch still turned to lock. She looked back into the mirror, and suddenly someone—or something—else was there, scuttling in through the door and flopping abruptly up against the glass, its mouth open wide.

Addy got off the bus when it made the next stop in Kenora, and she refused to get back on. She let it just leave without her, with all her luggage still in it: and to this day, she refuses to tell me exactly what she saw in that mirror.

I

*The family gathers for a wedding in Whittle;
Jack feels sorry for a neglected dog*

IT'S TRUE THAT Jack once asked Addy to marry him, but he
insists it didn't really mean anything. This was over the weekend
of his Aunt Tracy's wedding out in Whittle, when they were
both only nine years old, too young to understand what marriage
actually meant anyway. Besides, when he asked her it was late in
the evening after a long and exciting day, and he had been half
delirious with exhaustion.

They were staying with his grandparents for the weekend, and
because his mother and his little sister were both in the wedding
party—Nora a bridesmaid and Natalie the flower girl—he and
Addy had been stuck with one another for much of the day,
surrounded by drunk and giddy adults whom they had never
met but who had known both Jack and Addy's mothers way back
when, and who kept looming up and telling them what a cute
couple they made, and were they going to have a wedding like
this one day too?

The whole day had seemed to consist of being dragged in a
great rush from one place to another, and then forced to wait; at
any given moment Jack had felt like he was either being told to
hurry up, or told to sit still. It was a hot day, cloudless and bright,
too hot by far for early June, and Jack in his black suit had suffered
horribly. He'd never worn a suit before, and he was shocked at
how stiff the white shirt was, and the cuffs chafed his wrists and
the collar rubbed a little raw patch on the back of his neck, but

he didn't complain. Addy did: she was wearing black too, a puffy black gown with a thick white bow in back that Nora had bought for her especially, complaining bitterly about the cost, and that Addy had flatly refused to wear right up until the moment that she did. She even let Nora wash and thoroughly brush her hair without a battle—whether because she sensed that Nora was near the snapping point and wisely decided not to push her, or for other reasons all her own, was hard to guess.

The first thing that people always noticed about Addy was her hair, the colour of red wine and tumbling halfway down her back, thick and unruly. She refused to have it braided or pulled back in a ponytail, and usually refused to let anyone brush it, either. Her mother would sometimes threaten to chop her hair all off if she wouldn't take better care of it, just shave her completely bald; but Addy would invariably say, quite cheerfully, "Okay, sure, I'll go get the scissors," and then Casey would snap and say, "We're not cutting off your hair," and throw the hairbrush furiously across the room.

The other thing that people always noticed about Addy were her eyes, because they were two different colours: the one on the left was a kind of hazel just like Casey's, the sort of eye colour that people sometimes call green but isn't really; but the one on the right was green for real, green as a pine needle. Addy in fact made sure that people noticed her eyes, because she was very proud of them, she knew it was very rare to have eyes that are two different colours, and she solemnly insisted that it was the sign of a curse. "Probably my father committed some horrible crime," she would say happily. She knew absolutely nothing about her father and she liked it that way, since it meant that she could imagine him any way she wanted.

THEY HAD DRIVEN out to Whittle the day before the wedding; Nora had picked the children up from school at three o'clock with the car already packed and ready to go.

Natalie was so excited she couldn't even walk properly, she had to go backwards, hopping, facing her mother at a forty-five degree angle, babbling something about a bird that had gotten into the school somehow and flown up and down the hall in a panic, beating its wings wildly, and all the kids in her class had rushed out to watch as the caretaker tried to get it to fly out again, using a broom stretched over his head to try and sweep it towards the open doors.

It should have been a three-hour drive, but it took them more like four, and it felt more like five. To Jack the longest part of the drive was just getting out of the city, a slow interminable crawl through rush-hour traffic, with Natalie in her booster seat complaining that she couldn't see out the windows, and Addy on the other side complaining that she didn't want to go to a stupid wedding anyway, and why did *she* have to go, it wasn't *her* aunt, and Natalie asking every two minutes if they were out of Winnipeg yet, and when were they going to be there, and when were they going to have dinner because she was *so* hungry.

Then, once they finally did get past the perimeter and out onto the highway, Natalie announced that she had to go to the bathroom *really bad*. So they had to stop at the Tim Hortons in Headingley so that she could pee, and Nora made Jack and Addy go too even though they said they didn't have to, but Nora said she was damned if she was going to stop again. Since they were there anyway, she lined up and bought herself an extra-large coffee, and one donut each for her and the kids. Then they had to stop again ten minutes later so that Natalie could be carsick at the side of the road. You could still see chunks of double-chocolate donut, Addy reported with cheerful interest, that hardly looked chewed, let alone digested.

After that Natalie slept the rest of the way, which was a blessing. Nora began to speed to try and make up for lost time. As the speed of the car picked steadily up, Jack felt a fierce exhilaration rising steadily in him along with it. He stared at the birds skimming over the farmers' fields, the horses standing in small clusters, the grazing cows, while Nora and Addy entertained themselves by counting how many times the road had crossed over the winding Whitetail River, and arguing about whether it was three times or four.

Jack even saw a deer at the side of the road, a white-tailed doe all speckled and gold, standing along the edge of a woody stretch. The doe startled as the car got near, and darted into the bush. He had called excitedly to his mom and Addy to look and see, but by the time they turned their heads the deer was already gone. Then Addy started teasing him, pretending that he had just made it up. "It probably wasn't even a real deer," she scoffed.

"It was too a deer."

"Do you even know what a deer looks like? It was probably just a big dog or something."

"Shut up."

"Hey!" said Nora angrily. "Don't tell people to shut up."

"River!" yelled Addy excitedly again. "Is it the Whitetail?" They watched for the signpost as they approached the bridge: it *was* the Whitetail. "That's five," said Addy. "We've crossed the same river five times."

"Four," said Nora.

"Maybe we've entered, like, a time warp in the universe or something, and we're cursed to keep passing the same river over and over again. And, like, a hundred years from now people will say this is a haunted highway because if you drive this way you'll pass an ancient car with three screaming kids doomed to cross the Whitetail River forever and over and never get to their destination."

"You'd better not be screaming," said Nora.

Soon they could see the silhouette of Riding Mountain in the distance, a long flat unmountainous ridge, and Nora said that meant they were getting close. They were driving straight into the sun now, low in the sky and right in their eyes, and the low-lying clouds on the horizon were smeared with streaks of deep pink.

Because they were running so late, they had to skip dinner and drive straight to the wedding rehearsal. It was almost seven o'clock when they finally pulled up outside the church. Natalie cried at first when they woke her up to get her out of the car, and Nora had to hold her for a minute and whisper softly to soothe her.

"See?" Addy said, "If *I* was the flower-girl, I wouldn't be puking and crying all over the place."

Nora said, "Shut up, Addy."

Jack had never been inside a real church before. It was bigger than he imagined, especially the ceiling that seemed to stretch up forever, and he desperately wished no grown-ups were around so that he could give a really good holler and test for an echo. It smelled a little like old ladies' coats, and Nora sat him and Addy on the smooth wooden pews and told them not to move. "This won't take long," she said, and then added, less comfortingly, "I hope."

"I'm starving to *death*," said Addy.

"Join the club," said Nora irritably. And then, relenting a little, she said, "I think there's some gum in my purse, you can have that if you can find it." So while she and Natalie joined the rest of the wedding party up at the front, whispering hurried apologies to her sister and to the minister for being late, Addy rooted happily through her purse. She found the gum straight off and stuffed three pieces in her mouth before offering the last piece to Jack, and then kept searching the purse, but she was disappointed.

"Your mom doesn't have anything interesting in here," she said to Jack, in a voice made thick and slobbery by all that gum.

"What did you think you'd find?" he asked.

"I can't hear a word they're saying," Addy complained, ignoring the question and leaning forward to stare at the minister, who was talking in a low voice and gesturing broadly. "Can you hear what he's saying?"

Jack had picked up a book from the back of the pew in front of them, and was looking idly through the pages, understanding nothing. "No," he said.

"Is it gonna be like this at the wedding tomorrow? 'Cause if I can't even hear what they're saying during the wedding, this is going to be seriously boring."

Jack put the book back where he'd found it as his mother looked over towards them, frowning. Natalie had finally let Nora put her down, but she was standing hugged tightly up against her mother's leg, sullen, shy, and probably still half-asleep, looking warily at her grandfather who had had the temerity to try to hold her, despite being a virtual stranger.

Jack rather liked his grandfather, who looked so much like Nora: tall like her, with the same blond hair and the same pale blue eyes. Now he stood off to one side, his face turned slightly down and his lower lip jutting out in a cartoonish pout that more than ever made him resemble Nora. It was, Jack thought, as if his mother were standing in front of a magic mirror that showed what she would look like if she were an old man: still just as tall but fleshy, fat, and saggy instead of lean and athletic, her fair smooth skin turned leathery and speckled with brown spots, her long blond hair cut short and beginning to rust, her beautiful face all pouchy, veiny, and wrinkled, and yet somehow unmistakably still *hers*, with the same wide expressive mouth and the same pale blue eyes. And then Jack remembered that he had thought the exact same thought he had seen his grandfather, a year or so ago, giving him a strange sensation of déjà vu; and it occurred to him that even though he had his own father's black hair and light brown skin, he too had the same light blue eyes as his mother and her father, the same shape of face, the same long mouth, and—as he had often been told, usually to his irritation—he had that same unconscious habit of pushing his lower lip out in an exaggerated pout that made him look uncannily like his mother. And now he noticed that his grandfather had raised his head and was looking at him, smiling, and Jack wondered if the old man was thinking the exact same thoughts that Jack had just thought, applied to him. Perhaps that same thought, right down to the detail of looking into a magic mirror, had been thought in much the same way in their family for generations, each person supposing it was an original idea when in fact it was no more unique to them than their pale blue eyes or distinctive habitual pout. Perhaps *every* thought and idea he had ever had or ever would have had been thought by one ancestor or another, and ideas were passed down through the genes like pigmentation; and that would have to include *this* thought, and also this thought about that thought about those thoughts, and so on.

The minister started leading the wedding party down the long aisle now, towards the back of the church. Nora and Natalie came last, and Nora gave Jack and Addy a meaningful look as she walked past, mouthing the words, "Don't move," and jabbing her finger at the pew.

Addy spun round to kneel on the seat, arms folded over the back of the pew and chin resting on her arms, watching them go. "This would be an awesome place to play hide and seek," she whispered loudly out of the corner of her mouth.

"No it wouldn't," said Jack quickly.

As soon as Nora and Natalie had filed out with the others through the heavy oak doors at the front, Addy said, "You're it!" and sprung over the back of the pew, dropping lightly to the floor and ducking down, disappearing from sight.

IT WAS LATE when they finally got to his grandparents' house, where his grandmother had dinner all laid out and waiting. "Well," she said, with a kind of breathy and self-deprecating laugh, "I was beginning to think you weren't even coming. I hope the children like perogies. I had to just guess. Of course if I ever got to see them, I'd *know* what they like to eat..."

"I'm sure they'll love it," Nora lied firmly. It was disgusting: flabby pale perogies with thick-cut undercooked onions, all caked with congealed grease, slices of some kind of sausage the colour and consistency of pencil erasers, broccoli that had been mercilessly boiled into a repugnant green mush, overdressed salad all soggy and wilting at the edges. His grandmother informed them all that it probably wouldn't be any good, because she'd had to keep it warming for three hours, but Jack was fairly certain it would have been just as disgusting served fresh.

"So? How was the rehearsal?"

"It was fine," said Nora, spooning heaps of sour cream onto Natalie's plate, taking great care not to let it touch the other food.

"Of course I would've liked to have been there, but I had to stay here and watch the food."

"Honestly, Mom, you didn't miss anything."

"Oh, don't worry about me, I'm just the mother of the bride, that's all. It's not like *you*'ll ever have a wedding rehearsal I can go to."

Jack's grandfather, who had yet to speak a single word the entire evening, abruptly asked his wife to bring him something to drink.

"Of course, of course," she said apologetically, "where's my head?" And she bustled off to the kitchen, coming back with a bottle of wine. "What about the children, Nora? What do the children like to drink? It's not like *I* would know, I'm just their grandmother. Don't worry about me."

"I don't know, Mom, why don't you ask them yourself? They're all old enough to talk, you know."

"Anything is fine," said Jack quickly. "Thank you."

"I'll try some wine," said Addy brightly.

"Milk," said Nora. "They would all love a glass of milk, thank you, Mom."

"Now tell me," said Jack's grandfather abruptly. "Tell me, how is your mother?" It took everyone a moment to realize he was addressing Addy, who sat at his left.

"Oh, you know Casey," she said through a mouthful of half-chewed perogies, sketching a little hieroglyphic in the air with her fork: "Always with her trees."

"Well," he said solemnly, "it's a shame she couldn't be here. I can't tell you how many times she sat right there where you are, eating dinner with us. You look a lot like her, young lady. Just like her." This was patently untrue, as everybody at the table knew: Casey's hair was boring old black, and both her eyes the same colour.

Hungry as he was, it took Jack a real effort to choke down as much of the food as he could and try to smile while doing it. Natalie wouldn't even try, she put a piece of sausage in her mouth and rapidly took it out again, ate about half a cup of sour cream, and then burst into tears when Nora told her to at least *try* the perogies.

"What's wrong with her?" asked Grandma, who had yet to sit down, fussing back and forth from the kitchen to the dining room, talking rapidly in a stream of constant complaint, peppering everyone with questions and hardly waiting for any answers. She was short and round as a rubber ball; she seemed not so much fat as inflated, and Jack's eyes were constantly drawn to her forearm, fascinated and horrified by the way the band of her thin silver watch bit into the flesh of her fat wrist, she wore it so tight; and the skin on her arm was taut and smooth.

"She's just tired," Nora said apologetically, picking Natalie up and moving her to her lap. "She's exhausted. It's way past her bedtime, and…"

"Well, don't worry about me…"

"…all this excitement, it's a lot for a little girl."

The three kids slept down in the basement, all sharing the one hide-a-bed that folded out from the old orange couch. Natalie was long asleep when Nora took Jack and Addy down; she was lying diagonally across the bed on her back, arms and legs splayed out like a starfish, somehow taking up two-thirds of the large mattress with her small little body.

"You're sleeping next to her, not me," said Addy, as Nora prepared to move her.

"Why me?" said Jack.

"If she pees the bed, I'm not getting it."

"She's not going to pee the bed," said Nora impatiently.

"Oh, she's gonna pee the bed," said Addy.

"She's sleeping in the middle," Nora insisted. "If she does pee the bed you should both get peed on, it's only fair."

In the end they agreed to lay her at the very head of the bed, along the couch-back and between the arms, and Jack and Addy slept with their feet by her body and their heads at the far end, safely out of pee's reach.

Jack slept poorly. Perhaps it was all the excitement, and sleeping in a strange house; perhaps it was the mattress, musty, lumpy, and thin, and the crossbar beneath it that dug into his hip all night, no matter which way he tried to position himself; and then, if he was turning around too much, Addy would dig her elbow into him and tell him to stop flopping around already.

When he finally did begin to drift off, Addy dug her elbow into him again and woke him up. "I can't sleep," she whispered. "Can you?"

"Yes," he said furiously. "Leave me alone."

"Liar," she said cheerfully. She woke him a second time, much later—he had no way of knowing when, but he had been deeply asleep this time, and it felt like the middle of the night; it was dark as hell and the house was quiet and still. It took him a few moments to remember where he was, and Addy was standing by the side of the bed, prodding him in the shoulder and whispering his name excitedly. "You'll never guess what I found," she said excitedly. "Come see."

But he was still half-asleep, and he rolled over, turning his back to her, and mumbled something about leaving him alone.

"Fine," said Addy, obviously disappointed. "You're no fun." She disappeared for a few minutes, and he lay there wondering furiously what she was up to. A minute later he felt her climbing back under the covers beside him. "Natalie would have got up and come with me," she complained.

"Then why don't you wake up Natalie?"

"No no," she said. "We can't do that, *flower* girls need their *beauty* rest. That's okay, it'll just be my little secret."

When he finally woke in the morning, he was alone in the bed, sleeping diagonally across it, arms and legs splayed out, the blankets twisted in a lump by his feet. Daylight seeped in through the basement windows, and above him he could hear the sound of an argument raging: voices raised and overlapping, something banging, feet stomping across the ceiling. He couldn't make out any words, but he could hear the unmistakable sound of his mother trying to suppress the urge to yell. And he lay there a minute or two, soaking it in, happily savouring the anticipation of a day out of the ordinary. And then he noticed something placed on the pillow beside his head: a tooth, a human tooth, adult-sized, white, and dry.

BREAKFAST CONSISTED OF dry brown scrambled eggs, some kind of crumbly toast, and those same rubbery sausages from the previous night, half-heartedly reheated. Jack couldn't stand the thought of eating them, but not wanting to hurt his grandmother's feelings, and being afraid too that if there were too many of them left over they would simply be served again at the next meal, and the next, Jack discreetly slipped as many of them as he could into his pocket unnoticed, to dispose of later.

After breakfast, Nora told them to go run outside and play for a couple of hours, just stay close enough so that they could hear her when she called for them. Go run around and get it out of their systems now, she said, because there was going to be a lot of sitting around and standing around the rest of the day, and once they were all dressed up in their good clothes she didn't want them climbing trees or rolling around in the mud or doing anything else fun. For just one day, as she had said to them over and over in the car, for just one day she wanted them to pretend that they were nice, civilized, well-behaved children, and not a pack of mad animals.

Addy decided that they should go explore the cemetery down the road. She had been to this town many times before, but not since her own grandfather's funeral, and it turned out to be a little farther away than she had remembered, more like a ten or fifteen minute walk than "right around the corner" as she kept saying it would be. The further they got from the house the more anxious Natalie got, but Addy told her not to worry. "We won't stay long," she said. "Besides, your mom yells pretty loud, I bet we'll hear her anyway."

As they walked, Jack asked Addy about the tooth on his pillow; instead of explaining she said, "I found another one," pulling a second tooth out of her pocket in conspiratorial fashion, letting him take a furtive look, and then pocketing it again.

"I found this one in the bathroom," she explained, "on top of the medicine cabinet." It had been wrapped up in an old piece of newspaper and completely caked under dust.

"Why were you looking on top of the medicine cabinet?"

"That's not the point," she said impatiently. "The point is, why do your grandparents have teeth hidden all over their house? Maybe it's like a voodoo thing, maybe it's the teeth of their enemies."

"I think that's supposed to be hair. How would you even get your enemy's teeth?"

"Maybe it's more than just teeth," she said dreamily. "Maybe your grandfather killed a guy, and there's bits of bones and stuff stashed all over the house—like a whole skeleton, in tiny little pieces."

"My grandpa did not kill a guy."

"Why not?" said Addy shrewdly. "Somebody has to."

The homes along this stretch of road were mostly drab little bungalows. In the small and unfenced front yard of one house, the smallest and dingiest house of all, with flaking paint on the side and no curtains or blinds in the window and dead brown grass all around, a dog was chained to a stake. It started to bark frantically, half strangling itself on its choke collar, when it saw the three kids coming up the street. Natalie and Addy moved nervously over to the far side of the street as they passed, but Jack inched closer, carefully.

The dog was at least as big as Jack was, with short yellow dirty fur, and it was obviously starving, you could see the outline of its ribs and everything, and what looked like a nasty scab running along its left haunch. Its chain was so short it could hardly move around, and there was no shade anywhere in reach, no food or water either, with the sun already hot in the cloudless sky and climbing higher. Jack felt sorry for it, and he felt indignant at whoever lived in the house and would treat a dog that way. It didn't even look like anybody was home to take care of it, there were no vehicles in the drive and the house had an empty, almost abandoned feel.

Remembering the sausages in his pocket, he crouched down just a foot or so beyond the dog's reach and began talking to it in a calm and friendly voice, saying, "I've got something for you." He pulled out a piece of sausage and held it out for the dog to see, and then tossed it to the ground. The dog sniffed it, and then snapped it up and swallowed it down, scarcely even chewing. So Jack took another sausage out and, still in a crouch, inched closer, holding his arm stretched out so the dog could eat it out of his hand.

"And now we're friends, right?" Jack said, coming closer yet as the dog licked at his hand.

"Come on," Addy called impatiently from behind him.

"Just go ahead," Jack called back, not bothering to look around. "I'll catch up in a minute." He dumped the remainder of the sausages on the ground beside it. "See?" he said, stroking the dog admiringly as it frantically gobbled the last of the food. Glancing underneath, he decided the dog was a girl. "See?" he said, "You're a good girl, aren't you? You just need someone to take better care of you."

He wished he had more food to give her; he especially wished he had some water, she probably needed water more than anything else, her nose was completely dry. He felt another little surge of anger at the poor dog's owners, they didn't deserve to have a pet if this is how they treated her. He looked up and down the street and checked to make sure that there was no sign of anyone at home in the shabby little house; he looked at the houses on either side and across the street to make sure no one was watching him out of any windows. Then, confident that no one would see him, he rubbed the dog's neck affectionately and unclipped her choke collar. He just couldn't bear to leave her chained up like that. And if the dog ran off and never came back, Jack thought, it would serve her owners right. "Go find some water," he whispered to her. "And be a good girl." Then he sprinted away up the road, turning to look behind him as he went around the bend. The dog was still standing there in the yard, wagging her tail and watching him, but not following. She barked, once, and he waved and ran on.

This time the cemetery really was around the corner. It was nothing like the cemeteries they sometimes played in back home, like the one in St. John's Park not too far from their house, or the one in Elmwood across the river. This one was open, and airy, lush and green and meticulously groomed; it was more like a flower garden that just happened to have headstones in it. It even had picnic tables, as if coming for a nice lunch in the graveyard was a normal sort of activity around here. In almost every direction, the view was exhilarating. Looking north, they could see Riding Mountain silhouetted against the horizon; to the south, the ground spilled down into the winding valley of the Whitetail, a lush green gash in the earth. To the east, across the river and perched at the top of a high ridge, sat a solitary and imposing old building, sprawling and immense, clearly derelict even from this distance: its crumbling face lit up by the rising sun, it seemed to be brooding over the town below it, sinister and grim. Addy told them it was a prison, a prison for people so dangerous there weren't even guards inside, the prisoners had to fend for themselves, and once they went in, no one ever came out.

And Jack scoffed and said, "Then where do they get food?"

And Addy said, "They drop it in through the roof once a week, and the prisoners have to fight over it. And if there isn't enough to go around, sometimes they eat each other."

And Jack didn't believe her and said so, and Natalie wasn't sure if she believed her or not, so she said nothing.

First they split up to see who could find the oldest headstone: Addy had a theory that if you found the very first grave in a graveyard, you got to make a wish on it. The problem, of course, is that the oldest headstones are always the ones that the letters have all worn off of, the ones that have been worn down by years and years of wind and rain and sun and ice and snow until they're just a flat and blank-faced slab of stone. So you can never be completely sure, all you can do is make your best guess. Over the last couple of years Addy had made wishes on more than a dozen different headstones in the cemetery at St. John's; since none of the wishes ever came true, she simply figured that she hadn't found the right one yet. She also had a theory that if you searched a cemetery at midnight under a full moon, you'd find your own headstone, and it will tell you what year you're going to die. This theory she hadn't gotten around to testing yet; and as Jack pointed out, who the hell wants to know what year you're going to die, anyway?

When they got tired of searching the headstones, Jack drifted off to scramble around the edge of the grounds, where a precipitous slope loomed over the snaking Whitetail far below, while Natalie began picking fistfuls of flowers from the various garden beds, ignoring Addy's dire warnings—delivered from near the top of a tall tree that she had shinnied up and disappeared into the leaves of, so that it seemed like the tree itself was speaking—that it was desperately illegal to pick those particular flowers, and the cops might show up any minute, and she'd have to spend the wedding in prison, and Aunt Tracy and Uncle Anthony would have a terrible marriage and have to get divorced because everyone knows that it's bad luck not to have a flower girl at your wedding, and it's probably especially bad luck if you were supposed to have a flower girl but she couldn't make it because she got tossed in jail for stealing flowers. By the time they started heading back, Natalie's hands were stained green from the juice of the stems, and she had amassed a bouquet that was half as big as she was, dribbling a trail of petals all along the dusty road.

The sun was already hot in the cloudless sky and climbing higher. Conscious that they were probably late and already in trouble, they walked as quickly as they could. Coming around the bend, Jack was curious to see if the dog was gone, or if she would still be sitting there in the little yard. But not only was the dog not there, the little yard wasn't there either, and neither was the dingy little house with flaking paint. The houses on either side of it were there, exactly as he remembered them, the one on the left with the green vinyl siding and the one on the right with the purple curtains and the flower boxes in the windows, but now they stood next to one another, with no house between them, just a narrow strip of lawn.

He stopped, puzzled and feeling uneasy; he looked up the street one way and down the other, wondering if his memory was playing tricks on him. But Addy and Natalie were impatiently yelling at him to hurry up, and though he was virtually certain this was the same street they had come down earlier and that this was exactly where that dog's house ought to be, it simply wasn't.

2

Two brothers found a town;
Nora finds out about her grandfather

THERE WAS A STORY behind Whittle's famous cemetery. Nora had learned all about it when she was in university, doing a research project on the history of the old Stone School.

The town had originally been founded by a pair of wealthy speculators out of Ontario, a couple of brothers named Howard and Jonathon J. Afton. This was about 1881. The "settlement" when the brothers arrived was little more than a handful of farms and homesteads scattered around the area, the original Indigenous inhabitants having already been forced out, further northwest, to the area that's now the reservation called Waabishkigwan.

Slightly east of the townsite was the future residence, then just beginning construction, of Sir Colin Craig McKenzie, formerly the Chief Trader and District Factor for the Hudson's Bay Company. It was Sir Colin Craig himself, who would be travelling back to Scotland to secure a marriage while his house was being built, who had proposed the idea to the brothers, offering to underwrite them financially and to use his influence with the nascent Manitoba and Northwestern Railway to extend their line and build a station in the would-be town. In exchange they promised to establish, before McKenzie's return from Scotland, the two amenities he would most require for his wife: a general store, and a Presbyterian Church.

They purchased land and surveyed town lots along the east side of the Whitetail River, both north and south of Sally Creek, and established a general store where the Sally and the Whitetail met—not far from the site where the grain elevator is now. Included in the land they purchased were the salt springs, which had long been a resource for the local Indigenous peoples, and which Howard Afton in particular believed could be profitably exploited.

In fact, there appears to have been some friction between the brothers: Howard, being the younger and more practical of the two, was focused primarily on salt, believing that the best and fastest way to establish a town was to establish an industry and let the town grow up around it. Jonathon J., under the spell of Sir Colin Craig, had visions of a more genteel and agrarian community. If they could please McKenzie—or more particularly, McKenzie's wife, whoever she might turn out to be—the railway was certain to follow, and their investment would be secure.

The result was that they started to build what were in effect two parallel, adjacent towns on either side of the Sally. On the north side, Howard established his saltworks, bringing in one of Joseph Monkman's sons to supervise the construction and production. Reservoirs were dug; two evaporating furnaces, fired by wood, were housed in a log cabin; labourers were brought up from Brandon, and quick shoddy shacks thrown up for them to live in. The salt produced was soft, flaky, and had a yellow tinge; in advertising materials from the time, Howard hinted that the local peoples had long prized it for its "vitalising and aphrodisiac qualities," a piece of traditional lore that he appears to have concocted out of thin air.

The belching smoke and acrid stink of the furnaces were a source of bitter complaints from Jonathon, as were the manners, habits, and "low character" of the labourers, to whom he referred as "drunks" and "scoundrels;" he worried incessantly that Sir Colin Craig and his wife would object to living in the vicinity of such people, that they would lose McKenzie's favour and, with it, the promised railway. Howard was dismissive: they wouldn't need McKenzie's influence; the M & NR would see the value of establishing a station where there were goods to be shipped, like bushels of salt; and if they were still reluctant, a small bribe would settle the matter. That was the way business was really done.

Jonathan, meanwhile, on the south side of the creek, was focused on building the church, a small hotel, and a series of homes, designed by Sir Colin Craig's architect—homes far too large and elegant for the salt-workers, even young Monkman; or for that matter to house the carpenters and other builders who were brought in to build them, and who inevitably established themselves in Howard's half of town, which he wished to name Afton after himself, now rapidly thriving.

For the church, Jonathon had initially chosen the site where the cemetery still sits, up on the ridge, overlooking the valley, and where the Allisons would be able to see its spire from their home. And since it seemed to him that a church was incomplete, almost fraudulent, without a churchyard, he actually purchased several dozen graves and had them transported, coffins, headstones, and all, to the newly consecrated ground. Not only graves, with coffins, bodies, and headstones, but statuary and monuments as well. He even appears to have made rudimentary inquiries about the character of the deceased, where possible, wanting to populate his new town only with dead people of decent breeding, unimpeachable character. His brother accused him of becoming morbidly fixated on his "pet graveyard," which he built up like a park, eventually even relocating the church to make more room. The expense was enormous, and drove him deeply into debt.

But Jonathan won out in the long run. When the town was incorporated in 1885, following the establishment of the railway station, it was under the name Whittle, not Afton—Jonathon had suggested Whitetail, but Sir Colin's wife had advocated for the more whimsical Whittle, which was how the locals pronounced it. A few years later, following a fire that destroyed half a dozen homes on the north side of town—the neighbourhood officially known as Afton and still to this day referred to colloquially as "Half-town" by the locals—changes were made to the town's building code, requiring all new buildings to be made of brick rather than wood. Gradually, the older wood-frame structures built on the north side were abandoned, only occasionally to be replaced with brick structures. The saltworks, now modernized and requiring fewer workers, continued its steadily less profitable production into the 1950s before it was finally shuttered; while the cemetery remains, even to this day, the pride of the town, and a profitable source of tourism.

THERE IN THE CEMETERY, among so many others, was the grave of Nora's grandfather, Jack Fleisch, her mother's father, her amma's husband: a slab of dark marble with a cross etched in relief, and with his rank, regiment, and war record so proudly emphasized.

Nora's grandmother had kept a framed picture of him, dark and handsome and solemn in his uniform, on her bedside table her entire life. After she died, that picture was the one thing Nora had wanted, but her mother never let her take it, and later claimed that it had gotten lost. When Nora's own son Jack was growing up, there were many times she thought she saw an uncanny resemblance between him and that picture of her grandfather, and she would wish that she could get her hands on it to compare.

At some point in her childhood Nora had got hold of the notion that this grandfather had died in the War. *The* war, *a* war, any war; all wars were one war, all long ago and across the ocean, one motley war that her imagination had subconsciously stitched together from scraps of old movies and tv shows and from half-comprehended readings and recitals at Remembrance Day services. And her grandfather had been a fighter pilot, brave and handsome, heroic and stoic and solemnly sepia-toned, who had sacrificed his life for Canada, freedom, and the Queen: shot down behind enemy lines, burnt and spattered and scattered across the poppy fields of Flanders.

She had believed that for so long, she couldn't remember where she'd first got hold of the idea. No doubt she had misunderstood something her grandmother or mother had told her, or perhaps she had been merely misled by that headstone. It was not something she thought about often, or talked about really at all; it didn't even interest her particularly, except occasionally in idle, day-dreamy moments, or around Remembrance Day. And so there was never any occasion for her grandmother, her parents, or anyone else to notice and correct the misconception, and it quietly lodged itself in the back of her mind and put down deep tenacious roots.

And so, years later, when her own son Jack was growing up, she would tell him sometimes how he had been named for his great-grandfather, who had been a brave fighter pilot and had died in the war. And one day when he was three or four, and they had come back to Whittle for a rare visit, then she had even taken him to see her grandfather's grave. And only then, noticing the dates engraved on that headstone, had it occurred to her that the Second World War, in which her grandfather had fought, had been more than a decade over when he had died. She noticed it as an odd discrepancy, the first seed of niggling doubt or wonderment, but didn't think too much of it at the time. She made a mental note to ask her mother about it, but quickly forgot, never got around to it. It was only four or five years after that, when she was back in town again for her sister's wedding, that she finally remembered to bring it up, to ask about it, and only then that she learned she had been completely mistaken all those years. It was her Aunt Bonnie who told her the true story in the end.

And yet this new, truer version of her grandfather's death could not wholly displace the old, mistaken one. From then on, in her mind, the two existed side by side, and it was as though her grandfather Jack had both died in the war and survived it, uninjured, at least in any visible or tangible way; had been left behind in the killing fields of the western front as carrion for the crows, and had also returned to Canada, there to resume his mundane old job at the saltworks, to rekindle the flame with his once and future sweetheart Alma Arnason, and to marry her, to build a house together, and have a son and a daughter; and late one autumn night, to slip quietly out of the house where his wife and children lay sleeping peacefully, and follow the low slow river out of town, and walk across a farmer's field, and climb atop a bale of patiently rotting straw, and there beneath the vast indifferent sky, spattered with cold bright stars, to place the muzzle of his old service revolver against his right temple and blow out his brains.

3

A rare condition;
a recurring dream

NORA'S GRANDMOTHER had been born with a rare condition that
caused her body to constantly produce new teeth.

It was so rare the doctors couldn't agree on a name for it. It's
not that uncommon for a person to have a few extra teeth; it's not
unheard of for a person to grow a complete third set of teeth over
the course of her life. But that wasn't what Nora's grandmother
had. She had been born with half a dozen teeth already poking
through her gums, and couldn't be breastfed for the biting. She
had a full set of teeth by eight months, and lost her first baby
tooth before she turned one year old. From then on and for the
rest of her life, she kept constantly producing new ones, pushing
the old ones painfully out as they emerged. The front teeth would
come in every ten or eleven months, the molars at the back might
take anywhere from a year and a half to two years. And because
they came in at different rates, there was never a time when she
didn't have one or two old ones coming loose, and one or two
new ones cutting through. She always said it didn't bother her,
not really, but that couldn't have been true: the lower half of her
face was almost always swollen and blotched, and her gums bled
so regularly that Nora grew accustomed to seeing that little swirl
of red and pink in her grandmother's glass of milk. She always
only drank milk, as cold as she could get it.

How many teeth did she go through in the course of her life?
Nora tried to do the math more than once, and she was sure it

must have been over fifteen hundred, as impossible as that seemed. When she was young enough to still believe in the tooth fairy, she thought her grandmother must be rich. But the old lady just laughed and said that the tooth fairy had put her on a blacklist years ago or she would have gone bankrupt.

She used to pull the old ones out herself, just as soon as they were loose enough. Nora asked her once how she could stand it, but she said it made the new ones come in much less painfully, and straighter, too, and that it was better that one sharp pain of pulling the old tooth out, than a constant aching as the new tooth tried to push it out of the way.

Years later, Nora would always think of her grandmother sitting in that faded yellow and red armchair in the evening with a glass of bloody milk at her side, holding a tatty old paperback in her left hand, and her right hand in her open mouth, the long thin thumb and forefinger absentmindedly wiggling a loose tooth back and forth, back and forth, back and forth—and then, at last, with a sharp deft tug and a gout of blood, out the tooth would come. She'd drop it with a clatter in the ashtray next to her armchair, all without her eyes leaving the page of the book, and the rest of the evening you could hear her sucking gently at the hole, preferring to swallow the blood than spit it out.

Towards the end, the last couple years of her grandmother's life, the teeth seemed to come in faster than ever. She didn't read anymore, hardly ate, didn't cook or bake, didn't do anything but sit in that old armchair, shapeless as a heap of dirty laundry, hands groping in her mouth. She started keeping the teeth she pulled out—at first in an old jam jar, but later she would hide them around the house. She'd wrap each one up in a square of old newspaper with a piece of tape or elastic band around it and hide the little packets in the clothes drawer, under couch cushions, tucked inside the heating vents or taped behind the pictures on the wall, behind the books on the shelves, under the carpet, even at the bottom of the flour canister and the back of the freezer; and if they discovered one, they had to be careful not to disturb it, for Amma would check on them frequently and fly into a rage if one was missing or even just moved out of place. She forgot so many things towards the end, sometimes even forgot who her daughter and granddaughters were, but she never seemed to forget where she'd hidden each and every precious tooth.

Nora had nightmares sometimes, horrible vivid dreams that her grandmother's body had started to produce so many teeth they were coming out of her palms and her armpits, her stomach and her back all down the spine, cutting through her cheeks and coming out of the soles of her feet; and Nora would have to help pull them out with a small black pair of pliers and wash the wound with warm salt water, kneeling on the floor.

4

Nora and Casey grow up in Whittle;
they hear stories of the old Stone School

GROWING UP, NORA'S BEDROOM was at the back of the house, above the pantry and the mudroom. Long and narrow, it was a late addition to the original structure, unconnected to the air ducts. It had to be warmed on winter nights by a clumsy old space heater that took forever to get going, but once it did would hum loudly and grow dangerously overheated, no matter how low it was set, so that Nora often went to sleep shivering and huddled beneath her blankets only to wake a few hours later in a stew of sweat, half-suffocated from the heat.

Her room was separated from her sister's bedroom by a large window, remnant of the original house design. Their father often threatened to take the window out and board over the opening, or at least nail the sash closed, but he never did get around to it and so the girls would regularly slide open the window and slip through from one room to another.

From the rear windows in Nora's room, if you carefully removed the screen, you could lower yourself down onto the gently sloping roof over the back verandah; as teenagers they would sometimes spread a blanket over the shingles on a hot summer day and lie in the sun. It was Nora's friend Casey Mack who first saw that you could edge your way down to the eaves, take a short hop across to the roof of the bicycle shed—taking care to keep your weight away from the middle, or the cheap tin roof would buckle and dent—and from there reach the tall wooden fence and climb that down to the ground. Nora at first was frightened to try, but soon became so practiced at it that by the time she was eleven or twelve, it was her preferred method of coming and going.

Their house, with its pink and pockmarked stucco façade, pea-soup coloured shutters, and that one incongruous window next to the front door, circular with an old-fashioned ship's wheel mounted around it for a frame, sat at the blind end of a short cul-de-sac. The street had only eighteen houses in total, no fences separating the front yards, and a dozen kids living on it, ranging in age from five or six years younger than Nora, to five or six years older. It was a perfect street to play road hockey on, or football across the rows of yards, or—on those long summer evenings when the mellow twilight seemed to linger on for hours—for elaborate games of hide and seek. They took their hide and seek with deadly seriousness, going so far as to improvise camouflage outfits, draw crude maps, and conspire codes of whistles for one hider to let another know whether the seeker was approaching, or if it was safe to make a break for home. Home was always the steps and stoop of Nora's house since it marked the end of the street and since no one was allowed to hide in their yard anyway, with its profusion of immaculate flowerbeds. Casey, on nights when she stayed over at Nora's, was allowed to play too, but only if she partnered with Tracy or one of the other young kids to keep it fair, for Casey had an almost preternatural gift for disappearing and an animal-like patience to stay hidden and immobile for hours at a stretch, silent and unminding.

Behind the house, on the far side of the back fence, there was a short patch of ground that fell away abruptly, running three feet down to the road. They were forbidden, of course, to climb over the fence, but of course they did so anyway, going up in the back corner behind the greenhouse, where they were mostly hidden from sight, swinging over, hanging down, and then, when they were sure there were no cars or trucks coming in either direction, dropping to the ground and as often as not tumbling right out onto the road.

From there they could cut across the road and go right into the park, where the ground sloped gently and unevenly down towards the Whitetail. North of town, the Whitetail was just a creek; down here, after it was joined by the Sally Creek, it was officially a river, but it only really earned that title for a few months of the year, swollen with spring runoff, sometimes swamping half the park and swallowing the little footbridge. Then it was fun to watch the bits of dirty ice, branches, plastic bags and other debris glide rapidly along the water's deceptively placid surface, and place bets as to how high it would reach this time, and tell again the same handful of stories about kids who had supposedly drowned in it over the years. It was hard to believe that by late summer this same river would be little more than a sleepy, shallow stream you could hop across on a few big rocks.

On this side of the park the trees were mostly willows, with their forked and angled trunks so excellent for climbing, and a handful of gnarled thick and twisty oaks, planted long ago by an act of town council, that in the autumn provided fistfuls of acorns that were perfect for smuggling to school and whipping at one another over recess. And the trees here were well-spaced and groomed, the grass kept trimmed and weeded, and a path was maintained along the river. Follow that path north, and it would take you all way up a gentle hill to the cemetery; follow it south and you'd come to the old jungle gym and swing set, some picnic tables, and a pair of ornamental cherries by the footbridge; a little further south than that, past the soccer field and almost at the highway, was the town's only swimming pool, open from the May long weekend to Labour Day. When Nora and Casey were old enough to take Tracy with them to the playground without any adults, often there would be other kids there, closer in age to Tracy, like their cousin James Mazur or her friend April from school or the Anderssen girls, and then they could leave her playing on the swings or the slides, or digging in the sandbox or playing lava tag, and they would drift a little ways off on their own and play on the wooden footbridge, or climb in the trees, or later in the summer when the sun was high and the water was low, pick their way down along the creek bed, all the while talking indefatigably, an endless stream of conversation that no matter how trivial, silly, or repetitive it might get, always seemed to them somehow secret, urgent, and indispensable.

The road between the park and Nora's house came north from the highway and roughly followed the course of the Whitetail all the way to Riding Mountain. Scenic and gently winding, it was a popular route for day-trippers. Past the park, it would take them up the hill, past the cemetery, on the way out of town. It was often remarked that when Whittle's founders chose the site for the cemetery, they picked the prettiest spot for miles around, either as a consolation to the dead themselves, or as an enticement to the living. From here you could look south down the spilling ground into the valley where the Sally Creek flowed into the Whitetail, the valley so spectacular in autumn with its brief and glorious blaze of red, yellow and orange, and the sky blotted over with the thick squalling flocks of migrating geese congregating by the hundreds around the water traps and covering the course with their thick and slimy shit. North of the golf course, across the river valley from the cemetery, perched at the top of that same unclimbable ridge, they could just see the old Stone School, perched at the top of its high ridge, solitary, sprawling and immense, clearly derelict even from that distance, sinister and grim; or they would scramble around the edge of the grounds, where the precipitous slope loomed over the snaking river far below, or simply lie in the grass, lazy and peaceful, gratefully soaking up the heat of the sun.

It wasn't actually stone, that old Stone School: the original building had been, but that was gutted by a fire way back in the nineteen-twenties. The building they replaced it with was made of buff-coloured brick, but the locals had gone on calling it the Stone School anyway. It had been sitting empty now for twenty years, sprawling sinister and grim, accumulating darkness: all smashed glass, splintered rotting wood and crumbling plaster, guarded and half-hidden from sight by the unchecked growth of skinny tilted poplar trees, wild and overgrown lilacs, and dark stalks of thistle as tall as a man and thick as his arm.

It was a subject of frequent discussion among Whittle's children, almost all of whom managed to convince themselves that they had heard the sounds of ghostly drumming coming from the empty building on full moon nights. Others said those drumming sounds came not from the school itself but from a thick grove of crabapple trees behind the building, with dark purple leaves and little nasty apples, that was believed to be growing over the site of a mass and unmarked grave where the bodies of schoolchildren had been surreptitiously and unceremoniously buried—many who had died in the fire that had destroyed the original schoolhouse, others who had died over the years from malnourishment, beatings, and disease, or had been molested, murdered, and discarded; and a boy in the fifth grade said he knew another boy, since moved away, who had once taken a pocket knife to one of those trees, and dark red blood had come spurting out of the cut. There was also a boy Nora knew who said that his cousin knew a kid who had spent a night in the empty school on a dare and came out the next morning completely naked, covered in bruises, and his head shaved bald; and the boy could no longer speak any known language but only a kind of urgent, anguished gibberish, and he had been locked up ever since in Selkirk, hopelessly insane.

Nobody really believed that story, for the boy who told it was a notorious liar who also claimed to have an uncle who had broken into that empty school years ago, not long after it was first closed: he and some of his buddies broke into it one day, figuring they might find furniture and fixtures and stuff they could take and sell up in the city, or if nothing else gut the place for wire and scrap; and this uncle said that it was pitch-black inside even though it was the middle of the day and there were no blinds or curtains on any of the windows, and they were forced to go back to their truck for flashlights, and he also said there were strange markings and stains on the walls and even the ceilings, and when they went back in with their flashlights there was a dog there, a yellow dog, big and yellow and ugly, with filthy matted and patchy fur and its long pink tongue lolling out of its mouth, showing its dirty long teeth. It didn't bark or growl at them or try to chase them out of the building, but it followed them silently around from room to room, walking with a limp but somehow getting ahead of them even when they closed the doors behind them, they would think they had it trapped and then they'd come around a corner and there it would be waiting for them, and it wouldn't let them go in to certain rooms at all, squatting in their path and staring them down; and it spooked them so much they left without touching or taking anything. So nobody believed that story either, even though it was a pretty good one.

The most popular and well-believed story, the one told and retold by all the children with varying details but consistent conviction, was that if you went up to the second-floor dormitories on certain nights—exactly which nights varied from telling to telling—and if you went into the washrooms and said a certain combination of words, or performed some simple ritual—this too changed from telling to telling, and was often a matter of heated controversy—but if you did this right, you would see reflected in those bathroom mirrors the horrible crimes of long ago being re-enacted before your eyes. Nora and Casey knew many kids who claimed that their older siblings had done exactly that and told them all about it; and when they were old enough, they told Nora's little sister Tracy that they had too, and Tracy believed them, or half believed them, and told her friends so. And so the old abandoned school had become a great gift to the local children, for winters in that town were long, cold, and profoundly boring, and the time had to be whiled away somehow; and when those same kids grew up to become bored aimless and destructive teenagers, then the Stone School became the Stoned School, a perfect place for them get drunk and fucked-up and party in secret, and the walls inside and out were gradually covered over with obscene graffiti, and those forsaken, smashed-up classrooms with the old scarred desks and busted chairs and tumbled down chalkboards gradually filled up with beer bottles full of cigarette butts, candy wrappers, chip bags, roaches in tinfoil ashtrays, homemade hash pipes, used condoms, and the lingering persistent stink of adolescence.

5

Casey sees a stillborn foal;
she makes the woods her wild kingdom

BEFORE SHE STARTED SCHOOL, Casey Mack had hardly ever
met or even seen another child her own age. She hadn't gone to
kindergarten, not because her parents opposed it, but because it
simply hadn't occurred to them that they ought to send her. Her
parents had seemed to feel that so long as she was well-fed and
watered, had a good run at least once a day, and was washed and
brushed down before bed, their job was done. Back then, Casey
was a shy, sly child, more at home around dogs and horses than
other human beings. She was small for her age, thin as a garter
snake, brown as a squirrel, and her flat black hair was cut short
as a boy's.

Her father was a gentle man, affectionate even in his awkward,
mumbling way, an affection he generally could find no other way
of expressing than by giving his daughter an occasional furtive
candy from one of his many secret stashes, and then tousling her
dark hair roughly with his calloused and enormous hands. He
had a great weakness for candy himself, especially lemon drops
and wine gums, and Casey knew that she could always find some
in the pockets of his big blue coat, jumbled up with dog biscuits,
sugar cubes for the horses, stray flakes of blonde tobacco and bits
of straw.

Casey's mother was something else. She was a small woman
with an extraordinary mass of hair, the colour of clotted blood,
that she wore in a braid hanging down past the small of her back.

Unbraided, her hair was twisty, dark, thick, and delinquent: snagging and tangling, falling forward to hide her face, winding itself lovingly around her neck as she slept, or slipping into her open mouth and snaking down her throat to choke her. She often talked to herself out loud, like someone who has lived alone for many years, and she had the habit of pinching Casey on the arm or the slope of the neck, hard enough to leave a nasty little mark, whenever the child left a mess, or talked back, or got in her way, or sometimes for nothing at all that Casey had done but simply as a convenient way to relieve her compressed and private frustrations. And so Casey early learned to stay out of her way, except when absolutely necessary.

Her mother was restless, always on the move, always coming around unexpected corners, noticing everything; always busy, preoccupied, complaining, impatient, irritable. At meals, she would eat her share of the food mostly in snatches standing up as she prepared and served it, and as Casey and her father sat at the table eating, her mother would already be at the sink, scouring the pots and pans. The only time she ever sat down was in the evening, before bed: then Casey's father would put a game on the tv, baseball or hockey depending on the time of year, with the sound turned all the way off, while her mother on the sofa would sit down to do her hair, unbinding the braid, shaking it out, and then patiently and thoroughly brushing it in long powerful strokes.

She told Casey once that Casey's father had married her for her hair. He had bought her at an auction when she was eighteen, she claimed, going deep into debt to outbid a prominent broom manufacturer, all on account of that extraordinary hair. They had lived in the big city back then, happy and poor, until one cold and sleeting day Casey's father gave a few bucks and his umbrella to a beggar who turned out to be a wealthy and eccentric man in disguise. Having lived a life of meanness, greed, and grasping foreclosures, this rich man had been given a revelation in the form of a tumour the size of a lime pressing on the back of his brain.

After his diagnosis he had gone about the city in disguise, posing as a poor homeless man and rewarding anyone who showed him kindness. To Casey's father he had given the deed to this PMU farm. They had planned to sell it, knowing nothing about horses or farming either, but could never find anyone willing to take it off their hands, and had been trapped out here ever since: and that, Casey's mother told her, is why you should never be kind to strangers, for in this life no act of generosity goes unpunished.

IN WINTER, when it was too cold to play outside, Casey often followed her father on his rounds, making a third with Rusty and Mud, the shaggy, matted, and boisterous mongrels who were always at his heels. Her father didn't mind her tagging along; he even seemed to like it in his quiet, awkward way.

It would still be dark when they left the house. The dogs would be waiting for them in the mudroom, where it would already be cold enough to see your breath. They knew better than to bark, but their excited panting would fill the little room, nails scrabbling on the unfinished plywood floor, always in imminent danger of knocking Casey down as she tried to pull on her boots.

Outside, the black sky above would be spattered with stars, and the floodlight from the house would cast long black shadows, and the only sound in the world would be the scrunching of their boots on the hard packed snow and the heavy panting of the dogs. Or sometimes the sky would be covered over with soft black clouds, and the wind would come scouring across the empty field, cutting through her little thin body and whipping the snow and ice into her face; then her eyes would blur over with tears, and she'd struggle not to slip.

Coming into the stables out of the cold was always a keen pleasure. She loved stepping into the warm wet air, heavy with the smell of straw and dung, and the sounds of a hundred and twenty horses, nickering and snorting hello. She would follow her father silently as he walked up and down the rows, saying good morning to each mare, looking her over, making sure she looked healthy and well, and finally checking the rubber boot beneath her tail, the one used to catch her urine, make sure it was properly in place and hadn't become plugged up with dung, as they often did. As he worked, the horses would shift uneasily; heavy and swollen in the later stages of pregnancy, their eyes would be glazed over with sullen resignation, listless, bored, unhappy, and trapped.

This would take a couple of hours, to check each and every mare. By then the farmhands would have arrived—interchangeable young men who rarely took much interest in Casey, and never seemed to stick around long enough for Casey to take much interest in them either. Then the horses would be fed, and a row of them turned out to exercise, and Casey and the dogs would crouch at the gate and watch them gambol and roll in the snow while her father and the hands scraped out the stalls and scrubbed the boots.

In late winter and early spring, the mares would grow restless, moody, rebellious, some even a little vicious, and they'd all be turned out into the pasture for the season, where soon the foals would come. Sometimes, out of curiosity or boredom, Casey would go with her father when he drove the old orange truck out to check on them. It was fun to squat in the back of the truck with the dogs, jostled and bounced and tossed about as they drove over the bumpy muddy fields, cool in the soft spring air, the low sun spilling bright.

Once they came across a mare, alone and separate from the herd, straining in violent distress. Casey spotted her from far away, watching her lie half-down and scramble back up again, skitter backwards and forwards, thrashing her head and contorting her body wildly as if in a desperate fight with some fierce invisible enemy. The dogs saw her too, and started to bark; and her father turned the truck and slowed down to a crawl as they got closer, approaching in a wide and cautious circle. The mare was making a keening and unearthly moan like no sound Casey had ever heard; the sound poured over the pasture, and filled her head, and disturbed her sleep for a long time afterwards.

The mud and melting snow were churned up beneath the mare's hooves. Beads of sweat stood out all over her body, despite a cool west wind; her eyes rolled and bulged, showing the whites all streaked with red, and her lips were pulled back from her teeth as she twisted her body to bite at her own sides. Here and there she had bitten herself hard enough to break the skin, and her lips were slobbered with a sort of foam of saliva and blood. As they continued to circle around, inching carefully closer, they could see now that the head, neck, and one leg of an enormous foal were sticking partway out of her, stillborn and stuck; and the dead foal's head lolled limply back and forth as the mare tried desperately and futilely to squeeze it out.

THAT SUMMER when she was six, her last summer before she started school, Casey spent most of her time in the woods behind their house, down past the vegetable garden and the half-dozen apple trees they called the orchard.

They weren't much for woods, just a long and narrow stretch of ash trees, skinny tall poplars and scrubby brush that ran all along the east side of their property, hiding it from the highway. Just inside the treeline there was a little clearing, an enclave, where a long-abandoned outhouse was patiently and peacefully rotting away. In this clearing Casey made a home for her doll Polly and her two stuffed animals, constructing a sort of lean-to out of sticks, and a bed of moss and leaves, with an old tree stump serving for a table; and she would spend long hours in solemn play, having deep and intricate conversations with Polly, lunching off handfuls of raspberries from the garden. Sometimes her father's dogs would join her, and she would pretend they were Polly's brothers; she would give them dog biscuits she'd taken from her father's pockets, and pick the swollen ticks from their bodies, as big and round and smooth as purple grapes, and roughly brush their knotted fur, just as her own mother would check her for ticks at bedtime and then roughly brush her brown tangly hair until the tears sprang out in her eyes.

Gradually, surreptitiously, Casey added more items that she magpied out of the house: a pair of tea towels to serve as a blanket and a tablecloth, a few pieces of cutlery that she would pocket while helping clear the dishes after dinner, a cracked old cup here and a rarely used saucer there. Taking one dish from the back of the china cabinet, she would apologize to all the other dishes that she was leaving behind, untouched, whispering urgently and plaintively to them, with one eye out for her mother. She hated to think that she must be hurting their feelings by not choosing them, and tried to assure them that it wasn't because they weren't good enough, but what could she do? She couldn't choose them all.

As the days gradually got longer and her parents seemed content to turn a blind eye, she got a little bolder, adding a small pot and wooden spoon, and some of her mother's good Tupperware to use as bowls, and a spare flashlight from the mudroom in case Polly got frightened at night; she improved the bed with an old throw pillow and made a floor of sorts from a stiff blue blanket that she quarried out of the back of the linen closet. She began to smuggle out food, too, from the depths of the pantry, anything that looked like it had been in there a long time, collecting dust, and that her mother seemed unlikely to miss: cans of soup and beans and pineapple slices, a box of crackers, a bag of dried apricots, a jar of applesauce and one of hot dog relish. These she stacked carefully inside the old outhouse, except for the crackers: the crackers she just ate.

The summer wore on, July seeped into August and her parents were starting to talk of how she would be going to school, soon. At first they said little to her directly, and she was left to glean what she could from their conversations. All she could tell for certain was that one day soon, a bus would pull up at the end of the drive, and she would be put on that bus and driven away—an image that in her mind was mingled, in a confused but insistent manner, with thoughts of the weanling foals being herded onto trucks every October, to be taken off to auction and never return.

Then her mother would entertain herself sometimes by telling Casey what school would be like: "First," she might say, "they'll teach you how to stand up straight, without slouching. And you'll have to stand in a long row with books on your head and recite the alphabet, and if the book falls, you'll get a whack across the back with a whippy stick and have to start over again, and if you cry you'll get more whacks across the back with the stick until you stop."

Casey was unsure what an alphabet was, or what it meant to recite one. Or her mother might say, cheerfully, "Every Friday morning they'll have a spelling test, and math and such, all the things you'll have been learning during the week. And whatever child does the worst on the test has to spend the rest of the day sitting in a cage that hangs down from the ceiling, about four feet above the floor, and they call it the Stupid Cage, and whatever child does the best on the test gets to poke the stupid child through the bars of the cage with a big long stick, and they call it the Smart Stick." And it would be obvious that her mother was enjoying herself very much.

CASEY BEGAN EXPLORING deeper into the woods. She went cautiously at first, a little further every day, finding narrow paths through the brush, making herself familiar with the face of each individual tree. She learned that if she went straight north, away from the house, she couldn't go very far at all before she came to a barbed wire fence, and beyond that a dry and shallow ditch, and then the highway. She could have gotten past the fence without a problem, it was as old and neglected as the outhouse, the round wooden posts spongy to the touch and tilted over at precarious angles, the two lines of barbed wire all rusted and tangled, in many places trampled down and grown over by brambly weeds or outright snapped, but she had no real interest in going past it. She preferred to stay out of sight of the road, pretending it was a wide river that marked the boundaries of her wild kingdom, and the rumbling sounds of occasional passing traffic she transformed in her imagination to the sound of rushing water.

The greater part of her kingdom lay to the west, where she could ramble for hours undisturbed. Go far enough and the ground would begin to rise, rolling gently at first, the poplars now interspersed with jack pine, and then abruptly, all steep and forbidding. She scrambled up this escarpment one day, a taxing climb that left her covered in scratches and dirt, her eyes stinging with sweat. At the top, she found herself on a ridge looming high above the pasture where a band of horses grazed languidly in the afternoon heat. She lay on her stomach in the scratchy grass and looked out over the fields, feeling drowsy, hot, and happy, entirely empty of thoughts and wants. As sleep overtook her, she had the curious illusion that she could hear the horses' hooves thundering across the turf, though the animals themselves continued to stand listlessly in the grass below. The next day, she broke out in a wicked rash that covered most of both her legs, and patches of it on her hands, her arms, and even her belly: swollen and stinging, red as a hot stovetop. It itched and burned so bad it felt like fiery tiny ants had burrowed beneath her skin and were biting her from the inside out; her mother made her soak in a hot bath mixed with slimy oatmeal, and covered her with pink stinky lotion, and kept her inside the house for four tedious and excruciating days, making her wear oven mitts to stop her from scratching the seeping and waxy blisters.

6

*Nora and Casey attend a wedding in Strathdale;
the minister gives Casey advice*

THIS HAPPENED ONCE when Nora and Casey went to a wedding
out in Strathdale. Casey wasn't actually invited, but she went
along anyway. They were fifteen at the time, but you wouldn't
have guessed it to look at either of them: Nora was half a foot
taller and looked very much like a young woman; Casey, though
actually slightly the older of the two, still looked like she was
twelve: short, lithe, and boyish. She didn't really own any nice
dresses or dressy clothes, so she'd had to borrow a dress from
Tracy for the occasion.

It was late July. For several days the weather had been hot,
airless, almost unbearably muggy. The sky that morning was
thinly smeared with weak white clouds; by the time they left
for Strathdale, a little after two o'clock, the wind had kicked up
from the west and fat black clouds were making evening out of
the afternoon.

They drove down to Strathdale with Nora's favourite cousin,
Katharine, who had moved to Winnipeg four years before to go to
university. This was her first visit back in a year and a half. Nora
adored her. Like most of her father's side of the family, Kat was
unreasonably tall; she had a gawky long neck, a moony round
face, and clunky glasses perched on a wedge and pointy nose.
Casey thought she looked like a nerdy and good-natured ostrich.

Kat's car was a clunky old Crown Victoria with one cracked
headlight and a suspect muffler that she called the Queen Vic.

They stopped on the way out of town to fill up with gas, and they bought red licorice, slushies, cigarettes, and barbecue-flavoured sunflower seeds for the ride. Nora peppered her with questions about what it was like to go to university and to live in the big city, and Katharine happily regaled them with not entirely improbable tales of her fine bohemian existence: sharing a rented house with three other students and hosting epic parties, attending openings at the WAG and first nights at the Warehouse, going to hear music at the Main Spot and then staying after closing to drink on with the staff and whatever musicians had been playing that night. She smoked five menthol cigarettes over the forty-minute drive and between cigarettes drummed the steering wheel with the side of her thumb; she wore a flimsy beige and brown sundress, a matching floppy sun hat, no makeup and most certainly no bra; her fingernails were cracked and stubby and her fingers paint-stained, and all in all she was utterly glamorous.

A fork of lightning flashed over a field of canola just as they were approaching the outskirts of town, followed by a crack of thunder so loud it seemed to make the Queen Vic shake. Fat rapid splats of sudden rain came bursting across the windshield, and soon they could barely see through the downpour.

They circled the church for a while, but the closest spot they could find to park was several blocks away, and they were forced to run for it through the driving rain, laughing helplessly, instantly drenched. The outline of Katharine's body was clearly visible through her soaked dress, and they shook themselves out in the vestibule like wet dogs, unchastened by the disapproving glares of the ushers. The ceremony had already begun, and the pews were packed to capacity anyway, so they had to stand at the back, still dripping.

They spotted Nora's family sitting five rows up, along the aisle. Her father was idly gawking this way and that, looking at the flower arrangements. Tracy looked pouty and bored, probably still sulking that she hadn't been allowed to go along in Katharine's car with the older girls. Her mother was following the sermon with a show of prim and purse-lipped interest, and her grandmother, hand in her open mouth, was absent-mindedly worrying at a tooth. Flashes of lightning sent pulses of coloured light through the stained-glass windows, and there was a near-simultaneous barrage of thunder so loud and rattling it startled a collective gasp from all the guests, followed by a hushed and nervous giggling.

The minister droned on for what felt like forever, punctuated by the occasional awkward cough or murmur from the wedding guests. Standing at the back, they could barely make out anything he was saying, but it was fascinating to watch him. He was elderly and obese, his balding head combed over with a few sad strands of greasy grey hair and his fat pouchy face jiggling as he spoke, glistening with sweat. When he would lean forward to emphasize a point, sometimes stabbing the air sternly with his finger, then his whole body would tremble. He looked angry, as if he had forgotten that he was supposed to be presiding over a joyful celebration and not denouncing a sinful and backsliding congregation. The bride and groom stood patiently before him, looking shiny, terrified, and slightly nauseous. The overcrowded church was airless and hot, thick with the stewing smell of wilting lilies, discount perfume, and fresh sweat.

"Poor thing," Katharine whispered as they got to the vows at last, and the groom bent over to place the ring on his bride's finger. But later, when they filed through the receiving line, she would hug the bride with a squeal of delight and say, "You must be *so* so happy! I'm *so* jealous!" The groom was burly, stiff, and pink as a pencil eraser; the bride looked tiny standing beside him, pudgy and freckled, and their faces shone whenever they looked at one another: joyous, grateful, and amazed.

By the time the ceremony was finally over and the guests had begun to shuffle slowly out of the church, the rainstorm was over too, as brief as it had been violent. There were great slashes of blue sky through the clouds, and the puddles were so deep in the streets that in some places they overwhelmed the curbs and spilled onto the sidewalks.

Katharine's parents joined them at the bottom of the steps, Bonnie and her husband Geoff, a wisp of a man with a perpetual, expectant half-smile on his face, as if he went through life in constant anticipation of a pleasant surprise that never quite arrived. Nora told him how much she liked his bowtie, and he beamed, and launched into a long, quite earnest explanation of how he had been practising all week to learn to tie it. It was one of his more endearing qualities that he never suspected anyone of teasing him, and assumed that everyone in the world was just as simple, sincere, and well-meaning as he was himself.

Bonnie, who gloried in her great height and was wearing heels to accentuate it, greeted her daughter. "My dear," she said, "everyone can see your nipples right through that thing."

Katharine laughed. "You look lovely, too, Mom."

Bonnie put an arm around her daughter's shoulder and kissed her lightly on the side of the head. "And Nora," she said affectionately, turning her attention to her niece: "Nora, you just look more beautiful every time I see you. I always said you reminded me of Sadie, but I think you might turn out even lovelier, poor thing." Sadie was another of Nora's many aunts; Nora had never actually met her, though she'd often heard stories about her.

The sun poured warmly through the rapidly dissipating clouds, shimmering off the oily surface of the puddles; the ground was littered with leaves and small sticks, torn down by the violence of the storm. Most of the wedding guests chose to walk from the church to the community centre across town, crowding the sidewalks and fanning out to fill the middle of the street like an impromptu parade, strolling slowly in groups of four or five, chatting and gossiping pleasantly. Katharine took her shoes in her hands and waded through the deepest part of every puddle, some coming up past her ankles; Nora and Casey took off their shoes and socks too and did what she did.

Tracy spotted their cousin James Mazur, walking with his parents and grandparents, and went over to join him, glad to have someone she could talk to. A gangly boy in a poorly fitting suit lingered back to walk alongside Nora, making charmingly fumbling attempts to strike up a conversation. He knew her name; he looked about fifteen too, and talked as if they had met before, maybe more than once. Nora couldn't remember him for the life of her, and she felt bad about it, so pretended that she knew him.

Outside the community centre, a pair of young boys, maybe three and four years old, raced and chased each other up and down the long, low wheelchair ramp, and up and down and up and down again, shrieking happily while their mother stood warily and wearily at the bottom of the ramp to make sure neither of them darted suddenly out into the parking lot.

The dreary, concrete, barn-like building sat at the very edge of town. It had been decorated earlier with streamers and a banner that now lay torn and sodden in the puddles all around. At the back of the building, past the parking lot, there was nothing but a deep uneven field sloping down, all seedy grass, large stones, and scraggly weeds, with one solitary tree in the distance, a forked and leaning cottonwood, imposing and aloof.

The doors to the centre were open, but no one was in a hurry to go inside. Nora's uncle Matt, his wife Louise, and both their sons were there. There was Mark, the younger boy, who had gone straight into his father's business out of school, just like everyone always knew he would. Nora had never particularly liked him: he was athletic, slightly stupid, and handsome enough in a blocky sort of way, with none of his father's effortless charm. But she adored Nathanael, his older brother, dark dreamy slouchy slender Nat with his sleepy eyes and soft voice, and his beautiful, slightly feminine face. It was as if Uncle Matt's personality had been carefully divided between his sons, with Mark getting all the bad parts, and Nat all the good. Nat and Katharine had been inseparable growing up, as close as siblings, as close as Matt and Bonnie themselves had been when they were children; now he was living out in Montreal, studying to be a dentist at McGill. Bonnie, who loved Nat dearly, was fond of speculating how long it would take before he announced to everyone that he was gay. Though in actual fact he was thoroughly, even boringly heterosexual, he always told Kat not to disillusion her mother: "Let her keep thinking she's right," he said. "It makes her so happy and smug."

Dinner was a typical country spread of chicken wings, bratwurst, and ham, garlic potatoes and knobby glazed carrots and mushy green peas, coleslaw, caesar salad, cabbage rolls, and crusty buns. They sat near the back, nine of them at a table set for eight: Kat and her parents, Nora and her family, and then Casey the extra and uninvited guest, squeezed in anyhow. Casey and Nora were permitted half a glass of wine each and had to pretend they were unused to alcohol. The wine was red, acidic, and nasty, and it brought a delicate blush to Nora's cheeks, and she looked beautiful. Tracy wasn't allowed to have any, but Kat let her try a sip when her mother and grandmother weren't looking, and she grimaced with violent disgust, and shuddered.

Casey sat between Nora and Nora's uncle Geoff, who fussily cut his food into very small pieces before he ate it. He used his knife and fork to tease the meat off the chicken wings, pushing the crinkly skin and bones to one side. He had always been fascinated that Casey lived on a PMU farm, and peppered her with endless questions whenever he saw her.

Kat and Nora were talking about high school, which Nora and Casey would be starting in the fall. Whenever Nora was around Katharine, she would unconsciously adopt some of her cousin's mannerisms and her way of speaking. She drummed her thumb against the edge of her plate; she held her chin slightly up and her shoulders down to accentuate the full length of her neck; she used phrases like "poor thing" and slipped the occasional casual "fucking" into her sentences.

"Now tell me," Geoff was saying to Casey, "do all the horses have names?"

"Yes, of course."

"All of them. You said you have, what, almost a hundred of them? And you can actually remember all their names, just by looking at them?"

"Yes, I guess."

"Amazing," he said, shaking his head incredulously. "*I* couldn't do it," he said confidentially. "I couldn't do it. No way," he added with a sort of breathy laugh, as if Casey had tried to argue with him.

Bonnie had brazenly co-opted an extra bottle of wine and kept it by her hand so that she could constantly top up her and her brother's glasses. Simon, who had been looking so glum and uncomfortable in his good suit, was smiling happily now and even laughing quietly, and the skin would crinkle charmingly at the corner of his eyes: Casey didn't remember ever having seen her friend's father laugh like that before. He and his sister were reminiscing about the numerous family weddings they'd been to over the years, including two for John, their oldest brother and now the father of the bride. Their brother Matt at the next table over had turned his chair at an angle so that he could listen to Bonnie and Simon's conversation and periodically chime in.

Across the table, Nora's mother was shooting nasty glares at her sister-in-law every time she topped up Simon's wine glass. Lynn had permed and coloured her hair for the occasion but had not bought a new dress, feeling she was hardly justified spending such money for the wedding of a niece they almost never saw. Because she'd put on a fair bit of weight over the past few years, a fact she was still in some denial about, she'd had to let her dress out a little, but it was still too tight, so that her bosom seemed to squeeze out the top like toothpaste from a tube, and she was forced to sit rigidly upright in her chair and breathe in shallow, emphysemic fashion. She nagged at Tracy to eat her food properly and fussed over her mother, who was drinking cold milk out of a thermos they'd brought from home, and who was telling Katharine a rambling anecdote about a recent trip to the hospital down in Brandon.

"Eight hours we had to sit and wait there," Alma was saying. "Eight hours. Well, I thought they had forgotten about us entirely."

"Terrible," said Katharine politely.

"Don't mind us, I said to them, we only drove an hour to come here and get x-rays, it's not like we're in a hurry. And poor Lynn here with her arm swollen up like a beach ball and nothing to eat since breakfast."

"Tracy."

"What?"

"*Tracy's* arm all swollen up."

"That's what I said."

One part of the story she didn't mention was the fact that she wasn't supposed to drive at all anymore and hadn't renewed her driver's license in half a decade; nor had she left any kind of note or indication where she had gone off with Tracy and the car, so that for the dozen or so hours they were away, the rest of the family was in a terrified panic, phoning everyone they knew.

Tracy had landed awkwardly when climbing over and dropping down from their back fence, twisting her ankle and tumbling head first into the road. Flinging her arm out to break the fall, she had ended up breaking her wrist, and had to wear a cast for ten weeks: it had only come off, in fact, the week before the wedding.

Since it was strictly forbidden to climb over that fence, Tracy had lied, pretending she had been going to cross the road to the park properly, at the intersection, and was almost run down by a speeding car that had come whipping recklessly around the curve and sped right on, not even slowing down after it could have *killed* her. Tracy was not a practiced and effortless liar like Nora or Casey, and she was naïvely proud of this effort, which had been accepted by their grandmother unquestioningly and even caused a minor stir around the town.

The whole experience had been the highlight of Tracy's young life so far: not so much the trip to the hospital, although that had been exciting and different at least, but all the commotion it had caused at home, and showing up at school wearing the cast, and all her friends signing it, and getting a pass on homework because it was her right hand and she was right-handed, and James Mazur offering to help carry her books and stuff around school every day, and just generally being the centre of concern and attention.

"Anyway," said Lynn, bristling visibly and breathing heavily, "they're thinking about putting up a crosswalk at that intersection after Tracy's accident. Ever since they put in that gas station and motel across from the golf course it's been an accident waiting to happen, it's just a blessing no one's been killed already the way those people will come whipping around that curve, but like I said to them, I said if you're not willing to put up traffic lights or at *least* a stop sign there then you're better off not doing anything, because with that sort of driver, you know, a crosswalk won't mean anything."

They were interrupted by a raucous clatter of cutlery on glasses, and laughs and cheers around the room as the bride and groom stood and kissed yet again, and Katharine slipped a little more wine into Nora's glass with a sympathetic wink, and then Geoff was questioning Casey again, asking her how they got all the mares pregnant all the time: did each mare have their own mate, or was it just one stallion for all hundred of them, like a kind of equine harem? And what did they do with all the baby horses—or did they force the mares to have miscarriages?

One of the front doors had been propped open for a while, but the mosquitoes were starting to come in, and it had to be closed. Now it was hot and claustrophobic inside the community centre, which was packed to capacity if not past. The toasts and speeches were underway, that purgatorial stretch of embarrassing anecdotes, awkward jokes, and sentimental testimonials, with occasional painful bursts of semi-drunken emotion; seated near the back, they could hardly make out half of what was being said, but it seemed to drone on forever.

Katharine excused herself to go outside for a cigarette, and Nat and his brother both followed her out. Matt had turned his chair completely around now, the better to join in the conversation with Bonnie and Simon. Quite a few people around the room had left their seats to stretch their legs, slip outside, or use the facilities. The bar wasn't open yet, but several men were lounging around it, waiting to be first in line; a few others had gone back to the buffet table to help themselves to the remnants of the feast, eating straight out of the enormous aluminum foil trays. The minister was one of these, hovering over the tray of ham with a proprietary air and feeding fatty scrap-ends into his mouth with quick, jerky motions. Casey had been watching him for a while now, more than ever convinced that he was going to have a massive heart attack at any moment, and both longing and dreading to see it.

Nora touched Casey on the elbow and asked her to come to the washroom with her. The ladies' room was up near the front of the hall, on the far side, and Nora led them on a deliberately circuitous route along the tables, so that they passed close to the boy who had come and spoken to her earlier. He saw her coming; he waved earnestly as she went by and she sort of waved back as she hurried past, holding her body stiff with embarrassment. Once inside the safety of the washroom, she whispered to Casey, "I didn't recognize anyone at his table, either. I don't remember him at all."

"So you think he's cute?"

"*No*," said Nora, as if outraged. "God no. Do you?" The ladies' room was fairly busy, not a good place to have a private conversation. Having come there anyway, Nora decided she might as well use the toilet. While Casey waited for her, she watched a fly skittering across the surface of the dull and smudgy mirror. Someone had left half a glass of white wine on the counter by the sink, and Casey sipped from it experimentally; finding it far less nasty than the red wine had been, and pleasantly cool besides, and since there was no one watching her at the moment, she took a large quick swig of it and then put it back in place and started to wash her hands. A woman in the stall next to Nora's seemed to be in some kind of discomfort, letting out occasional low moans. It really was unbearably hot, Casey thought; she was all sticky with sweat, and she felt a wave of nausea wash over her, and for a brief terrifying moment she thought she might puke all over the sink.

When Nora was done they didn't go back to their table; Casey said if she didn't go outside and get some fresh air she was going to be sick. On their way out they passed the buffet, where the waiters were clearing away the dinner trays and setting out the coffee urns and the wedding cake to be cut and served, while those three- and four-year-old boys scampered on their hands and knees beneath the tablecloth, pretending to be dogs, and the minister was snatching up as much of the remaining ham as he could before they took it away, cramming the scrap ends greedily into his mouth, which was ringed round with shiny grease. His face was beet red and his eyes were bulging, his whole body trembling ominously. Casey snagged a handful of sugar cubes from a bowl as they walked by, popping one into her mouth and putting the rest in her pocket.

Coming outside from the dimly lit building, the bright flat light struck their eyes painfully at first. Kat, Nat, and Mark were still out there, standing in a little circle smoking, probably on their second or third cigarettes by then. Mark was holding forth on the relative merits of the bridesmaids, and making them sound like the three bears' bowls of porridge: one was much too pretty, and unlikely to be available; one wasn't pretty enough to be worth the effort, though not so unattractive that she wouldn't do in a pinch, at least after a few more drinks; but the middle bridesmaid was just right: pretty enough that you'd want to make love to her even totally sober, but not so pretty that she's probably got too many better options and offers.

"You're such a fucking pig," Katharine said cheerfully.

"If you can't get laid at a wedding, you aren't even trying," he retorted. "Heck, I bet even *you* could get laid tonight if you wanted to, Kat." She replied with her middle finger. This was the affectionate sort of way they always bantered when they got together, that Nora and Casey found so glamorous and sophisticated.

There were a dozen or so other people outside as well, some of them smoking, some of them just standing about chatting. Casey slapped a fat mosquito on her arm, leaving a starburst of blood. Half a dozen kids were playing tag in the parking lot, darting in and around the parked cars, up the ramp and down the stairs. One kid racing up the ramp almost barrelled into Mike Mazur, who had come out of the building not long behind Nora and Casey; he had to jump back smartly to avoid a collision. The kid charged heedlessly past him and launched himself over the railings on the far side, tumbling down to the damp grass below, then rolling up to his feet and running off around the back of the community centre. His pursuer, who looked a little younger and slightly chubby, wasn't bold enough to go over the railings, but instead leaned against them, craning his head over and yelling, "Out of bounds! Out of bounds!" with a wild indignation.

From inside the building, there was a burst of wild applause and clatter on glasses, even louder and more sustained than ever. "Does that mean the speeches are over?" Kat wondered hopefully.

"It probably means they opened the bar," said Nat. "We'd better get in line."

As they headed back in, Mike Mazur stopped Nora and Casey to say hello. He had taken off his suit jacket and had it draped rakishly over his shoulder as he leaned against the railing and puffed at a fat cigar that smelled reminiscent of a tire fire. He asked Casey how her father and mother were doing, and asked after Rusty, whose eyes had lately clouded over with cataracts. The way the sun was striking his straw-coloured hair made it look golden, it practically glittered, and he complimented Nora on how beautiful she looked. He must have been pretty drunk already because he leered at her and laid it on fairly thick and creepy, and told her she was the loveliest girl at the wedding, and was probably making the bride and her bridesmaids all jealous.

Inside, they were clearing most of the tables away to make room for a dance floor, leaving only a handful at the back and along the side for people to rest their drinks on. There were two long lines for the washroom, and an even longer one for the bar; Nora noticed that her father and her Uncle Matt were at the front of that line. Their table was one of the ones that hadn't been moved. Three plates of cake had been saved for Nora, Casey, and Kat; of the others, only Tracy had eaten more than a few bites: she had finished hers and was now eating her grandmother's slice. It was dense, stale, and sickeningly sweet.

"You're supposed to save a piece of that and put it under your pillow," said James Mazur's grandfather, Jim Ritchie, who had wandered over to join them. "Then you'll dream of who you're going to marry when you get older." And he smiled with melancholy affection at Tracy and his grandson, who were sitting next to one another, whispering and giggling madly. He had aged immensely in the years since he had retired, and the feistiness and irritability was all drained out of him: he looked so old now, so tired, listless, and grey. He had lost a lot of weight as well, far too much weight, so that his skin sagged alarmingly, as if his face was in danger of sliding right off his skull.

Up at the front the first dance was beginning, the bride and her father alone on the floor, turning slow unrhythmic circles to a sticky mournful tune. The bride's mother looked on and cried, as brides' mothers must.

Alma was gazing vaguely in the direction of the dance floor, her mottled hand jammed shamelessly and probably unconsciously into the back of her mouth. Matt and Simon returned from the bar triumphant, skillfully carrying an array of glasses: beer for Matt, plastic tumblers of whiskey for Simon and Bonnie, a glass of white wine for Lynn, and a Shirley Temple with extra cherries for Tracy. She was a great addict of maraschino cherries, so much so that they couldn't keep them around the house, and only bought them on special occasions like Christmas, Easter, and her birthday: she would even drink the pale red syrup out of the jar when all the fruit was gone.

There was a smattering of applause as John passed his daughter's hand gallantly to the groom and retired from the floor, and the newlyweds finished the dance alone together, the bride resting her face in a capitulation of love and exhaustion against her husband's chest, leaving a smear of sweat and makeup on his wide lapel. A new song began, even more languorous and doleful than the first, and the bridesmaids and groomsmen paired off and joined them on the floor.

Nora was anxiously scanning the crowd for a glimpse of that boy, so that she could force Casey to go over and talk to him, find out who he was. She dreaded, for some reason, the idea of having to admit to him that she couldn't remember him: she couldn't stand the thought of hurting someone's feelings, and she felt certain he would be crushed. And so she gave a startled little jump when he suddenly surged up behind her, looking ganglier than ever, all elbows and sharp angles. Before Nora could even say hello he was asking her if she would dance with him, bursting the question out in a strained and slightly manic voice, without warning or preamble, and with an air of having screwed himself up to a pitch of desperate bravado. Nora just stared at him blankly for a few moments, startled and embarrassed, and then stammered out, "I need to pee." She turned and walked quickly, rigidly away, not turning her head to see if anyone was following.

"I'll dance with you," said Katharine cheerfully. The poor boy was looking utterly crushed, and like he wished he could just disappear; he looked at Katharine now as if uncomprehendingly, and it was all she could do not to laugh out loud. "Come on," she said, taking him by the hand and pulling him along.

Casey followed them slowly towards the dance floor. As she

went along, she kept an eye out for unattended, half-empty glasses of white wine that she could surreptitiously finish off. Nobody paid any attention to her.

Nora, who had mostly recovered her composure, joined them just as Katharine and the boy were coming off the dance floor, one song ending and another starting up. Katharine said to her, "Steven and I were just arguing about who's the best dancer on the floor." And Nora, relieved that she knew the boy's name at last and could now at least better pretend to remember him, happily joined in.

The next song to come on was the chicken dance, and Katharine gave a whoop and pulled Steven back out onto the dance floor; Nora took Casey by the hand and pulled her out there too, and Casey had no choice but to go along and try to dance with her, for it would have been more conspicuous to refuse. She managed to slip off when that song was done and the next one came on. Steven moved over so that he and Nora were dancing next to one another, if not actually together. Katharine grabbed that boy who had been playing tag outside earlier, the slightly chubby one who had cried, "Out of bounds!" She took him by his hands and was forcibly dancing him, working his arms back and forth like mad pistons. Mark was out there doing a kind of slick and slinky mating dance in predatory circles around the just-right bridesmaid; even Bonnie and Geoff were on the dance floor together, twisting earnestly. Everyone looked happy; everyone, it seemed to Casey, knew that they belonged and knew the secret of simply enjoying themselves: everyone except for her. She felt dizzy, nauseous, and hot, the floor listing beneath her feet, but it didn't occur to her that she was simply drunk. She could feel beads of sweat springing out all over her face.

She made her way out of the community centre as quickly and discreetly as she could, threading her way through the maze of people. Once outside, she kept going, down the ramp and around the side of the building. Behind the centre, by the garbage bins, she passed close by a group of maybe half a dozen young men—the groom among them—who were standing in a loose circle, talking loudly and smoking weed. Their faces loomed out of the long shadow of the building; she could feel them leering at her as she walked quickly on through a pungent cloud of mingled stinks, of skunkweed, garbage, and cheap cologne, but she kept her head rigidly forward and her feet moving, through the parking lot, between the cars, and out into the field. There was a rough path that had been walked down through the weeds and seedy grass, made muddy by the recent storm; she was thronged by mosquitoes, but she ignored them too, not checking her pace until she had reached the cottonwood tree. Behind the tree, safely out of sight, she leaned forward and violently puked: once, twice, three times.

Her head throbbed painfully, and her nostrils burned, but still she felt a little better. She pulled some leaves from the tree and used them as makeshift tissues to wipe her mouth and blow her nose; she spat as much of the vomit taste away as she could, and then moved away from the tree, so that she couldn't smell her own puke anymore.

It was a warm evening, but deliciously cool compared to inside the community centre. There was a strong breeze now, soothing and dry, that helped with the mosquitoes. She noticed now that her shoes were caked with mud and the skirt of Tracy's good dress was wet, grass-stained, and splashed with flecks of puke, but she couldn't care.

Past the cottonwood, the field began to slope down even more dramatically; the ground became rockier, more weed than grass. Further down, maybe forty or fifty yards from where she now stood, the path disappeared into a line of trees, tall pliant poplars that gently swayed and rustled in the wind. Soft grey clouds were smeared across the sky, and beneath the clouds a scattering of gulls flew playfully back and forth, darting and circling. The upward slanting rays from the lowering sun illuminated the gulls' white bellies and the white undersides of their wings, so that they seemed to glow, luminous against the backdrop of the clouds.

Casey looked behind her; the community centre and the town were entirely, blessedly out of sight: she could almost pretend she was in the middle of nowhere, lost in the wild, miles and miles from any human presence, except that she could still clearly hear the pulsing and pounding of the tightly repetitive music and the din and clamour of raucous voices. The sun in the west was just beginning to take on a reddish tint as it inched toward the horizon; in a half an hour or so, it would throw a spectacular sheet of colour across the sky. She knew that she really ought to be heading back now, get back to the reception before Nora started to miss her or worry, but just the thought of going back inside the hot, loud, crowded building, being crushed and surrounded by all those people, all those strangers, made her feel a little sick again. She told herself that Nora wouldn't even notice she was gone, not for a while yet: she was having fun, she was dancing, she was surrounded by family and friends and people who wanted her attention; and if Nora wouldn't notice that Casey was gone, nobody else would either. Nobody else would notice if she never came back at all. Above her one of the gulls squawked with surprising violence, its playfulness turned to sudden aggression. The group broke up, most flying back towards the town, a few others out over the trees.

She thought that if she went just a little further, just down the hill and into the woods a little ways, she wouldn't be able to hear the noise from the wedding any more: then she would enjoy the peace and quiet for five minutes, that was all, and then she'd feel completely better, and she'd have the strength to go back and try and enjoy herself the way a normal person would. But she only got a few steps further down the path before she was startled by a voice at her back, saying gravely: "A beautiful evening, isn't it?"

It was that minister, though she couldn't believe he could have gotten so close to her without her hearing or sensing him approach. "It's always so lovely after a good hard rain," he went on pleasantly. "The air always smells so clean."

Casey agreed politely. Up close he looked even more obese, if that were possible: even his wrists and fingers were fat; even his head was fat. His suit jacket was hanging open, and she could see the enormous yellow circles of sweat beneath his armpits and around his collar. His face was blotchy, his breathing was laborious and asthmatic, and he leaned on a plain aluminum walking stick. She found him repulsive and also spellbinding, like a toad or a ghost.

He said, "Now tell me, young lady, why are you out here alone, and not in there dancing with your friends? Is everything all right?" She assured him it was, slightly alarmed by this show of concern.

He turned his face to cough slightly, and then said, with a heavy-handed attempt to sound playful, "I suppose you're out here daydreaming about your own wedding, are you?"

"I just wanted some air," she said meekly. "It was getting so hot in there."

"Indeed it was," he agreed solemnly. "Hot and loud. It gives me a headache," he told her, leaning forward as if confiding a secret. She could smell the ham on his breath, and see a ring of grease around his mouth, embedded with crumbs and smears of icing from the wedding cake. "Like someone hammering a nail, right here," he added, lightly brushing the end of his fat thick finger between his eyes. His hand was trembling, and his cheeks were starting to shiver and shake. Yet again, Casey was seized by the certainty that he was about to have a massive coronary or stroke, and so close and confidingly was he leaning over her, she became abruptly terrified that he would collapse on top of her and crush her.

"Do you know why they need it so loud?"

She shook her head.

"Because they're terrified of being able to hear their own thoughts. And so they should be," he added, straightening up slightly and removing his hypnotic gaze from Casey's eyes. "So they should be. You're not from around here, are you?"

Again she shook her head. "Not really," she said meekly.

"Never trust anyone who's afraid to be alone with their own thoughts," he told her sententiously. "That's my advice to you in this life, young lady. Never trust anyone who can't stand silence and solitude. I've been stuck in this place for seventeen years, I know these people like the back of my hand. Every single one of them is small and mean and frightened and stupid. Their minds are like month-old cartons of milk, you open them up and the smell makes you sick to your stomach. I've married dozens of them to one another, God forgive me. If I could have had the whole lot of them sterilized instead, I'd feel like I'd accomplished something worthwhile in this world." All this poured out of him in a calm, dispassionate voice, but his whole body was shaking violently now, and the beads of sweat were bursting from his forehead despite the cool of the breeze.

The minister was seized now with a spasm of violent coughing, bending him forward, contorted. He made no attempt to cover his mouth. It was a raspy, rattling, bark-like cough, and large gobs of phlegm and spittle choked up out of his mouth and slobbered down his chest, and dangled from his chin. And in and with those gobs of snot and strings of spit Casey saw tiny black ants that scampered back up his chin, scurried over his lips, and slipped back into his mouth.

He looked at her again, smiling a ghastly smile that was probably intended to be avuncular. "I never caught your name, young lady."

"Casey Mack, sir."

"Well, it's been a pleasure to meet you, Miss Mack. I must be getting home now. I'll leave you to your thoughts. Remember what I said."

She watched him walk on down the path, navigating the rough uneven ground with surprising firmness until he was about half way between her and the trees, when his body suddenly crumpled up as suddenly as if he had been shot. She saw him drop heavily down, face first, making no attempt to break his fall.

Casey ran towards him in a near-panic, adrenalin surging through her body and the blood pounding behind her ears. She felt a terrified certainty that he was dead. But he was merely asleep: miraculously, he even seemed to have avoided serious injury from the fall, his forehead missing the edge of a large rock by mere inches. She could hear him snoring peacefully and rhythmically, a sort of scraping and rumbling sound like someone dragging a loaded sled over stones and gravel.

She gingerly touched his shoulder and tried to shake him awake; she thought she had succeeded when he coughed quietly and rolled over to a more comfortable position, but he instantly dozed off again, if he had ever really woken. His eyes were half-open and leaking tears, his jaw slack, mouth hanging wide.

As the minister's body relaxed into a deep slumber, dozens and dozens of those tiny black ants emerged from his mouth and nose, racing and scouring industriously over the surface of his face to gather the sticky crumbs and smears and remnants of his meal, and then carry the precious forage back inside his head. Casey was certain she even saw them come and go from inside the canals of his ears and from beneath his pouchy, swollen eyelids.

7

Dr Wellesley fathers nine children;
Simon Wellesley marries Lynn Fleisch

NORA'S FATHER, SIMON WELLESLEY, was the youngest of seven siblings. Or the youngest of nine, if you counted two acknowledged half-brothers, born to his father's long-time receptionist; or of untold more, if you put any stock in the old rumours, the nasty naughty long-forgotten gossip.

Lionel and Cicely Wellesley had moved to Canada when their eldest children, Frances and John, were four and almost two. They came first to Winnipeg, where they lived for three years and added two more children—the twins, Abigail and Sadie—before moving again.

Tall, dapper, and lamentably handsome, Lionel Wellesley was a doctor, and by all accounts an excellent one, ministering to his patients' ills as much by the gift of imparting to them his own abundant confidence and vitality as by the application of common sense and, in cases of last resort, actual medicine. He was selfless with his time and energy, known to make house calls at all hours of the night without complaint, never took vacation, and often accepted his fees in the form of eggs or quartered cows, market vegetables, homemade wines, and other payments in kind, if not quietly forgoing those fees entirely.

Lionel and Cicely never gave up the habit of dressing fully for dinner every night, eating late and alone by candlelight after the children were fed and sent upstairs. Then he put on his black tails and white tie, and she her gown and gloves, dressed as if guests at a wedding: all clothes that had come with them from England and that Cicely had painstakingly preserved and maintained, so that if they grew inexorably more threadbare and shabby over the years, it was so gradually that they themselves hardly perceived the difference. If Lionel received an emergency call during dinner, as sometimes happened, then he would attend to it without changing. For the people who lived in the town or neighbouring farms, the sight of Dr Wellesley arriving at their home in a tuxedo to tend to a feverish infant, stitch up a nasty wound, or on one memorable occasion, preside over a birth, all the while unflappably debonair, never failed to baffle and awe his patients.

Lionel was devoted to his wife; he adored her, he doted on her. Few days passed that he did not bring her home a bouquet of flowers, box of chocolates, or other gifts, ranging from dubious knick-knacks that he had accepted from patients in lieu of payment, to the latest expensive kitchen gadgets. Their intimate and formal evening dinners never entirely lost the quality of romantic liaison, a faint warm glow still enduring from the heady days of their first courtship. He often told his children how lucky they were to have a mother so beautiful, intelligent, talented, and gracious, and he meant it fervently.

In his children themselves he took only a mild and friendly interest between the hours of five and seven, primarily appreciating them as proofs and tokens of his wife's unending excellence, that naturally extended even to being a mother. Fanny, the eldest, was the serious and sensitive one, who never entirely forgave her parents for uprooting her from their English home, and then uprooting her again from Winnipeg just when she had begun to make new friends; she was painfully self-conscious of her lingering accent and gawky unfeminine height, and resentful of the constant responsibility heaped on her to shepherd and tend her younger brothers and sisters. John was the one who liked breaking things and putting them back together when he could. The twins, Gail and Sadie, were the pretty and popular ones, confident, vivacious, and carefree. Bonnie was the smart one, observant, detached, and perpetually amused. Matthew was the scamp, a schemer; he and Bonnie were an inseparable pair, partners in crime. And Simon was the baby, his mother's favourite and everybody's favourite: by nature as serious and sensitive as Fanny, but unlike her always doted on, loved, and indulged.

Alma, who in those days had taught at the local elementary school, enjoyed telling her granddaughters stories of when their father had been a young boy, and she had had him in her class, as she had had all his brothers and sisters before him, all but Fanny, the eldest. She remembered them all, all the Wellesley children, including Fanny, who had a reputation among the other schoolchildren, and even among the teachers, for being insufferably stuck up, snobbish—"but of course they said the same sort of thing about me when I first moved here, and it was all nonsense. I felt bad for that child, I could tell she was suffering. I wish I'd had her in my class, I could have really helped her."

Very different from her brother John, who knew the two sure ways to gain the respect of his peers: to do poorly at his schoolwork and make a great show of not caring; and to start frequent fights in the playground, and hit hard. "Horrible child." She also remembered Matt well, and more fondly: he was "a clever little devil, always up to no good"—the sort of child you knew would go far in life, because he was "smart as a whip and had no scruples at all." Bonnie was another one, smart as her brother Matt but not so ambitious. She was the sort of child, Alma would say, that you couldn't do anything for: schoolwork came too easily to her, everything was effortless, nothing was going to convince her that someday, sooner or later, she'd have to learn to work hard or suffer for it.

Then Tracy, who'd been listening in with genuine interest, asked if their father had also been the sort of kid that schoolwork came too easily to. "Certainly not," Alma said emphatically, with a little glint in her eye, perhaps because Simon happened to be in earshot: "Quite the opposite. And I strongly suspected," she added, narrowing her eyes, "that your aunt Bonnie did his homework for him. She coddled him horribly, you know. But I could never prove it." And Simon, gazing off into the middle distance and trying to disguise the urge to smile with an exaggerated pout, said that he didn't know what she was talking about.

"Am *I* the sort who schoolwork comes too easily to?" Tracy asked hopefully.

"I wouldn't count on it," her grandmother replied drily. "I do worry about your sister, though."

"Hey!" Nora said indignantly, looking up from the book she was reading. "That's not fair, I do too work hard."

But Alma just pursed her lips, and shook her head slowly, and continued on as if Nora wasn't in the room: "Too smart, too pretty, too popular. If I've seen it once, I've seen it a hundred times. Thank goodness she's got a friend like Casey, here. Casey's the lucky one: she knows what it's like to have to tough things out and work hard for what you get. Life won't catch *you* off guard, will it?" she added, turning her face to Casey with a little wink.

AMONG THE LOCAL FARMERS and poorer residents of the town, it was widely believed that Dr Wellesley and his wife enjoyed a glittering and busy social life. Among the wealthier and more prominent residents of the town, it was believed that the Wellesleys were incurable snobs—or rather that she must be, for he was so immensely and effortlessly charming and convivial he was impossible to blame or dislike, while very few people knew Cicely at all, beyond a handful of polite words exchanged at the store or on the street, so that it was easy to assume the worst of her.

In all her time in the town, Cicely made but one single friend, an independent-minded woman named Peggy Afton who shared with her a fondness for gardening, classical music, and lovely objects, and who was virtually the only woman Cicely had ever met who did not find her husband the least bit fascinating. Behind her brusque informality, Peggy had a kind of canny and natural tact that was better than any learned and external courtesy. When she felt like visiting Cicely, she would merely show up unannounced and let herself in, always in the mornings or early afternoons, when Lionel was sure to be out and the older children at school. She never cajoled Cicely to leave the house or visit her, nor ever attempted to interrupt her evenings; she never tried to elicit confidences under the guise of presenting a sympathetic ear, and because she had no husband or children herself, nor any particular interest in either, her conversation did not revolve endlessly around those two monotonous topics.

Together they would have a pot of tea, if it were in the morning, or some gin and tonic if it were after lunch, and talk of flower gardening and fine cooking, or discuss music and books, or Cicely might play her beloved Schubert on the piano while Peggy listened appreciatively, or Peggy might relay all the latest local gossip, something she did very adroitly, so that between her friend's anecdotes and the tales her husband brought home from his work, Cicely often felt she knew every person in that town fondly and intimately, the very people she so assiduously avoided meeting in person—knew them the way she might have felt she knew the characters in a long-running soap opera to which she was secretly devoted.

But as for Lionel's serial and compulsive infidelities, Peggy of course never alluded to them in the slightest. Such an indiscretion would have been irreparable, unforgivable, though of course Cicely knew perfectly well that her friend must have known all about them, that in fact everybody did.

When Lionel had first fathered a child with his young receptionist, the scandal had been immense. They had been living in the town only three years then; Bonnie was still an infant when Pearl Mikolash's swelling belly became too obvious to be ignored. Pearl was a local girl, barely twenty, small, mousy, and slightly cross-eyed; she had been raised on a nearby farm, her mother was dead and her father was a notoriously brutal and tyrannical man. She herself was meek, conscientious, and eager to please, she had a grateful gentle nature and a gift for hero-worship. When she became pregnant, her family disowned her completely, which was a blessing without disguise.

The uproar was enormous. More than half of Lionel's patients announced they were leaving him in outrage. Another doctor would have let himself be run out of town; another doctor's wife might have died of shame. Perhaps it was Lionel Wellesley's very foreignness that allowed him to withstand the scandal; perhaps there was a sense that a man who would travel eleven miles through a winter storm in white tie and tails to deliver a baby on an isolated farm could not be expected to be held to the same social or even moral conventions as mere mortals.

He relocated his doctor's office to a converted house with living space on the second floor, and Pearl lived there with the child, a baby boy they named Ronald, who Lionel quite openly acknowledged as his own; the second boy, named Rudy after Lionel's favourite author, came two and a half years later, when Matt was one. He treated them as a sort of second family, lunching in the small neat apartment with them every weekday. Four times a year, at Thanksgiving, Christmas, Easter, and Lionel's birthday in late August, this second family would join the first for a day. Pearl regarded the doctor's wife with slightly awe-struck admiration and shy devotion, an attitude that gratified Lionel and amused Cicely, who generally referred to her as "that poor thing." To Cicely's children she was "Auntie Pearl" and Ronald and Rudy their cousins, a polite fiction that was never particularly expected to fool any of them.

Lionel Wellesley died when Simon was seventeen years old: died in a car accident while returning home from one of those late night calls. What precisely happened to make him drive off the road and into the river was never determined. Perhaps he swerved to avoid an animal, oncoming vehicle, or will-o'-the-wisp; perhaps he had a stroke or a heart attack; perhaps he simply nodded off. That he was at least partly inebriated was certain enough, for he pretty much always was. He wore no seatbelt, and his face was half-shredded from its passage through the windshield.

Only after his death was it discovered that they were crushingly, overwhelmingly in debt. His office was on a second mortgage, their house on its third. Neither his life insurance nor the auctioning of all their possessions, including Cicely's beloved piano, was adequate to pay off the multitude of loans that had been keeping them afloat. Simon dropped out of high school and got a full-time job with the town's parks department, and supported his mother in a small apartment for the last ten years of her life. He was helped out in the beginning by his Auntie Pearl, who had also lost her home but who had always very scrupulously husbanded her salary over the years—financial help that Simon accepted furtively and shamefully, but not ungratefully, though he kept it a deadly secret from his mother and even allowed her to believe that *he* was continuing to support *them*. Cicely was easily deceived, no doubt in part because she chose to be; but it was true too that the early encroachments of old age and the accumulated years of steady stealthy alcoholism, combined with the abrupt profound grief of losing her beloved husband, her home, and all her lovely things in one devastating blow, had seemed to leave her with little more than a tenuous and twilight grasp on reality.

Fanny had married the young veterinarian Jim Ritchie almost immediately after finishing high school, and now had children of her own only a few years younger than Simon himself. Fanny was the one who had suffered the most keenly from that long-ago scandal over her father and Pearl, for she had been on the cusp of adolescence when it happened, of both an age and a temperament to be excruciatingly vulnerable to the teasing and mockery of her peers, the protracted humiliations, the painfully self-conscious sense of being ostracized and pitied. As soon as she was old enough, she had married and left her parents' home; as soon as she was married and had left her parents' home, she distanced herself from them completely, maintaining from then on no better than a cool polite estrangement with her mother, father, and most of her siblings, all but John.

John, who had always had a mechanical bent and a greater feeling for gears, gaskets, and pistons than for people, owned and operated a garage over in the nearby town of Strathdale. He had inherited something of his father's profligacy but none of his generosity, and rather cruelly blamed his mother after it was discovered how disastrously in debt the family was.

Gail became an airline stewardess, flying internationally; for some time at least she was living in Toronto, but her cheerful random phone calls and brief occasional visits, always unannounced, gradually became less frequent over the years, and finally stopped altogether: where she lived now or what had become of her, no one in the family could say.

Sadie had moved to Winnipeg to get her nursing degree. It was she who would introduce her brother Matt to his future wife, Louise, a fellow nurse. Sadie was the wild one, and seven years of heavy drinking and hard drugs were followed by a sudden and violent religious conversion. She married a much older man, older and chronically ill, a lay preacher in a small apocalyptic sect. He believed that the physical entrance to Hell lay at the north pole, huddled amid the arctic ice; he preached that Canada was the special domain of the Devil, who had let it to the French and the British under terms of an infernally negotiated lease, claiming as rent the lives and souls of so many Indigenous people per annum, the whole system of reserves and residential schools having been established as a means of collecting and delivering that due. This preacher was Métis himself, or claimed to be at any rate; the two of them were last heard of living in a trailer park outside of Prince George, in a state of grinding poverty, debilitating illness, and unflagging faith and righteousness. Among all the siblings, only

Matt, Bonnie, and Simon remained really close, friendly, and affectionate throughout their adulthoods.

By the time Cicely finally passed away, Simon had been engaged to Nora's mother for close to a year: Lynn Fleisch. She used to bring him lunch to the cemetery or the riverside park, or wherever he happened to be working that day. Lynn had fallen a little bit in love with Simon before she even really knew him because he was so tall, and handsome, and faintly tragic. He looked so much like his father. She remembered his father well; Lionel Wellesley had been her doctor when she was young, and she remembered the shock that had gone through the town when he had died, and again when it was learned that he was bankrupt, and all the fascinating old scandals that were dredged up and whispered over again. She lost her virginity to Simon in the garden shed at the edge of the cemetery one day when they were caught in a sudden and violent rainstorm. After that, Lynn began to talk of their getting married as an agreed and settled thing, and Simon obediently gave her his mother's old engagement ring, though he couldn't remember ever actually proposing to her.

8

Sadie introduces her brother to Louise;
Louise goes to work for a wealthy family

NORA'S UNCLE MATT had first met his wife Louise in Winnipeg. He was in university then, supposedly studying to be an architect but not actually attending many classes; she was a public health nurse, not long out of school, working out of a clinic in the North End. He met her through his sister Sadie, who was still a few years away from her religious crisis and subsequent marriage: back then Sadie was still the life of every party, with a voracious appetite and fearsome tolerance for alcohol, weed, hash, acid, mushrooms, and mescaline, all of which she took a warm-hearted amusement in introducing to her younger brother.

Matt himself was more interested in being introduced to her friends and fellow nurses. More than any of his brothers, Matt had inherited his father's gallantry, charm, and compulsive libido. He had already been with half a dozen of his sister's friends and acquaintances before he even met Louise.

Louise was different than those others. She was small, smudged, and mousy, with the timid melancholy of the frequently overlooked. Why he took notice of her, she who was so rarely noticed by anyone, was hard to say. Perhaps she reminded him, in some way and subconsciously, of his Auntie Pearl. At any rate, notice her he did: he turned on her the full force of his not inconsiderable charm, to which she responded with a seeming display of polite and guarded disinterest. In actual fact he frightened her, and she fell in love with him almost immediately, but he didn't realize it at first.

Louise was the adopted daughter of an aging couple who had never been able to have children of their own: Dean and Beverley Frere. She had always known that she was adopted, of course, but that was really all she knew: she had no idea who her biological parents were, where they came from, or really anything about them, and had never been particularly interested. Her adoptive parents were kind, gentle, and deeply conventional, quietly religious and prone to long comfortable silences. They lived just outside of Birds Hill, not far from the city, in a snug little bungalow on several acres of mostly poplar and scrub brush. Her father had been a mechanic in the war and drove a delivery truck in peacetime; her mother had been a kindergarten teacher. Her childhood had been happy enough, if rather lonely. Her father had passed away when she was fourteen, of a sudden and massive heart attack; her mother was still alive, after a fashion, at the time she met Matt: eking out an existence at the Riverview Health Centre in a state of advanced dementia.

Growing up, it had been Louise's ambition to become a doctor; or perhaps it had been her parents' ambition for her, she couldn't remember any more. Schoolwork had never come easy for her, but she was diligent and dedicated enough to get the grades she needed, and she managed to scrape into pre-med at the University of Manitoba on a scholarship. But her mother could no longer manage on her own, and so they sold the house and she moved into Riverview.

University was hard, harder even than Louise had expected. She was lonely, too: shy and quiet, she had always found it difficult to make friends and felt painfully aware of being different from the other students, out of place; at best overlooked, if not actually unwelcome. She stuck it out as much for her mother's sake as for her own, and with a helpless inability to imagine trying anything else, it had been so long settled in her mind that this was what she was going to do. She often took her textbooks and lecture notes with her to Riverview and studied in her mother's room;

then, if the gentle old lady was having one of her good days, she would watch her daughter in loving silence, looking for all the world like a new mother watching her infant sleep: the pride and adoration would glow so clearly on her face that when Louise would go home at last to her tiny, tidy, antiseptic apartment in St Vital, she would cry helplessly, she would sometimes cry so hard it hurt her stomach.

By the beginning of her second year in pre-med, Louise could no longer study at her mother's side at Riverview. Her mother's bad days outnumbered the good ones now, and what was worse, she had been moved into a room she had to share with a bloated old woman with a congested face and a look of stupid cunning, out of whose mouth there flowed a constant torrent of astonishing and humiliating obscenity: anyone who entered the room, whether strangers, staff, or even members of her own family, she would compulsively accuse of an endless array of sexual crimes and deep perversions, from bestiality, coprophagia, sadism, and necrophilia, to acts and desires so bizarre, grotesque, and vicious as to defy belief. She made her accusations sometimes in a sly insinuating wheedle, sometimes in a hoarse and thundering tone of denunciation, occasionally with a kind of whimpering terror, but always with a wealth of obscene, graphic, and intimate detail.

It was around this time that Dr Hensel from the university took Louise aside, entirely out of the blue, and made her an offer. This was a woman who Louise admired very much, everybody did: though still relatively young, Dr Hensel was a rising and respected figure in the world of medical research and a vocal and frequently published advocate for public health and women's rights issues. That she was a fairly terrible educator didn't diminish her authority or reputation among the students in the least; if anything, it increased her prestige, it being a commonly held belief that only mediocre doctors and scientists made good teachers.

That Dr Hensel was even aware of Louise's existence was baffling to her. She wasn't in any of the professor's classes, and certainly she had done nothing to distinguish herself academically; she was barely keeping her head above water and had hardly scraped through with good enough grades to continue on to her second year. But Dr Hensel not only knew her name, she seemed to have somehow informed herself of Louise's circumstances: her financial difficulties, her mother's living situation, all of it. She took Louise out for coffee, away from the campus, so that they could talk privately; after coffee, they drove out to Riverview, where Louise had a brief visit with her mother while the professor had a word with the administrators about moving the poor woman to a private room. She had no qualms about pulling strings or throwing the considerable weight of her personality around; she was able, with tart and clipped satisfaction, to inform Louise that the change would be made within a day or two at the latest. She would not allow Louise to thank her, either, she had no patience for displays of gratitude.

Leaving Riverview, they took a walk down along the river path. It was a soft, still day, the ground slightly damp underfoot; the dirty brown river flowed sluggishly along, and a scatter of orange and yellow leaves was just beginning to appear amid the thick and overhanging green.

Louise would one day confess to Matt that she began then to indulge a childish fantasy: the idea that this accomplished and celebrated doctor was actually, secretly, her birth mother. There were fairly obvious reasons why this was improbable, to say the very least, but it wasn't *impossible*; Dr Hensel was about the right age, if nothing else, and certainly it would have explained, as Louise thought nothing else could, the professor's sudden and seemingly generous interest in her. Of course it wasn't so, and even years later, as she told Matt about it, she was embarrassed to admit how intensely, if fleetingly, she had felt certain of it. She was thankful only that she had said nothing out loud. Her head was bowed as they walked the path, trying to hide the fact that her face was flushed and hot; her body was trembling slightly, she could feel the blood pounding behind her ears, and she felt a spasm of anxiety so acute it made her stomach hurt: for a brief terrifying moment she thought she might actually lose control of her bowels and shit herself a little.

"Now that that is off your mind," the professor was saying, referring to her mother's private room, "I would like to offer you a job. Two jobs, really; or one job with two parts…"

The first, and most straightforward, was as a live-in nanny. They'd had to let the last one go in the spring, after they had caught her stealing from them. She had been the third they'd had to fire in the past five years. They had muddled through the summer without one, but it would be impossible to keep on any longer. Her husband split his time between Winnipeg and Ottawa, where he served as a backbench MP with aspirations to cabinet; she herself had numerous obligations and calls on her time, conferences to attend and boards to sit on, her research to conduct and analyze, her columns to write, and all her obligations as a tenured professor.

Louise, of course, protested that she had no experience whatsoever dealing with children, not even to the extent of having younger siblings or cousins: none whatsoever.

"You're kind, you're conscientious, and I believe you're honest," the professor had replied, in the same brusque impatient tone with which she would correct a particularly obtuse student in the lecture hall. "If I tell you that you're qualified, you're qualified."

The work would not be particularly demanding, she assured her: the children were well-behaved and largely self-sufficient. The youngest had just turned six and was now in full-time school. "I'll arrange your schedule at the university to ensure there are no conflicts." Louise would have her own room, all meals provided, the use of a car, generous pay, and plenty of time to study and maintain her coursework. Her scholarship would not be endangered; Dr Hensel went so far as to personally guarantee that her marks would not suffer, and would in fact likely improve. "I'll see to it personally," she added, with the imperious confidence of someone wholly unused to opposition. All of this, of course, assuming that she was also willing to take on the second part of the job. This part would be even simpler and easier than the first: Dr Hensel merely wanted Louise to sleep for her.

The fact was, that even apart from the calls on her time as a mother, she had so many pressing demands as a researcher, educator, writer, organizer, and activist, she often got no more than three or four hours of sleep a night. Not even she, with her indomitable willpower and easy access to pharmaceuticals, could maintain that pace for much longer. She was already starting to feel its effects on her energy and her concentration, and that was intolerable. She knew from experience that she could manage, even thrive, on five or six hours a night, but not less. And so Dr Hensel wanted Louise to sleep for nine or ten hours every night, for so long as she was living with them: seven or eight hours for herself, and two more as a surrogate for Dr Hensel. Nothing could be simpler; Louise herself would probably hardly even notice the difference, but to the professor it would be truly invaluable.

Louise accepted, eagerly. Even if the terms and money had not been so very generous, she would have accepted anyway, if only for the relief of her intense loneliness and out of sheer gratitude at being singled out, being noticed and chosen.

The Hensels lived on Wellington Crescent, in a sprawling two-storey house, grey brick covered in lush green creeper. Set well back from the street, backing onto the Assiniboine River, it was screened from sight by an orderly row of stolid pine trees. Both Dr Hensel and her husband had come from wealthy families; it might not have been the largest or the grandest house on the Crescent, but to Louise it was practically a mansion.

She was given a comfortable room on the second floor, right among the rest of the family, with an antique roll-top desk and the softest, widest bed she'd ever slept on. What little furniture she owned was put in storage, except for the old wooden rocking chair that had been her mother's: there was space enough in her bedroom for that.

Her greatest misgiving was the fear that Dr Hensel's children would take a disliking to her. She needn't have worried. The children never became especially fond of her, nor she of them, but they all got along well enough, on terms of slightly impersonal cordiality. There were three: Esther and Ruth were identical twins, nine years old, and their little brother Isaac was six. The twins were inseparable and serenely independent of anyone but each other. They chose their own clothes and coordinated their outfits; they had the same friends, took all the same classes, slept together in one queen-sized bed. Though they could have had separate rooms if they chose, and indeed could rarely be found more than a foot or two away from one another, always close enough to reach out and touch. When dressed in their school uniforms, with their kinked and thick black hair tied back in identical ponies, it was impossible to tell them apart. If one had a cut or a scrape, the other would wear a matching band-aid. They finished one another's sentences; they spoke to one another in a kind of private language, consisting not of invented words but of a compressed, allusive, and telegraphic way of speaking, such that they could communicate a wealth of nuance and meaning to one another using one or two words only, laconically exchanged and virtually incomprehensible to outsiders.

The girls' lives were a heavily scheduled round of clubs, classes, recitals, and social occasions: Louise felt less a nanny than a glorified chauffeur. At first she was sorry for them, supposing it was their parents who kept them enrolled in so many activities that they were barely ever at rest; soon she came to realize that it was Ruth and Esther themselves who wholly determined their own schedules, choosing and enrolling themselves in their own activities, filling out the registration forms, and even, when it was more convenient, confidently forging their mother's signature on cheques and permission slips. When an alarmed Louise first became aware of those occasional forgeries, she immediately told Dr Hensel, who merely responded by saying, "Yes, they're very clever, aren't they?" in a distant and preoccupied way.

As for Isaac, his sisters managed him with ruthless efficiency, and he adored them, and lived for their approval and for their occasional cursory displays of indulgent affection. Because it was convenient for their schedules, the twins had registered him for several classes at the Royal Winnipeg Ballet at the same time as theirs; on Saturdays, Louise would spend virtually the whole day there, camped out in the foyer with her textbooks and lecture notes, a duffel bag full of clothing, and a small cooler of drinks and snacks. Sundays were supposed to be her free day, though Ruth and Esther often asked her to drive them to friends' homes, drop them off at birthday parties, or the like, and she never refused. The remainder of the day she would spend at her mother's side in Riverview.

The husband was no problem, either, even when he was around. To Louise he was always polite and amiable, and appeared to be largely uninterested in her existence. Louise in return considered him a benign nonentity, almost wholly eclipsed by his brilliant wife, and seemingly content to be so; his sole endearing characteristic was the obvious, bemused delight he took in his daughters, who in turn rewarded him with the same mild, slightly contemptuous affection they showed for their little brother, and for nobody else.

For six or maybe eight months, everything went as well as Louise could have reasonably hoped. She never quite learned to feel at home, but she had never felt at home in her old apartment, either. She fell into a comfortable routine, was happy to be kept busy, slept well, rarely had the time to feel lonely. Cleaners came in to do the house three days a week; their laundry was all sent out. When Mr Hensel was at home, he would cook, and was a rather excellent amateur chef; when he was away in Ottawa, all their meals were take-out from a select rotation of Vietnamese, Indian, and Italian restaurants. Louise was served wine with every meal, a wholly new indulgence that seemed to her the very height of gracious living. Her grades at school did not get worse, as Dr Hensel had promised they would not, though in truth she thought they probably ought to have: not for lack of time or effort, she was feeling increasingly out of her depth.

Dr Hensel would often largely ignore Louise for days or even weeks at a time, barely speaking to her, but now and then would grace her with the warmth and force of her full attention, inviting her to spend the evening in the study together while the twins put their brother and then themselves to bed. She would ply Louise with more wine, entertain her with fascinating anecdotes and expansive ideas, and gently encourage Louise to open up about herself. This might happen two or three evenings in a row, and then not again for several weeks, but that was enough and more than enough for Louise to love her, and to feel a boundless gratitude.

It was in the late spring that Louise began to notice that she was feeling tired and run-down. She ascribed it to the stress and pressure of school, of term papers and final exams, and didn't think much of it; but the school year ended, spring turned into summer break, and still there was no improvement. She spent three weeks with the family at a cottage on Lake of the Woods, the loveliest and most restful place she had ever been in her life, yet even there she hardly felt an improvement. By the time summer was over and school resumed, a deep and helpless lassitude had taken over her life: she was simply tired all the time, out of sorts, lethargic, passive, and forgetful. She began falling asleep in classes: first her eyes would refuse to focus, her vision bifurcating, and the lecture she would be trying to follow would become mere sound, devoid of meaning, like waves lapping against the shore or the rustle of the wind through the trees; then her head would suddenly and painfully snap back up, and she would realize that she had already been asleep for a minute or more. Sometimes she would wake to find her classmates smirking at her, or the professor glaring, and she would wince and burn with shame and embarrassment.

Trying to think was like trying to run along the bottom of a murky lake. She had long since stopped dreaming; no matter how long she slept, it would seem to pass in a blank and empty instant, leaving her just as tired and hopeless as before. She began to wonder if perhaps she had contracted mononucleosis, or developed some other disorder; the actual answer, which ought in retrospect to have been painfully obvious, did not occur to her for a long time. By Christmas, she had dropped out of school. It was meant to be a brief hiatus, just until she felt better; Dr Hensel had no difficulty in making her believe that it was her own idea, and in her own best interest.

Looking back, telling all this to Matt, Louise could not remember many details of her life from that winter: it was a kind of strange haze, as elusive as trying to remember a dream. She almost never left the house except to chauffeur the children around or to run errands for the twins; she rarely even visited her mother. She functioned like an automaton, getting through each day on coffee and Benzedrine, counteracted by red wine and benzodiazepine at night, all generously and freely provided by Dr Hensel.

Louise was sleeping eleven or twelve hours a night now, but it hardly mattered, for Dr Hensel was taking eight of those hours for herself, and had been for close to a year. The professor no longer even bothered to lie down in her bed or to close her eyes at all, except to fool her husband when he was home: she worked all through the night, every night, while draining the rest from sleeping Louise without restraint or compunction. Dr Hensel had never felt better in her life than she did for those two years, never felt stronger, keener, more perceptive or more powerful, and the work she accomplished, the research she completed and the papers she published during that period made her more celebrated and renowned than ever.

This might have gone on indefinitely, had the twins not intervened. They chose a weekend when their mother was away at a conference in Geneva and their father home in Winnipeg.

Parliament was in recess, and rumours of an impending cabinet shuffle had Mr Hensel nursing great hopes of being elevated at last. To have his famous and distinguished wife involved in a scandal, especially one as grotesque as this, would have been disastrous. His daughters easily convinced him that people were already starting to talk.

He acted decisively, the only decisive action that Louise had ever known him to take. Not only did he pay her out a generous severance—they had always been more than generous with money—he even set her up in a new home, the bottom half of a little duplex not far from Riverview. The owners of the duplex lived upstairs, a pleasant and complacent couple in late middle age, and Mr Hensel paid them a little extra to keep a discreet eye on Louise and check in on her periodically. He even, shrewdly, bought Louise a dog.

This was Ruth and Esther's idea, Mr Hensel told her: "The kids picked him out themselves." He was a Cairn terrier cross with a coarse and shaggy coat the colour of a storm cloud, and they told her his name was Smokie. It was true, too, that their mother was allergic to dogs and disliked them, and that her children had always wanted one. For a while they visited regularly, once or twice a week, and perhaps it was as much to visit with Smokie as to see Louise.

They always came alone, just Esther and Ruth and Isaac. There was no new nanny to chauffeur them around: instead the twins had bus passes, and the freedom to come and go as they pleased, and full responsibility to care for their little brother, and to boss him around without check or interference. Sometimes when they came over Louise would ask them about their mother, but she never got a satisfactory answer. She missed Dr Hensel immensely, and never completely rid herself of a lingering feeling of guilt, a feeling that she had let her down by leaving. If she had only been a stronger, better person she would have insisted on staying, and continuing to sleep for Dr Hensel's sake: but she had been too weak, and she was worthless.

That winter she was almost completely adrift. It took months and months to wean herself off the bennies and the benzos. She lost weight, she shivered and sweat, she cramped and puked. The bright winter sun reflecting off the white snow would slice into her skull and make her want to cry. When she looked in a mirror, she would see shadows moving behind her, sometimes flitting past like bats, sometimes crouched and creeping in the corners, watchful and predatory. Her landlords' footsteps on the floor above her would fall into the clacking pattern of a funereal tango, persistent as an earworm. There were days when she could hardly bear to get out of bed, let alone leave the house, if Smokie had not been there to drag her forth, all bossy, exuberant, and aggressively cheerful. There were long nights when she would lie sleepless, listening to massive black wings beating against the windows, thumping and rattling the panes; then Smokie would guard the foot of her bed, protective proud and fearless, barking at those phantoms with his piercing, bullyish yap.

She had no friends; apart from the Hensels and her landlords, her only human contact was with her mother, who was hardly even human any more: a mere shell of herself, a bashful stranger in her mother's body. Louise spent long hours at her side anyway, almost every day, for there was nothing else to do, and the muffled, dim, and antiseptic atmosphere of the health centre had a soothing effect on her. Her mother never remembered her, and usually took her for just another one of the nurses. It was best when she slept; then her face would relax and take again its old familiar shape, and Louise would watch her sleep with love and grief.

Leaving Riverview, she would walk home along the side of the street by the riverbank. It would already be night, even if it was still afternoon. The trees on the riverbank would stretch their thin bare branches up towards the dark and purple sky. She would crunch through the snow that would sparkle under the lights from streetlamps and passing cars; and the lights from streetlamps and passing cars cast long black shadows that would writhe and intertwine like copulating snakes, and she would imagine turning away from the street and trudging down the bank, walking out onto the frozen river, and breaking through the ice, letting the frigid black waters suck her under and smuggle her away.

At night, when she was trying to fall asleep, she would run a particular fantasy through her mind like a lullaby: she would imagine that she was lying in the bunk of a houseboat drifting aimlessly out to sea, or on the sleeping berth of a train, heading west through the mountains. Her eyes closed, she would meticulously conjure up every detail, every sound sight and smell as she imagined they would be: sometimes she would even convince herself that she could feel the surge and roll of the boat on the waves, or the rattle and sway of the train; and she would imagine taking a whole bottle of sleeping pills, one at a time, picture herself swallowing each pill down with a sip of red wine, unhurried, almost luxuriating, savouring each and every swallow, tasting the wine on her lips and tongue, feeling each pill pass down her throat, counting them the way someone might count sheep.

But always there was Smokie waiting impatiently to wake her in the morning, waiting to be fed, watered, or run, played with or scolded or loved. He would stare at her with his limpid black eyes like she was a puzzle he was trying to solve; he would lick her hand with his little pink tongue, leap on and off the bed, bark at the shadows of sleep still gathered around her head. And eventually spring came, the days got longer, and she discovered, to her surprise, that she was sometimes happy, even for an hour or more at a time: taking Smokie for runs through the park or along the river, watching him sniff and root through the piles of rotted leaves, still half-frozen with cakes of snow and ice, and then sneeze his ludicrous little sneeze; or when he would scamper frantically after a half-glimpsed squirrel or rabbit, barking ferociously, his fierce little body all coiled and exuberant.

And she discovered, to her surprise, that many of the nurses and other staff who worked at Riverview had come to know her, took a friendly interest in her, called her by name, and actually wanted to have conversations with her; and that sometimes as she showered in the mornings, she found she was actually looking forward to having those conversations later in the day. They told her she would make a great nurse, she was so gentle and patient with her mother. One young man who worked in housekeeping even asked her out for coffee; nothing much came of it, except for Smokie biting him just above the ankle, but it felt good to have been asked. Sometimes at night she wouldn't even need her suicidal fantasy to lull her to sleep, though she often put herself through the motions anyway, almost wistfully, it had become such a comforting habit.

10

Dr Wellesley dies in a car accident;
the whole town turns out for his funeral

THE NIGHT WHEN MATT'S FATHER DIED in that car accident, the phone call came at five in the morning. Louise happened to be there in Matt's bed at the time, sleeping beside him, when the phone rang. She would never know it, but he had been planning to break things off with her that very evening, had been thinking about breaking up with her for weeks, but when the moment came he had lacked the courage to do it, and had weakly put it off for another time.

In the beginning, Louise's story had inspired him with both pity and a perverse excitement; he had been excited, too, by the challenge of gaining her trust and lowering her defences, and by the novel thought of seducing a woman who was several years older than him and yet still a virgin. He was helped by the fact that Smokie took an immediate, irrational, and almost passionate liking to him. Smokie, who was normally so jealous and protective of Louise, so vigilant and mistrustful of any man being near her: but from the very beginning he adored Matt. He would yap enthusiastically at the mention of his name, leap with frantic playfulness when he saw him approaching; he loved to dart and scamper between Matt's long legs, nip at his shoelaces to try and untie them with his teeth, or lie on his back at Matt's feet, wiggling and squirming. If Matt sat down, Smokie would be sure to scamper onto his lap; if Matt tried to stay the night, Smokie would bark frantically at the bedroom door until they let him in.

But now that the challenge and novelty of seducing Louise was over, Matt's interest and excitement were ebbing rapidly away, leaving only the pity and a frightened realization that she had fallen deeply and irreparably in love with him. He might have known, of course, that this could be the result of his actions, but back then he was young, stupid, and thoughtless. Still, thoughtless and young as he may have been, he was not entirely heartless. He had no desire to cause her more pain than he could possibly avoid. How to extricate himself as delicately as he could from the relationship had been his sole preoccupation for a month now, but his courage failed him every time he saw her face; and the longer he put it off, the harder it became.

He had been deep in sleep when the phone began to ring, so deep it failed to wake him. It was the stuttered ring of a long distance call. Louise had to shake him gently by the shoulder, whispering in his ear; whispering at first, then shaking harder and repeating his name loudly: "Matt. Matt. Matt, it might be important."

It was his sister Bonnie. She was calling from the hospital in Brandon. Her familiar voice still held to its habitual intonations of dry and drawled amusement, as if helpless to sound otherwise, but it was strangulated, stretched tight as a guy-wire. In his still half-sleeping, hungover state, he completely failed to comprehend what she was saying. Behind him, Louise was gently, lovingly kissing his shoulder and back. She could hear what Matt's sister was telling him over the phone, for Bonnie was very nearly yelling now, but she told herself that she didn't need to hear it, that she had known the moment the phone began to ring, that she had had a premonition, a prophetic dream. Or not exactly prophetic, though she was convinced that she had indeed been dreaming that Matt's father had died, and that she alone could console him, and it was sweet. No, it was more like the ringing of the phone had cracked the shell of her sleep and allowed the dream to seep out into reality. And now she was feeling, mingled with genuine concern and compassion, a triumphant tenderness, a joyful grief. For she, too, had once lost a father: this not only bound them by a common experience, but it placed her, for the first time since she had met him, in a position of relative strength.

Drawing on her training and experience as a nurse, as well as her personal experience of loss and death, Louise took Matt entirely in hand. She didn't ask him if she ought to come or if he wanted her to, she simply took charge and went. She dressed him, fed him, and packed for him. And he found that he was grateful, after all, to have her with him, to tell him what to do, to say, and even to feel. He was dazed and passive; he felt stunned, stupid, and useless, incapable of either wholly believing or disbelieving that his father was really gone.

Louise drove the whole way out, stopping first to pick up Smokie, who sat in Matt's lap the entire drive, unusually subdued, almost solemn, barking only occasionally at the sight of birds skimming by beneath the low grey sky and at the clusters of somnolent and grazing cows along the side of the highway. Then they could make out the silhouette of Riding Mountain in the distance, a long flat unmountainous ridge, and Louise's heart soared. She placed her hand over Matt's and squeezed it gently, silently.

The town reminded Louise of where she had grown up in Birds Hill, but even prettier. She fell in love with it at first sight, she knew instantly that this was where she wanted to spend the rest of her life. Of course she didn't say so out loud.

Matt directed her to his family's home, a buff brick house with a wrap-around porch, ornate gables, and a stately bay in the middle of the second floor, with a red door opening onto a small patio. That red door came off the master bedroom; there, Matt told her, his mother and father would have their coffee every morning and their brandy at night, and the children were forbidden to set foot. A carefully trimmed hedge of lilac fenced the yard from the street, bursting with white and purple flowers, and the air was thick with their deep narcotic scent; behind them, a pair of crabapple trees flanked the walk, spilling over with lush and burgundy blossoms; tulips, hyacinth, and prairie crocus overwhelmed the flowerbeds and window boxes. An extravaganza of colour and smells, spring incarnate, that helped mask or distract from the many small signs of shabbiness and disrepair in the house behind it: the crack in the foundation near the northeast corner of the house, the sag at one end of the porch, the faded and flaking paint on the trim, the curled or missing shingles, the awry and neglected eavestroughs.

THE WHOLE TOWN came out for Dr Lionel Wellesley's funeral, the whole town and more. People drove in from miles around. The church wasn't big enough to hold everyone who wanted to attend the service, and the street filled with farmers dressed stiffly in their Sunday best, hair slicked down, staring at their shoes or quietly exchanging news with one another. The men stayed outside so that the women would find room inside, holding on their laps or in their arms the children that Dr Wellesley had delivered. After the service was finally over, everyone followed the hearse in slow procession up the hill to the cemetery, like a subdued parade.

It was a beautiful day, mild and blue and a riot of birds, and the solemnity of the occasion could hardly suppress an almost festive atmosphere. Only Pearl Mikolash openly showed her grief; still in shock, helpless to restrain it, she sobbed and whimpered and gulped for air, and her face was streaked, puffy, and crumpled. She was dwarfed by her hulking sons, who flanked her like a pair of prison guards and glared and scowled at anyone who so much as glanced at their mother in her bereavement.

There was a reception afterwards at the Wellesleys' house, the doors were thrown wide open. People who had been friends with the late doctor for almost three decades saw the inside of his home for the first time ever. Peggy Afton oversaw everything, fussily tidying the house as people came and went, making sure there was always plenty of food and drink set out, keeping a protective loving eye on Cicely. She co-opted Louise as her assistant, peremptorily ordering her about, getting her to wash dishes, fetch bottles, fill trays and ice buckets and so forth. And Louise was grateful to be made use of that way, to be kept busy and allowed to be helpful, and it was the beginning of a long friendship between Ms Afton and herself.

Matt's oldest brother John made nasty remarks to Louise in the kitchen and yelled at his wife for allowing their children to play in the muddy back yard with a dozen other kids, all dressed in their finest formal clothes. He prowled around the house, rifling through drawers. He drank straight whiskey with a mechanical rapidity; he stood by the sideboard with his brother-in-law, Fanny's husband, the stocky chain-smoking veterinarian with that look of perpetual irritation, and exchanged low conspiratorial remarks and quiet disparagements. Fanny herself, who had entered into a premature middle age and carried herself like a caricature of a prudish and old-fashioned schoolteacher, stood near the vestibule the entire evening with her adolescent daughter Annaliese, a spindling gloomy girl with a long splotchy face and a mouth full of braces. Fanny had been amiable enough to Louise when they had first been introduced, or civil at least in her own glacial way, until Louise had tried to be friendly to Annaliese.

Pearl Mikolash did not show up to the reception, but her sons came, later on in the evening. Fanny, Annaliese, and the veterinarian had gone home by then; so had John and his family, though not before he had slapped one of his young sons for knocking over a drink and had made an unpleasant scene with Sadie, who had been snorting coke in the upstairs bathroom and flirting sloppily with her father's friends.

It was getting late then, but the reception was showing no sign of winding down. The farmers and people from out of town had all filed through, paid their respects, and gone home; the townspeople who had young children had gone home too, to put those children to bed, and then many of them had returned.

Benji Pettinger, who in those days owned the town's only liquor store, had come back with more bottles. People recounted stories of Dr Wellesley to one another: his quiet heroics, his medical acumen, his boundless generosity, his gallantry and charming eccentricities. They remembered, and spoke loudly of, how he had adored his wife: how after almost forty years of marriage he had still been as much in love with her as if they had only just gotten engaged; how whenever he spoke of her or looked at her his face would glow; how at even the slightest hint of a word against her he would blaze with cold fury. Everyone had a story to tell about him, as a doctor or as a friend; they laughed, they got teary-eyed and boozily sentimental, they sang his praises. And if anyone said well, it was getting late, they really ought to be going, Cicely would urge them to stay, with an unmistakable sincerity and an undercurrent of terror, as if this reception, this gathering, were her last stay of execution, the last thing holding off the black loneliness and bitter grief that were stalking patiently in the background, waiting to engulf her.

When Pearl's sons arrived, they didn't enter the house at all, they went around to the back yard where Matt was, and Sadie and Gail, and Simon and Bonnie and Bonnie's soon-to-be-husband Geoff, and many of their friends. Matt and Simon had started a bonfire, but the wood was wet and green, and gave off more smoke than light. Ronald and Rudy were already drunk when they arrived, they didn't need to catch up. They still wore the sullen, pugnacious expressions they had worn during the funeral procession. Ronald lurched and swayed unsteadily, Rudy carried himself with his shoulders hunched up and his head low, like a boxer waiting for the bell to sound and the round to begin, ready to hit or be hit. Smokie began to bark frantically when the two brothers came through the gate, baring his teeth, straining at his leash, and Louise had to take him away. The sky was bunched with stars and the moon was a tilted sliver. A cold damp wind was coming down from the mountain; goosebumps stood out all along Louise's bare arms. In the front yard, under the apple trees and away from the family, a clot of older gentlemen were smoking cigars and reminiscing about a different side of the late Dr Wellesley than the one they had been discussing in front of his widow: in low smirking voices they were exchanging tall tales of his sexual escapades, his philandering, his conquests and infidelities. The men were recalling all this to one another, in winks and circuitous hints, with an air of drunken titillation; and they made sly repulsive allusions to the old persistent rumours that he had been, back in the days when it was still illegal, a suspected abortionist, and not only in cases where he might have been the father.

II

Louise learns about the old Stone School;
Matt loses his job

LOUISE WOULD COME TO REMEMBER that first year they lived in Whittle as perhaps the happiest of her life. She and Matt lived in a small house on the north side of the Sally; they bought it cheap, using as down payment what money she still had left from the Hensels. In fact it was a drab, draughty house, poorly designed and shoddily built, but the passing of the years would invest it in her memory with a cozy romantic glow. It had been built, she was told—it and the houses around it, some of which were already tumbling down or had been demolished—for workers at the old Afton saltworks. From their back yard, Louise could see the tops of the old pumps, the red tin roofs of the abandoned sheds, and that cold grey smokestack stretching up into the sky.

The breezes that swept down from Riding Mountain were soft and warm and stained a piney green; the vast silence of the nights sounded in her ears like a lullaby. She made no attempt at first to find work, as a nurse or anything else. She spent the summer luxuriating in a joyful idleness; she put on a little weight, she radiated good health and happiness.

Together with Smokie, she would take long rambling walks around the countryside. Once or twice a week she would dutifully visit Matt's mother, who treated her with a vague and formal politeness. She would always go to see her in the mornings, when Cicely would still be mostly sober; then she would help her with the grocery shopping, surreptitiously adding some of her own money to cover the bill, or she would quietly and unobtrusively tidy and clean the apartment. If Peggy Afton happened to be there, and she often was, that was best. Ms Afton alone seemed to have the capacity to pull Cicely out of the narcotic haze of her grief and her intrusive consuming memories, and back to the present moment.

Matt had found work with a contractor down in Brandon. He got the job through his half-brother Ronald, who would pick him up in the mornings, before Louise was even awake, to take the long drive to town; he wouldn't return until late in the evening, exhausted and sore, smelling of sweat, sawdust, plaster, and paint. He worked six days a week, sometimes twelve hours a day. He told Louise that he had better take all the hours he could get now, because when the work dried up in the winter, he would be the first one they laid off. Last one in, first one out. On Saturdays he actually only worked half-days, but Louise didn't need to know that.

They had their Sundays together. They would sleep in, lounge in bed all morning, luxuriantly lazy; in the afternoon they would take Smokie on long walks out into the country, going any direction at all, it didn't matter. They walked, and they talked, and they lost track of time; in those days, they never seemed to have any lack of things to say to one another.

One day, this was near the end of August, they ended up on the grounds of the old Stone School. Smokie had caught sight of a jackrabbit and disappeared off into the tall prairie grass. The school had only been closed down a few years then, and most of the land it sat on had not been sold off yet. There were several hundred acres; it had been a working farm, with the schoolchildren for labour, back in the day. Some of the outbuildings, the barns and sheds and outhouses, were already starting to rot and crumble, but the main school building itself did not yet wear that look of sinister dilapidation it would take on in later years. From a bit of distance, with the sun behind them illuminating the school's face, Louise thought it looked beautiful, more like a mansion than an institution.

The original stone building, the one that had burnt down back in the twenties, that *had* been a mansion, apparently, before it had been taken over as a school. There was a whole story about it that Matt didn't remember at the moment. Louise's hand was around his waist, she leaned lightly against his body; they were slowly drifting closer to the school, trying to follow Smokie, whose little form they would periodically glimpse above the shuddering grass, like a dolphin breaking the surface of the waves for a breath before submerging again. Now that they were getting closer, Louise could see the first signs of disrepair on the building: a broken windowpane here, a scrawl of graffiti there.

Matt had started talking about one of his grandiose ideas. He was saying that if someone was smart, they'd buy the building up, gut it, and turn it into a hotel, a luxury resort. If he had the money, he'd do it himself. He often talked like this, Louise didn't think anything of it, she was hardly paying attention.

"I wonder what it was like to go there," she said. She was thinking of the sort of books her mother had given her to read as a child, set in English boarding schools, Enid Blyton and the like. She had adored those books. At this time, she knew little or nothing of the real history of residential schools, even though—had she not been adopted out as an infant—she might well have ended up in one herself. Later in her life, she made it a point to learn everything she could about them, with a bottomless, almost vertiginous, sense of grief and indignation: but that would come later.

Matt, too, knew little at the time. His father had gone there a few times to attend to some of the children as a physician, when he had first moved to town—this would have been before Matt was born even—and he had apparently been disgusted and outraged by the conditions the children lived in, and refused to have anything more to do with it.

They were circling the building to the north, now; Matt pointed in the direction of a meadow a little ways off, just outside the school land itself, down a slope and half-hidden by a belt of trees, where the children's families used to come sometimes. They'd pitch tents, camp out for a day or two, and their kids would look for opportunities to slip out of the school and come visit them.

Why the kids had to sneak out, why their parents couldn't just come right up to the school to see them, Matt didn't know. That was just the way it was. The people who ran the place must have known it was going on, anyway. Everybody knew. It had apparently been going on for years and years like that. They would come from thirty, forty, fifty miles away or more, come every weekend to be close to the children who had been taken away from them, and for the hopes of catching a few stolen moments in their company. Matt had a vague memory of coming out to that campsite one time with his father—he didn't remember why, he must have been very young—but he remembered seeing from a distance the pillars of dark dull smoke rising towards the sky, and the flickering lights of campfires, and the dark huddled shapes moving to and fro in the half-light of early dawn. And he remembered that there was a touch of frost, so that the grass crunched under your feet, and he remembered the kind sad smiling faces, patient and melancholy, and he remembered trying a piece of fry bread made over the fire, so hot it singed his fingers.

Matt and Louise had come around the back of the building now, and Smokie was just outside the crabapple grove, barking ferociously at something that wasn't there. He sprang from side to side, his little body tense and coiled, his teeth bared, barking now not playfully but almost frenzied; but whatever it was he had seen would not emerge from the grove, and Smokie would not go in.

The crabapple trees were heavy with fruit that looked more like overgrown cherries than little apples. They were, Matt told her, completely inedible: woody, dry, and "bitter as fuck."

"I'd cut them all down," he said, returning to his idle daydream of converting the old school into a luxury hotel. "You could make a hedge maze out here, it would be incredible." This was, secretly, his greatest ambition in life, to be the sort of person who owns a property with a grand and elaborate hedge maze on it.

Louise was attempting to calm Smokie; she had crouched down beside him, futilely trying to contain his furious body, to soothe or distract him. The sun had dipped behind the roof of the school now, leaving them in shadow and a shudder of cold: it was getting later than either of them had realized.

It was only a few weeks later that Matt returned home early from work in Brandon one day. He had a black eye and a new used pickup truck. On the side of that truck he would later have painted the words *Matt Wellesley—Independent Contractor*, followed by their phone number.

The black eye had come from the fist of Matt's boss, or former boss, in Brandon, who had apparently come out of the fight even worse, with three lost teeth and a splattered nose. Louise learned this not from Matt, who refused to discuss it, but from Ronald, who showed up the next day looking for him in a state of drunken rage: he had lost his job too, because it was he who had brought Matt on to the crew in the first place, and so had been held guilty by association.

Rudy came with his brother; said nothing, just stood a few feet behind him, with his shoulders hunched up and his head low.

Matt wasn't there, he'd taken his new truck out to Strathdale to get his brother John to look it over. Louise told them this, standing in the doorway and blocking the entrance with her body, blocking the brothers from coming in and Smokie from getting out; but Ronald either didn't hear her or didn't believe her, he just kept yelling past her into the house as if Matt was hiding inside. And Smokie was trying to squeeze between her legs and the door held slightly ajar, forcing his head into the gap, his little body shaking fiercely, growling and barking at the brothers with his piercing, bullyish yap.

Abruptly, Rudy took a few steps closer to the doorway and leaned forward into a simian crouch, looking straight into the little dog's eyes, and began barking back at him, a deep, violent woofing. It should have been ridiculous, comical, but instead it was deeply unnerving. Rudy's face became congested, it swelled and turned purple and his fat brown eyes bulged out of their sockets, flecks of foamy white spittle flew from his blubbery lips as he leaned in and barked and barked. Then Smokie became frantic with rage, he completely lost his mind, and his claws dug painfully into Louise's leg as he tried to climb and squeeze past her to get at Rudy; and she was trying to push him back so that she could close the door.

She didn't think she could hold him back much longer, and she was certain that it was going to end horribly; no doubt it would have, if Peggy Afton had not happened by at the right moment, coming up behind Rudy, grabbing hold of his earlobe and twisting it sharply. She sent the two brothers, sullen and suddenly deflated, home to sleep it off.

12

Matt meets the Hensels;
Matt and Louise are married

THAT DECEMBER, Louise's mother finally passed away. They got the call one Wednesday evening, just after dinner, to say that the poor woman had collapsed on the way from her bed to the bathroom and would probably not last the night.

Matt drove. Blowing snow streamed back and forth above the surface of the road, ghostly and luminescent in the headlights, shifting, swift, sinuous, and hypnotic. Near the turn on to the Trans-Canada they passed a car that gone off the highway into a snowdrift-filled ditch, its hazards blinking, the vehicle abandoned. It was after midnight when they arrived at Riverview.

They spent the whole night in Beverley's room. Her skin had taken on a nasty yellow tinge, mottled with patches of purple and red. Her breathing was thready and weak, and her body gave off a faint odour of urine, as if it were seeping steadily from her pores. Louise held her hand and talked to her all night. Her voice took on the soft, lulling, sing-song rhythm of a parent telling a bedtime story to an infant. Louise's mother never woke up; Matt struggled not to fall asleep. Louise was telling her mother all about the life she was currently living with Matt, and she reminisced about the life she and her mother and father had lived together in Birds Hill, and she talked about the future she and Matt were going to have together, the wedding they were planning for the spring and the children they were going to have after that, and she moved back and forth freely in her talk between the past, the present, and the future, so that all three seemed to merge into a single vision of a serene and happy life.

Matt felt stiff and sore in the hard plastic chair. His socks and pant legs were wet, his feet itched. It was warm inside the room, too warm, he felt slightly feverish. Occasionally he stood up and went over to the window, watching his dim reflection get larger and then disappear, merging with the blowing snow outside as he approached. And he would press his face against the pane for the relief of the cold of the glass.

Louise's words became mere sound, devoid of meaning, they merged harmonically with the solemn metronomic beep of the heart monitor and the occasional rattle of a cart or gurney being wheeled past the door. He drifted in and out of consciousness. Low-flying birds, black and fat, began to circle his brain. Then he opened his eyes and there was a nurse in the room, she and Louise were talking like old friends, they were smiling quietly and it seemed unbearably sad. Matt would have liked to get up and use the bathroom, but he didn't want to disturb them. Then he closed his eyes again and dreamed that Louise was giving birth in a hospital bed, her whole body contorted, writhing, shiny with sweat, she had bit her lower lip half off and foamy blood was dribbling down her chin, she was thrashing her head and churning at the bed and sobbing in pain as Matt watched a pair of long skinny arms emerging from between her legs, bony grasping hands with yellow fingernails like claws that sank into the inside of Louise's thighs to try and pull the rest of its body out, and Louise was screaming and Matt felt sick and the doctor and nurses were doing nothing, just smiling fatuously and saying, "Isn't it beautiful?" and, "The miracle of life," and, "You're a lucky man, Mr Wellesley."

When he woke up that time he went to the washroom and splashed cold water on his face, and almost vomited in the basin. He went back to the window and he saw that it had stopped snowing, the clouds had tattered apart to expose patches of stars. He didn't sit down again.

As the sky began to subtly lighten with the first approach of dawn, there was a change in Beverley's breathing. It became harsher, more raspy and grasping; her eyelids fluttered and her face twitched. Then her tongue began moving in and out of her mouth, as though she were trying feebly to lap up more air. This only went on for a minute or two, but to Matt it seemed like forever. Then it stopped, her face was slack, her half-open eyes were glassy and she was gone.

Louise cried a little, but more out of tiredness and relief than grief for it seemed to her that her mother had really died a long time ago and had been mourned for already.

Outside it was bright and bitterly cold, the fresh snow sparkled in the sunlight and the skin on their faces tightened painfully as soon as the air touched it. Their truck was half-buried in a snow drift. They had to trudge up to Osborne with their bags to catch a cab, and then it took almost two hours to get to the hotel, a drive that normally would have taken maybe fifteen, twenty minutes at most.

The Christmas tree in the hotel lobby looked as if it had been constructed entirely out of stiffened tinsel; the piped-in Christmas music sounded like a fixed grin. They made love as soon as they got to their room, as much to warm themselves up as anything, and Louise was later convinced that this was the moment when Nathanael was conceived. She fell asleep and Matt let her sleep.

THE FUNERAL SERVICE was held the following Monday, three days before Christmas. No one wept. It was a brief, melancholy service; it had the sad, shabby air of an afterthought, perfunctory and lonesome. Hardly anyone came; apart from the Hensels and themselves, there was no one but a stumpy, garrulous, slightly ghoulish old lady who claimed to have known Louise's mother as a neighbour back in Birds Hill, and who evidently pored over the obituaries daily, looking for just such opportunities as this.

It seemed to Matt then, as they sat in that dingy little funeral parlour, going weakly through the dutiful motions of mourning, it struck him that there were two paths in life, and only two: one led to a funeral like his father had had, where a whole town and more had turned out in lamentation, in spontaneous grief and celebration. The other led to this.

But the Hensels had come, the whole family. Matt found it amusing to compare and contrast the actual them with the pictures he had formed of them in his mind, from the many stories Louise had told him. Of Dr Hensel he supposed he had been foolishly expecting or imagining something along the lines of Baba Yaga in a lab coat: someone tall and bony, angular, pointy, and sinister. He had very definitely expected, for no particular reason, an eagle's beak of a nose and a long pointy chin, great heaps of curly and unruly hair, and at least one prominent mole, probably hairy. He had not even realized what a complete picture he had formed of her in his imagination until he met her in the flesh and found out how wrong he had been. She was, it turned out, surprisingly non-descript: of average height and weight, smartly and neatly dressed; she had well-kempt, sober hair that was a mousy brown colour with a respectable touch of grey; she had an unremarkable chin and an utterly normal nose in a perfectly pleasant, garden-variety face. Only her keen brown eyes and her confident, decisive manner suggested anything out of the ordinary about her. She might, Matt thought, even have been pretty when she was young, but not *too* pretty: just normally, averagely attractive, as her daughters now were, the twins.

Matt supposed those twins must be nineteen or so now, give or take a year, and they matched more closely with the way he had always imagined them. There on their heads were the wild black masses of kinky curly hair that he had expected to see on their mother; and they had the smallish breasts, muscular legs, and out-turned feet he associated with ballet dancers. Still inseparable, still standing or sitting always together and almost touching, still speaking to one another in exactly that secretive, hermetic, cryptic and supercilious way that Louise had described to him.

Their brother he found more likeable. Isaac had something of the hang-dog manner that Matt had expected in him, now joined to the hapless awkwardness of adolescence: an outsized head and orangutan arms, livid pimples and the faint premature wisps of facial hair; an air of tortured bashfulness, a breaking reedy voice, a ready tendency to blush.

But it was Mr Hensel, or rather the Right Honourable Leonard Hensel, that interested Matt the most. He had had no need to try and imagine what the man might look like, for he had seen his picture in the newspapers and on the television often enough, looking vaguely like a brainy and distinguished bison. Louise had told Matt something about him that few people knew: that Leonard Hensel's distinctive eyeglasses were in fact plain glass, and that his vision was actually perfect. He had taken to wearing them at the outset of his political career to make himself appear smarter and credited much of his subsequent success to that simple ruse. Louise had told Matt this because she thought it was funny, but Matt considered it admirable, even inspiring.

Since the days when Louise had been the Hensels' live-in nanny, a pair of elections had sent Hensel's party first tumbling down onto the lowly benches of the opposition, and then surging triumphantly back into power; and it had sent Hensel himself into cabinet at last, as the Minister of State for Regional Economic Expansion and Development.

Louise *did* cry when she saw the Hensels arrive at the funeral parlour, cried as she had not even done when her mother had died. In her memories, she had successfully effaced or erased the deep unhappiness, even misery of that last year or more that she had lived with them; and so too, in her current state of happiness, in her memories and their absence she had amplified the fondness

and affection that she had felt for each member of that family.
And so she was genuinely and deeply moved that they had come
now, she was surprised and grateful, she was so happy to see them
again. She had in fact thought of calling them, of trying to get
in touch, but she hadn't had the nerve, hadn't wanted to bother
them. Nobody told her then that in fact Matt had contacted them
and urged them to come: they all allowed her to assume that they
had just happened to notice the obituary in the papers and had
come of their own accord.

"It was so kind of you to come," Matt said gravely, after Louise
had introduced him, shyly and proudly, as her fiancé. "I know
you've done so much for Louise, I'm sure it means the world to
her that you would be here for her." He had his arm around her;
he was looking down at her with grave and loving affection.

"Of course," said the Minister, perhaps a little warily. And to
Louise, gruffly but kindly, "It's good to see you again, young lady.
And looking so well. I wish it were under happier circumstances.
We're so sorry for your loss. Though I know you must feel you
actually lost your mother a long time ago, still it's..."

"Yes," said Louise.

"...it's always difficult, that final.... Well. It's hard, I know. But
it's wonderful to see you again. And looking so healthy, so well.
You oughtn't to have lost touch with us like that, we've worried
about you."

"Rice," said Esther confidentially to her sister.

"Shoes," Ruth agreed; and then, to Louise, she asked peremptorily, "How's Smokie?"

After the service was over, Matt invited the Hensels out for
dinner. He insisted on paying, something he certainly couldn't
afford, but he looked on it as a sort of investment—or perhaps
more like a gamble. They hesitated whether to accept, but he was
gently insistent: "I know it would mean so much to Louise if you
joined us," he said. "It would mean a lot to me, too. You know,

she's told me so much about you all—told me everything about you, really—I feel like I already know you."

He took them all to Rae & Jerry's. He could hardly have justified paying to eat there alone, let alone afford to buy steak dinners for seven people, along with several bottles of good red wine, but he managed to convincingly appear blithely unconcerned about the cost.

After they had placed their orders, Matt suggested a toast in memory of Louise's mother. "To Beverley Frere..."

As they awaited their appetizers, he told them the story about his truck, how it had been buried in the snowstorm the night that Louise's mother had passed away, and they had had to leave it on the street in the morning and take a cab to the hotel. After lunch, as Louise slept, Matt had taken the bus back out to Riverview to pick up her mother's few last effects and borrowed a shovel to try and dig his truck out.

He had to trudge through the middle of the street to reach the truck, half-buried in a snowdrift. The sun had come out; the fresh and untouched snow, swept by the night wind into great peaks, ridges, and valleys, sparkled all lovely and clean. In the distance he could hear the incessant grind, beep and rumble of the snowplows at work, but they had not gotten near this side street yet.

As he approached his truck, about ten feet or so away from it, the strangest thing had happened: a dog stood up in the back of the truck and started barking ferociously at him. Scared the hell out of him. He thought for a moment that he must have the wrong truck, maybe even the wrong street, but he looked closer and sure enough, there was his name painted on the side, only half-covered by the drift: it was his, all right. But where the dog could have come from and how the hell it had ended up in the back of his truck, he hadn't a clue.

"And this was a big dog," said Matt. A big yellow dog, big and yellow and ugly looking. He couldn't see a collar on it or anything, and its fur was all patchy and dirty and matted with snow and ice, and it had ice on its eyelashes, and what looked like a nasty scab running along its left haunch, and it looked half-starved, half-frozen to death. He felt sorry for it, he said, but he wasn't about to go up and pet it. It was staring him down now, front paws up on the side of the cargo bed, its flabby speckled lips pulled back in an ominous grin. Unsure what else to do, Matt gingerly took a slow step closer. The dog began growling warningly at the back of its throat, and then it began to bark: ferociously, savagely, thick white spittle flying from its lips.

"I was just glad I had a shovel in my hand," said Matt. "I was ready for it to jump out of there and come at me. It looked hungry enough to try and eat me even." So he had stopped moving, frozen in place, and the dog subsided into a low premonitory growl, showing its dirty long teeth, saliva dripping from its flappy and black-speckled gums.

And now Matt had no idea what to do. Not a clue. "You know, I don't even know how long I just stood there, not moving, me and the dog just staring each other down."

There was no one else on the street, nobody else in sight. He was getting cold, too. He considered just saying fuck it, taking the bus back to Louise in the hotel, and trying again the next day. And maybe that's what he should have done, too, but he didn't. Instead he trudged over to Osborne Street and found an open convenience store, bought a packet of sandwich meat and a box of milk bones—both egregiously overpriced. And a hot coffee for himself. Stood inside the store for fifteen, twenty minutes to drink his coffee and warm up a little, chatting with the man behind the counter, who had apparently been stuck there, alone, for over sixteen hours, the day staff having been unable to make it in to relieve him because of the blizzard.

"I was putting it off, a little," Matt admitted. But he couldn't put it off forever. The sun was already beginning to get low in the sky, and even after he had gotten the dog out of there, he still had at least a couple of hours of hard digging before he'd be able to get his truck out.

"Now here's the crazy part," said Matt. "I get back to the truck, I've got the shovel in one hand and a fistful of sliced ham in the other, and the dog's gone. I'm whistling for it, calling it, I even try barking a little bit. Nothing. No dog anywhere. Right? So that's not so crazy, but then as I'm looking around, I realize: there are no dog prints leading away from the truck. None. No dog prints, no footprints, nothing at all. I made a big circle all around, and the snow is totally undisturbed on every side. And this—you know, this was soft, deep, powdery snow. And that dog must have been fifty pounds if it was an ounce. So what do you make of that?" he said. He was looking at Isaac now, on his left.

"You imagined it," squeaked the boy. "There never was a dog, you were just hallucinating or something."

"Right? That's what I thought. I thought, I must be going crazy. I'm dreaming on my feet from lack of sleep or something. But then I go right up to the truck—still a little cautious, you know, in case the dog's just laying low in the back or something, like maybe it went to sleep or even froze to death while I was gone—I go right up to the truck and look in, and there's no dog there now, but you can see paw prints in the snow in the back of the truck, and the snow's been kicked around and packed down, and right there—right in the middle of my truck bed, there's a big fat steaming pile of fresh dog shit. Swear to God." He leaned well back in his chair as the waitress placed his bowl of French onion soup in front of him. He spread his both hands out and wide as if to demonstrate that there was nothing up his sleeves. "Swear to God," he said again.

"It's true," Louise said eagerly. "He told me the whole thing as soon as he got back to the hotel."

"Swear to God," he said again. "I wish I'd had a camera. I almost saved that pile of dog shit to show people, because I knew that nobody would believe me."

"You're not going to pull out a pile of dog poop at the dinner table, are you?" asked Esther.

"Because we believe you," said Ruth. "Really."

"Don't need to show the shit."

"Not before dinner."

"Maybe after dessert."

"Maybe don't and we'll say you did."

Later, Dr Hensel asked Louise whether she was still working as a public health nurse. She seemed disappointed, disapproving, when Louise admitted that she hadn't been working at all; and Matt could sense that Louise felt that disappointment, that despite everything that had happened between them, Louise still longed for Dr Hensel's approval.

Matt said, "To be fair, it hasn't been for lack of trying." This wasn't entirely untrue: since the fall she had applied at various schools in the area, to work either as a nurse or a T.A, and had been rebuffed at every turn—Matt hinted that there was perhaps a little racism at play. The nearest doctors, hospitals and health clinics were as far away as Brandon; they had been hoping she wouldn't have to make such a long commute, but it was starting to look as if it might be the only option. And Matt talked about how badly underserved the region was by physicians and medical facilities. His own father had complained of it often, to no avail: and since Matt's father had died, the town had been unable to attract another doctor to take his place, to take over his practice. It was getting to be a desperate situation, to be honest. His own sister was now pregnant, due in the spring, with no local doctor to provide prenatal care. And when the time came to deliver, they would have to drive all the way down to Brandon and just hope there were no complications.

The problem, of course, was that no young doctor just out of medical school wanted to bury himself in a small town out in the country, far from everything. "We don't even have a golf course to dangle in front of them."

He spoke, too, of how they had wished they could have had Louise's mother closer to them during these final months of her life, but there was nowhere anywhere near to place her, and no doctors to look after her.

All this was of great interest to Dr Hensel. Since Louise's time, Dr Hensel had given up doing research and had cut back greatly on her teaching, preferring to focus now on her writing and her advocacy work: going to conferences, appearing on the radio, giving talks and speeches, sitting on panels and committees. The problem of underserved rural communities, of rural, northern, and isolated communities that had little or no access to proper medical care: this had been a recent and persistent theme in a number of her weekly columns, as Matt was well aware.

"Of course," she said now to Louise, a little severely, "you could always go back to medical school and complete your degree. You could fill that gap yourself. I'm sure your fiancé would happily support you."

"Of course I would," said Matt, placing his hand over Louise's and giving it a gentle squeeze. "I've always said I would support Louise in anything she wants to accomplish. Whatever it is and whatever it takes, we'd make it work somehow: right, sweetheart?"

"And what do *you* do, young man?" asked the Minister of State for Regional Economic Expansion and Development.

"I'm an architect, actually," Matt said, squeezing Louise's hand again as he said it. It was, of course, technically untrue: he had never bothered to finish getting *his* degree, either. And afraid that Louise might naïvely interject here, he followed it up quickly by adding, "Not practising, yet. At the moment I'm working as a general contractor. Fixing roofs, doing renovations, that sort of fun stuff."

The Minister grunted. He speared a hot snail on the end of his fork and waved it in Matt's general direction, saying, "Good money in that, I suppose," before popping it into his mouth.

Matt shrugged, as if modestly, and took a sip of wine. "Mostly

I like to think of it as practical experience, practical know-how, to complement the theoretical. And to be honest, there aren't a lot of opportunities for an aspiring young architect in our little town, either. Not yet. But they'll come, and I'll be ready to take them. I'm a great believer in making opportunities happen."

"Yes," said the Minister, "I suspect you are."

As they parted company at the end of the night, Leonard Hensel pulled Matt to one side for a brief and private conversation. And he closed that conversation by saying sternly, "I hope that you're good to her."

The two men looked over at Louise, who was embracing the twins and chatting animatedly with them as they got on their winter coats: giggling, bright, affectionate, and happy.

"I hope I am, too," said Matt, quite seriously. "I hope I am too." He was almost somber, and for that moment, at least, wholly sincere.

"She's a loving, generous girl. Very giving, trusting nature," the Minister continued carefully. "Just the sort of girl who a lot of people might take advantage of."

"Yes," agreed Matt. "And have. I won't let anyone do so again."

The Minister grunted, and there was a heavy silence between the two. Looking at one another, sizing each other up. Then he said at last, with an effort to make his tone a little more friendly, he said, "You really love her, do you?"

"I love her for the dangers she has passed," replied Matt lightly, "and she loves me, that I do pity them."

AND SO THAT WAS HOW it came about that when Matt and Louise were married at the end of June, Ruth and Esther Hensel were her bridesmaids, and it was the Right Honourable Leonard Hensel, Minister of State for Regional Economic Expansion and Development, who walked her solemnly down the aisle and gave her away.

It made more than a little stir among the locals, particularly since almost no one had known beforehand. It wasn't easy to

keep such a secret, or any secret at all, in a small town, but Matt
had managed it: the effect was at once more subtle and more
devastating that way, as he had known it would be. For he knew
exactly what so many people in that town thought of his bride
behind closed doors, and some of them quite openly. And when
those same people, those same narrow nasty provincial bigots
came up to him after the wedding and asked him was that really
the Leonard Hensel, the Cabinet Minister, who gave her away?
and was that actually the Minister's wife, the famous Dr Hensel,
with the monthly column in *Maclean's* and everything, who
sat beside Louise at the head table and made that long speech
after dinner?—then Matt's carefully rehearsed, casually blasé
response—"That's right, Louise is a close friend of the family,
you know. She's been almost like a niece to them, really."—gave
him a full and gratified satisfaction.

He had another, greater reason to be glad the Hensels had come
for the wedding. It was an idea that had hatched in his brain that
evening after the funeral, and which he had been nursing ever
since: secretively, assiduously, meticulously. It was in some sense
a desperate gamble. Without telling Louise, he had put them
deeply, deeply into debt in the trust that his idea would pay off.

He had had to take four people into his confidence, or partial
confidence. The first two had been Bonnie and her husband Geoff.
Bonnie was easy: it had always been his habit to tell her almost
everything, anyway, and she had always been an eager participant
in his plots and plans. Geoff was necessary, for he was a loan
officer at the local bank and was able to help smooth over the
fact that Matt had almost no collateral to speak of. Geoff might
have been reluctant to do it, for he was a conscientious, timid, and
fairly unimaginative man: luckily he not only adored Bonnie, his
trust in her judgment was boundless; and Bonnie, who was then
seven months pregnant with Katharine, bored and housebound
through the long winter, made it her personal mission to win his
full support for her brother.

The next person that Matt had approached was Peggy Afton. He was frank with her and made no particular attempt to charm or mislead her. He counted on both her deep, longstanding love for his mother, and her obvious and growing fondness for Louise.

She heard him out with amusement, over tea. She said, "Do you remember the summer you started that lawn care business?"

"Of course," said Matt. He had been fourteen. "You were our first customer."

"I was," she said. "I even let you overcharge me. Your brother did all the work, didn't he?"

"Well..." said Matt. "Most of it, I suppose."

"All of it."

"He always did enjoy that sort of thing. It was fun for him."

"It must have been. Did you pay him at all? Share any of the money with him?"

"Well, that was a long time ago," said Matt. He had in fact paid Simon entirely in occasional ice creams and bottles of root beer, and with vague, never-realized promises to help buy him a new bike at the end of the year. This he had justified, retroactively, by "allowing" Simon to take over the business the following year, Matt having long since grown bored with it anyway.

"If I agree to this little plan of yours," she said, "why should I believe you'll treat me any better than you did him?"

"Because you're sharper than he is, for one thing," said Matt. "And most of all, because it'll be in my best interest to make sure you do well out of it. Believe me, Ms Afton," he said in a spontaneous burst, gambling that allowing her a glimpse—just a glimpse—into the scope of his ambitions, would ultimately work in his favour: "Believe me, Ms Afton, I'm only getting started. I'm only getting started."

And so two weeks later, Geoff brought the necessary papers to Ms Afton's house, and the deal was discreetly made: Matt became the owner of the old Afton salt mine, along with the abandoned refinery and adjacent buildings. He paid rather less than the bank had assessed its current market value as, which was already fairly low, for the properties had sat unsold, unused, and unwanted for some time.

The last person he brought into his plans was Benji Pettinger. It was Benji Pettinger who had purchased Matt's family home when it was auctioned off by the bank, after his father's death: the house and half the furniture in it, including Cicely's beloved piano.

Benji Pettinger's real name was Vanya Perevezev. The Perevezevs had been farmers in the area for several generations, farmers and moonshiners, bootleggers. It was said that the family had been among the Doukhobor refugees who flooded into the province in 1899. If so, they must have turned apostate almost as soon as they arrived. Perhaps it was something in the land itself that made them wild. Benji had been the youngest of eleven, all boys. The runt of the litter. He always put Matt in mind of Rumpelstiltskin. He might have been an inch or two over five feet tall, but that was all. High-heeled cowboy boots, a shoelace necktie, and tinted glasses; a pockmarked face that looked as if it had been crudely carved out of a potato. His father used to lament not having fed him to the pigs when he was still an infant. That same father died when he was ten or so, his mother a few years later, leaving Benji to the mercy of his older brothers. He ran away from home, made his way to Winnipeg and eventually out to Calgary, and returned twelve or fifteen years later with a wife, a young son, a great deal of mysteriously acquired money, and a new name.

His wife was a slip of a woman with protuberant eyes and a breathy, ingenuous delight in all things great and small: easily moved to exclamations of wonderment and easily moved to tears, whether happy, sad, or some mingling of both.

They moved right into town. He made no attempt to get in touch with his brothers, refused to acknowledge or have anything to do with them. By then the Pereverzev brothers had moved on from moonshining to growing marijuana crops. Most of them had been in and out of prison, several were dead, one of them murdered by another at the tail end of a drunken fistfight: knocked him down, dragged him out of the farmhouse by his heels, and calmly backed his truck over his brother's body.

Benji bought several properties that he fixed up himself and rented out, but his main business in those days was the liquor store. He would sit behind the counter with an open volume of Tolstoy beside the cash register, reading it slowly, painstakingly, his lips moving as he silently mouthed each word. He had never learned to read at all until adulthood. He might get through half a page in the course of a day.

It was there, over the counter of the liquor store, that Matt struck up a friendship with him. It wasn't difficult: they took a genuine liking to one another. Matt said to him once that if there was a magic mirror that could show, not your external appearance that everybody saw, but a projection of your true and inner self, then Benji would appear just like Matt, and Matt would look very much like a younger version of Benji. He might have been drunk when he said this.

From chatting over the liquor store counter, they soon graduated to poker games in the back room after closing. Matt often brought Ronald and Rudy to these games, mostly because he couldn't afford to always lose, modest as the stakes were, and Benji always won.

In April, a new sign went up in the storefront next to the liquor mart. This was another building that Benji owned. The sign read:

Wellesley & Pettinger
Design and Construction

At the beginning of June, Benji Pettinger took his wife and son on a month-long vacation. They sent postcards back from the CN Tower and Niagara Falls, from the Parliament Buildings in Ottawa and La Citadelle in Quebec City. While they were gone, Matt and his half-brothers—now his and Benji's employees—re-shingled the roof of the Pettingers' house, fixed the eavestroughs, patched the foundation in the northeast corner, painted the exterior; Simon mowed the lawn, trimmed the hedges, weeded the flowerbeds, painted the fence. And then, when this work was done, together with a handful of small and largely cosmetic repairs to the interior of the home, then Louise, Matt, and Matt's mother moved into the house for the remainder of the Pettingers' vacation.

This was said to be Benji's wedding gift to Matt and Louise, to allow them to be married out of the house that Matt had grown up in. The ulterior reason was this: that it allowed Matt and Louise plenty of space to put up the Hensels as houseguests for the wedding, something they could certainly never have been able to do from their draughty little shack with the view of the derelict salt refinery.

Of Matt's ulterior motives and machinations, his hopes and wild schemes, Louise was blissfully unaware. She seemed radiantly happy, seemed so even to herself: as if she were not experiencing her own happiness, only observing it, at a slight remove and with mild surprise.

She was unused to being the centre of attention, unused to being surrounded by people keeping her in mind and making an effort to be kind. Playing hostess in a make-believe house. Up early, before anyone else was awake, to take Smokie out for his morning run. Louise moving slowly, frequently stopping to rest, shyly greeting the occasional fellow early riser and hoping they wouldn't try to engage her in much conversation. Smokie would scamper ahead and circle back, or trot beside her all conceited and protective, or dart off barking at the glimpse of a squirrel or a rabbit, or to chase after the long shadow of a low-flying bird.

Louise was then six, six and a half months pregnant. The stage of nausea had passed, and the stage of heartburn, back spasms, and muscle cramps had not yet fully set in. She was experiencing now a pleasant lull of occasional sleeplessness, dreamy lethargy, and heightened sensuality. Tastes and smells had taken on an almost tangible sharpness, an intense pungency; sounds were louder, lights were brighter, shadows darker, the colour of everything deeper, as if supersaturated.

Back at the house, she would tie Smokie up in the yard—he wasn't allowed inside the house, not that house—and bring him his food, fill his water dish. Then she would make the coffee, carefully make it, as she did everything carefully in this home that wasn't her own. Hovering by the pot as the coffee slowly dripped and drizzled down, her eyes half-closed, luxuriating in the earthy fragrance. That smell of the coffee brewing would trigger an almost painful but intensely pleasurable excitement in her saliva glands, and she would feel the baby shift and wiggle inside her as if it too was excited by the smell.

Then she would prepare the tray to take upstairs to Matt, doing it with exaggerated and loving attention, making sure everything was just so: the coffee mug that he particularly liked, precisely the right amount of sugar and cream, a plate with two chocolate-covered digestive cookies, his favourite. A banana for herself. And together they would have their coffee on the small patio outside the master bedroom, above the porch, just as Matt's own mother and father used to: the cool and lovely morning, listening to the chorus of birds, looking peacefully out over the slowly rousing town. Talking softly, desultorily, about nothing of importance. And once they'd finished their coffee, and Matt had eaten his cookies and smoked his second cigarette, then they would go back into the bedroom and make love—as perhaps Matt's father and mother had done every morning as well, in that very same bed.

Louise would stay in bed afterwards, resting, neither wholly asleep nor fully awake, for two hours or more. She liked to listen dreamily to the sounds of the house stirring below her, sounds that would start out quiet and intermittent, and gradually build. Cicely playing the piano, usually something gentle, melodic, and melancholy. Matt and his mother exchanging a few words, gentle and confidential murmurs; a cupboard door opening and closing, the flush of water from the taps, the subdued clatter of dishes in the kitchen. Then the sound of the front door opening and Bonnie's voice would join them, turning the duet into a trio, and with her the pettish cries or cheerful gurgles of little baby Katharine: baby Katharine who was just three months old and already so bright, chatty, and self-confident, Katharine with her ridiculous long fingers and toes on the end of her impossibly pudgy arms and legs, Katharine always so ready to be doted over and adored. The three of them talking away now, raising their voices to be heard over one another; more dishes, cups, and cutlery clattering, cupboards and doors opening and closing, chairs scraping across the floor, occasional bursts of laughter. And the smells of bacon frying and bread toasting and more coffee coming down, and the sound of Smokey yapping outside in the yard and the front door opening again and Peggy Afton's voice, always louder and more decisive than the others, turning the trio into a quartet. And Louise would stay in bed as long as possible, luxuriating in the music of it all, and thinking to herself that this was the essence and audible distillation of happiness itself; and she would spend a long time suspended between the desire to join them downstairs, and the desire to extend this exquisite luxury of distant listening. She would lie in bed until the baby inside her, stirred and excited too by the increasingly boisterous sounds and tempting smells coming from downstairs, would allow her to rest no more.

Louise often wondered, then, if she herself had been so alert and active when she was inside her own mother, her real mother, birth mother, the one she'd never known and knew nothing about. She found herself thinking about her birth mother frequently in those days, someone she had hardly thought about at all in years: not so much about what sort of person she might have been, or what the circumstances of her life were, or why she had given Louise up for adoption, the sort of idle speculations that she'd sometimes indulged in as a teenager; rather she thought about her now almost solely and wholly as a physical body. It was hardly even thinking, really: only she would catch sight of herself in the mirror with a certain characteristic expression on her face, or become conscious of herself making a long-habitual gesture, as the way she lowered her head to the left and looked towards the floor if someone said something kind or complimentary to her, or how she would tilt her head to the right and look upwards smiling whenever Matt said or did something that made her feel particularly in love with him: then she would be struck by a sudden, uncanny, baseless but absolute certainty that her birth mother had made precisely those same gestures and expressions under precisely the same circumstances. So, too, when she had gone through those early months in her pregnancy of abrupt and frequent vomiting, or now when her feet ached if she stood for too long or her buttocks were sore if she sat too long, or when the baby squirmed inside her, or she felt that nasty surge of heartburn after eating too heavy a meal, or experienced a certain embarrassing but undeniable increase in her libido, especially in the morning as she stood over the coffeemaker, breathing in the brewing aroma: then she would be irrationally but absolutely convinced that her mother had experienced those exact same physical sensations; more than that, convinced that she and her mother in such moments were for all intents and purposes the same interchangeable body, merely transposed in time and space.

And then, for several days, it was not just Matt and Cicely and Peggy Afton and Bonnie and baby Katharine and sometimes Simon, it was Dr Hensel too, and Dr Hensel's husband, and Ruth and Esther and Isaac. And Louise would not allow herself the luxury of lying in bed all morning. But she had to allow herself to be fussed over, with the wedding just days away: last-minute dress fittings and adjustments, hair appointments for herself and the twins, manicures and pedicures; last-minute decisions to be made or unmade about the seating arrangements, the speeches, the music, menu, flowers, and so forth. And there was the obligatory afternoon tea-party at Fanny and Jim Ritchie's house, hastily thrown together when Fanny discovered that the role of Louise's family was being played by the famous and distinguished Hensels; and there was the rehearsal at the church, and then returning to an extravagant dinner that Ms Afton had prepared in their absence.

And throughout this, there was also the pleasurable but slightly unreal sensation of watching Mr Hensel engaged in long, thoughtful conversations with Matt's mother, or seeing how Dr Hensel and Peggy Afton took an instant if slightly combative liking to one another. Of watching Esther swoon and squeal and coo with delight over little baby Katharine, always wanting to hold her, even eager to change her diaper; and the strangeness of seeing the twins for the first time not of a single mind, for Ruth took no interest in the baby whatsoever, and even seemed slightly frightened and disgusted by her. And then there was a simpler, more straightforward pleasure, joined to a profound authentic feeling of pride, at watching both the Hensels getting to know Matt, how they seemed to listen to him with interest and genuine respect. The afternoon that Louise was out with the twins getting their hair and nails done, Matt took the Doctor and the Right Honourable for a long walk to show them the town: they were apparently gone all afternoon.

That same evening, Dr Hensel and Louise sat alone together for a few hours, as they occasionally had in the old days; and just as she had back then, Dr Hensel was not only charming, witty, and attentive, she gently coaxed Louise to open up about herself, to talk of her life now, her hopes, dreams, and ambitions, ending the conversation, when she saw that Louise was rapidly fading into exhaustion, with a blunt straightforward question: "Tell me this, and tell me honestly: is he good to you? Does he treat you well—always, not just when other people are around?"

"He is," said Louise, her tired eyes getting wet. "He is, he does. He treats me like the world." What she meant was, *He treats me as if I mean the world to him*— And she deeply, sweetly, completely believed it. The words hadn't come out quite right, but she was too sleepy to try and correct herself. It didn't matter, Dr Hensel understood her, and she was satisfied, or seemed to be at least, and told her to go to bed.

In early September, Nathanael Leonard Lionel Wellesley was born in the hospital in Brandon: eight pounds seven ounces, healthy happy squirmy and funny, long and brown like a baby otter.

At the end of September, plans and funding for a major new project were announced to great fanfare, a joint initiative of the municipal, provincial, and federal governments, made further possible by the generous support of a private donor: the construction of the Joan Hensel Regional Medical Clinic and Beverley Frere Memorial Long-term Health Care Facility, to be constructed on the land formerly occupied by the now-derelict Afton saltworks and refinery, designed and built by the firm of Wellesley & Pettinger.

Within the year, using most of the profits from his sale of the salt works property to the provincial government, Matt purchased the old Stone School and all the land still remaining to it from the federal government. It was done cheaply, with the help of a few well-placed words from the Rt Hon Leonard Hensel. Frankly, the government was glad to be rid of it. Done cheaply and in complete secrecy, not even Louise knew anything about it, or ever would. For having bought the place, Matt had neither the time nor the ready funds to do anything with it right away, but always waited for the right opportunity. And the years slipped by, as years do; children grew, governments changed over, new schemes and projects intervened, and the right opportunity never seemed to arrive; and the old Stone School sat untouched, accumulating darkness, patiently and peacefully rotting away, its ownership a mystery.

13

A young man is kissed in a maze;
Maureen and Kenneth Mack take over a farm

TRENT PETTINGER WAS A HALF-FOOT TALLER than his father:
he took more after his uncles Pereverez, at least to look at; only
he had his mother's protuberant eyes. His hair was so fair and so
fine it almost looked pink. But though he may have looked like a
Pereverez, for a long time he didn't know he was related to them.
His father never mentioned it; his mother had no idea.

There were several of his cousins at school with him, but
none in the same grade. Michael Pereverez was three years older
than Trent but only two grades up, he'd been held back a year. A
notorious bully and universal bastard, bulky, sweaty, swaggering
and angry, he had a special hatred for Trent and made him his
favourite target, tripping him in the halls and knocking him into
lockers, slapping the books out of his hands, cornering him in
the washroom or the playground to twist his nipples or punch his
shoulder, or to grab the back of his head and shove his face into his
armpit, holding it there and rubbing his nose in the acrid stink,
barely able to breathe, calling him bug-eyes and cocksucker but
most often *Cuz*, investing the word with a kind of obscene relish
and contempt. Trent in his ignorance assumed Cuz was some
obscure or private slang, probably sexual from the lascivious way
Michael pronounced it, maybe an amalgam of cum and jizz. As
they got a bit older, Michael began to "borrow" money from him
with increasing frequency, looming over him with a menacing
intimacy and saying, "You don't mind, do you, Cuz? Your daddy's

rich, isn't he?" It got so bad at last that even the teachers started to notice. Then, when Trent was in ninth grade, early in the year, Michael stopped showing up at school. A rumour went around that he had been busted for dealing weed to a twelfth-grader; whether the rumour was true, or there was some other reason, he never did come back.

Trent back then was an awkward, dreamy kid, bashful and bookish. His father, to compensate perhaps for the fact that *he* had never learned to read until adulthood, forbade him the television and inundated him with books. Any books would do, Benji made no discrimination, if his son had asked him to buy him *Venus in Furs* or the *120 Days of Sodom* Benji would have happily complied: a book is a book is a book. Happily, Trent's tastes didn't run in that direction. When he was younger, he lived off *Robin Hood and Knights of the Round Table.* Later he made his way through Tolkien, and Conan too. In eighth grade, his English teacher introduced him to Sherlock Holmes and Edgar Allan Poe, Ray Bradbury and Isaac Asimov. In eleventh grade his class studied *Great Expectations*, and he fell desperately in love with Estella, and saw her in his dreams, looking very much like Vivian Heidecker. At sixteen he had never yet had a girlfriend, or kissed a girl, or held a girl's hand even, not in that way. In June his parents dragged him along on a month long trip out east, to the CN Tower and Niagara Falls, the Parliament Buildings in Ottawa and La Citadelle in Quebec City.

They travelled mostly by train. Trent's mother was a born tourist, with her stacks of brochures and a brand-new polaroid camera and that breathy, ingenuous delight in all things great and small, easily moved to exclamations of wonderment and easily moved to tears, whether happy, sad, or some mingling of both; and then, too, she had both her boys at her side, her husband and her beloved son all to herself, with no work or school, no friends or obligations to pull them away from her: it might have been the happiest month of her life. Her name was Grace.

On the train way out, Trent read Agatha Christie and met a girl named Denise. She wore an oversized old hoodie, gold coloured, with a faded University of Alberta crest across the chest. She was perpetually slouched, hunching her shoulders, her stringy brown hair falling forward to obscure her face. Her legs were too long for her body, awkward and gangly; her face was shaped like a wedge, wide at the temples and narrowing down to a pointy little chin. Their families had been assigned adjacent tables in the dining car. And she glared at Trent, that very first morning over breakfast, as if she hated his guts.

They were the only teenagers on the train. She was travelling with her mother, her annoying little brother, and her mother's new husband; in fact her mother and stepfather had only just got married and this was sort of their honeymoon. To be dragged along on her own mother's honeymoon, when Denise was more than old enough to be left alone at home for two weeks and take care of her brother, seemed to her the apex of humiliation. Her little brother was an annoying brat, and a nerd to boot: he and their stepfather were both obsessed with model trains, they'd practically taken over the basement. Her mother and stepfather were forever holding hands, or making moon eyes at each other, or sticking their tongues in one another's mouths, it was utterly disgusting. They'd been on the train since Edmonton, it was only a few days but it felt like forever.

She told him all this in the observation car after lunch, where he'd gone to read his book. She had just plunked herself down next to him, though there were plenty of other empty chairs: sullen and hostile, slumping her body so far down that her backside was off the edge of the seat, hands jammed in the pocket of her hoodie, the drawstrings of the hood wet and frayed from chewing. She had hardly even looked at him before she started talking, didn't say hello or introduce herself, just launched into her litany of grievances and resentments. She was sitting so close to him he could smell a faint aroma of black licorice emanating from her pores. Since breakfast she had applied black eyeliner with a heavy hand and some sort of pale lip gloss; her neck was long and supple; there was a small and incandescent scatter of acne across her forehead, mostly but not totally hidden by her falling hair. The train rattled and swayed past jagged looming rockface and tall skinny pine and multitudinous lakes, sometimes glimpsed in the distance, sometimes emerging suddenly right beside them, almost as if beneath them, so close it created the illusion that the train was skimming across the waters, deep blue and serene, the sunlight dazzling off the rippling surface. Now for a brief, furtive moment the girl turned to look at him, and her eyes were the shape and the colour of almonds and swallowed him up like a sandstorm, and the sun striking her hair brought out a hint of bronze, and she quickly looked away again, and looked down at her hands in the pocket of her hoodie, and said, "I guess my name's Denise."

He admitted his name was Trent. His heart was thumping wildly, as if he were having a panic attack, and he turned pink as a pencil eraser. She said, "So what's your story, Trent? Where are your parents dragging you to?"

He told her that his father had lent their house to his business partner to use for a month, so they were temporarily homeless and were going to spend the month travelling all over Ontario and Quebec like a bunch of tourists. He was, in actuality, quite excited about the trip, but he tried to make it sound as if he resented it.

"Seriously?" said Denise eagerly, letting herself glance at him again, and this time not looking immediately away when their eyes met. "So there's just some strange person right now using your room, sleeping in your bed?"

"I guess."

"Ugh. That's so creepy." She blew upwards at the hair falling over her face, making it flutter. "Parents are the worst."

She took him on a tour of the train, which mostly consisted of two or three identical cars repeated over and over again, with only the dining car in the middle and the observation car at the very back to break the monotony. She told him she had been playing a game to pass the time: she was pretending that she was a secret agent, and that one or more of the passengers were foreign spies, but it could be any of them, and she had to figure out which. Trent threw himself into the game with great enthusiasm, and for the next day and a half they stalked up and down the corridors of the train together, whispering and giggling. Their suspicions were chiefly centred on an elderly couple from Colorado—at least that's what they claimed to be—who said that every year for the last eight years they'd fly out to the west coast of Canada so they could ride the train all the way to the east coast, and then fly back home. He was flabby and gregarious, and seemed to chiefly enjoy the trip as an opportunity to chat up strangers and meet new folk; she knit. This was all very suspicious. It was Trent's suggestion that she could be knitting secret coded messages into the pattern of her scarf, or sweater, or whatever the hell she was supposed to be making. Then the train arrived in Toronto, and they went their separate ways.

He saw Denise again at Niagara Falls. They were staying, briefly, at the same hotel. It turned out this wasn't just a coincidence: his father had apparently struck up a conversation with her stepfather on the train and found out where they'd be staying. In a strange reprise of their first encounter, the two families found themselves seated at adjacent tables over breakfast. Denise was no longer wearing her hoodie, just a t-shirt, and the sight of her bare arms made Trent feel light-headed. She had her hair pulled back in a ponytail, making her face look sharper and more triangular than ever. The acne on her forehead was mostly cleared up.

It turned out that this was their last full day in Niagara, they had to leave early the next morning to start making their way back to Edmonton. "Honeymoons can't last forever." But since they had the whole day ahead of them, and nothing really planned, they offered to act as tour guides of a sort and show the Pettingers around.

The dull roar of the Falls in the distance followed them around town; a fine mist hung in the air, though the sky was blue and the sun blazed. Every surface seemed faintly damp and slick to the touch. Their parents, and Denise's little brother, strolled up ahead in one group, talking energetically; Denise and Trent followed up twenty feet behind. They passed the Ripley's Museum, and Denise complained that it was *so boring*, but that her little brother and stepfather both had been so geeked out about it they had to spend almost a whole day in there. Then there was the wax museum, and that wasn't just boring, it was creepy too, and she shuddered demonstratively as they passed it on the street. She had put her hoodie back on after breakfast, but had changed into shorts and flip-flops, and the sight of her pale and gangling legs made him even dizzier than the sight of her bare arms had, it was all he could do not to stare at them. They had lunch on a patio, and discussed the afternoon. It was decided that they would stroll down to walk along the river and see the Falls themselves, but Denise declared that she wanted, instead, to take Trent to the Mirror Maze and maybe the Haunted House. Her stepfather was amused; he said, "When *we* went to those, you said they were stupid and boring." Trent's mother was doubtful, too, about leaving her little boy in a strange town—what if they got lost, or something happened to them? But Trent's father said, "Why not? Let the kids have their fun, if that's what they want to do," and Denise's mother said, "They won't get lost, Denise knows her way around by now." She gave Denise some money, and Benji gave Trent some money too and made sure it was more, and they made the teens promise faithfully to meet them back at the hotel at six o'clock. "Six o'clock in the lobby, no excuses."

She took him through the haunted house first. He had great hopes that she would actually get scared and want to hold his hand, or maybe even cling to him, but of course she had been through it before and knew what to expect. She only wanted to mock it and whisper sarcasms to one another. But at least the narrowness of the corridors with their frequent twists and turns forced an intoxicating closeness on them. And it was dark, too, so that sometimes they bumped up against one another. Along the walls of one long and narrow corridor, lit only by strobe lights that flashed blindingly bright at slow intervals, there were the usual threats and dire warnings scrawled in what was meant to look like blood, while a series of gibbering noises and whispers of "Get out! Get out while you still can!" seemed to emanate from every direction and no direction at once. Then Denise did take his hand in the dark, and he could feel a faint prickling that ran from the touch of her hand, up his arm, and down his back to the base of his spine, a pleasurable electric pulse. The smell of black licorice was coming off her body in waves. Around a bend, a life-sized doll was dangling from the ceiling, hanging by the neck from a noose and gently swaying back and forth; she was dressed in a drab and ragged slip and her stringy black hair artfully concealed her face, no doubt because the face was the hardest part to make look realistic. A pressure plate on the floor, when Trent stepped on it, triggered a loud and high-pitched giggle that startled him; a mechanical clown sprung out from behind a trap door, holding a bloody and decapitated head in one hand and a meat cleaver in the other.

When they finally emerged back into the daylight, dazed and giggling, it took a few minutes to adjust to the brightness of the sun. Denise took off her hoodie and tied it around her waist, complaining of the heat; when she pulled it over her head, for a brief moment her t-shirt lifted too and he caught a fleeting glimpse of her navel, and his knees nearly buckled.

In the Maze of Mirrors she took his hand again, and this time she didn't let it go. They'd had to leave their shoes and sandals at the entrance; Denise, since she wasn't wearing socks, had to pay an extra two dollars to borrow a pair of felt slippers: for not only the walls and ceilings but even the floors of the maze were made of mirrors. A sign at the front door asked the customers not to touch the walls, but they were smeared with fingermarks anyway. Several times they passed a harried looking mother trying to keep up with two young boys whose excited, belligerent voices echoed loudly through the corridors, arguing incessantly and insultingly about which was the right way to turn. Trent and Denise made their way very slowly through the maze, savouring the vertiginous, heady sensation of infinity and speaking only in low voices. Trent would have been content to stay in there with her forever, surrounded by the kaleidoscopic sight of infinitely repeated Denises, and the boundless multiplicity of her bare arms and legs.

The middle of the maze, when they reached it, was a relatively open room with a wall of funhouse mirrors that distorted and distended their bodies into grotesque shapes. It had been a little while since they'd seen anyone else, or heard any other voices: they seemed to be, at least for the moment, alone in the maze. Without warning or preamble, and with an air of having screwed herself up to a pitch of desperate bravado, she suddenly kissed him.

LEFT TO HIS OWN DEVICES, Trent might have liked to go to university, take a variety of different courses, spend some time trying different things and figuring out what he'd like to do with his life. It didn't matter. He knew, and had always known, that his father was counting on him to join the family business.

Benji wanted him to learn a bit of everything they had a hand in. For a couple of summers he caddied at the new golf course and learned to play the game passably, if never very well. He stocked the shelves in the liquor store and did inventory in the back, before graduating to sitting behind the counter, greeting the customers and working the register. When they expanded the store, he was there to help knock down the adjoining wall and haul away the debris. Sometimes he would be invited to sit in on those poker games with his father, Matt, Matt's half-brother Ronald, and whoever they happened to be working on at the time. There he would be expected to smoke his share of cigars and drink his share of drinks, Benji firmly believing that knowing how to gamble, smoke, and hold your liquor was an essential part of any business education. One winter they stuck him down in the main office, back then a little hole-in-the-wall on 2nd Ave between Gerry Shaw's office and the Lucky Panda, where they served an American-style breakfast for under five dollars, if you got there before 8.30: watery coffee, two eggs any style, hashbrowns, two small and flabby sausages or three thin strips of bacon, and two slices of toast—all vaguely and indefinably redolent of egg rolls—and served with a fortune cookie for dessert. There at the office Wanda Dueck patiently taught him the rudiments of filing documents and organizing a calendar, preparing leases and invoices, collecting rents, running a payroll, and balancing the books. When they had a construction project on the go, then sometimes Trent would be sent along to serve as Matt's joe-boy—or Ronald's, who was acting foreman whenever Matt couldn't be on site—to lend a hand with any random, relatively unskilled task that needed doing at any given moment.

Or sometimes Matt would just show up wherever Trent happened to be, tell him to hop in the truck, and take him along on whatever jobs or errands he happened to have going that day, just for the company. Matt seemed to enjoy having him around, a fact that Trent found at once flattering and confusing. When he had turned eighteen, Matt and Ronald had taken him to Brandon and got him tremendously drunk at a pub near the University; there he met a soft and slightly older woman named Paula who smelled like a bar of soap and told him he was sweet. He ended the night at her apartment, which also smelled of soap. It was his first, and until Marian his only, sexual experience. Only later, piecing together as much of the evening as he could remember through the haze of alcohol, did it occur to him that Matt and Ronald had probably engineered the whole encounter.

One spring, a few years later, they got a job repairing and modernizing the stables on the old PMU farm north of town. The farm had formerly belonged to Stan and Boris Pereverez before it was seized by the RCMP. That raid, which had included an eighteen-hour armed stand-off and a helicopter circling overhead, was the most dramatic thing that had happened in or around the town for many years. It was something of a mystery, too: only later did it come out that, in addition to the drugs seized, the stolen property and illegal firearms, human remains had been found on the property. The bodies were eventually identified as Rhonda Lepine and Fawn McKee, two young women who had gone missing from Brandon and Waabishkigwan respectively, seven years and three years before. Trent had a vague memory of several posters for Fawn McKee briefly appearing on telephone poles around town, back when she'd first gone missing, but they had been quickly taken down. As soon as the nature of the crimes had become apparent, a collective determination had settled on the town not to know more about it. The trial, which took place in Brandon, was neither followed nor discussed.

The day that Matt went out there to meet the new owners and discuss plans for the stable, he brought Trent along for a sidekick. Matt picked him up after breakfast. It was early April; there were still heaps of snow on the fields and in the shady places. Trent wondered if the people who now owned the place were aware of its history. "I have no idea," said Matt, "but we're not going to tell them." Obscurely, Trent had expected that the evil that had occurred there would be palpable in the place; he wasn't sure if he was relieved or disappointed to find that the sun shone down equally on this farm as on its neighbours, that it looked and felt no different than any other he'd been to.

The new owners seemed tremendously young, especially the woman, who emerged from the main house holding an infant and who looked, to Trent, like she could have been fifteen. The man kept his hands in his pockets and his eyes on the ground, smiling bashfully and agreeing to everything that Matt proposed, only occasionally glancing over at his young wife for approval.

She said little, but watched and listened with evident amusement, occasionally jiggling the infant in her arms. She was short, slender, and lithe as a young cat; her lightly freckled face had something feline about it too, in the shape of the face and in the wide green eyes with their look of mischief and contempt; when she stood near him, Trent could smell a strong odour of freshly cut grass emanating from her pores.

Later, when they went inside the house to sit at the kitchen table, drink some coffee, and finalize some numbers and other details, Maureen quite casually pulled up her shirt and began feeding the baby, making no attempt to obscure herself or even to warn her guests, so that Trent, though he quickly looked down, got a clear and vivid glimpse of one full and lightly freckled breast and a protuberant and milky nipple, a brief and inadvertent glimpse that lodged somewhere deep in his brain and haunted his dreams for many years after. It fused in his imagination with a story that Matt had once told him, over a few drinks, about his university days in Winnipeg: how he had heard a rumour then about an expensive and exclusive brothel, of sorts, that ran only during office hours, Monday to Friday, and was staffed exclusively by bored and well-heeled housewives in their second trimesters. Matt had never managed to find this mythical bordello, though not for lack of trying, and he had eventually dismissed it as an urban legend or undergraduate fantasy. He told Trent the anecdote offhandedly, as an example of a young man's gullibility, not suspecting the secret and disproportionate effect it would have on Trent's imagination. And so it would be a deep and permanent disappointment to Trent that Marian, after he married her, proved, like her sister Vivian, to be incapable of having children—not because he wanted kids particularly, but because the idea of making love to a pregnant woman, or a breastfeeding one, had become for him a persistent and ineradicable erotic fantasy. Of this disappointment he was deeply ashamed, and lavished all the more devotion on his wife by way of compensation.

14

Maureen makes a fire;
she educates Casey

IN THE AUTUMN ESPECIALLY, but really any time of the year, Maureen enjoyed burning things. Then she might spend hours roaming the property, collecting deadfall, sometimes taking Casey with her to help gather the fallen sticks and twigs, and she would spend hours more in front of the burn barrel, tending the fire and feeding it with loving care and attention.

Jammed thick with branches, brambles, and dead leaves, old papers, napkins, and cardboard boxes, a dense, languid smoke would seep out the airholes at the bottom, yellowish and acrid; then a few flames would start to flicker clear, and she might pick out a hefty branch from the pile, snap it over her knee with a satisfying crack, and stuff it into the burn barrel, dried-out pine needles crackling into a quick surge of flames that would leap up and nearly lick her face. And she would keep feeding it until it was in full blaze, crackling and popping loudly; and to Casey looking up at her, it would seem as though spurts of flames were surrounding her mother's body like a nimbus, and smoke pouring from the top of her head.

She told Casey about a house that had burned down on the street where she grew up, back when she was a child. Then, after they had cleared away the debris, the lot stood empty for many years, no one wanted to build a new house there. There were still the remnants of a wrought-iron fence separating the property from the sidewalk, but nothing behind that fence but broken ground, burdock and cigarette butts, thistle, bits of smashed glass and other garbage.

She and her brothers and sisters used to cut through the lot all the time, she said, on their way to school and back. Of course they weren't supposed to, their parents forbid it, with the broken beer bottles in the weeds and everything. And Maureen said that whenever you passed through the property, as soon as you went past the fence, if you were quiet you could hear a voice. It was faint, you had to really listen for it, but it was definitely there, always there, it never stopped so long as you had a foot on the property. It was a man's voice, but thin, whiny, and high-pitched, and it talked rapidly, babbling almost, a steady stream of complaints, usually bitching about trivial things: the weather, money troubles, that sort of thing. "I swear to God someone's been moving my shoes," she heard it say once—the only time she was ever able to pick out a complete sentence. And even though the voice never really said anything menacing, or meaningful, or even particularly interesting, there was something about just hearing it that gave you a creepy cold shiver.

The legend was that after dark, the voice got louder. A handful of teenagers in the neighbourhood made a bet once, who could stick it out the longest. Her oldest brother was one of them. Apparently the closer it got to midnight, the louder and angrier and more insistent the voice became, until it was yelling obscenities, almost incoherent with rage, and they all felt a kind of tightness in their chests and a blind building terror. Only the moment they stepped back onto the sidewalk, they couldn't hear a peep, like someone had pressed a button; even leaning over the fence they couldn't hear a thing.

Sometimes when Maureen told Casey stories about her childhood, she said that she had grown up in the city, sometimes she said it was in a small town, sometimes it was on a farm. Sometimes she said she had grown up in a large family with lots of siblings, sometimes that she was an only child, sometimes even an orphan.

If Casey questioned her, she would flatly deny ever having said anything different. "I don't know what you're talking about," she'd say coldly, "and neither do you." And she might quite likely give Casey a hard, twisting pinch, or slip her hand into Casey's hair, grab hold, and give a painful yank, hard enough to wrench the child's head, twisting her neck and bringing tears to her eyes. And so, of course, Casey learned very quickly not to question her, or bring up any contradictions at all.

Back then, before she started school, Casey's hair was still quite long and unruly, and always a mess of knots and tangles, twigs, leaves, burrs, and bugs, and there would be a great battle every night as Maureen roughly brushed it out, callous to her daughter's cries of pain. This went on until one day when Casey managed to get a hold of her mother's good scissors and disappear into the woods, up to her secret place on the escarpment, where she cut her hair all off, every bit of it, as close to the scalp as she could get it. And though she knew she would catch hell for it, still she felt a thrill of triumph, almost exultation, for she knew that not even her mother could put that hair back on.

IN THE GARDEN, Maureen grew only vegetables, and never planted flowers. She said that she had known a woman, once, who couldn't stand the sight or the smell of flowers, because they reminded her of funerals. But then over time, said Maureen, this woman got it mixed around in her head, and instead of hating flowers because they reminded her of funerals, she started hating funerals because they reminded her of flowers. In the end she completely refused to die, because she couldn't bear the thought of all those wreaths and bouquets; the last time Maureen heard tell of her, she must have been a hundred and something years old, still hanging on out of sheer bloody-mindedness.

Once Maureen had tried raising peafowl on the farm. There was no real purpose to it. It turned out that peahens lay so little, they reproduce so slowly, there's no value in them for eggs or meat either. It's true that the peafowl were meant to keep the pests down, eating woodticks, ants, even mice and small garter snakes, but that hardly justified the expense.

Her first attempt, she bought three India blues at great cost, all fully grown, a pair of peahens and one peacock. She gloated over them. She made Casey admire the "eyes" on the peacock's tail feathers. She said, "Many eyes make many spies." He had a tremendous squawk that sounded for all the world as if he were being murdered. The three birds flew up into a tree as the sun was beginning to set; by the next morning they were gone, never to be seen again, they had just flown off. Maureen was furious. For weeks afterwards she walked around in a kind of cold and tightly coiled rage, muttering angrily under her breath and slamming the pots and pans as she prepared meals. Casey's arms and shoulders were black and livid blue from all the pinching before her mother got over it.

She tried again the next year, this time getting four chicks from a hatchery. Impossible to tell, yet, if they were cocks or hens. They were funny-looking things, with their scrawny necks, curved beaks, big black shiny eyes, and that tuft of feathers like a samurai's topknot. Maureen kept them cooped for the first few months; she built a chicken tractor for them that she would drag around the property, patiently pointing out the various landmarks.

As summer began to wind down, she let them roam free, and they didn't fly away. In fall, when the geese in great flocks would be flying overhead, the peafowl would run after them, squawking wildly, as if begging them to come back and take them with them, it was funny to watch but horrible to hear.

They didn't fly away, but they didn't survive the winter either. Though Maureen had a heat lamp in the coop for them, they were too stubborn or too stupid to sleep there, insisting on roosting in the trees. After a particularly nasty cold snap in December they weren't seen for several days before Maureen finally spotted them up a tree, well away from the house, frozen solid; when she gave the tree a shake, they dropped like rocks, or like fat feathered coconuts.

She didn't try again. But one morning that spring, when she went out to feed the chickens and collect the eggs, she found a peacock among them, one of those original India Blues that had flown away two years before. How it had survived the winters, where it had gone and why it had come back, she could never get it to tell her. She named it Rama.

It seemed to Casey that Rama took on something of her mother's personality. He, too, would disappear for long stretches to God only knew where, and then suddenly appear as if out of nowhere, coming around unexpected corners. And he would come strutting right up to people, moving with surprising speed, fixing his gleaming black eye on them and looking for all the world as if he might give them a nasty peck for no reason. Even the dogs were wary of him. Mud would bark at him now and then, from a safe distance, but when he fanned his tail, Rusty would always avert his eyes. Or sometimes Rama would flutter up to the roof of the house and roost there, surveying the farm like a king his kingdom, loosing a great honking squawk, puffing up his chest, and spreading his magnificent tail, with its shimmers of amethyst amid the emerald, turquoise, and sapphire.

When Rama dropped his tail-feathers, Maureen would collect them lovingly and tacked them up all over the property and in every room of the house, even Casey's bedroom. "Many eyes make many spies," she said with satisfaction. Whenever she was alone in her room, Casey would drape a dishtowel or a t-shirt over the feather so it couldn't see her.

In the end, she slaughtered Rama, and his meat fed them for over a week, first as a roast, then as sandwiches, and pot pie, and a soup that she made from boiling his bones. It had pained her to do it, but his squawking had become intolerable. Casey's father had never actually complained, would never have complained, but you could see him wince with pain every time. He was tremendously sensitive to certain noises; the rooster's crowing didn't bother him, nor did the clucking or squawking of the hens, but Rama had an unholy screech that made him shudder and brought on his migraines.

ONCE A WEEK Maureen would drive up to Brandon in the morning and return in the afternoon with groceries and other supplies. But four or five times a year she would leave very early and drive all the way out to Winnipeg, not returning until Casey was already asleep. On those days Casey and her father would eat cold leftovers or sandwiches for lunch and dinner, and in the evening Casey would be allowed to sit on the couch with her father and watch the game with him, and eat wine gums, and if she had questions about what was happening in the game or what were the rules he would patiently explain, or if she just felt like chattering he would happily listen, and he wouldn't brush her hair or make her change into her pyjamas or brush her teeth but let her fall asleep there on the couch, cuddled up against him, and then carry her into bed and tuck her away without waking her up.

Only once ever, that August before she began first grade, Maureen made Casey come with her to Winnipeg, to shop for school supplies. "When we get to the city," her mother said, "watch for cars when we're crossing the street. They'll run you down every chance they get. And make sure you stick close to me the whole time, don't wander off or get ahead or fall behind. Because if somebody snatches you, that's just too bad. I'm not coming hunting for you."

"Snatches me?" said Casey.

"That's right," said her mother cheerfully. "Snatch you up and sell you on the black market. Lots of money in little kids, even the runty ones like you. If you're lucky, they'll auction you off to some rich folks to scrub their toilets, or sell you to a factory to sew buttons on blue jeans. If you aren't so lucky, they'll just harvest your organs to give to rich sick kids, and then make a nice soup

out of what's left of you. Farm girl soup is a real delicacy in the
big city. Forty dollars a bowl with fresh bread sticks and a poached
hummingbird egg, fifty dollars for a bowl with an eyeball in it.
The eyeballs are the tastiest part, but of course there's only two
to go around."

As they passed the cemetery, Maureen slowed the car so that
Casey could get a good look at the old Stone School in the distance,
squatting high on its ridge and brooding over the town. The sun
was behind it, so that its face was obscured in shadows and it was
lit all round with red like a hot glowing coal.

Her mother told her that that was where they'd be taking her
away to school soon. It wasn't true, but of course Casey had no
way of knowing that yet. And Maureen must have been in a good
mood, because she started to tell Casey a story: how a long, long
time ago, before the old Stone School was a school, it was a mansion,
and a very rich man had lived there, alone except for his cook.

This rich man was very lonely, because his cook was a very
good cook but not very good company. What he really wanted
was a family, with lots of kids, because he wasn't very bright. So
one day he went away on a trip, leaving the cook in charge of
the mansion, and when he came back he had a wife with him,
young and beautiful, with doe eyes like a china doll and a little
puckered mouth.

"What colour was her hair?" Casey asked.

Irritably, her mother said, "Red. All beautiful, good-hearted
girls have long red curly hair that they brush every day, everybody
knows that. Now stop interrupting," she added, reaching over and
pinching the underside of Casey's arm, hard.

For a while, Maureen went on, the man and his new wife
were genuinely happy. She was free to do as she pleased and for
a long time it pleased her to throw wild parties on the weekend
and spend the week tending her vegetable garden, going for walks
in the woods along the riverbank, and spending hours holed up

in the kitchen with the cook, concocting wonderful and exciting new recipes.

But time went by, and the rich man started to get sad again, because it turned out that his wife couldn't have children, couldn't get pregnant. It began to bother him more and more; it began to obsess him. It spoiled his sleep and ruined his appetite. They saw every doctor, herbalist and quack they could find, but no one was able to help and nothing worked. It was hopeless, that's what the doctors told them.

Soon he could think of nothing else, and he grew thinner and sadder every day, and his wife hated to see him so sad, because she had a good heart; so she and the cook talked it over and came up with a plan. One night, the two of them slipped out of the house after he was asleep, and rode their horses to a nearby village, and slipped silently into a tipi and stole a baby. And in the morning she proudly presented it to her husband at the breakfast table. But to her surprise, he didn't seem happy at all; in fact he was so shocked and horrified that something in his brain snapped, and he ran up to the highest room in the mansion and locked himself in and never spoke again. At night they'd hear his footsteps, pacing back and forth, back and forth across the floor.

Now, his wife and the cook were confused. After all, they had got him his baby—wasn't that what he had wanted? And the cook said, "Maybe we got a defective one. What do we know about babies?" And the wife said, "I guess that must be it, there must be something wrong with this one." She gave the baby to the cook and told him to take it back, and they'd go out that night and try to find a better one, they'd keep trying until they found one that made her husband happy, because she had such a good heart she couldn't bear to have him so sad. But the cook thought it seemed like too much work to return the defective baby, so instead he took it to the kitchen and cooked it in a roasting pan with carrots, leeks, celery, and parsnips, and a crabapple in its mouth, and served it for dinner with crabapple jelly and a nice Pinot Gris. It was delicious.

So the next night they went out and stole another baby. The cook thought that maybe the first baby had been too skinny, and that's why the husband hadn't liked it, so this time they looked around until they found a really plump one, but when they brought it home and took it up to show him, he didn't seem to like this one either: he just stared blankly into space, weeping silently, as if he couldn't even see them or hear them. So the cook made a pie this time, with potatoes and a rich baby gravy, and it was even better than the roast.

And the cook said, "Maybe an older kid would make him happy. Maybe he doesn't like the idea of changing all those diapers." And the wife said, "Maybe you're right. It's worth a try, anyway."

So they started snatching toddlers and even slightly older kids, but that didn't make the husband any happier or snap him out of his catatonic state, he still never left his room or ever spoke a word again, only paced silently back and forth, back and forth, all the damn time, it was very irritating. After a while they didn't even bother showing him the little children they had snatched, just put them straight into the pantry. The toddlers made for excellent eating but they found that any older than two or three years old and the meat started to get tough, greasy, and gristly.

Then one winter the cook passed away, because he was old, and the wife said, "What am I going to do now?" Because she had a whole pantry crammed full of kids waiting to be turned into meals, and even though she could have cooked them herself—she was an excellent cook, like all beautiful women with long red curly hair—she just couldn't bring herself to kill them, because she was such a kind, good-hearted woman. The cook had always done all the butchering, out back. So instead of killing them and cooking them, she kept the kids and raised them as her own, and since she was raising them she had to teach them too, and that's how the mansion became a school.

"What about her husband?" Casey asked. "What happened to him?"

"Well," said Maureen, "his wife walled over the doorway to his room, so that the kids wouldn't wander in there accidentally and get scared, because you know at that point he hadn't had a bath or a haircut in twenty years. And from what I've heard, he's still up there. So when you're at school, you should listen carefully some time and you might hear his footsteps pacing back and forth above your head…"

THERE WAS A STORY, or group of stories really, that Casey's mother used to tell her sometimes, if she was in a particularly good mood. Usually while Casey was helping her collect deadfall for the fire, or as they stood around the burn barrel, feeding the flames. This detail or that would vary from one telling to another, but the basic gist was always the same:

It all happened a long, long time ago, she said, in the far-away city of Winnipeg, and there was a poor young policeman, a simple constable, from good *canadien* stock, the son of a son of a voyageur. And he was in love with the mayor's only daughter. The mayor's daughter was wealthy, beautiful, and clever, with doe eyes like a china doll, a little puckered mouth, and long red curly hair; and she was in love with the young policeman back, because he was honest, brave, hard-working, handsome, and stupid. Unfortunately, they weren't allowed to get married because even though the mayor liked the young policeman well enough, he would only let his daughter marry someone very rich, and the policeman was really very poor, because he was so honest, and so were his parents. The mayor's daughter thought they ought to run away together and head off into the wide world and have adventures and be happy, but the policeman, being both honest and stupid, wouldn't hear of it.

Now, outside the city, across the river, through the woods, and under a hill, there lived a sort of ogre by the name of Baltasar. He was huge, misshapen, fierce and solitary. His head was covered with gnarly black hair like scorched steel wool. He lived in a cave under the hill far away from the city and always avoided being seen by people and other animals.

Baltasar had been there before the city, before the highways, before the rows of telephone poles stretching on into infinity. Baltasar hated the city. He never went there except once a year, at the end of winter, to snatch a couple of babies from their cribs as they slept. He would take the babies back to his cave, stew them to a paste and grind their bones, along with certain incantations, to make a magic fertilizer; and with this fertilizer, he grew in his garden the biggest, bestest vegetables you could ever imagine. Because Baltasar, of course, was a strict vegetarian.

He lived this way for many, many years; he had lived this way for longer than even he could remember. But he was lonely, and the building of the city made him feel even more lonely, for some reason; and as he was growing older, somehow his loneliness seemed to matter more. So, when he went into town one year, he stole an extra baby this time, a baby girl, to raise as his own; and he named her Ellen.

She grew up to be small and thin: thin as a garter snake, brown as a squirrel, with flat black hair cut short as a boy's. She called him Father, and helped him in the garden. She helped him in the garden and she helped him around the cave; and he taught her all he knew of witchcraft, of herb-lore, of spells and potions and all the magic secrets that he had learned over the course of a very long lifetime.

When Ellen was a teenager, Baltasar blessed her and then he passed away, old fat and happy. Ellen began going into town on market days to sell the giant vegetables she grew. The people in town didn't know anything about her, where she came from or how she had been raised, all they knew was that she was young, polite, shy, and a poor orphan; and they pitied her, and were friendly to her, and bought her vegetables. At night she would disappear back into the hills.

Among the many friends who came to visit her vegetable stand, there was one she fell in love with. It was the policeman, penniless and beautiful and young and dumb. Ellen fell madly, passionately, helplessly in love with him; but of course the policeman was already in love with someone else. He loved the daughter of the Mayor of Winnipeg, and every night he serenaded her from the garden outside her window. The Mayor's daughter loved the policeman, too, and they were as close to happy as any two idiots can be.

The policeman used to come and tell Ellen all about the Mayor's daughter, and how wonderful, lovely and perfect she was, and lament the fact that because he was poor, they couldn't get married; and he would ask Ellen's advice, and invite Ellen's compliments. He didn't mean to be unkind; he didn't know that Ellen was secretly in love with him, and that his words were like sharp slivers of ice stabbing Ellen's heart. And Ellen's love for him started to curdle into hatred, and ideas of revenge set into her joints like arthritis.

This is what she did: she continued going to the city to sell her vegetables every day, and when the policeman would come and blather on to her about his great love, like the boneheaded boob that he was, she would hide her true emotions and even encourage him to confide in her; not that he needed any encouragement. And in all her talks with him, in all the friendly comments, compliments, and seemingly tentative, well-meaning advice she offered him, she conspired to insinuate doubt like a seed or disease inside his mind.

This is what she did. This is what happened to the policeman: he came to "realize" that the Mayor's daughter was so wonderful, so impossibly lovely and beautiful and kind and intelligent and beautiful and perfect, that he—being, after all, but one man, and not even a particularly remarkable man at that—could not possibly have enough love and devotion inside him to do her justice.

So this is what he did, taking Ellen's advice: she led him out one night, under a full moon, to a particular clearing in the woods, that was good for magic spells; and she placed a wedge on the top of his head, right on the grain, and she hammered it down, splitting him in two, like an earthworm, and then sprinkled a certain magic fertilizer with a little spring water on the open half of each side, so that they grew whole again. Now there were two of him, two policemen, and twice as much love and devotion to offer the Mayor's daughter; and while one of them could continue his honest ways in the day as a poor, upright, and lovable constable, serenading the Mayor's daughter outside her window at night, and taking her out for ice cream and walks along the river on the weekends, the other one could be out in the world accumulating wealth the only way it's possible to get wealthy in this world, by robbing and cheating and stealing, so that together they could earn enough money to marry her.

The problem, of course, was that neither of him wanted to be the one who went off to rob and steal and get rich, because both of him wanted to be the one who got to buy her ice cream and go for strolls along the river with her, holding her little hand and feeling his heart thump. So finally, after some very heated arguments and a round of rock-paper-scissors that went on interminably because both of them always picked rock every single time, finally the two of him agreed to take turns, one for one week and the other the next. This worked for a little while, but eventually it grew intolerable. It turned out that skulking around the highways and waylaying strange travellers to murder them and steal their money is not nearly as fun and exciting as it sounds: it's actually tiring, unpleasant work, with a lot of down time, a lot of just waiting around feeling bored and lonely and wondering if your other self is out holding the hand of the woman you love at that very moment, and seething with jealousy; and sometimes you'd get caught in the rain, and you'd get soaked and cold to the bone, and sometimes when a traveller finally did come by he'd put up a fight, and you'd get some nasty bruises, and sometimes they'd barely have enough money on them after all that to have made it worth your while, it was all very depressing.

The back and forth of it grew too much for him, in the end; and Ellen made sure that the end came quickly enough. He started arguing with himself constantly, and trying to steal one another's turns, and sabotaging one another's time. Instead of going out along the highways and earning a fortune like he was supposed to, he'd hide in the bushes by the river and when the other him and the Mayor's daughter would come strolling by, holding hands and gazing dreamily into one another's eyes, he'd huck acorns and pinecones at their heads and then run away.

Finally—on Ellen's advice—he admitted that it could go on this way no longer. So he went out to that same clearing in the woods, and he drew a circle in the dirt, fifteen feet across. He agreed with himself that whoever was the victor would get to be with the Mayor's daughter forever and always, while the loser would give up the struggle, leave the country, and never be seen nor heard from again.

So he fought himself. He wrestled and wrestled all day inside his circle, each of him trying to beat the other down; then at night he slept just outside the circle, too exhausted to dream; then he woke at dawn, ate a quick breakfast of bread and cheese and apples that Ellen would leave in a basket every night, because he went on like that, wrestling from sun-up to sun-down, for days, and weeks, and months—because, of course, each of him was the exact same person and so each of him was exactly the same in strength and in skill and endurance and luck, and neither one of him could possibly ever best or beat the other. He fought himself so long he forgot what he was fighting about; he fought so long that he forgot his name; he fought himself so long that he forgot that there had ever been anything in his life except fighting from sun-up to sun-down.

He fought so long that the Mayor's daughter, who had no idea where he had gone or why, believed that she had been abandoned by her beloved. She had wept for days, and then she had got bored, and tired of crying, and she slung a knapsack across her shoulders and slipped away in the night, setting out into the wide world to find a new life—one without stupid policemen. And still he fought himself; he'd probably be fighting himself to this day, if Ellen had not intervened.

One night, after the Mayor's daughter had been gone months, gone long enough that the Mayor had given up trying to find her and Ellen felt certain that she would never return, she decided to bring the fight to an end. Perhaps, in her heart of hearts, she believed that with the Mayor's daughter gone, the policeman might now fall in love with her: for even though she hated him, she was also still in love with him, because that's the way love works in this world. She brought the usual picnic basket at night as he slept, and she put it down and went over to one of the sleeping policeman and carefully wrapped his hand around the handle of an axe. Then she took a certain potion and she poured it into his ear, and that potion made him dream this dream:

The dreaming policeman dreamt that he was wrestling himself, as always, but as he wrestled water began rushing in from somewhere, flooding the clearing: cold brown water that quickly covered the ground, and then was above his ankles, and soon up to his knees. Above it was all dark swollen clouds that swirled and churned swiftly across the sky, and midday was now dark as dusk, and the wind was blowing and buffeting him relentlessly, drenching him with cold spray, and still the water was rising, as if the Great Flood had come again. But even then he didn't stop wrestling.

A jagged flash of lightning scratched across the sky, bathing the world in a blink of brief light, followed quickly by a crack of thunder so loud and close that it rattled the bones in his body. Now the water was rushing past him as if he was standing in the middle of a vast fast river, and he was sort of wrestling weakly and clinging to himself for support at the same time, as dirty ice, branches, plastic bags and other debris shot by. He could feel the ground disintegrating beneath his feet, scoured by the icy water; then the dreaming policeman lost his footing, and fell down to one knee, in the icy water up to his neck, holding desperately on to his other self to keep from going under; and then a heavy branch struck him across the face as it careened by, and he was beneath the water, dark and cold, and he could feel the other policeman's foot on his chest, holding him down, until light was bursting inside his brain like rockets going off; and then he woke with a sudden start, and the dream was over.

When the dreaming policeman woke up, it had started to rain. He interpreted this dream, as Ellen had intended him to, as a sign that God wanted him to win the fight; and when he found that an axe had appeared in his hand over night, as if by magic, he considered it settled.

He walked over to the other policeman, who still lay sleeping; he leaned over and with one hard swop, he chopped his head from his shoulders. The head rolled away from the circle, down a slight slope, and rolled off into the bushes and down a gopher hole, and it was gone.

As his opponent's head rolled and separated, memory came rushing back, and the victorious policeman remembered who he was, and where, and why he had been fighting in the first place; the only thing he didn't remember, was just how long he had been out there. So he went home, and cleaned himself up, and went to the Mayor's mansion to ask if he could speak with the Mayor's daughter. And that was how he learned that she had gone away months and months and months ago, that she had left no word of where she was going, and that no one had heard from her since.

The victorious policeman felt as though he had been kicked in the stomach, and he went home and vomited in the corner. Ellen came to try and console him, but he was inconsolable; and to her rage and bitter disappointment, instead of staying with her and falling at least a tiny bit in love with her, he vowed to go off into the wide world and search for the Mayor's daughter, to either find her or die trying. He packed his bags and off he went.

Ellen went home to her cave and tore out her hair in great fisty clumps and howled with anger and rolled and tumbled and cried all night. She went to a patch of rose bushes near her home, and threw herself in and rolled about the thorns until she was scratched and bleeding all over. She swallowed handfuls of hard dirt that she dug out of the ground until her fingertips bled. She cast very many curses: she cursed the policeman and she cursed the Mayor's daughter in very many ways, so many curses she kind of lost track of them; she conjured a hellhound and set him on the policeman's trail, ordering him to hunt down not only the policeman himself, but everyone the policeman was related to, and everyone he had ever loved or ever would love, down to the eleventh generation. It was all a little excessive, and she felt vaguely embarrassed about it the next day, but of course by then it was too late. Because that very night the hellhound showed up at her cave, an enormous yellow dog with long sharp dirty teeth and lots of drool: not just any hellhound, but the seeing-eye dog of the very Devil himself; and as it killed and ate her up, only then did she realize that the policeman really had loved her after all, in a way, just not quite in the way she had wanted; and so in a moment of rage she had cursed a curse that had curved back to curse herself, only to repent when it was too late. And that's why when you curse somebody, you should always take the time to choose your words carefully and set very clear parameters, and not just go off half-cocked tossing curses left and right like a crazy person.

The victorious policeman had gone east, for no particular reason: he had to pick some direction, and that seemed as good as any. He had many strange adventures over the course of his journeys. In the lowlands he was tricked into building a house for a wily old widow; in the highlands he was made witness to an impossible marriage contract. In a pond near a forest, he saw the reflection of the most beautiful woman in the world, and seeing that its owner was nowhere about, and had apparently forgotten her reflection behind her, he folded it carefully up and kept it in his breast pocket for safekeeping.

In another town he met a one-armed man, who hired him to steal a pair of rare gloves from the museum. In the mountains he was chased up a tree by a bear and kept there for five days and two nights. Back in the lowlands, he met that same wily old widow, sitting in a rocking chair on the porch of the house he had built for her, with a shotgun across her lap. In yet another town he was mistaken for a notorious horse thief, and narrowly avoided a hanging. He fled into the forest, where he was caught in a terrible storm. Thrashing about desperately for some sort of shelter, he came upon a cleverly hidden cloister, built out of pale red stone along a cliff-face.

He knocked on the door feverishly—and to his surprise, it was opened to him by the most beautiful woman in the world, wearing a nun's habit. He pulled her reflection carefully from his breast pocket, unfolded it, and gave it to her, bowing slightly. "I thought you might have missed it," he said gallantly, as if he had come there on purpose to return it.

The nun told him that she had lost it many years before, when she was young and thought nothing about the next day, and that she had long prayed that someone would find it and return it to her.

Time had passed, and she had sworn an oath that whoever returned her reflection to her, she would give all the money she had in the world. But no one came. She swore an oath that whoever returned her reflection to her, she would teach to speak the languages of the birds. Still no one came. Years passed, she told the policeman; the years passed and the promises multiplied; but no matter what oath she swore, what promises she made, no matter how sincerely and devoutly she prayed, still no one came.

And then just that very morning, in a burst of frustration and anger, she had sworn an oath that whoever returned her reflection to her, she would kill. "And here you are," she said delightedly, "and now I have to fulfill my promise." She cried crocodile tears when she ate him, roasted on toast with a little red pepper jelly. She buried his bones in the usual place nearby the cloister, and returned her reflection to its place in the pond, and waited for the next chivalrous idiot to find it and return it to her.

Meanwhile, when the headless policeman had woken up, he had been unable to find his head anywhere, which was very disconcerting. Ellen and the other policeman were nowhere to be seen, either. So he stumbled off, along the great main highway to the west of the city, where he had formerly gone to skulk in the ditches and hide in the bushes and waylay lonely travellers in order to murder them and steal their money. Only now he wanted to steal their heads, so that he could replace his own. And he also stole their money, because after all, it seemed wasteful not to.

When he would steal a head, then he would fit it on his shoulders, and go off and look in a mirror to see if he liked it. But he was vain, and picky, and tossed away a good many perfectly decent heads until he finally found one he really, really liked: the head of a handsome young Anishinaabe warrior.

With his new head and all the money he'd saved up, he headed further west, far away from the scenes of all his crimes and heartache. He came at last to a city in far-away Alberta, possibly Edmonton but probably Calgary; and he found a job there as a policeman, because he still had his old uniform, and he got married to a pleasant, not particularly interesting woman, and bought a house, and together they had two boys, identical twins: identical in every way except that one of them was *canadien* and the other one was Anishinaabe, but other than that you couldn't even tell them apart. And the four of them were fairly content, and reasonably happy.

Then, one day, when the Mayor's daughter and Winnipeg and Ellen and his headless days were all barely even a distant memory, like a dream, one day he went to answer a knock on his door.

"Who is it?" he called out.

"Meter man," said a deep, rumbly voice he didn't recognize. "Come to read your meter, sir."

And then when he opened the door, instead of a meter man he saw an enormous yellow dog, with long sharp dirty teeth and lots of drool; and the dog leapt onto the policeman's chest and pinned him to the ground and bit off the policeman's borrowed head with one snap of his jaws, and swallowed it whole. The policeman's wife sent her boys fleeing out the back, while she fought the hellhound off with a frying pan, giving them time to make good their escapes before she, too, was eaten up. One of the boys fled north and the other went south, and they also had remarkable adventures that Maureen would occasionally make up, but usually by that point she'd had enough, and just wanted Casey to go away.

As for the Mayor's daughter, and what became of her: well, she was that same beautiful young woman who married the rich man, and went away to live in the old Stone School, or rather the mansion that would later become the old Stone School. Maureen would retell that story sometimes too. And even though she always made a point of insisting that the Mayor's daughter had long red curly hair like all beautiful and good-hearted young women, Casey always pictured her as looking exactly like Nora, with pale blue eyes and blonde hair, long and straight and the colour of straw, and that was just one of the reasons she enjoyed it when her mother told her those stories over and again.

15

Nora visits the farm and sees a familiar face;
Casey dreams someone else's dream

ONCE NORA WENT OUT and stayed at Casey's place for the night. She had begged her parents to let her go, for she desperately wanted to see the newborn foals.

Nora's father drove her out on the Saturday morning. They found Casey waiting for them at the side of the road—practically in the middle of the road, stepping out and waving excitedly as soon as she caught sight of Simon's truck approaching in the distance.

Casey had walked out to the road to watch and wait for them because there was nothing to mark which driveway was hers, and she didn't want them to miss it. She said she hadn't been waiting long, but that wasn't true: she had been out there for well over an hour. It was a beautiful morning, dry and warm; a light breeze was enough to make the tall, skinny aspen sway precariously, waving their crowns of infant leaves.

Nora tumbled out of the truck and the two friends ran hand in hand down the long and curving driveway, talking over one another, the words tumbling giddily out of them, as Simon brought the truck along slowly and carefully behind them.

Rusty and Mud burst into a sudden frenzy of cheerful barking as they came around the corner. Rusty, slightly the larger of the two dogs, had a reddish-brown coat and looked tremendously fat, though Casey swore it was mostly fur. His bark was a booming thing, and his fur was filthy: thick, coarse, and matted, all tangled with burrs and twigs and ticks. Mud was brown and black in patches, with a long tapering snout that he plunged shamelessly into Nora, sniffing her all over with such aggressive friendliness that he very nearly knocked her to the ground, while Rusty stayed a little further away, moving back and forth in a rapid little dance and barking with frantic enthusiasm.

"Are your parents in the house?" Simon asked, getting down from the cab with Nora's overnight bag. He had been looking forward to meeting them, but they were nowhere to be seen; her father was out in the fields with the horses, Casey said, and her mother was somewhere, who knew where.

That left him at a bit of a loss. It didn't seem quite right, somehow, to simply leave his child there without even seeing the parents first, and saying hello, and thanking them, and assuring them he'd be back the next morning to pick her up, and don't hesitate to call if there's anything at all; but Nora was urging him to leave, assuring him it was fine, with that air of patient, barely suppressed exasperation. And then Casey was taking Nora by the hand and saying, "Come on, let's go see the foals," and the two girls raced off and were gone, the dogs scampering alongside them, and Simon was alone. And he could hardly just wait there indefinitely, alone and uninvited; so, with one last look around and a helpless shrug, he climbed back into his truck and drove away. When he got home later and his wife asked him eagerly what Casey's parents were like, he said, "They seemed nice enough." And she said, "Is that all? What did they look like, what did they say?" And he said, "I don't know, just normal. Shy, I think. They didn't really say much."

CASEY LED NORA OUT between the barn and the garage, past the old plow rusting peacefully in the weeds and the ramshackle chicken coop where one fat rooster lorded pompously over seven hapless hens. The chickens were Casey's responsibility: she brought them feed and kitchen scraps and fresh water, collected the eggs, mediated their disputes, listened to their troubles and little triumphs, and periodically cleaned out the muck and laid down fresh straw.

In a mood to admire everything, Nora was even delighted by the chickens. She thought they were adorably ugly, and laughed happily at the jerky way they moved, and said Casey was lucky that she got to take care of them, and Nora wished *she* had chickens.

Leaving the chicken run, they went past the old pump where there was once a well, and where Nora nearly trod on a dark green garter snake that flashed suddenly across their path, and then they cut out across a low uneven meadow dotted with bright yellow dandelions. The dogs, who had been sticking close to Nora in their gregarious way, sniffing at her with good-natured curiosity, licking at her hands and face, and occasionally nudging and bumping up against her experimentally to see if they could knock her down, now rushed ahead, disappearing into the wild grass and willows in the distance.

Nora was smitten with the dogs, she adored them. "You are *so* lucky," she told Casey. It was the great sorrow of Nora's life that she wasn't allowed to have any pets. Her father would have let her, but her grandmother had a ridiculous prejudice against letting animals inside a house, and anything her grandmother thought, her mother would think too. Sometimes when Casey came over, they would pretend that *she* was Nora's pet, a half-dog half-cat called Ruffpuff—the outcast offspring of a star-crossed and forbidden love affair—and Casey would scamper around the basement on all fours, and lick her paws and wag her tail, and chase a ball and eat goldfish crackers out of a bowl and say, "Mraowff! Mraowff!" and let Nora scratch her behind the ear and rub her tummy. That was fun, but not the same as the real thing.

The ground now was getting spongy; just a little further south, Casey said, was a kind of slough that separated their property from the next farm over, a hog-farm: in the summer, when the wind was from the south, you could smell the ammonia blowing over, so strong sometimes it made your eyes sting. In the blue sky above them, Nora spotted a hawk, making wide and languorous circles above their heads before dipping suddenly down and darting out of sight beyond the trees.

The dogs rejoined them just as they were about to enter the narrow strip of woods along the western edge of the property. They were soaking wet, especially Rusty, panting happily, pleased with themselves, reeking as if they had been rolling on something dead and decomposing. The trees here were all poplar and aspen, many dead, some growing at strange precarious angles; and the deadfall crunched satisfyingly beneath their feet as they walked.

"We can't get too close to them," Casey said as they made their way north through the woods. She explained that the mares were very protective of their foals for the first little while, sometimes even vicious. She had already explained this several times to Nora over the past week, but Nora listened as solemnly as if it were the first time she'd heard it. "Are we almost there?" she asked, and Casey nodded. They could have gone straight out by the same route her father took the truck and been there twenty minutes faster, but she had wanted to take Nora the long way around.

Mud darted off in pursuit of a small brown squirrel; Rusty had turned back not long after they'd entered the woods, probably to return to the slough and roll on that dead thing again. And then they were out of the trees and standing at a wooden fence on the edge of the pasture, barely ten feet from where a mare, her back to them, waited patiently as her foal stood at her flank and craned its head underneath her to suckle. The foal was so skinny they could make out its ribs beneath its short brown coat, and its head jabbed back and forth as it sucked and lapped greedily at its mother's teats, until at last she gave a squeal of impatience and started to walk away, the foal trotting after her.

Casey climbed easily over the fence, and Nora followed her. They drifted slowly along the edge of the pasture, back in the general direction of the farmhouse, not talking much, and often stopping to watch the horses for five or ten minutes. The foals, with their spindly long legs, mostly stuck close to their mother's sides, moving lazily about the pasture in matching pairs; only the slightly older ones would occasionally break away and skitter off in sudden irresistible bursts of energy, their short tails twitching happily, sometimes attempting awkward leaps and wheels and then circling back to their mothers as if to solicit their admiration.

Eventually the girls met up with Casey's father, emerging from the midst of the horses in the company of the veterinarian, Jim Ritchie. Ritchie was wearing a light grey canvas jacket and oversized rubber boots and appeared to be lecturing Casey's father angrily about something; then he stopped abruptly when he saw Nora and Casey there by the fence. He was obviously surprised: he knew Nora, of course, she was one of his many nieces. Nora's father was his wife's youngest brother; his own grandson, James, was just a year younger than Nora's little sister Tracy, they played together at the park sometimes. He said, "Good morning, ladies," with heavy courtesy and the ghost of a bow, then reached into his pocket, took out a handful of sunflower seeds, and popped them into his mouth.

Then Casey's father looked up and saw them, too. He had been staring at the ground this whole time, patiently listening to Ritchie's lecture like a penitent schoolboy, one hand rubbing the back of his neck and other patting a gentle rhythm against his thigh. And if Ritchie had been a little surprised to see Nora, Casey's father was obviously shocked. His face registered confusion, disbelief, and what looked like fear, all in rapid succession; he opened his mouth as if to ask his daughter a question, then closed his mouth again without saying anything, and jammed his hands into his pockets as if to hide them, and looked back down at the ground, blushing fiercely. He was shorter than Nora had imagined he would be, sort of stumpy looking, brown as a squirrel, with a bit of a stoop. His head was too large for his body—perhaps that was why he kept looking down, perhaps his head was simply too heavy for him to keep upright for long; and his hands were far too large for his body, they were simply enormous.

Addressing not her father but Jim Ritchie, Casey said, "This is my friend Nora. She came to see the horses, we're having a sleepover." She said it a little louder than necessary, perhaps, with a touch of something like nervousness and defiance in her voice, but also pride; she had taken Nora's hand again, and gave it a gentle squeeze.

Ritchie spat out his shells into the mud, looking at the two girls speculatively but not unkindly. "Is that a fact?" he said at last. "Well, you picked a lovely weekend for it, anyway. I'm sure you'll have a wonderful time. You know," he said, turning slightly and addressing Casey's father now with conspicuous cheerfulness, "you know, Mack, Nora here is a niece of mine. I never realized that she and Casey were such close friends."

And Casey's father lifted his head slightly, making brief and furtive eye contact first with Casey and then with Nora and then quickly looking away again, mumbling something that sounded like, "Yes, lovely." He smiled a fleeting smile and looked up at the sky, squinting. "Lovely weather," he said. Then he shaded his eyes with one enormous hand and looked obliquely towards the sun. "Almost lunchtime," he added.

Nora very nearly burst out laughing, but managed to hold it in. Casey had warned her that her father was painfully shy. But Nora decided that she would like him anyway, his eyes were kind and so was his funny, furtive, bashful smile; she even decided that he was secretly sort of handsome, or would have been if his body was the right size for his head.

"Stay for lunch?" he asked the veterinarian. And if Ritchie had been a little surprised to see his niece here, now he was flabbergasted. In all the years of tending to Kenneth Mack's animals he had never once been offered so much as a cup of coffee, let alone invited to stay for a meal. And he thought that there was something wistful, almost pleading in the way that Mack had asked him; and Casey quickly, eagerly chimed in, saying, "Yeah, you should stay for lunch"—Casey who had never yet addressed more than two words consecutively to him in her life, and then as if under duress; Casey who usually bolted for the woods like a frightened rabbit when she saw him approach.

The girls sat in the back of the pickup truck for the brief ride back to the house. Nora felt a tickle on the side of her thigh and found a flat black wood tick crawling up her shorts. She squished it between her thumb and forefinger, digging her nail in to break its little body, but for the rest of the day she was haunted by the constant phantom sensation of little legs crawling all over her.

FROM THE OUTSIDE, the farmhouse looked fairly large, if rather plain and desperately in need of paint. Inside it seemed much smaller. The ceilings were low, and everything was dim and airless, even with the windows open in the middle of the day. There were too many corners, too many walls; there were far too many rooms, connected by an excess of cramped and twisty hallways and low and narrow doors. Years ago, Casey's mother had told her that there was a hidden room somewhere inside the house, the entrance walled up and papered over, and that she forbade Casey to carefully measure all the outside and inside walls and study the layout of the rooms and corridors to figure out where that hidden room must be, because whoever had sealed it up and hidden it must have had a very a good reason, and God only knew what—or who—might be inside it. She had told Casey this because it amused her to watch the child make her futile, secretive and persistent attempts to solve the puzzle, for back then Casey had been still too young to be entirely sure when her mother was just making things up.

On the kitchen stove, they found a pot of beef stew gently simmering, giving off a dark, warm, almost malty aroma, all mingled with the smells of garlic and caramelized onions; beside it was a sheet of biscuits, still warm from the oven. On the counter next to the stove were four small plates, four large bowls and spoons, four cups, and a pitcher of iced tea, all laid out and waiting for them, as though Casey's mother had somehow known that there would be two guests joining them for lunch—but Casey's mother herself was nowhere to be seen.

They ate outside in the yard. The sun was directly above them, and surprisingly hot; here in the shelter of the yard there wasn't more than a faint breeze. The men sat on precarious old aluminum lawn chairs whose vinyl seats were sagging and frayed, with a rickety and rusted round table at their elbows; the girls sat on the steps, Casey on the top step and Nora on the second from the bottom. The dogs lay demurely in the middle, with their heads between their forepaws and their wide faithful eyes gazing from one person to the next, waiting for some food to fall. Mud kept his eyes most keenly on Casey's father, who in his shyness found it difficult to eat in front of other people and was toying with his food in a wistful way; Rusty was staring particularly at Nora, who was devouring her food wolfishly. And Nora thought that it was the best food she had ever tasted; she ate it up so greedily she was almost embarrassed, but she couldn't seem to help herself. She had scarfed down her biscuit and emptied her bowl long before anyone else was finished; and she had hardly swallowed the last bite when she heard a voice saying, "Casey, aren't you going to offer your friend seconds?"

It was Casey's mother, who was suddenly standing right there. Nora hadn't noticed her coming from the house, or anywhere else, though she'd been half watching out for her: just suddenly she was there, as if she'd been in their midst all the time, or as if she had materialized out of thin air.

Casey was on her feet in an instant, taking Nora's bowl and plate and hurrying into the house, head down. And Casey's mother said, "Well. It's a pleasure to meet you at last, young Nora."

"Yes, Mrs Mack," said Nora meekly. "Thank you," she added,

unsure of the proper response. Nora had often tried to picture Casey's mother to herself, but had never imagined that she would be so pretty or look so young. She looked more like a teenager than a real grown-up. She was short, slender, and lithe as a young cat; her lightly freckled face had something feline about it too, in the shape of the face and in the wide green eyes with their look of mischief and contempt. She was barefoot, her faded sundress clinging lightly to her body. Her hair was lit by the sun so that it flickered and glowed as though it were made of hot coals; and it seemed to Nora that she stood among them like a deer, her body simultaneously relaxed and alert, graceful, effortless, poised, and ready to explode into motion at any moment.

"Please, call me Maureen. I was just telling your friend," she remarked to Casey, who was returning from the house with more food, "I was just telling your friend what a pleasure it is to actually meet her. We've heard so much about you," she said to Nora. "I could have sworn that Casey was making you up. You *are* real, aren't you?" And she stepped lightly forward and gently poked Nora in the shoulder: "Yes," said with an air of whimsical amazement, "Yes, you seem real enough. Wonders never cease." Then she took Nora's chin in the palm of her hand, opened her mouth, and peered inside. "Well," she said, taking a step or two back and looking down at her, "Go on and eat. Eat it all up like you want to."

So Nora, feeling horribly awkward, resumed eating. Her appetite had abruptly disappeared, but she felt compelled. The dogs had lowered their eyes forlornly; Casey was holding herself completely still, in an agony of suspense; Jim Ritchie was shifting peevishly in his chair, ominous storm clouds gathering on his face; Kenneth Mack was gazing at his wife with a kind of dumb, yearning, bovine admiration. And Maureen never moved from the spot, but stood in front of Nora the entire time, standing and watching intently with her head tilted slightly to one side, quizzically, one corner of her mouth just the slightest bit turned up in a smirk, one thin eyebrow arched impishly and her eyes unblinkingly green as they looked straight back into Nora's eyes: green, cool, amused, and unkind.

When at long last Nora could eat no more and put her half-empty bowl and half-eaten biscuit to one side, Maureen said, "You have such lovely hair, young lady. You must brush it every night. Don't you think she must brush it every night, Casey?"

"Yes, Mom."

"I'll enjoy watching her brush that beautiful hair tonight, won't you? Lovely girl, good manners, good appetite, strong healthy teeth, beautiful hair that she brushes every night—and yet she's *your* special friend. Astonishing. The age of miracles is upon us, my girl."

"Yes, Mom," said Casey. Perhaps she ought to have felt humiliated, but in that moment there was no room in her heart for any sensation but a vast relief and a fierce secret triumph: for unbeknownst to Nora, she had never asked her parents if she could invite her friend over, terrified that they would say no, certain that they would say no; she had instead made a desperate gamble. That her father would be too shy and too kind to turn away a guest once they had already arrived, of that she had felt pretty sure, but how her mother would react had been too hard to predict. Anything was possible. And now it seemed that it was going to be okay after all. She would no doubt pay for it later, but Casey didn't care: she was sure now that Nora would be allowed to stay the night, and that was worth any punishment in the world.

"Yes," Maureen was saying, turning around now to look at their other guest: "A really lovely girl. Excellent breeding. She must have good genes, don't you think, Dr Ritchie?"

Ritchie's face gave a little spasm of irritation at being addressed as "doctor", but he restrained himself, merely grunting.

"You can always tell by the teeth," she added cheerfully. "Would you care for more stew? Another biscuit? Beer, perhaps?"

"No, thank you," said Ritchie grumpily. "I seem to have lost my appetite." He placed his half-eaten bowl at the foot of his chair and beckoned to Mud, who glanced quickly and warily at Maureen before hurrying over to lick it clean.

AFTER THEY SAW RITCHIE OFF, Kenneth slipped the girls half a pack of wine gums to share between them. Casey took Nora to show her the woods behind the house, down past the garden plot and the half-dozen apple trees just starting to blossom.

She didn't take Nora to that little clearing where she used to play with her dolly by the old outhouse, because in that rotting and tumbling down outhouse now she kept a secret cache of dozens of small objects that she had pilfered from other people's homes, mostly Nora's. These were small, unimportant items, unlikely to be missed, things such as nail clippers, combs, and souvenir fridge magnets, bottle-cap openers and half-used books of matches: anything that she could slip furtively and unnoticed into a pocket, taking them opportunistically, impulsively, almost unconsciously, not because the items had any particular value or attraction for her in and of themselves but because they possessed a kind of magic or talismanic significance, as being fragments of other people's lives.

In the woods, they pretended to be spies, deep behind enemy lines—keeping low and sprinting from ash tree to ash tree, crouching for cover, speaking in giggling whispers. Every time they heard a bird calling out, they froze; every bird that flew above them was an enemy spy to hide from.

Casey led her friend up the escarpment, patiently helping her climb, and at the top they lay down on the ridge and watched the mares and their foals in the pasture below. They pretended that this was the enemy stronghold below them, that they had been sent to gather information about; but soon they forgot their game, they let it go, right then it was more pleasurable to just lie on their bellies in the young grass and gaze lazily down at those beautiful animals, gossiping idly about the inner lives of horses.

And Casey confessed to Nora that this was her favourite place in the whole world, and Nora said that they should build a lean-to or a little fort and it could be their secret place together, and that made Casey's heart so happy it almost hurt.

BEFORE BED, the girls checked each other carefully over for ticks, finding three: one behind Casey's ear and two on Nora, one nestled in her armpit and the other on the back of her neck, crawling up into the thickets of her hair.

Casey's bedroom was not only small and cold, but almost completely devoid of comfort or personality. There were no pictures or posters on the walls, no shelves, no books, no toys or trinkets or games. The bed was too small for both of them, too small even for Nora alone, so they slept together on blankets laid out on the floor.

It was the first time that Nora had ever slept away from home. Casey's parents did not come and say goodnight to them. The silence of the night was overwhelming, almost terrifying: it was so immense that Nora started talking compulsively to try and fill it, the whispered words just tumbling out of her. She asked Casey questions about the mares and the foals, questions she had already asked and had answered many times in the past; she told bad jokes, and they both giggled. She talked about school, and their teachers, and their friends, and her sister's friends; she repeated bits of garbled gossip she had picked up from her mother and grandmother. She talked about what they had done yesterday, and what they were going to do the next day, and the next week, and that coming summer. She talked about the distant future too, what they would do when they were grown up: how they would move away from this boring horrible place, move to the big city, go to university, get glamorous exciting jobs, be rich, maybe travel the world: see the mountains, see the oceans; she was thinking of her aunts Gail and Sadie, whom she had never met but had often heard stories of. And because she and Casey happened to be together at that moment, Nora spoke as if they would be together always. Her words started taking on a languid nonsensical quality as she floated over the periphery between waking and sleeping, and then she was mumbling something about shirts and pants, and then she was finally asleep.

It was a curious fact that Casey never dreamed at all, her nights passing in a blank and empty instant, as if she hadn't even slept—except those nights that she shared a bed with Nora. Nora always had an abundance of dreams: they would spill out of her head all night, enough and more than enough to spill into Casey's head beside her. Then Casey would dream too, only in her dreams she was always Nora, while somehow also still herself.

That night Casey dreamed that Tracy was waking her, urgently whispering her name: "Nora," she was saying, "Nora, I think it's almost time."

She could hear the trepidation mingled with excitement in her sister's voice, and she sat up, suddenly alert. The pink-tinged light of early dawn trickled between the curtains and seeped across her room. Tracy took her impatiently by the hand and pulled her to the window.

Even though it was Nora's room in Nora's house, outside the window it was Casey's farm, and in the dream that was the way it was and the way it always had been. She looked out over the roof of the barn, past the thin line of trees, and into the field, where she could just make out pillars of dark dull smoke rising towards the sky, and the flickering lights of campfires, and dark huddled shapes moving to and fro in the half-light. What at first glance resembled heaps of yet-unmelted snow were actually tents, and the huddled shapes moving between them were people.

Then she was hurrying downstairs, already dressed somehow, moving quickly and quietly so as not to disturb her parents or her grandmother. She pulled on her rubber boots, draped a coat loosely over her shoulders, and tumbled out the back door: across the yard, past the clothesline and the old tire swing, around the barn, through the stand of naked trees, and onto the edge of the field.

There were hundreds of tents, hurriedly and inexpertly erected, stretching across the acres of churned and fallow field, and among them dozens of small incipient campfires, and men and women moving happily and unhurriedly about: making coffee, readying simple breakfasts, greeting one another with low joyous voices: "Good morning... peace be with you." Tracy was with her again, and she felt her sister's small soft hand slip into hers.

One of the men noticed the two girls now and ambled over, waving cheerfully. He was slouchy, pouchy, and stiff-legged, but there was a jerky exuberance to his steps, and his stubbly face shone gratefully in the spreading red of dawn.

"Peace be with you," he called out as he approached them. "Welcome, welcome," he added, as if the land they stood on belonged to him and his fellow squatters, and not to her and her family.

She and Tracy hurried across the litter-strewn field, threading their way between the tents. More people were emerging every moment, their faces creased with sleep and their bodies hunched against the cold but their chorus of "Good morning" and "Peace be with you" was relentlessly, almost maddeningly cheerful.

On the far side of the field, past a windbreak of blue spruce, lay a meadow that was used in the summers for making hay. In the middle of that meadow, the melting snow had revealed a massive sinkhole, four metres across and God only knew how deep. It was half-filled with brackish water, icy and black, and the ground around it was shifty and unstable. No one would have dared camp in the meadow itself, nor were the many camera crews permitted to bring their heavy equipment past the spruce line, for fear a second sinkhole might abruptly open and swallow them up; yet some could not resist the urge to approach dangerously close, braving the treacherous earth. Already dozens of people had arrived at the meadow before them, inching forward on their hands and knees: reverential, eager, and greedy.

She would have liked to stride boldly past them to the edge of the pit, brave and territorial, but she knew it was her responsibility to keep Tracy at a good safe distance. At her back, the hundreds of squatters were now amassing, sipping coffee, some cradling infants or propping bleary complaining toddlers on their shoulders to see better. The television crews were setting up their equipment, the reporters checking their makeup and rehearsing their lines in hushed and muttered voices.

Slowly behind them the sun continued to rise, until at long last it showed its face just above the trees, its rays slanting down to strike the meadow at the briefly perfect angle, and for a precious fifteen or twenty minutes before the sun rose too high and the angle was lost, they could see revealed, faint but unmistakable, the shimmering flickering translucent form of a ladder, emerging from the gash in the earth and stretching up towards the sky; and they could see too the colourless, almost transparent forms of the angels that moved silently and purposefully up and down it: beautiful, flawless, grim, and terrifying.

16

Alma has trouble with her teeth;
Nora and Tracy get a special treat

ONCE EVERY SEVEN YEARS OR SO, like some astrological con-
vergence, more than a dozen of Alma's teeth would all want to
come through at the same time. Then for several days she would
run a low-grade fever, lose her appetite, have difficulty sleeping,
get bouts of diarrhea. Tired and testy, she would retreat to her
armchair, shifting uncomfortably, wincing and hissing, trying
to read but finding it difficult to focus, her conversation reduced
to irritable grunts and mumbles. Even her customary glasses of
cold, cold milk could give her no pleasure.

This time it happened at the height of summer, during a stretch
of weather so hot, sticky and humid that it was difficult to breathe,
and everyone was listless and irritable to begin with, stewing in
their own sweat. Even at night the temperature would hardly
drop, and not a breath of a breeze to give relief. The Whitetail
had dwindled to a bare trickle, the muddy banks dried, fissured,
and crumbling; the sun scorched the grass, and Simon, with a
nasty sunburn and the skin peeling off his bright red shoulders
and the bridge of his nose, fussed and pouted over his lawns and
flowerbeds like an anxious father with a sick infant. It was too hot
to cook, or bear to think of turning the oven on, so they lived off
salads, fruit, cold cereal and cold sandwiches. Casey was home
on the farm; Alyssa and her family were away at the lake, in fact
half the girls' friends were out of town, and how come *they* didn't
have a lake, how come *they* never went on vacation? It wasn't fair.

Bored, with no one but one another for company, Nora and her sister could only squabble listlessly.

So at first they hardly noticed that their grandmother was becoming testy and withdrawn, though usually it wasn't like her to let the weather affect her, she was too tough, too stubborn. Then one morning Nora was up at the crack of dawn. The curtain on her window didn't quite reach the sill, leaving a slit for the early morning sun to slip through, a narrow slice of hot bright light that cut right across her face as she lay in bed. She sat up, defeated. Dust motes danced in the shaft of light; the air was humid, dense, and difficult to breathe. Her sheets, and pillow, and pyjamas were all soaked through with sweat; she felt shiny, sticky, and disgusting. She didn't think she'd be able to get back to sleep anyway, so she got out of bed, put on some light dry clothes, and slipped out to the bathroom.

The house was quiet and still, quiet except for the sound of her father's rattling snores from down the hall. Nora's was the only bedroom with an east-facing window; she assumed that everyone else was still asleep, and padded as softly as she could so as not to wake anyone up.

Down in the kitchen, she went to the fridge to get a glass of cold milk, and then saw that the jug of milk had been left out on the counter. It must have been left out all night, she thought, it was sure to be spoiled and her amma would be furious; but when she touched it, it was still cool to the touch. Beads of condensation had formed a ring of water where it sat on the counter. Then she noticed a low moaning come from the living room, and found her grandmother sitting in her armchair, wearing only a thin pink nightgown, head back and eyes closed but evidently awake, shifting uncomfortably. The room was dim, just a little light from the rising sun was leaking between the slats of the blinds. But even in that dim light, Nora could see that the lower half of her grandmother's face was swollen horribly, all splotchy and distended; her hair was matted and wet with sweat, her hands tremulous. She had her feet up on the ottoman; Nora couldn't remember having really noticed her grandmother's feet bare before: they were ugly and misshapen, the knuckles protruding obscenely, the toes huddled and cramped, the nails yellow and thick. Her legs, sticking out from under her nightgown, were mottled and frail, the meat sagging limply off the bone. She looked, in fact, tremendously, horribly old, in a way that Nora had never seen or thought of her before, and that frightened her terribly, she felt bewildered and alarmed. Alma was breathing deeply and slowly, the breath whistling between her teeth and rattling in her chest, and she was wincing and hissing in obvious pain; she started to bring her shaking hand up to her mouth, and then changed her mind, and lowered it to her lap, holding her breath as she shifted in her chair, then releasing it slowly with a low moan. A sickly odour was wafting off her body, a baby's smell, a smell of sour milk and thin seedy feces.

Nora, still unnoticed, slipped quietly out of the room and quickly back upstairs, to her sister's room, and sat on the side of the bed and shook her awake: "Tracy," she was saying, "Tracy, wake up. Amma's downstairs and I think she's really sick, I think she might be dying."

THAT DAY and for the rest of the week, Lynn took the girls to work with her, down at the library, so that Alma could have the house to herself. There was no air conditioning at the library either but at least there were ceiling fans, and a dehumidifier, making it just a little more bearable than it was at home.

The library in those days was right on 1st Ave, right downtown, in a buff brick building that had been the old town hall, before the town outgrew it and built a new, larger town hall over on 4th that did have air conditioning. The copestone was inscribed 1908. Just a single storey, but you had to climb a dozen grand limestone steps to get to the entrance, double doors of dark and heavy wood. The library shared the building with the town's permit offices and building inspector, and the place where you came to pay parking tickets. Lynn and the girls arrived at eleven, an hour before the library was open to the public. They would walk into a musty, almost sweet smell. Lynn deputized the girls to gather the books from the overnight return bin and carry them up to the desk: this being Wednesday, and the library having been closed since Saturday, there were at least ten or eleven books there. While they were doing that, Lynn went and emptied the dehumidifier. It had to be emptied three times a day, that's how humid it was during that heat wave. Then she would unplug it and roll it to a different section of the library before plugging it back in, and hear it lurch back to life with a satisfying hum. How much good it actually accomplished would have been difficult to say, but it was better than nothing.

Then Tracy wandered off to the children's section and started pulling picture books off the shelves, but Nora preferred to help her mother at the desk, going through the returned books and checking them back in. It was Nora's job to skim through each book looking for signs of damage and removing forgotten bookmarks, and then place the book on the shelving cart: nonfiction on the top rack, fiction in the middle, children's books on the bottom. Any bookmarks she found she placed in a small pile on the desk. People would use just about anything for a bookmark, her mother told her, and then forget that they were in there: business cards, shopping lists, receipts, unpaid bills; once she had found a child's dirty sock, another time a butter knife, and not even a clean one either, it still had bits of dried crusty food on the blade.

It being a small town, Lynn could generally remember exactly who had checked out each and every book. She had decided opinions, too, about everybody's reading habits, their taste in books and what it said about them, and was happy to share those opinions with Nora, who absorbed them with interest and amusement. Thus Nora learned that that Ted Tibbett was addicted to *How-To* and *Build Your Own…* books, though in Lynn's opinion he probably couldn't change a lightbulb; that Desirée Friesen—a teenager who Nora was vaguely aware of as a good friend of her cousin, Kat—that Desirée's parents ought to be worried about her, the sort of books she read: horror novels of the lowest class, morbid nasty and perverse, quite possibly Satanic; and that Shannon Laurence's mother was addicted to trashy romance paperbacks whose covers were graced with pictures of chiselled, bare-chested men, long hair flowing in the wind and a constipated expression on their faces, typically clutching a bodice-wearing, bosom-heaving maiden in one strong arm: books she typically checked out four or five at a time, and invariably returned late. "I feel sorry for her husband," Lynn added; Nora supposed because it must have been her husband who had to pay all those late fines.

Once all the books were checked back in, and any late fines owing duly noted in the ledger, then Nora helped her mother wheel the cart up and down the rows, replacing the books in their proper place on the shelves. By the end of the week Nora could do the job just about all by herself and put each book in its rightful home almost every time, her mother looking on approvingly.

When it was noon and they unlocked the door to the public, then it was time for what Lynn called, in all seriousness, the "lunch rush": perhaps four or five people over the course of the next hour would wander in to the library, mostly people who worked close by and were coming in on their break. Each would stop first to chat with Lynn for several minutes, always beginning with near-identical complaints about the weather. Some, as far as Nora could tell, didn't even look at the books, but had dropped in solely to pass the time of day.

Soon enough Tracy grew bored of looking at books, dozens of which were scattered face down around her in heaps on the carpet. She was bored, and hungry, and hot, and restless, and starting to complain. Of course their mother wouldn't allow food or drink in the library. Lynn had brought a couple of peanut butter and honey sandwiches and two limp, speckled bananas in a plastic bag and was going to send them outside to sit on the front steps and eat their lunch. But it happened that one of her good friends was in the library at the moment: Vivian Heidecker, who cut hair in the salon one street over and had popped in, as she often did, for a nice visit or quick gossip.

She had been there for ten or fifteen minutes now, probably telling Lynn all about her latest misfortune, for Vivian's life seemed to lurch from one crisis to another. Bad luck followed her around like she had it on a leash. Her car was sure to break down whenever she needed it most; she might no sooner have scraped together the money to get her car up and running again, than her hot water tank would stop working, and she would have to take cold showers for a month and boil water in the kettle to wash the dishes before she could afford to get that fixed. Not long after her divorce, she had been in a car accident, barely even her fault, it was true that she had slid into the car in front of her on an icy street, but that was just a fender-bender, barely a love-tap; only then the car behind had slid into *her*, slamming into her with a lot more force, and her back and neck had never been right since; she still had to see the physiotherapist on a regular basis, and some days after standing all day at work she'd have searing pains shooting up and down her spine, but it wasn't like she could just find another job where she didn't have to stand so much, it wasn't that easy, she wasn't trained to do anything else. That was the sort of luck she had. And Lynn would listen greedily to each latest tale of woe with lips pursed and eyes lit, her bosom rising and falling in deep even breaths, just occasionally tossing in a sympathetic, "Oh *no*," or an indignant, "Well!" It was like catnip to Lynn, she couldn't get enough, she'd practically start purring.

Vivian offered to take the girls out for lunch, at A.C's, the little diner up the block. "You don't have to do that," said Lynn, but Tracy was already begging her mother to say yes, hopping up and down and saying, "Please please pleaseplease*please*." And Nora too joined in the pleading, for even though it meant having to spend time with Vivian, eating out in any kind of restaurant was such a rare treat for them that it was worth the price.

Vivian insisted: it would be a favour to her, honestly, she had been planning to have her lunch there anyway, she'd enjoy having the girls for company. She had no children of her own, was incapable of having children, having had to have a hysterectomy due to polyps in her uterus; that was why her ex-husband had left her for a younger, more fertile woman, and she had moved back to Whittle.

"At least let me give you some money," Lynn said reluctantly, for among Vivian's other misfortunes, she was perpetually in debt and always scrambling to meet her bills. But Vivian refused: she'd done Peggy Afton's hair that morning and the old lady had given her a very generous tip, as she always did.

Stepping outside, the heat of the sun was like a punch to the face. The leaves and branches of the trees drooped listlessly; it was too hot for the birds to fly about, too hot even for the bugs to buzz. The downtown had a half-abandoned feel, and the click of Vivian's high heels echoed loudly on the pavement. She lit a cigarette as they started up the street, saying, "Look at me, I can hardly breathe already in this heat and here I am smoking, I must be crazy." She said it with a wide smile, as if it were funny. She said, "Don't you girls follow my example, believe me, don't ever start smoking, you'll regret it." By the time they reached A.C's Diner, she wasn't even halfway through the cigarette, and she sent them in ahead, telling them to find a table and she'd join them in a minute.

Coming out of the bright midday sun that dazzled and reflected off the metal of parked cars into the dimly lit diner was almost like going blind: it took their eyes a while to adjust. It was blissfully cool, and there was an appetizing smell of grease and salt coming from the kitchen. Tracy went up to the front counter, where there were pies and dainties in a refrigerated display case next to the register, and she leaned her forehead against the chilled glass,

looking greedily at the desserts; but Nora, who was old enough
to understand a little about money, went and fetched her sister
away, making her promise, in a whisper, not to ask for dessert
unless Vivian offered first.

They chose a booth away from the windows and near a vent so
they could savour the cold air blowing close to them, and it was
the best feeling in the world. The seats were covered with a sort of
burgundy pleather that their bare legs stuck to, peeling painfully
off when they moved. There were only a few other customers
in the diner. Near the front, there was a trio of slender men, all
tremendously bald. They might have been forty, or fifty, or sixty
years old; they must have been brothers, or a father and two sons,
for they looked very much alike, and were even dressed alike, in
blue jeans and button-up blue shirts. They had a single pair of
eyeglasses between them that they passed from one to the other
as they took turns looking over the menu, talking the while in
low slow mumbly voices. At another small table, a pair of ladies
were sipping coffee and picking wistfully at the last remnants of
their lunches. Vivian stopped at their table to say hello and pass
the time of day; Nora vaguely recognized one of them as the
mother of one of the kids at school. Everyone spoke in hushed
voices, as if not to disturb the loud hum and occasional rattle
of the air conditioning: as if the sound it made was inseparable
from the coolness it created and you had to hear the one in order
to feel the other.

Nora ordered root beer, Tracy a Seven-Up. Their grandmother
would never have let them order soft drinks, she would have insisted
on juice, milk, or just plain water. The waitress asked Vivian if she
wanted a coffee, and Vivian, smiling widely, said, "I do, believe
me, but I'd better not. You know what my stomach's like."

"Just water, then?" But she had hardly turned around to walk
away when Vivian called her back and said, "You know what,
maybe I will risk just one little coffee. But don't let me have any

refills, or I'll be up all night." The waitress, who seemed to have been expecting this, briskly agreed. When she was gone, Vivian picked up the metal napkin holder to use it as a mirror, fussing at her hair with her long red nails and lamenting how frizzy it looked from all the humidity. She had great abundances of bronze-coloured hair, professionally curled and poofed high in the front. "Believe me," she said, "I wish I could just cut it all off, especially in this heat."

The girls lingered over their menus, not because they had difficulty deciding, but because it was a small luxury in itself to be looking at a menu at all. These were just flat laminated sheets, breakfast and lunch on one side, dinner and drinks on the other, with a few very small photographs inset: a plate of bacon, eggs, and hash browns; some kind of sandwich—impossible to tell what kind, the photograph was too small; a plate of perogies and fried onions; and something that might have been shepherd's pie, or possibly not. In several places on the menu, the prices had been covered over with liquid paper and new prices handwritten in their place; in one spot on the dinner side, an entire item had been liquid papered out of existence and left blank, and Nora was desperately curious what it once had been.

In the end, Tracy opted for a grilled cheese sandwich and fries, just like Nora had known she would, and Nora herself, feeling wildly sophisticated, asked for the half-sized Caesar salad with strips of grilled chicken. She wanted fries, too, but she was confident that she'd get to eat half of Tracy's anyway, Tracy would never be able to finish them. Vivian ordered a steak sandwich, rare, and a side salad.

Tracy pulled the bowl of creamers towards her and began stacking the little plastic containers on top of one another to make a tower. "I hear your grandmother gave you quite the fright this morning," Vivian was saying. "I remember the first time I ever saw her like that, believe me I was frightened too, I was terrified."

"How old were you?" asked Nora. It was the only thing she could think of, and it seemed rude not to say anything at all. "Oh, gosh," said Vivian, "I don't know. Ten or eleven, maybe?"

Lynn had often said that when they were both young, Vivian had been a great beauty and all the boys had been in love with her, but Nora had difficulty picturing that, and privately doubted it was true. Back in those days her friends had called her Vee, but now she didn't care for it. Her face seemed imperfectly attached to her head, like a poorly fitted rubber mask, the skin stretched too tight in some places, sagging off in others. When she smiled, it was a mechanical, over-wide smile, a sort of rictus almost aggressive in its rigidity, displaying her unnaturally white and even teeth; but apart from that smile, the only other facial expression she seemed capable of was a look of slack and unnerving blankness, and that was somehow even worse.

Tracy had built her tower five containers high, and then run out of creamers. Looking around, she spotted the table where those ladies had just finished their lunch and left: the table hadn't been cleared yet, so she peeled herself off her seat, ran over, and returned triumphantly with four more creamers to add to her tower.

"Isn't that clever?" said Vivian blankly as Tracy added a sixth, and then a seventh. The tower now was beginning to lean precariously.

"It's gonna fall," said Nora, as Tracy was preparing to add the eighth.

"It's not gonna fall," said Tracy.

"It's gonna fall," said Nora.

It fell. Two of the creamers skittered off the table and onto the floor, and Tracy hopped down with a giggle to pick them up; while she did, Nora quickly swept the others over to her side of the table, and began stacking a tower of her own. "Hey!" said Tracy indignantly. "That was my idea!"

Unlike Tracy's tower, Nora stacked them so that every other container was upside down, wider top to wider top, narrower bottom to narrower bottom. She had just added the sixth one to the top when Tracy reached over and snatched the bottom one out. "Hey!" said Nora indignantly as the tower crashed down. One of the creamers rolled into her lap. Tracy snatched another, and now she had four of them that she cupped her hands over protectively.

"Come on, I just wanna try," said Nora, but Tracy just narrowed her eyes all sinister and said, "Get your own. I got these, get your own." Nora half-stood in the booth and craned her neck to survey the restaurant, but none of the other tables had bowls of creamers on them. "Fine," she said with disdain, and pushed the rest of the containers over to her sister, who smirked triumphantly.

"I'm sure Carol would bring you more," said Vivian. "Do you want me to ask her?"

"It's never gonna work that way," said Nora to her sister. She was slumped back petulantly in the booth, arms crossed over her chest.

"Is too," said Tracy. But this tower attempt had started to go crooked almost immediately, so she broke it down and started over, slowly and carefully.

"Wanna bet?" said Nora.

"I'll ask her the next time she comes around," said Vivian.

"I'll bet you a quarter," said Nora. "Quarter it won't work."

"Shut up," said Tracy. "It will too." She was up to four and adding her fifth, and it was straight and steady.

"Bet me then," said Nora.

"I don't wanna bet," said Tracy.

"Chicken."

The waitress had come out to clear the dishes off that other table and wipe it down, and Vivian waved to her, saying, "Carol honey, could you bring the girls another bowl of creamers?"

Carol grimaced with brief irritation, but all she said was, "Sure, why not?"

"Thanks, honey."

Tracy had successfully brought her tower back up to seven, and it was looking pretty solid: not perfectly straight, but straight enough. Nora sat up and leaned in and began to gently blow in the direction of the tower.

"Stop it," said Tracy.

"I'm not doing anything," said Nora. And then she started doing it a little harder. She wasn't blowing hard enough to topple the tower or even really make it sway, but it sent her sister into a rage anyway. "Stop it!" she yelled.

Carol arrived then with another bowl of creamers, and the coffee pot, and she topped up Vivian's cup and then watched as Tracy successfully placed the eighth creamer. "You oughta reverse them," she suggested: "You know, so it's top to top, bottom to bottom." She had watched many many kids build many many creamer towers over the years.

"I know, right?" said Nora gratefully, but Tracy just shot her a look of searing contempt and made ready to place the ninth. Carol shrugged and wandered back to the kitchen.

Tracy put the ninth creamer in place, then held her breath as they all watched to see if it would hold steady. The tower swayed ominously for a moment, and then settled. It held. "I did it!" she cried triumphantly. "You owe me a quarter!"

That started a new argument, but thankfully their food arrived at the table, the creamers were put off to the side and the bet was at least temporarily forgotten as they ate. Vivian slid the slice of garlic toast out from under the steak, took a bite, and put it off to one side, then began industriously slicing the steak into the thinnest pieces she could manage. The pieces around the edge, that were most thoroughly cooked, she ate herself; the slices from the middle that were still at least a little pink—she had ordered it rare, but they had served it more like medium—these she pushed off to the side of the plate, these ones were to take with her for Lancelot.

Vivian's one saving grace, in Nora's eyes—and her only flaw, as far as Lynn was concerned—was her dog Lancelot, a stout and ardent pug whose middle-aged spread and tendency to wheeze were a source of constant worry. Vivian was worried about him now, during this heat wave, so she had been bringing him to work with her every morning: unlike her claustrophobic and airless little bungalow, the hair salon was air conditioned.

She had adopted Lancelot right after her husband moved out on her. She was still living in the city back then and was unaccustomed to living alone. So she had set out looking to adopt a collie or something of the kind, the sort of dog who would not only give her some company and keep her from feeling lonely, but could also intimidate potential intruders and dangerous strangers, help her feel safe at home and out walking on the street. That was the sort of dog she went looking for, but then when she saw Lancelot, it was love at first sight, she couldn't resist.

He turned out to be a real ladies' man, too. Any man he encountered, he would be at best stand-offish, if not downright hostile, puffing out his little chest ridiculously, growling and yipping at them for no apparent reason. Even men he came to know well, like nowadays when Lynn would send Simon over to her house to fix this or that for her, or when her brother-in-law would stop by, Vivian would still have to lock Lancelot up in the bedroom or put him out in the back yard. But the ladies were a different story: any woman he saw, even a complete stranger, he would sidle up to right away with a happy little swagger, rolling his big brown eyes seductively and looking for affection. In a way, he reminded Vivian of her ex-husband, only Lancelot at least had been fixed and couldn't get anyone pregnant.

When it came to children, Lancelot had no pre-conceptions. Boy or girl, so long as they weren't too boisterous, too loud or unpredictable, he was content to play with them, to let them rub his tummy and give him treats. Tracy and Nora both adored him, and since he considered that the right and natural attitude for anyone to have, he was even a little fond of them. So when they found out that Lancelot was at the hair salon, they begged Vivian to take them back with her so they could visit with him.

"Why not?" she said, hitching up her lips and baring her bright square teeth. She had no appointments booked for that afternoon, it was the deadest time of year, half the town was out of town, she'd probably just be sitting around bored, waiting for walk-ins that wouldn't come and flipping through magazines she'd read a million times. "I know," she said, leaning in with a spark of genuine enthusiasm: "Why don't you let me do your nails and do up your hair all fancy? Wouldn't that be fun?"

The idea didn't appeal much to Nora, but she didn't say so: Vivian clearly believed that she was offering them some great treat, and if it was the price she had to pay to get her hands on Lancelot for an hour or two, she was more than willing to put up with it with a good grace. Anyway, it would be better than going back to the library and hanging out with their mother the rest of the day. Tracy, on the other hand, didn't have to pretend, she was genuinely excited by the idea.

The salon was one block over and up the street. Vivian didn't really own it, the building and the business both were owned by her brother-in-law, Trent Pettinger, but he let her run it just as if she owned it, and never interfered. He was married to Vivian's youngest sister, Marian; she was younger than Vivian by half a decade and the bane of her existence, a spoiled brat as a child and not much better now. Vivian often had to call Lynn up to vent about the latest catty or condescending thing that Marian had said to her, and how all she could do was grin and bear it, because even apart from the salon, Vivian was in debt to them for thousands of dollars, a hole she'd probably never dig out of and all three of them knew it, so Marian had that to lord over her, and she had the ears of their parents too, so that their mother was forever calling Vivian up and saying, "Marian tells us *this*," or "Marian says you did *that*," in disapproving fashion.

Vivian's father, after decades working at the grain elevator outside of town, had arthritis in his hips and both hands, his knuckles looked like red grapes; and worse yet, he was deaf as a post, grouchy and demanding. Deaf as a post but didn't want to admit it, wouldn't see a doctor or wear a hearing aid, and conversations with him were a kind of slow torture. Her mother had become nagging and quarrelsome, forever complaining, finding fault and picking fights. It was her great disappointment in life that she had had three daughters and no sons; and that of those three daughters only one had given her grandchildren, including a grandson, but they all lived out in Calgary, so that she barely got to see them.

When Vivian had decided to move back to Whittle, after the car accident, it was Marian and Trent who found her little house for her. At the time it had seemed a great kindness, she even cried with gratitude, of course she was on a lot of painkillers. And it was Trent who rented the truck and drove her out, with Lancelot and everything she owned. She hadn't yet replaced her own car, and even if she had, her back was still too messed up to drive. Sitting in the passenger seat, every bump the truck went over sent the muscles in her back and neck into painful spasms that left her wincing and gasping for breath. Trent drove as carefully as he could, but roads are roads.

It was a little house in Halftown, just north of the Sally, Trent had bought it for her from the bank, using his own money as a down payment: she could pay him back whenever she got around to it, he wasn't worried. "Not a bad little house, I hope." And then, after some brief silence: "We fixed it up some."

"I'm sure it'll be wonderful," said Vivian. "I'm sure I can't thank you enough."

"Nice big yard," he said. "Lots of room for Lancelot to run around."

Lancelot, in a travelling cage in the back of the cab, heard his name coming out of a man's mouth and growled and yipped menacingly.

When they pulled up outside the house at last, and she saw it for the first time, then Vivian had to hide her disappointment by smiling as widely as her face would stretch. The house was so small it was almost comical. There were no front steps, the front door was level with the ground. There was only one small window, as if whoever had built it had been allergic to sunlight and fresh air. The brown paint on the outside of the house was dingy and flaking off. "Have to take care of that for you when the weather turns," Trent said apologetically.

But inside the house it wasn't so bad, at least it was clean and freshly painted, and all the floors had been redone. There was a lingering peculiar odour: apparently, just that morning, Marian had come and smudged it for her by burning sweetgrass, to get rid of any bad energy left over by the last owner. And then, the house had sat empty for almost a year, and you never know what kind of spirits will invite themselves into an empty house.

Everybody was there to welcome Vivian home and help move all her things inside and unpack her boxes: her sister and her parents, of course, and Lynn and Simon and Alma too, with sweet little Nora who was a chubby funny toddler at the time, and Tracy just a baby, barely four months old. Alma had baked some pies and brought her some jars of saskatoon jam and sweet pickles; Simon said he had some rose bushes and a lilac set aside to plant in the yard for her as soon as it was warm enough. Even Marian's father-in-law Benji was there, and Simon's brother Matt, who was Benji's business partner and had helped Trent fix up the house, and Matt's family for some reason, his wife Louise who had knit Vivian two tea towels and a dishcloth as a housewarming gift, with both their sons, Nathanael and Mark, who might have been ten and eight but did their best to carry some of the smaller boxes and miscellaneous things, like cushions and table lamps and the toaster, from the truck to the house. They had all gotten together and stocked her fridge and pantry with some basic necessities: milk, eggs, bread, butter, coffee, sugar, salt, all that sort of thing. Marian had brought wine and beer for everybody. They ordered pizza. It was all so kind it made her cry again, and for one afternoon and evening at least, the house didn't seem small and dingy at all, it seemed cozy and welcoming.

The house itself was barely ten years old, but it was already starting to fall apart, despite the patchwork repairs that Trent and Matt had made. It was not a well-built house. Its one and only previous owner, a widower named Walt Gotthelf, had built it more or less himself. He was notoriously a crank and a loony old coot, who tried to disguise his miserly impulses behind folksy sayings about thrift and hard work being good for the soul, and grandiose blather about the joys of self-sufficiency and good old-fashioned ingenuity. When his wife was still alive, she was a good woman and a good influence, and he was just a little eccentric; but after she had passed away, then he couldn't stand to live in their old home without her, and there was nothing and no one left to help him restrain his worst impulses, he had no other family. Gossip had it that in his cheapness he had stolen a good portion of the building materials from the old Stone School, pillaging wires, pipes, and fixtures. Vivian knew none of this at first, knew only that the previous owner had passed away almost a year ago, leaving no heirs, and that was why she had got it so cheap.

The land he had built on was lower-lying than any of its neighbours, so that in the spring when the snow melted the yard became a marsh, all mud and breeding mosquitoes, and hardly dried out some years until summer was almost over. After she had lived there a few years, it became evident that the south side of the house was sinking, and ominous cracks were starting to appear in the plaster. It was a porous sort of place, in the winter cold air poured in from every corner, in the spring and summer water seeped into the basement. And it wasn't just wind and water, she couldn't keep the mice and ants from getting in either.

The wiring was a fiasco, too. She couldn't run the washing machine without turning out the bedroom lights, or it would blow a fuse. There was no dryer at all and no place to install one, so that she had to hang her wet clothes out in the yard in the summer and on a line in the basement when the weather went below freezing. The first time she tried plugging in her toaster, sparks shot out at her, leaving behind an acrid smell and a black scorch, and she was never able to use that toaster *or* that outlet again. She had to set up her coffee maker in the living room.

But worse than any of this, when she learned more about Walt Gotthelf, she managed to convince herself that the house was haunted, Marian's smudging be damned. Doors opening and closing on their own, which happened all the time, that could be chalked up to how draughty the house was, and the fact that none of the door frames were perfectly square, nor any of the doors hung very nicely. But it was true that Lancelot often seemed edgy and restless at night, whimpering, growling, or sometimes even breaking out into frenzied barking—barking and growling at something that simply wasn't there. He'd never done that sort of thing when they lived in the city.

Gotthelf, of course, had died in the house. Who knows how long his body might have gone undiscovered—for he had grown increasingly withdrawn and antisocial those last few years—if a neighbour hadn't noticed his front door wide open one morning. Freshly fallen snow covered the yard and had collected in a little heap inside the entranceway of the house. Strangest of all, there was a single set of paw prints, like those of a large dog, leading through the snow, up the front walk, and into the house—but no prints coming out again. Yet the neighbour could find no trace of a dog or any other animal when he went inside, concerned and more than a little nervous, calling out Walt's name again and again and getting no response. He found the old man, who wasn't really that old after all, only just sixty or so, bunched up on the floor beside his bed, wearing nothing but boxers, his lips blue and his eyes glassy. The coroner determined it had been a massive heart attack, probably as he was getting out of bed. Certainly there were no signs of violence on his body, nor anything in the house disturbed, but no one ever could explain those paw prints.

17

*A birthday present;
a bit of jealousy*

FOR TRACY'S EIGHTH BIRTHDAY, her father bought her a kitten: calico, with a splotch of black fur across her eyes that gave her the look of a bastard half-raccoon. He had smuggled her home from the Brandon humane society in complete secrecy and hid her overnight in his greenhouse, braving the very real fear that she would wreak havoc with his plants. Luckily, she was too frightened and confused to do anything but hide.

His plan had been to get up early and slip the kitten into Tracy's bedroom as she slept, so that she would wake on the morning of her birthday to the sight of her new pet, perhaps curled up at the foot of her bed, or perhaps even sniffing with shy curiosity at her face. He had vividly imagined his reward: sitting at the kitchen table, drinking his morning coffee, and listening to his daughter's delighted squeals of discovery, and the thunder of her excited feet as she rushed downstairs to tell everyone. But when morning came, he was unable to find the stupid animal anywhere. She had hidden herself so effectively inside the greenhouse that he was forced at last to wake both his daughters and ask their help to hunt, having first removed his bottles of scotch from their stashes and hid them temporarily behind the seat in his pickup truck, wrapped in an old wool blanket.

It took nearly an hour of careful searching for the girls to discover the kitten at last, filthy and terrified: she had crawled into an almost empty bag of potting soil in the back corner, beneath a table of cattleya, behind a stack of empty clay pots. It took another half an hour almost to coax her out, Tracy having received a ragged nasty scratch on her wrist when she had first reached into the bag recklessly to grab her. Her grandmother put iodine and a band-aid on the scratch, and Tracy named the kitten Pudge.

Once inside the house, Pudge went into hiding again and wasn't seen for two whole days. It was Nora who finally found her for the second time, hidden in the furnace room: actually inside the ceiling, having gotten into the rafters where several tiles had long ago fallen down. It was Nora who was able at last to coax her out, and got her to eat, and Nora alone whom she would allow, at first, to hold her and stroke her fur. It took a good month before the poor thing was comfortable enough not to startle and flee at any unexpected sound, and another month after that before she felt confident and secure enough to become playful and affectionate, like a real pet. The day she knocked a saucer off the end table where the girls' grandmother had placed a newly pulled incisor, still wet and bloody at the root, and batted and pounced the tooth around the room as if it were a mouse, was celebrated as a kind of milestone.

Their grandmother never did like cats, or pets of any sort: she firmly believed that all animals were dirty, carried disease, and had no place inside people's homes. She was eloquently, elaborately silent in her disapproval of Pudge, regularly announcing, when the topic came up, that it wasn't her place to say anything, and thereby saying everything she needed to.

Lynn, who had been raised with the same belief about pets, felt perhaps less strongly about it but was considerably more vocal. For the rest of the winter, Pudge became one of the most prominent items in her customary litany of complaints; for a time she even tried to convince her family and herself that she was allergic to the animal and suffering martyrously. Simon as usual submitted to her complaints with a sullen, mountainous, and infuriating passivity, but beneath it Nora thought she could detect an uncustomary undercurrent of satisfaction, even smugness, as if this too was some small part of his reward.

Nora could not help adoring Pudge, even if partly against her will, nor could she help being touched by the fact that from the very beginning Pudge clearly loved her best. Their father may have given Pudge to Tracy, but Pudge gave herself to Nora. It was to Nora's lap that Pudge would leap when feeling affectionate or wanting to be brushed, and it was on Nora's pillow that she would curl and nap during the day when the girls were at school; and though Tracy continued to take her into bed with her every night, she was forced to leave the connecting window open so that Pudge could slip into Nora's room, or else she would keep them both awake scratching at the sash and mewling like a banshee. By the time spring came around and Tracy's initial burst of passionate enthusiasm waned, it would be Nora who would take over sole responsibility for feeding the cat, filling her water dish, and even cleaning her litter box; and if she complained about it when she remembered to, adopting her father's habitual pout and even trying a touch of her mother's air of martyrdom, it fooled no one, not even herself.

As for Casey, perhaps there was a little mutual jealousy and mistrust there. And the first time that Casey had a sleepover after Pudge arrived, and she and Nora shared the hide-a-bed in the basement like they always did, then Pudge peed in Casey's shoes as she slept; and the next time Casey spent the night after that, Pudge sat on her face and tried to suffocate her in her sleep, and when Casey pushed her off, Pudge gave her a nasty scratch that went from the inside corner of her eye, down the side of her nose, past the corner of her mouth, and all the way down to her jawline, and the scratch hurt like a bugger and bled freely, and it gave new fuel to Lynn's complaints and to Alma's deafening disapproving silence. Alma cleaned and bandaged the scratch, grimly predicting that it would probably get infected, cat's claws are so filthy and full of feces, and Casey would no doubt end up in the hospital getting antibiotics through an IV; and Lynn said that if that damn cat scratched one more person just one more time, she'd take it back to the humane society where it came from, or maybe out to the dump where it belonged; and Tracy cried and said it was all Casey's fault, and even Nora was briefly worried. So after that Casey made it her great mission to win Pudge over and make friends, because she couldn't stand to see Nora worried, and every time she came over she would bring a tin of tuna or flaked salmon that she would steal from her mother's pantry, and she would put the fish right in the cup of her hands, sitting cross-legged on the floor, and let Pudge eat it out of her hands, gobbling up the meat and then lapping and licking her palms clean with that raspy, tickling tongue.

18

Tracy gets a crush on her new teacher;
Miss Atcheson misses home

IN SEPTEMBER, Tracy started grade three and immediately had
a mad crush on her new teacher, Miss Atcheson, who was bright,
young, and relentlessly bubbly. Miss Atcheson was notorious for
singling out one favourite each year and making a pet of her.
Always it was one of the girls. In Nora and Casey's day, when
they were in her class, it had been Alyssa Shaw, of course. Now
all the early signs were pointing to Tracy as this year's chosen one:
already, in just the first week of school, Tracy had been chosen
three times to take the class attendance sheets to the office, and
on Friday she was asked to stay ten minutes late at the end of the
day and help Miss Atcheson tidy the classroom. Casey and Nora
had waited for her on the playground. When Tracy finally came
out she was beaming, her hair bouncing.

"Did she ask anyone else to stay and help, too?" Nora wanted
to know.

"Just me," Tracy said smugly. Miss Atcheson wore her hair
in a high, jaunty ponytail; she had a perfectly round face, just
slightly pudgy, and she often wore overalls to school: that day
she had worn her purple corduroy overalls with the sunflower
embroidered on the pocket.

"Miss Atcheson said she knew she could count on me," Tracy
boasted. Her exact words had been: "Well, I'm glad I've got *you*
in my class, Tracy. I know it's going to be a good year if I've got
you to count on." The nameplate on her classroom door read

H. Atcheson. There was a rumour that the H stood for "Helga." She was unmarried, lived alone, had no family in the area: she'd moved there seven years ago for the job. Some people thought that she was actually from Saskatchewan. One of the Tibbett kids said his father said he often saw her early in the mornings, when he was out walking their dog, jogging along the Whitetail or up the hill towards the cemetery, huffing and puffing and wearing a sweatband, her ponytail bobbing and flopping.

"Did she sort of crouch down when she said it, like this?" Nora asked shrewdly. "So she's, like, eye to eye with you? Did she kind of whisper it, like she's telling you a secret?"

Tracy was vaguely aware that her sister making fun of her, but she didn't care, she felt too happy and proud to let it spoil her mood. When she got home, she asked her grandmother if she could buy her some overalls: a considerable shock to Alma, for Tracy had always been addicted to pretty dresses and only ever wore long pants with reluctance.

Miss Atcheson lived along the northwest edge of Halftown, out past the community centre and the health clinic, where a couple of small apartment buildings had gone up in the last decade or so. She did not attend any of the many churches in town, but spent her Sundays either alone at home or out for a drive in the countryside. It was one reason why, even after seven years, many still considered her a stranger. She was once spotted taking photographs of the old Stone School with a heavy, expensive camera, walking around the grounds and even going inside the building; that was on a Saturday.

Nora herself had briefly been in the running for Miss Atcheson's favourite of the year, along with Alyssa Shaw and Shannon Laurence. And in truth Nora had been just as ready as Tracy to adore Miss Atcheson, who had a cooing, confidential way of making a girl feel special and important, and who radiated a kind of infectious good cheer to those she chose. But one day, when Nora had stayed late alone to help tidy the classroom, Miss Atcheson had tried to coax her into saying unkind things about Casey, and had asked her all sorts of snooping, prying questions about Casey's home life; and however Nora had responded, it must have been unsatisfactory, for she had dropped Nora soon afterwards, and Alyssa alone received her special attention and was designated Miss Atcheson's special helper for the remainder of the year.

Because, just as much as she was notorious for choosing a favourite pet every year, Miss Atcheson was equally notorious for singling out one or two students to pick on and to constantly hold up to the class as an example of what not to do, and how not to behave, and how not to do your schoolwork. Always with a tone of kindhearted regret, as if more in sorrow than in anger. She would invariably choose shy, quiet children for this purpose; she wouldn't pick on the real troublemakers, who might rebel and give her a hard time, but only the sort who are too bashful to talk back, the kind who just hope to go unnoticed. She liked bright, confident children with happy dispositions, not the meek who she considered sneaks and mopes: never trust a quiet child, that was one of her mottoes. And she had pounced on Casey immediately and singled her out relentlessly all year long, with an even more blatant than usual antipathy, an almost visceral dislike, so that when it had become apparent to her that she would be unable to detach Nora from her friend, Nora had dropped precipitously in her esteem.

ONE DAY, A MONDAY, Casey was riding home in the back of the school bus, feeling pleased. The bus was only half full now, she had a window seat and no one next to her, and she passed the time by staring contentedly out the window, thinking about nothing in particular. She had spent the weekend at Nora's, she hadn't been home since Friday morning. The leaves were turning colour, and here and there she spotted a bush with a blaze of bright red leaves, standing out brilliant among the pale yellow and yellowish-brown and brownish-orange leaves on all the other bushes and trees. An occasional raindrop would hit her window, and then she could watch it drag sideways across the glass, moving slowly, stopping, quivering, and starting again, dissipating itself in a thin and zigzag line. It had been like this all day long, threatening to rain but never mustering more than a few drops here and a few drops there.

The bus rumbled over to the side of the road, the doors wheezed open and let the Kerry brothers out, the bus driver wearily telling them not to push, as he had to almost every day. Through the window, as the doors wheezed closed and the bus slowly lurched back into motion, Casey watched them heading up their driveway, hoods up, saw the younger brother, Derek, give his older brother a sudden shove, so that he almost lost his footing and tumbled into the ditch, and then begin sprinting towards the farmhouse, his older brother abandoning his backpack and running hotly after him, hollering. And then the bus was picking up speed, and they slid out of her line of sight, and out of mind.

There were only a couple more stops to make, and then it would be her turn to get off. In the pocket of her thin vinyl jacket was a hair scrunchie that she had stolen from the bedroom of Nora's cousin, Katharine. The fabric was a kind of iridescent silver, with shimmers of blue and green, that crinkled satisfyingly to the touch. She slipped it around her wrist, as she had once seen Katharine wear it, then quickly slipped it off again, almost alarmed by her own boldness. They had gone over to Katharine's house on Sunday, all of them after church, had lunch and stayed through the afternoon and into the early evening. The adults were celebrating some occasion, Casey wasn't sure what, some piece of good news for Katharine's parents. Casey had never been to their house, had barely even met them before, but they had treated her like one of the family.

Now the raindrops were striking the window of the school bus more frequently, covering the pane with streaks. The bus pulled over to the side of the road outside the farm, rumbling to a stop.

She didn't go straight up the driveway to her house, but putting up the hood of her jacket, cut across the field towards the trees. She wanted to add Kat's scrunchie to her secret stash before anybody knew she was home, in that secret cache in the old outhouse. There, together with the nail clippers, combs, and souvenir fridge magnets, the bottle-cap openers and half-used books of matches, Casey had three of Alma's teeth. She had a fourth, a molar, that she kept in her pocket and carried around with her: whenever she was feeling a little anxious or afraid, then she would slip her hand in her pocket and fiddle with the tooth, cool and smooth, rubbing its side with her thumb; or sometimes when she was very anxious, almost overwhelmed, then she would put the tooth in the palm of her hand and squeeze as hard as she could, pressing it into the flesh, so that it was almost as if Alma herself was biting her hand. Something about it made her feel braver.

Of course she could have had more of Alma's teeth if she had wanted them. This was years yet before the old lady started jealously hoarding her teeth; in those days she took no particular interest in what happened to them after she had pulled them from her mouth. Casey could have asked to have them, or just taken them openly, and Alma would almost certainly have let her—at worst she might have chided the girl gently, or laughed at her a little, but not in an unkind way. It didn't matter: Casey would have sooner died. Though she could never have articulated it to herself, and never even tried, in an inchoate way she felt certain that such things only had magic in them if they were taken illicitly and in complete secrecy, that her little rituals only had power if nobody knew about them, that nothing in this life has any real meaning unless it goes unnoticed.

By the time she reached the woods, it was starting to rain in earnest; the wind had come up, rustling the leaves of the aspen trees loudly. But when the old outhouse came into sight, as she approached it from behind, then she stopped, suddenly alert, inexplicably aware that something was wrong. A strange man emerged from the outhouse, *her* outhouse. At first she could only see him from behind, see the back of his green rain poncho with the hood up, and she had no idea who it was; then he turned a little as he flicked the butt-end of a cigarette into the bushes, and she saw that it was that new farmhand her father had hired at the beginning of the month: she didn't remember his name, Kevin or Trevor or something like that. She wasn't worried about him seeing her, she stood completely still and knew she was invisible. He turned and walked briskly away, heading in the direction of the stables; she waited a minute to make sure he was completely gone, and then ran swiftly and silently to the outhouse.

It had been a week or more since she had come to the outhouse. Inside, it stank like an ashtray, and she spotted several old and crumpled cigarette butts in the dirt. The rain was striking the roof in an intricate patter, and in half a dozen places weakly pissing right through. Sure enough, her treasures had been disturbed; nothing seemed to be missing but everything had been looked at, pawed through, touched, examined. Casey could feel her cheeks blaze hot and red, and the blood pound behind her ears, her thin little body shaking with outrage and dismay. Furiously, she began throwing those treasures, one by one until every last one was gone, into the old toilet, down the dark hole to disappear into the depths of decades old shit. All that was left to her was Katharine's scrunchie in one pocket and Alma's molar in the other, that nobody had seen and so still had their magic. She would have to start over, somewhere new, somewhere safer.

Nora and Casey were in fifth grade now: now for the first time their classroom was on the second floor with the older kids, and for the first time they had real lockers, with combination locks and all. The two friends were assigned lockers not quite right next to one another, but only a few feet apart. Nora could never remember her combination and would always get Casey to open it for her. And the number on their classroom door was 207, and it seemed to Casey, cautiously, that this could be a good year, because of course 207 is a terribly lucky number. Casey knew that the luckiest of all numbers is nine: in fact she knew it is so lucky that it's actually unlucky, dangerous, that like the sun you shouldn't look at it directly, and that what is really lucky are larger numbers, the digits of which add up to nine: thus, the 18th and the 27th day of every month were bound to be good days, but the ninth was a dangerous day, a day on which she was always extra-careful not to call attention to herself, just as September, the ninth month, was the most dangerous month.

Of course she kept all this strictly to herself: like all magic, it had to be completely secret to have power. It had been the dread Miss Atcheson, ironically enough, who had given Casey her first glimpse into this mystic insight, back in grade three. One day in class, when they were working on math, she had taught them this trick in a kind of enthusiastic digression, her ponytail bobbing as she slashed the numbers onto the blackboard, actually snapping a piece of chalk in her exuberance: she taught them that if you take a large number and add all the digits together, and keep doing it until you finally reduce it to a single digit, it makes no difference to the final result if you simply toss out any nines, or indeed any groups of digits that combine to make nine. She wrote on the board the number 7 729 836. If you add all those digits together, she showed them, they add up to 42, and then you add four and two together and you get six. Then she erased the nine, leaving 772 836, and walked them through it again: now those digits added up to 33, and three plus three is, what? Exactly! Six. Still six. Now, we know that two plus seven equals nine, so we can cross those off, and that leaves 7 836; and three plus six is also nine, so we can cross those off too, and that just leaves 78. Seven plus eight is 15, one plus five is six. See how that works? "Isn't that neat?" she had finished triumphantly, turning to look at the class. Some of the kids were blank-faced, some bored; some looked faintly embarrassed and others anxious, as if wondering whether they were going to get tested on all this. She giggled a little, apologetically, and erased the board. "That's okay," she said. "You don't really need to know that, I just thought it was interesting."

Casey's face was as blank or blanker than anyone's, it betrayed nothing, but in fact she did find it interesting. It happened that math was the one subject at school that she had a natural aptitude for, that came easily to her, though she was always careful to work a few deliberate errors into every test or assignment, since she knew that perfect marks would draw as much attention to herself as failing.

On the walk back to Nora's house for lunch that day, she had tried the trick out on the addresses of every house they passed, silently and rapidly adding the numbers up in her head, and she found it strangely satisfying, the way it worked out every time. And it happened that Nora's address was 378 McKenzie St, which reduced to nine itself, nine or nothing, and that was somehow the most satisfying of all. She later worked it out with Nora's phone number as well, and at first it reduced to three, which was a little deflating, but then she thought to add the area code, 204, and felt a happy, foolish little thrill when Nora got her nine again, the feeling of something clicking into place.

Some time later, she tried playing around with names, changing each letter into a number, so that *A* became one, *B* was two, *C* three and so forth, but that didn't work out in a satisfying way. Nora's name added up to a three, *Nora Wellesley* to a four, and if she added Nora's middle name, Diane, which Nora hated anyway, then it went all the way back around to one. Worse yet, she discovered that while the name *Casey* was an eight, *Casey Mack* was a perfect nine. She had no middle name, so far as she knew. This was proof enough that trying to apply the game to names and words was no good, and from then on she stuck to numbers, pure and simple.

At first all this was just a sort of pointless but mildly amusing game she could play in her head when she was idle or bored, casting her eyes around for any visible number, such as the time on a clock, adding and reducing it, and if it reduced down to nine, she always felt a silly little thrill of satisfaction. She found, too, that it was a useful trick for helping to remember numbers, such as combination locks or somebody's phone number: once she had played her game with it, it stuck effortlessly in her head, easy to recall.

At other times, times not of idle boredom but of acute pressure, misery, or humiliation, as when Miss Atcheson was singling her out in front of the class; or when Shannon Laurence would go out of her path to pass near her, not looking at her but stopping next to her, and then wrinkle her nose with disgust, and in a loud ingenuous voice ask, "What's that awful smell?"; or when her mother was in one of her moods of cold fury, thankfully less frequent these days: at times like those Casey found a kind of refuge or solace in the game, much the same sort of solace she got from squeezing Alma's tooth until it bit into her palm.

It was only gradually, by imperceptible degrees, that nine and the multiples of nine took on, or revealed, a larger, more mystic significance to her mind. And many years later, well into adulthood, when she knew full well that numbers, like everything else, were merely meaningless, and she had mostly put her intense, childish and idiosyncratic superstition behind her, fragments of it still persisted in certain small compulsions that she could laugh at herself for, but could never quite give up, compulsions such as only ever setting her oven to 315, 360, 405, or 450 degrees, and never cooking anything at any other temperature; or setting her alarm clock to go off at 6:03 or 7:02, instead of simply six or seven o'clock.

ON THE LAST DAY OF SCHOOL before the holidays, Miss Atcheson's class had a Christmas party. They wore their pyjamas to school, and brought their favourite stuffed animals, and they were invited to bring cookies and dainties to share, and they exchanged cards, played games, and watched old Christmas movies and cartoons.

Miss Atcheson brought hot chocolate for everybody, in a big metal urn. Tracy brought vinarterta that her grandmother made, and Miss Atcheson said that it was the most wonderful thing that she had ever tasted, and Tracy said that she had helped her grandmother make it, and Miss Atcheson said, "Well, if you're as good a helper with your grandmother as you are with me, I'm sure it must make her very happy."

Miss Atcheson was wearing not just any pyjamas, but a one-piece sleeper in the shape of a fuzzy pink bunny rabbit, with a fluffy white rabbit tail and all. She, too, had brought a stuffed animal, a funny little penguin with very wide eyes and a little black bowtie. Tracy had brought her a Christmas gift; Miss Atcheson put it aside and said she would open it later.

At the end of the day, of course the classroom was an ungodly mess. Miss Atcheson said, "I can't ask you to stay and help clean up *this* mess, it will take much too long. I'm sure you can't wait to start your holidays." But Tracy insisted that she didn't mind staying, she wanted to stay, she almost pleaded to be allowed to stay and help. Miss Atcheson, looking at the earnest young girl fondly, said, "Well, I suppose it would be all right. Why don't you go and tell your sister not to wait for you, I'll walk you home when we're finished."

When Tracy returned, Miss Atcheson had poured a little cup of hot chocolate for each of them, saying, "We might as well finish it off." There were a few stray cookies left, and one butter tart, and she put these on a paper plate and said, "Let's have a picnic." They sat cross-legged on the carpet. The hot chocolate was no longer hot, it was just barely warm, but it still tasted wonderful because Miss Atcheson had given it to her.

She opened her gift from Tracy: there were several cakes of homemade soap, scented with rosehips and citrus, and a charmingly ugly little elf figurine on a string. "It's for your Christmas tree," Tracy explained. She had picked both gifts out herself at the annual Christmas craft sale, after spending hours agonizing over the choice, drifting fretfully from table to table. "Do you like it?" Tracy asked hopefully.

Miss Atcheson said, "I love it. It's wonderful, thank you so much." She said, "I have a present for you too. But you have to promise not to tell your classmates," she added in a whisper, holding her finger up to her lips. She had already given a small gift bag to every student, Tracy included: each bag had an eraser in the shape of a reindeer's head, two pencils, a few small chocolates wrapped in foil, a plastic whistle, and a rubber ball. But for Tracy she had something extra, something special. She had even wrapped it nicely, two small neat parcels, held together with a green cloth ribbon. After Tracy undid the ribbon, then Miss Atcheson took it and used it to tie Tracy's hair up in a jaunty ponytail, just like hers, except not really like hers because Tracy's hair was curly, thick, and unruly, and Miss Atcheson's hair was perfectly straight and always impeccably well-behaved.

In the smaller of the two parcels was a stuffed mouse, with a tiny little bell around its neck, and little reindeer antlers on its head. "That's for Pudge," Miss Atcheson said. "It has catnip inside it."

Of course Tracy had told her all about Pudge. One of the reasons that Miss Atcheson was so fond of her was that Tracy loved to babble happily about everything that was happening in her life. Miss Atcheson, too, had a cat at home, a hefty grey tom named Fitzie. Fitzie was growing old and crotchety, needed special food now, was half-blind, arthritic, and had started dribbling small hard turds and squirts of urine around her apartment.

In the second, larger parcel there was a thick hardcover book that said *The Nutcracker* down the spine, only it wasn't really a book at all: the pages were fake and the book was held shut by a clasp and a tiny little lock. There was a tiny little key, also attached to a green ribbon. Tracy unlocked it, and lifted the cover, or lid, and a small mechanical ballerina with a blank face stood up in the box and began slowly pirouetting to the tinkling dance of the Sugar Plum Fairy. Inside the cavity of the box, there was a folded note. Tracy took it out and read it: it said, "To Tracy. Best wishes for a wonderful Christmas. Your friend, Hannah." It was the best gift that Tracy could have possibly imagined, she wanted almost to weep with happiness.

The caretaker peered in at them through the classroom door with a doleful look on his face. "Oops," Miss Atcheson said with a giggle. "I think we're keeping Mr Wyatt waiting." Wyatt was the caretaker's first name, not his surname: a young man who had been a student there barely ten years back, under some of the same teachers still teaching, he preferred to let the kids call him by his first name; but the teachers, apparently uneasy with such informality in front of the students, always tacked that Mister on. It was part of his job, Miss Atcheson explained to Tracy, to be the last to leave the building every day, make sure it was really empty, set the alarms and lock everything up. Until they finished and left, he was trapped here.

They got busy and made brisk and cheerful work of it. As they tidied and swept, Miss Atcheson asked Tracy about her Christmas wish list, and what she was most looking forward to doing over the holidays, and Tracy babbled happily, and Miss Atcheson laughed and said, "Tracy, if I have a daughter I hope she's just like you."

Tracy asked her what *she* was hoping to get for Christmas, and she said, in a conspiratorial voice, "Well, there *is* something very special I'm hoping to get, but I'm keeping it a secret. If I say it out loud, it might jinx my wish. But I'll tell you in January if I got it or not."

By the time they finished cleaning the classroom it was already getting dark outside. When they left the room, they were a little startled to find Mr Wyatt right outside, waiting for them in the hallway beside his mop bucket, slouching back against the lockers, hands in his pockets. The lights in the corridor were dimmed, and his face was half in shadows, but he was staring and glaring at them glumly, and it was all a little creepy. Miss Atcheson seemed to feel it too, for she took Tracy's hand in hers, and when she wished Mr Wyatt a happy holidays it was with an unnaturally loud, bright voice, even for her. He only grunted by way of reply. They walked rapidly and silently down the dim corridor, their boot heels clicking and clacking on the polished floor, and only when they were out the front door did they look at one another and giggle with nervous relief.

Outside, a soft fall of fresh snow glittered beneath the street-lights. "I hope your parents won't be mad at me for keeping you so late," Miss Atcheson said. Tracy reassured her, almost shocked at the thought: how could anyone be mad at Miss Atcheson? They piled the metal urn, and Miss Atcheson's penguin, and her handbag, and all the gifts that the children had given her, into the trunk of her car, and left it there in the school parking lot, for though it was cold out it was a lovely calm evening without a breath of wind, and they would walk together to Tracy's house, and Miss Atcheson could come back for her car afterwards. Above them, the sky was not yet black but a very deep, dark blue, with a few remaining streaks of dirty ragged cloud and the first and nearest stars just winking into sight.

Tracy led the way. She very much wanted Miss Atcheson to come inside so she could introduce her to Pudge, and Miss Atcheson said, "Well, maybe just for a minute, as long as your parents don't mind. I wouldn't want to make a nuisance of myself."

They were coming up the cul-de-sac now, and Tracy pointed out her house at the end of the street, with a wreath in the ship's-wheel window, and strings of multi-coloured Christmas lights lighting up the pink stucco, and they could see half the Christmas tree through the living room window, looking cheerful with its blinking red lights and strings of glittering tinsel, and Miss Atcheson cooed delightedly over what an adorable little house it was.

Lynn must have been waiting and watching for them, for she opened the front door while they were still coming up the steps. She thanked Miss Atcheson for seeing her daughter home, so kind of her, and hoped that Tracy had made herself really useful, and had not been the sort of "helpful" that just makes it take twice as long to get anything done. She invited Miss Atcheson in for a drink, perhaps merely being polite and expecting Miss Atcheson to equally politely decline, but Miss Atcheson accepted without hesitation, strode boldly in and began taking off her things. Only then did she remember that she was dressed in bunny rabbit pyjamas, and she had to laugh at herself. Her cheeks and nose were bright red from the cold.

Tracy ran off to try and find Pudge, leaving her boots, backpack, mitts, hat, and coat strewn in a breadcrumb trail across the floor. Alma, coming out of the kitchen to greet their guest, yelled after Tracy to pick up her things, and Tracy yelled back, "I will, Amma," but didn't turn around to do it, just thundered on up the stairs.

Alma shook her head in exasperation, gathering up the girl's things. Miss Atcheson laughed. "I think she's a little excited," she said. Lynn offered her some eggnog—"Nothing in it, of course" Alma added, glancing meaningfully at Miss Atcheson's midsection, for she still got dribbles of gossip from her old cronies at the school. And Miss Atcheson, beaming and unembarrassed, put a hand to her belly and said she didn't think eggnog would sit very well, but she'd love a cup of tea. So Alma toddled back to the kitchen to put on the kettle, and Miss Atcheson invited herself into the living room, where Simon was sitting in his armchair. He made to stand up as she entered.

"Don't get up on my account," Miss Atcheson said merrily. "Just your friendly neighbourhood bunny rabbit, popping in for a visit." It was all very strange, if they didn't know better they might have suspected she was drunk. They had met her plenty of times, of course, under the semi-formal auspices of parent-teacher conferences, or perhaps exchanging a few polite remarks in line at the grocery store, but no more than that. "You have a lovely home, Mr Wellesley, I just love it."

"Call me Simon," he said, now standing, and giving the ghost of a bow. He invited her to have a seat with almost cartoonish gallantry. Guests always brought out his best, most antiquated manners, after the fashion of his mother and father; and after all Miss Atcheson *was* quite pretty, and looked particularly adorable in those pyjamas. She made a pantomime curtsy, and said, "Why, thank you," and made herself comfortable on the couch.

"I have to tell you," he said as he lowered himself back down in his armchair, "Tracy talks about you all the time, she thinks you're very much the most wonderful person she's ever met. You have no idea what an honour it is to get a visit from the Marvellous Miss Atcheson."

"Hannah, please," she replied. "And the feeling's entirely mutual. You have a wonderful daughter—*two* wonderful daughters," she corrected herself graciously, for Nora had just come downstairs, kitten in arms. "Or perhaps I should say two and a half?" she added, spying Casey in the background. "You know we call them Chang and Eng in the staff room. I see they're just as inseparable outside of school, aren't they?"

Tracy had found Pudge up in her sister's room, licking the last of the tuna juice off Casey's hands. She was so excited she was hopping up and down as if she had to pee and was almost squealing as she told them that Miss Atcheson was here to meet Pudge. Then she made a lunging grab at the cat, and Pudge gave a hiss and a yowl and hid under Nora's bed, and it had taken Nora a minute or two to coax her out, with Casey and Tracy guarding the other side of the bed to make sure she didn't make a break for it.

Casey could have stayed upstairs, but Miss Atcheson held no special terror for her anymore, especially not here, at Nora's house, the place she felt safest and most comfortable in the world. Now that Miss Atcheson had no particular power over her, Casey had been able to find her merely laughable, at least most of the time; and Miss Atcheson, too, now that she no longer had Casey in her class, seemed to no longer find the girl so aggravating, and occasionally made encouraging remarks to her in the hallways, and was once overheard congratulating herself, to the other teachers, for having helped Casey "come out of her shell."

"So this is Pudge," said Miss Atcheson in a cooing voice, reaching out and taking the kitten from Nora. Pudge looked back at Nora with a baleful sort of look, but didn't struggle to escape. "Yes you *are* Pudge, yes you are. Who's a beautiful girl?" Miss Atcheson said, squinting her eyes and holding the cat up so their noses nearly touched: "You *are* a beautiful girl, yes you are. You're just the sweetest little thing, aren't you?" Pudge mriaowed, bearing her sharp little teeth.

"Fitzie is going to be terribly jealous when he smells another cat on me," she said happily, leaning back on the couch and lowering Pudge to her lap, holding her firmly with one hand and stroking her gently with the other. "Fitzie's my cat," she explained to Alma, who had brought her that cup of tea, placing it down on the end table beside her.

"Yes," said Alma, forcing a polite smile, "I believe Tracy's mentioned him."

"Tracy does love to talk," laughed Miss Atcheson, turning to speak to Simon. "Such a ray of sunshine to have in the class, let me tell you. Both your girls, just a joy to have around."

Tracy, having just remembered Miss Atcheson's gift, had gone and dug the catnip mouse out of her schoolbag. She brought it over, holding it out and waggling it in the air, making the little bell around its neck jingle. "Look at what Miss Atcheson bought for you," she said, mimicking her teacher's cooing voice and shoving the mouse under Pudge's nose. Pudge mriaowed again. "Can you smell the catnip?" Pudge craned her neck to look back at Nora, as if silently pleading for help, but Nora could only shrug apologetically.

"Put it down," said Miss Atcheson, "and let's see if she'll play with it." It took a minute, for one of Pudge's claws had gotten snagged on the bunny pyjamas, but Miss Atcheson got her unhooked at last and placed her gently down on the floor beside the mouse. Pudge didn't look twice at it, but as soon as Miss Atcheson let go of her, she turned and darted off, running past Nora and Casey and darting up the stairs.

"That's all right," said Miss Atcheson to Tracy, who looked furiously disappointed. "I'm sure she'll play with it later, when there aren't so many people around." Pudge had left a little fur behind on Miss Atcheson's hands and lap, and she remarked again how jealous Fitzie was going to be. "In fact," she said, picking up her teacup, blowing across the surface, and then sipping tentatively: "In fact, I was hoping to talk to you about Fitzie." Because, she explained—speaking directly to Simon now, as if no one else were in the room—she would be leaving the next day to drive home for the holidays, as she did every year at Christmas; and normally of course she would take Fitzie with her, but he was getting so old now, she really didn't think he could handle the long drive any more—five or six hours, depending whether she stopped to eat along the way.

"Where is home?" asked Simon. "If you don't mind me asking."

"Oh, you wouldn't have heard of it I'm sure," said Miss Atcheson, waving the question away. It was so small, it wasn't even on any maps, that's how small it was. Anyway, she went on, what she was *really* hoping was that Tracy and Nora would agree to take care of Fitzie for her while she was gone, if it wasn't too much to ask. "I'd pay them, of course." They were both such good, responsible girls, there weren't any she trusted more, it would be a weight off her mind.

Tracy, of course, was ecstatic at the idea, begging her father to say yes, hopping up and down and saying, "Please please please-please *please*." Nora wanted to know how much they'd get paid; Alma retreated to the kitchen, as if to silently announce that she was staying out of it. Lynn frowned and said something about them being a little young, but Simon waved his wife's objections away and accepted the offer, and Tracy squealed excitedly and jumped on him, throwing her arms around him and saying, "Thank you thank you thank you."

"That's settled then," said Miss Atcheson, smiling at Simon and wriggling her nose at him, for all the world like a real rabbit. "Such a relief." They agreed that Simon would bring the girls over to her apartment in the morning so that she could introduce them to Fitzie and show them everything they'd need to know.

HANNAH ATCHESON lived in Halftown, along the northwest edge of town, out past the community centre and the health clinic, where Matt and the Pettingers had put up a couple of small apartment buildings in the past decade. She did not attend any of the many churches in town, but spent her Sundays either alone at home or out for a drive in the countryside. She was unmarried, lived alone, had no family in the area. Over the Christmas holidays, spring break, and all through summer, she would go back home. It was one of the reasons why, even after seven years, many still considered her a stranger. She could be spotted early in the mornings, when the weather was fair, jogging along the Whitetail or up the hill towards the cemetery, huffing and puffing and wearing a sweatband, her ponytail bobbing and flopping.

That had been her hobby when she first came to town, that was how she spent many of her Saturdays and Sundays those first few years, driving around the countryside, taking black and white photographs of derelict buildings, abandoned houses, rotting and decrepit barns. She developed them herself, weekends when the weather was too cold to go out, converting her bathroom into a makeshift darkroom. The day she had gone to photograph the old Stone School—it was in the spring, late May or early June, near the end of her first year in town—then she happened to bump into Matt Wellesley. What he was doing there, poking around the empty rooms, he wouldn't say, was very coy. She knew him, of course: he was her landlord, or one of them, and it was he who had shown her around the apartment building when she'd first moved to town. He was tremendously handsome. He asked her about her photography; they fell to talking of this and that, and ended up somehow back at her apartment, where she showed him some of her more successful prints, and then they made love.

For the next couple of years, they had continued their affair in a light and intermittent fashion. Sometimes Matt would call her up when he had spotted a particularly interesting old house or derelict barn he thought she might like to photograph, and then he might meet her there, and admire her as she worked. In the winter, there was always an excuse, as landlord, to drop by her apartment building and take care of something. It was just enough to assuage her loneliness in exile. That he was happily married suited her perfectly: she had no desire to get entangled with anyone in Whittle; all her hopes and aspirations were centred on home and someday going back home to stay.

The town she was from really wasn't on any maps, not because it was so small, but because the people who lived there paid handsomely to keep it off. Tucked in a small, deep valley, on the edge of a pristine lake, it was almost impossible to find if you didn't know the secret. It had no name. No plane ever passed overhead. The tall surrounding pines sheltered the town from the extremities of weather and stained the air with their green astringent scent. In winter it was always mild, in summer never too hot. At night, the sky was thick with constellations. No waves ever ruffled the glittering surface of the lake. Motor boats were forbidden; mosquitoes were banned. She had lived there from the time she was four until she turned eighteen, when her mother—who she adored—got remarried, this time to a much younger man. He, too, was terribly handsome, and seemed quite nice. Then her mother had sent Hannah packing; though nothing had happened between Hannah and the new husband, not so much as a giggle or a surreptitious glance, still, her mother said, it was only sensible to remove all possible temptation. And Hannah was sure that if her mother thought so, it must be for the best. She took Fitzie with her so she wouldn't feel lonely. For four years she hadn't even been allowed to come back and visit. When she did go back home nowadays, then her mother and stepfather would go off on their own vacations, to Mexico in the winter or the Mediterranean in the summer, and she would take care of her young half-brother, who called her "Auntie." It was more than worth it for the privilege of being permitted to return. Though she lived frugally and carefully invested a large part of her salary, she knew perfectly well that she would never be able to afford to live in that town on her own. She had no illusions that any of her mother's money would ever come to her: it would go first to the husband and from him to their son.

The affair with Matt gradually fizzled out, as these things sometimes must, for no particular reason. She had neither regrets nor resentments, but if the affair hadn't ended, she might not have made the misstep of sleeping with young Mr Wyatt from the school. It had happened in the dog-days of winter; for weeks it had been too brutally cold to go outside, except to hurry to work and hurry back home. It was her fifth year in Whittle; it was her ninth year in exile, and she was beginning to seriously question, perhaps for the first time, if that exile would ever end. Then one morning her car wouldn't start, and Wyatt, who lived in the apartment building next to hers, very gallantly got it started for her. That he was sweet on her, she was perfectly well aware, and had been for some time. And so, against her better judgment, she had invited him over that evening for a "thank you" dinner, as if jump-starting her car battery had been some arduous feat. Invited him to dinner and then, after dinner, invited him to spend the night. If he had been content, like Matt had been, to occasionally assuage her loneliness and lighten her mood when she was feeling down, it could have been ideal. But of course he had to go and fall in love with her, as deep down she must have known he would, and it was a messy and protracted business, ending the relationship without creating a scandal at the school.

Then just this past summer, at the end of her eleventh year in exile, something miraculous had happened. It was a resplendent night in early July. Her brother, now ten, was safely asleep in bed, and Hannah had brought her camera down to the beach to photograph the multitudinous stars in the sky, and their mirrored twins shimmering on the surface of the lake. Lately she had been trying to teach herself colour photography, so much trickier to develop. The first attempt was spoiled when, halfway through the long exposure, a figure had emerged from the black water, a midnight swimmer coming back to shore. It was a man named Allan Eider; she had known him since she was a little girl. He apologized for spoiling her photograph. Since his wife had passed away that winter, he had struggled to sleep at night, and a long late swim sometimes helped. That night they spent several hours sitting side by side on the beach, watching the constellations wheel slowly across the sky, relieving their consonant solitudes in low voices and unguarded conversation. They were still talking, and it seemed as though hardly any time had passed, when, across the lake, the black of the sky began to turn a deep and radiant blue, erasing the stars.

The remainder of the summer they met often. She, too, took to midnight swimming. Their lovemaking afterwards would be muffled, earnest, and tender, and proved the only effective cure for insomnia he had discovered. He really wasn't so old, only in his early fifties, and fit as a man fifteen years younger. He had no children to worry about: his wife had never been healthy enough to have any. Though she had died so young, she had outlived what she or anyone else had expected by a decade at least. Keeping her alive had been his sole occupation for so long, he now had no idea what to do with himself.

They carefully guarded the privacy of their meetings, not out of shame or fear, for neither had anything to be ashamed or afraid of, but to protect, nurture, and elongate the idyllic and dreamlike quality of that first night. They never spoke of the future for the same reason, but for Hannah, her secret hopes were almost overwhelming, much as she struggled to temper them. The summer drifted quickly by, July seeped into August and then August was already almost over, Hannah's mother and stepfather returned home from Monaco and it was time for her to return to Whittle, return to her life in exile. Only later, near the end of September, did she know for certain that she was pregnant. Then it was impossible to temper her hopes any longer, she was irreparably intoxicated with them, and along with those hopes came something new, a sort of blind incipient terror lapping at the edges of her consciousness: terror that Allan would reject the idea of being a father and starting a new life together; for if that happened, if the door closed on this one perfect opportunity of returning home to stay, she wasn't sure she would have the courage to keep living.

19

Pudge widens her worldview;
Nora goes to the lake with Alyssa

WHEN SPRING CAME, as soon as the snow was mostly melted, Alma began sending the cat outside. The first time, Pudge was terrified and hardly left the stoop, scratching and mewling at the door to come back in. The second time Nora sat with her on the stoop, patiently for an hour with Pudge on her lap, stroking her fur soothingly and laughing affectionately every time her little head would jerk up suddenly at some new or unexpected sound or sight: a car door slamming, the chitter of sparrows, a dog barking in the distance, a glimpse of a lean grey squirrel darting across the edge of the lawn and disappearing up their neighbour's elm. Then Pudge's body would stiffen, startled and alert, and her ears would stick up like a bat's as her head darted side to side, scanning the landscape.

The third time she went out she was bold enough to leave the stoop by herself, and even went as far as that elm tree next door, squatting beneath it and staring up. She apparently remembered seeing that squirrel run up it, and seemed to suspect it might still be up there. Tracy and April were trying to master double-dutch skipping, and Nora had let herself be coaxed into helping turn the ropes. It was a Sunday morning before church, there was nothing else to do anyway. There was a touch of frost on the ground but the air was still and the sky was clear; the swish and slap of the ropes and the tap and scuffle of their shoes on the pavement mingled with the morning chorus of the birds and the girls' half-sung, half-shouted chants of, "Bluebells taco shells, eevy ivy over," and "Strawberry shortcake apple berry pie, who's your lover who's your guy?"

Tracy and April were tremendous friends, especially when they were apart from one another. When they were actually together, then it seemed like they squabbled and bickered as often as they just had fun, and sometimes they lost their tempers, and it would end in tears—but as soon as they were apart they loved each other again, and only spoke adoringly of one another, and couldn't wait to get back together.

In April's house there was a laundry chute, tucked in the floor of the linen closet and going all the way down to the basement. April said she had slid down it a hundred times, and it was very dangerous, and if her mother ever caught her at it she'd be in so much trouble, but she did it anyway. Tracy desperately wanted to do it too, but it seemed that whenever she was over, there was never a good opportunity: either April's mom was always watching, or there was no pile of laundry that day to break the fall, or there was some other reason.

They had a freezer in the basement that always had ice cream bars and fudgsicles in it. There was a grand piano in the living room, and April had to take lessons, and actually she could play amazingly well but she always pretended that she was terrible because if her parents knew she had a talent for it they'd make her practice for hours a day like her sister Juliet. There was a pool in the back yard, a real swimming pool in the ground with a diving board and everything, one of only two real back yard swimming pools in the whole town, and there was also a trampoline and a treehouse, because April's family was very wealthy because her father had won the lottery before April was born and he was a millionaire now, but he and her mother still went to work every day even though they didn't need the money, they just did it because they didn't want to get bored.

April had flown on a plane four times. Once she got to go into the cockpit and meet the pilot and see how the plane worked, and now she could probably fly it herself if she had to. Another time they had turbulence and she puked all over the place. One winter they went to Disney World, and April went to a tea party with the real Snow White, Cinderella, and Sleeping Beauty. A different winter they went to Mexico, and April went swimming in the ocean every day and got crusted all over with salt, and she went scuba diving and saw an octopus *this close*, and she also found a real pearl, but word must have got out about the pearl she had found because when they went for dinner that night, their hotel room was broken into by burglars and the pearl was the only thing they stole, that's how valuable it must have been; and one day there was a shark in the ocean, and it bit a man's leg off, and the man had to hop out of the ocean on only one leg with blood gushing out of the stump of the other, and he hopped past April so close she got splashed with some of his blood and everyone was screaming, that's how lucky April was.

A sudden wild hissing and squalling startled all three girls. A tomcat named Farley from up the street had noticed Pudge beneath the tree and had come over to say hello, probably intending to flirt a little, for Farley was a notorious slut; but Pudge, not noticing him approach until he came swaggering around the trunk of the elm, had let out a frantic panicked yowl and strangulated hissing, her teeth bared, back arched, tail puffed out. Farley, startled, had growled back indignantly; and then Pudge flew at his head, claws out, with all the desperate ferocity of the truly terrified. There was a brief flurry and tangle of flailing bodies and paws, and then Pudge was darting blindly away, running between the girls, almost getting tangled up in the slack and hanging skipping ropes, up the stairs to their stoop, and began scratching madly at the door to be let inside.

From then on, Pudge did her desperate best to hide from Alma when no one else was home, knowing that if the old lady got hold of her, she would throw her straight outside. Then Nora and Tracy would find her waiting for them on the front stoop when they got home from school; she would start mewling complainingly as soon as she saw them coming down the street, then getting up to turn impatient, anxious little circles until they reached her.

This went on for several weeks, until Pudge found an unlikely ally in Simon, by digging up his freshly planted flowerbeds, chewing the green shoots and shitting in the dirt. Then Simon stormed and stamped his feet and slammed his hands and decreed that the cat was no longer allowed outside, ever. Alma ignored him, of course, and caught Pudge and put her out just two days later—so she went right back to digging, chewing, shitting, and pissing on what Simon had managed to salvage, restore, or replace. The devastation was thorough, almost systematic. Simon rarely lost his temper, not really, but when he did it was always fearsome: he was a tall strong man, and his whole body would shake with the effort of restraint; his voice would start out with tones of a sort of exaggerated and frigid politeness, and then steadily get louder until at last he was yelling, bellowing, banging the furniture and slamming doors. Tracy burst into tears, Pudge hid in the basement; Nora retreated to her room, Lynn tried to placate him. Only Alma remained unmoved, watching him from her armchair as she wiggled at a loose tooth with an expression of mingled contempt and amusement.

THAT SUMMER Nora spent a week at her friend Alyssa's family cottage, up at the Narrows on Lake Manitoba.

Nora was as disappointed to arrive as she had been excited to go: she had been imagining a place spacious and isolated, surrounded by pristine wilderness, perched on the edge of a blue and jewelled lake. But the cottage turned out to be small, cramped, and airless, perched on the edge of a rutted dirt road, and crowded by rows of almost identical cottages on every side. There was only a single bathroom for the six of them staying there, so that any time you needed to use it, it was invariably already occupied. And if it was one of Alyssa's brothers, then you had to wait another half hour at least for the smell to clear out before you could bring yourself to use it. There was no phone, no television, nothing but a small radio with dodgy reception. In the living room, the mounted head of a caribou looked down at them from on high. It had come with the cottage when they bought it, ten years ago. Then Alyssa's brother Anthony had been three or four, and when he had first seen it he had said, nervously, "Is that alive?" Told that no, it was not alive, he had narrowed his eyes ominously and, still staring it down, had said in a threatening voice, "It better not be." Alyssa's parents told that story to Nora three times over the course of the week, laughing heartily and lovingly each time.

The walls of the cottage were thin; at night, Nora could not only hear the sound of Alyssa's brothers snoring in the next bedroom and her parents boozily flirting with one another in the living room, but all the neighbours too, shouting, laughing, drunken and loud. It was too hot to close the windows, even at night, and it was Nora's first time so long away from home: she didn't miss her family, except maybe now and then her little sister, but she did miss her room, her own bed, and Pudge curled up beside her; and she was worried that Pudge would feel lonely without her, and that no one would take proper care of her while she was gone.

You couldn't see the lake from the cottage. It was a five-minute walk away, down the dirt road and around the bend, past the gas station and the grocery store, and a little park with an old swing set, slide, and monkey bars that were so rusted out and askew, they looked as if they might collapse in a heap should any kid be foolhardy enough to try and climb them. A finger of land had been built out into the lake to separate the marina on one side from the swimming area a scrubby little beach more rocks than sand, on the other. The water was dark, brackish, and weedy, at least until you got far enough from shore, but swimming was a pleasure anyway, especially first thing in the morning, before anyone else was awake except for two or three fishermen maybe, sitting on the end of the jetty, patient peaceful and unmoving, watching their lines in the water, so quiet they hardly counted as people at all, as if they were merely an extension of the landscape. Then the low sun would glance and sparkle off the unruffled surface of the water, giving it the illusion of being pristine and clean, and she and Alyssa could swim out well past the weeds and stony bottom, undisturbed by any boats.

Alyssa was the baby of the family, the youngest of four children, and the only girl, petted and spoiled by her parents and older brothers alike. She had been the first girl in their class to come to school wearing makeup, had the prettiest and most expensive outfits, and always got the highest marks in their class. At school she was bright, confident, and relentlessly chipper; at home among her family she was whiny, wheedling, and constantly indulged. She had the habit of dropping into a cartoonish lisp and using baby-talk when asking her parents for something; and then her parents would smile down on her adoringly and give her whatever she wanted. Alyssa loved Nora for coming to stay at the cottage with her and told her all her small and fragile secrets, her crushes and ambitions, and swore they would be best friends forever.

Alyssa's mother drank vodka and limeade out of big glass tumblers and spent the week reclining on the lounge chair reading a big fat book called *Flowers in the Attic*; Alyssa's father drank many cans of beer and puttered about the place looking for things to fix up, which he did ineptly and enthusiastically. They were incessantly affectionate with one another, always reaching out to touch or brushing up against one another, calling one another pet names, frequently kissing even in front of the kids. In the evenings they would turn the radio on, tuned to an oldies station, and dance stumblingly whenever a slow song came on. They were equally affectionate with their children, too, fond and indulgent and full of praise. By the end of the second day they had folded Nora into that same embrace, calling her "sweetie" and "sunshine" instead of her name, and randomly pausing to beam at her, and tell her how wonderful she was, how sweet and smart and lovely and well-mannered, which never failed to fill her with a kind of horrible frozen awkwardness.

Of Alyssa's three brothers, the oldest hadn't come out to the lake at all, and the second oldest was there but barely seen, disappearing all day with a gang of summer buddies and only returning occasionally to eat, steal his father's beer, and sometimes sleep; but Anthony, the brother closest to them in age, only a couple years older than Alyssa, followed the girls around constantly, teasing his sister, showing off for Nora, pestering them until finally even his father took notice and told him to give it a rest and leave them alone; and then he spent the last few days in a sulk, swaddled in his headphones, and Nora felt sorry for him. He was a chunky, clumsy, slobby kind of kid, with all the awkwardness of adolescence but no harm in his heart. The smell of him steadily intensified as the week went on, a sour and stinging miasma of curdled sweat and stale oily lake water, layered over with heavily scented deodorant.

In the afternoons, Alyssa's father would take Anthony and the girls out in his motorboat, pulling them behind on an inner tube; they rented water skis one day, going out before lunch and staying at it until the early evening, and by the time they had to quit Nora had almost gotten the hang of it. There was a horseshoe pitch in the back yard, and a croquet set that still had most of the pieces. After dinner they would spend the evening around the firepit. Anthony taught Nora the best way to build a proper fire, and they would toast marshmallows, and Nora would sit in companionable silence, slapping at the mosquitoes and watching the red and yellow flames lick and curl and consume the wood, and how the sap would boil out from the cut end of a log and bubble and sizzle in the heat, and the way the flickering lights danced across the faces of Alyssa's family that loomed out of the darkness; and she would think how those faces were kind, friendly, gentle, and slightly stupid, and Alyssa at her side would discreetly take her hand and give it a gentle squeeze, and that was okay too.

The last evening she spent at the lake it rained. The morning had started off grey and windy and kind of cool; by lunchtime the wind was blowing so hard it made the trees groan and flipped over the lawn chairs, and they had to bring everything inside. You could hear the crash of the waves all the way from the cottage, and Nora talked Alyssa into putting on their bathing suits and going down to check it out. Anthony went with them.

For a while they just stood at the edge of beach, inching closer and closer as the water dragged away and then scampering back when the next wave surged at them, laughing as it lapped around their ankles and the foamy spray burst up around them. The wind was cold but that just made the water feel warmer. Anthony threw off his towel and went charging in with a great goofy whoop, quickly stumbling and going face first into a whitecap that swallowed him over; and he burst out of the water a few moments later with a joyous holler. Then Nora went in too, not running in like Anthony but trying to walk. She didn't get far at all before a great wave knocked her flat on her backside. She couldn't believe how much force it had. The undertow as the wave went back out dragged Nora out with it, and then another wave picked her up and flung her back on to shore, and she lay there laughing so hard she could hardly breathe, and another wave was pounding right on top of her. Alyssa helped her to her feet, and she went right back in, this time running in so she got a little deeper, and diving forward when she met the next wave. She and Anthony stayed out there for well over an hour, letting the water toss them around, but they were having so much fun it hardly felt like fifteen minutes. Nora didn't feel it when it started to rain; she only realized it when she glanced back at shore and saw Alyssa with her towel wrapped around her, huddled under the shelter of a tree, looking miserable. Then she felt tremendously guilty and immediately headed in. Her towel on the beach was soaked and caked with wet sand. For the rest of the afternoon and through the evening, as the cottage shuddered and the rain slapped down, she made a special effort to be attentive to Alyssa and do whatever she wanted to do.

When they dropped Nora off at home the next day, sunburnt and covered in bug bites and tremendously sleepy, she felt as if she had been away for much longer than a week. As she got out of the van with her overstuffed duffel bag, thanking Alyssa and her parents for everything, then Tracy came barreling out of the house, the screen door banging against the railing on the stoop; she shot out of the house like she'd been shot out of a cannon, leaping down the front steps, yelling Nora's name: "Nora, Nora, Nora, you won't believe what happened while you were gone!"

What had happened was that Pudge had given birth to a litter of kittens. It was true that for the last month or so the cat had been acting strange, sort of listless, moody, and stand-offish, and getting kind of fat now that she thought about it, but they hadn't really noticed at the time. Then a couple days ago it had occurred to Tracy that she hadn't seen Pudge around for a whole day, and it didn't look like her food had been touched, and she was worried that Alma had thrown her outside and she hadn't come back, but then Tracy found her in Nora's bed; she had made a kind of lean-to or cave out of the blankets and there she was, with five little squirmy adorable kittens huddled around her, and Lynn was furious and said they'd have to throw away Nora's bedding and maybe even the mattress, and Alma just said that she'd told them so, this was what you got, and their father was furious too because he swore up and down that when he'd picked out Pudge at the shelter they had assured him that she'd been fixed, and Tracy said that the kittens were so adorable she could almost die.

20

Many pets go missing;
Ms Afton makes a fuss

ONE SPRING the town went through a mysterious epidemic of disappearing pets.

It had been a long and punishing winter, even colder than normal, and with twice as much snow. Casey had missed almost a month of school all told, when the great sweeps and drifts would bury their driveway and trap her family on the farm. So much snow fell, Simon would joke that it were as if God had decided to send another Flood, but this time a frozen one. He was worked off his feet all winter, with barely any time to spend in his greenhouse, there was always so much plowing and shovelling to be done. For as much as he complained about all the work, it clearly did him good: the bloated, puffy look went away from his face, he lost ten pounds, and he had more energy and enthusiasm than he had had in years.

In late February, a section of the roof of the health clinic collapsed under the weight of snow, and a whole wing had to be shut down. It was just lucky that no one was hurt. And even as late as the first weekend of April a blizzard had swept through town and closed it down, and it took three days to dig out from under.

That weekend, a large and not particularly good-tempered tabby named Simba went missing. He belonged to the family that owned the hardware store on 2nd Ave, and they were used to his coming and going as he pleased, sometimes taking off for a day or two before sauntering back home with a smug and rakish air, even in the winter. So when he went out the Thursday before that late and final snowstorm, and this time never came back at all, neither his family nor anyone else was particularly surprised. They blamed it on the blizzard, and maybe they were right.

When spring did come at last, it came abruptly. The weather seemed to go from midwinter bleak to midsummer warm in the space of a scant few weeks, and not even the threat of flash flooding could stop people from relishing it. The sky was blotted with returning geese; the Vermettes lost one of their cats, a sly grey tom named Westie, and no one thought much of that either, not even Scott Vermette, who was in Nora and Casey's class. Maybe he had caught a touch of spring fever and gotten struck by a car or truck trying to cross the highway, or wandered too far off into the woods or fields, maybe fell prey to a coyote or something. There were bound to be a lot of hungry and desperate wild animals out there after such a long relentless winter.

The first dog to disappear, of course, was Vivian's Lancelot. She was distraught. This is how it happened: an icejam, where the Sally and the Whitetail joined, had made the Sally run backwards, and half a dozen homes were flooded out on the Halftown side, including Vivian's. Then she had to move back in for a month or two with her parents, until the waters receded and the damage could be repaired. She blamed Lancelot's disappearance on this, for of course her mother wouldn't let the dog inside, she had to keep him chained up in the yard. If they had been in their own home, and Lancelot was sleeping curled up against Vivian's feet where he belonged, it never would have happened, that was what she firmly believed.

The night he disappeared she had taken a muscle relaxant and a sleeping pill, with maybe a glass of red wine or two to wash it down: the pain in her back had been terrible, sleeping in her childhood bed again with its thin and lumpy mattress, to say nothing of the stress of living with her parents. So though her mother complained bitterly the next morning that Lancelot had kept her up half the night, barking and wheezing until two in the morning, Vivian had slept through it like a stone. Otherwise she might have realized that something was wrong. When she went out in the morning to bring him his food, he simply wasn't there: his collar was still clipped to his chain, but he had somehow slipped it.

She showed up at Lynn's house in tears, almost hysterics. They organized a search party, with Nora, Casey, and Tracy scouring the immediate vicinity of the house, armed with flashlights to peer under porches and patios, and milk bones to lure him out; Simon, Matt, and Matt's son Mark fanned out west, along the outskirts of town and into the edge of farmland; and Trent Pettinger followed the banks of the Sally from the safety of the high south bank until it joined the Whitetail, scanning the surface of the water for any sign that Lancelot might have fallen in, trying to spot the little brown dog's body bobbing amid the thick and broken slabs of grey ice and the black sodden branches. Towards the end of the day it started to drizzle, and they had to call the search off, wet, cold, exhausted and disheartened.

Then there was Orlando, the Jack Russell terrier that belonged to Nora's second cousin James Mazur, who slipped his collar and escaped the yard one day when James was at school—not the first time that had happened, but the first time he hadn't come back by the evening, intensely satisfied and smelling like he had rolled on something dead. And the little black and white cat that belonged to the Anderssen family vanished around the same time. Her name was Merrykat, and she was a meek, gentle, and affectionate animal, who had never been known to venture much outside the Anderssen's yard or stay out longer than a few hours, and never after dark. The Anderssen children made up missing posters with Merrykat's picture on them, and put dozens of them up on telephone poles around town, and the town quickly had them taken down. Farley, who used to prowl around Nora's house and serenade Pudge through the windows, hadn't been seen on their street for weeks. That cat who lived with the Klassens, who had been given a different name by every member of the family and was known variously as Shadow, Blackie, Bob, and Dread, he went missing too. Some thought it must be a wild animal, a coyote or maybe even a lone wolf come down from Riding Mountain, driven to desperate hunger by the long and brutal winter—but no one could say they'd seen or even heard one, and it didn't make sense anyway, that a wild animal like that would come hunting in the middle of a town and leave alone all the animals on the farms around.

It was after both cats belonging to Peggy Afton disappeared that people really began to talk. Never were a pair of cats more assiduously spoiled and pampered, never had a pair of cats less reason to go wandering off; and when Ms Afton swore that neither one of them had ever so much as stepped a paw outside the boundary of her yard, no one doubted it. And yet disappear they did, first Olivier on a Monday afternoon, and then, only three days later, his brother Flamand, sometime in the evening—the very same evening, in fact, when Ms Afton was sitting next to Nora's mother in the basement of St Andrew's Presbyterian Church, discussing fundraising schemes to help the families who had been flooded out by the Sally, and telling anyone who would listen about her Olivier. What made Flamand's disappearance so especially shocking was the fact that Ms Afton had left him inside the house when she went out, not in the yard. It's true that she hadn't locked her doors—no one in that town was much in the habit of locking doors in those days—but the fact remained that Flamand could not possibly have gotten out on his own and must have been let out, lured out, or snatched. Even though Ms Afton was getting elderly, lived alone, and was beginning to go a little deaf, no one who knew her would have questioned her clarity of mind or the trustworthiness of her memory. She was generally considered sharper than most people half her age, and if she said she had left her doors and windows all securely closed and Flamand safe inside, then it was so.

Ms Afton lived alone and always had, in a tidy little bungalow at the top of the hill, three-quarters of her large yard given over to a vegetable garden of prodigious fecundity. She regularly drove the hour down to Brandon to see foreign films or go to recitals and all the way to Winnipeg a dozen or so times a year to do some shopping, attend the symphony, and spend the night at a fancy hotel. On Saturday afternoons she tuned the radio to the live opera broadcast and would allow no one to disturb her, unplugging her phone and cranking the volume on her stereo so loud that in the summer, it could be heard as far away as the cemetery: she owned a very excellent and expensive stereo. Ms Afton had no scruples about making a fuss when Olivier and Flamand were taken: she talked about it constantly, to everyone she encountered; she harried the police, she offered a reward, she paid to have a paragraph put in the *Whittle Tribune*, she even contacted the newspapers in Brandon and succeeded in seeing a few paragraphs put in about the rash of missing pets—a move that lost her the good will of a number of people who had otherwise been inclined to sympathize but felt she was airing the town's dirty laundry to outsiders and embarrassing them all.

A kind of vague disquiet was rippling out across the town now. Some were disturbed, even frightened, not so much by the unknown fate of the animals as by the violation of Ms Afton's home. They started locking their doors when they went out, even if they were only stepping down to the store for fifteen minutes, whether they had a pet or not. Others were morbidly excited, hiding their titillation with an outward show of voluble sympathy or righteous outrage, and indulging in endless speculation. But still there were a few who believed or claimed to believe that people were making a fuss over nothing, and just wished everyone would stop talking about it, even going so far as to hint that Ms Afton was likely a liar who had no doubt left a door ajar, a window open, or Flamand outside, and was now causing all this commotion simply to cover a bad conscience over her own neglect.

A few days later, another dog disappeared: a gregarious mongrel named Sloppy with a bit of terrier in him, a bit of spaniel, and God only knew what else. He was taken off his chain sometime in the middle of the night, snatched right out of his family's back yard, and no one even heard him bark. Once Sloppy had gone, another dog followed the next day, this one disappearing in the middle of the day from the front yard of the Tibbetts family on Queen Street: a tall black poodle named Cleopatra, notoriously nervous with anyone outside her family and known to bite. She was taken so quietly and so boldly that there seemed something almost uncanny in the way it happened, and the family was devastated.

Ms Afton went back to that Brandon reporter, and the follow-up piece in the paper was longer, and more prominently placed; this time the Winnipeg papers picked up the story too, and Cleopatra's family were interviewed on the radio, and the local RCMP were forced to release a statement to the press pretending to be very concerned and actively investigating. And many people didn't even want to think about what could be happening to those poor animals after they were taken, and other people didn't want to think of anything else.

Now there was an older kid named Landon Dueck who had heard his parents talking that it had something to do with all that construction across the highway from the golf course. They were putting in a new gas station with six pumps, with a restaurant and a grocery store attached to it, and next to that a new motel with eight rooms and mini-golf out back. They were supposed to have started working on it the summer before, but there had been all kinds of delays. There was a group of people in town who opposed the whole thing, loudly and angrily, including Lynn—which had caused a lot of tension in the family, for of course Matt was one of the main partners in the project, together with the Pettingers and a group from Waabishkigwan. So the start of the project had been delayed until after winter, and then the winter was so long and spring so late, that was another delay; and now they were working overtime to try and get it back on schedule, they had even brought in a bunch of workers from outside. What all that had to do with people's pets was another question. Nora remembered reading once that a long time ago, people used to bury the body of a small animal or even a human baby in the foundation when they built a bridge or a castle or something big like that, to sort of propitiate the devil, or the earth itself for building such a heavy weight on top of it; but that was a long long time ago, and anyway, it was always just one animal, not dozens of them. But according to Landon, his parents figured that it was probably one or more of those construction workers who they'd brought in, a group of mostly unskilled labourers off the reserve, and you know what *those* people are like.

Casey had her own idea about it, vague and inchoate, an idea she had avoided trying to think through even to herself, let alone try to articulate or express to Nora or anyone else. Her idea was that the animals were not being taken at all, but simply leaving, escaping—perhaps responding to the intuition of some impending disaster, or to some hitherto dormant instinct for freedom and independence. Sometimes she thought of it like the Underground Railway, sometimes almost like the Rapture. She expected it to keep spreading—perhaps it was already happening in other places, other towns and cities across the country, and they just hadn't heard about it yet. She expected to wake up any morning and find not only Panger, Rusty, and Mud but even all the mares and newborn foals on their farm vanished without a trace. If she had tried to ask herself where the animals were disappearing *to*, she could not possibly have answered, beyond a vague "Some place better"—meaning, probably, "Some place without people." She tried to avoid thinking too clearly about it, but the idea gave her a kind of grim exhilaration that, in turn, made her feel guilty when she remembered the sadness of Juliet and April, and James, and the Anderssens, and Ms Afton and the others, or when she thought of how devastated Nora would be when Pudge joined the others.

"I'm just glad that Pudge never goes outside," said Nora, not for the first time, late one night when she, Casey, and Alyssa were downstairs in her basement, pretending to be going to sleep.

It was the weekend of Nora's thirteenth birthday, and the three girls, along with Juliet, April, and Tracy, had spent the afternoon down in Brandon, where they had gone to a movie and spent an hour or two at the arcade before being driven back to Nora's house for pizza, cake, and ice cream, and a game of hide and seek out on the street, in the soft and fading evening.

"Of course she doesn't," said Casey, who was sitting cross-legged in the middle of the bed, teasing Pudge with a crumpled scrap of wrapping paper, holding it above her head, letting her bat it out of her hand before snatching it back and starting again. "You're too lazy to go outside, aren't you? Just a big fat lazy cat." It was true that Pudge had put on a lot of weight in the past year or so, after finally getting fixed; Nora suspected that her grandmother slipped her cans of tuna and other treats when no one was around to catch her at it.

Nora was sitting up against the couch back now, surrounded by a small pile of her birthday presents. Her father had bought her an acoustic guitar, all gleaming and new, and a book for beginners: she'd opened that present the evening before, and she and Casey had spent several hours taking turns plucking and pressing and strumming at it, eliciting noises that had some phantom resemblance to music, until their fingertips were too sore to continue. From Alyssa she had received a makeup kit in a lovely wooden box with a mirror on the inside of the lid; after the party, they had brought it downstairs with them and practised giving themselves and each other makeovers, caking the mascara, blush, and lipstick on with awkward and unpracticed hands. Nora sat now with the box at her side, occasionally glancing sidelong at the reflection of her now strangely unfamiliar face.

They had played with the makeup, and examined the other presents—music, a poster, two books, a locked and fancy diary from Juliet—and they talked about the movie they'd gone to that afternoon, and their friends, and school, and Casey made a joke about Alyssa's brother Anthony having a crush on Nora and Nora said shut up, he did not, but Alyssa was giggling and said, "Oh, he *so* does, it's so obvious." Nora herself had a bit of a crush on an older boy named Keith Lacoste who had recently moved there from Waabishkigwan, and whose sullen, inarticulate, and moody restlessness her imagination transformed into an air of brooding romance and secret tragedy. Keith's one real enthusiasm was a talent for drawing in the hyper-stylized fashion of comic books: mostly wild animals and grotesque monsters, wild foreboding landscapes, muscular men, and lithe, large-breasted women. His binders and notebooks were covered with such pictures, inside and out; he made them in pen on his backpack and his shoes, in pencil on napkins in the lunchroom, and even on his own arm, if he had nothing else handy.

Recently Keith had started putting this skill to use by offering to draw memorial pictures for kids whose pets had disappeared, if they had any photographs he could work from. The friends had seen one of these, a picture of the cat that had belonged to Scott Vermette: done carefully in pencil on a large sheet of paper and delicately shaded in with pastels, it was a bold departure from his usual violent style. He had evidently struggled with getting the right expression on Westie's face, for he had never before drawn an animal that didn't have its teeth bared in a threatening or savage manner, and that portion of the drawing showed traces of repeated erasures; but other than that, the girls agreed, it was perfect. Alyssa joked that they should spread the word that Pudge had disappeared too, just so Nora could have an excuse to talk to Keith and ask him to draw a picture for her. But Nora, who was getting tired now and felt abruptly sentimental, said, "Don't even joke about that." She leaned forward suddenly, scooped Pudge up from behind, and pulled her to her lap, wrapping her long arms squeezingly around the startled cat and kissing the top of her head, saying, "Pudge won't go missing, Pudge won't go."

Later that week, the town held an open meeting at the community centre, because there didn't seem to be anything else to do. Nora's mother was torn between not wanting to hear about it, and not wanting to miss out on anything; in the end, she attended, as Nora knew she would.

The mayor was there, and all five town councillors, together with a representative from the RCMP, all sitting behind a long wooden folding table at the front, looking tired, wary, baffled, and irritable. Ms Sawchuk had brought that reporter from the *Brandon Sun*, who sat next to her right in the front row; Lady's family had contacted CBC radio, who had sent a reporter and a sound guy, who was setting up his recording equipment at the back when Lynn arrived.

There were Fanny and Jim Ritchie and their daughter Annaliese. The Vermettes were sitting next to the Anderssens, such a nice couple, and there was that man who owned the hardware store, his name was Simmins. Sam Goode, of course, who ran the *Whittle Tribune*. Marjorie Jensen who ran the town's only bed and breakfast, sitting with the minister from St Andrew's and that young woman who worked in the bakery, the one with that mole under her left eye. And there were Matt and Louise, in a little group with Trent and Benji Pettinger and Albert Lacoste from Waabishkigwan, the four men talking to one another in terse low voices, and they had set tense faces like they had come expecting trouble.

The meeting was not much of a success. In the beginning, people were reluctant to speak much, being made cautious and self-conscious by the reporters and the microphones. Neither the mayor nor the mountie had any satisfying answers to give, any insights or useful suggestions to make. Graham Dueck, with his wife at his elbow prompting and prodding him, hesitantly floated the suggestion that it might be one of those construction workers come up from Waabishkigwan. This might have been a popular idea, but Benji Pettinger and Matt Wellesley were there to angrily and emphatically shut that down, while Albert Lacoste glared stonily and intimidatingly around the room. Matt personally supervised all those workers, he said, who were only there to do a hard and honest job and frankly didn't have the spare time to spend catching and diddling a bunch of damn house cats.

But most of the people in town felt certain that it must be one of the local teenagers who were to blame, likely while high on drugs of some kind; and one woman said she'd heard that it was all to do with some terrible Satanic ritual, and that the animals were being taken to sacrifice to the devil.

"Have you gone and looked at the old Stone School?" the same woman asked. "Because what I've heard is the old Stone School is where they're taking the animals to kill them, that's what I've heard." This was Ms Denison, who taught French of a sort at the high school, so it wasn't difficult to guess where she had heard it.

"Seriously?" said the mayor. "Seriously? I'm begging you, don't get started with that kind of shit." The mounties hadn't searched the old Stone School, he went on, and in his steadily mounting frustration with the whole meeting, he added that the mounties had more important things to do than waste their time chasing down every idiotic rumour and old wives' tales the town could throw at them, they had real crimes to worry about.

That brought an outburst of angry voices from the crowd that those microphones greedily and gratefully drank in, to be replayed on the radio three times the next day, at length, with the mayor's scabrous outburst even making a brief embarrassing appearance on the national broadcast in the evening, the obscenity prominently bleeped.

IT WAS CASEY who found the collar belonging to Olivier, caught on a branch downstream from the jungle gym. This was on a Friday in May, the warmest day of the year so far, and the river had slowly started to dwindle back down into a creek: the branch the collar was caught on must have been under water only a week or so before. Casey very nearly lost her shoe going down to retrieve it, the deep slick mud sucking it right off her foot as she leaned forward. She had to dig the shoe out and half-hop with it back up to the picnic table, scraping it clean as best she could with a stick before putting it back on her foot.

Those days Nora spent most her lunch hours at volleyball practice, so Casey, having no one to eat with, was in the habit of coming down to the park over the lunch hour, eating her sandwich on the way and then rambling by the river until it was time to return to school. Then she would lose track of time, and she was often late getting back for class; this day she didn't get back at all.

The collar was leather, studded with rhinestones, and Olivier's name engraved on a little nickel plate attached to the front. Casey's first impulse, of course, was to show it to Nora. But by the time she got back to school the bell had long since rung and classes begun.

If she went in, she'd be stuck there until the bus took her home and wouldn't have a chance to return the collar to Ms Afton until Monday lunch at the earliest. Casey had always found Ms Afton, or the idea of her at least, deeply appealing: she seemed to possess the secret of living precisely the way she wanted, gently and generously and utterly independent, without caring what anyone else thought. It would naturally never have occurred to Casey, young as she was, that this seeming secret could be explained by the fact that Ms Afton was lucky enough to be reasonably wealthy.

So instead of entering the school, Casey headed up the hill. Lilacs stained the warm soft breeze; green shot weeds pushed their way through cracks in the sidewalk. A red-winged blackbird curled overhead, gliding low past the Co-op and then climbing effortlessly into the sky. Ms Afton's home sat on the road that ran along the high south bank of the Sally, near where it went under the bridge and flowed into the Whitetail. It wasn't the largest house along that strip of road, but it was by far the prettiest and the best kept, painted a deep forest green and adorned with a smiling red clay sun above the picture window. An old-fashioned weather vane was mounted to the roof, rooster, rust, and all; the copper silhouette of a young deer stood in the flowerbed beneath the window, head bent to graze.

Casey had hoped and fully expected to find Ms Afton working outside in her garden on such a lovely day, but the yard was empty and the garden looked as though it had yet to be started that year. That Ms Afton was actually at home seemed almost certain: the living room window was open and the sound of the radio was leaking through, some kind of piano music, to Casey's ears tuneless, aimless, and melancholy.

She went through the gate and up the walk with some reluctance, suddenly shy. There was something about the mere act of ringing a doorbell that she found foolishly daunting: she had simply never done it before in her life, never had occasion to. She wished that Nora was with her. When she pressed the bell, she left a little smear of mud on it and was acutely reminded of just how dirty she was: both shoes caked with mud, both hands covered in it, smears of it on her jeans, her shirt, and almost certainly her face.

She heard the sound of the deadbolt turning back, and the door opened a few inches, just far enough for Ms Afton to put her face through the opening. "Yes?" she said loudly. "What is it? Who are you?" Her flat pale face was wrinkled and frowning, and Casey felt small, intrusive, and embarrassed.

"I found this by the creek," she began to say, holding up the collar, but Ms Afton cut her off.

"You don't look familiar," the old woman said coolly, almost accusingly. "I don't recognize you, you're not from here."

"My name's Casey Mack," said Casey timidly, unsure whether to add, "Ma'am."

"Speak up," Ms Afton snapped, opening the door just a little wider and turning her head slightly. "Stop mumbling."

"My name is Casey Mack, ma'am." She found that she was, absurdly, on the verge of tears. "We have a farm off 466…"

"Mack," repeated Ms Afton—at first blankly, and then once more, with the crisp satisfaction of recognition clicking into place: "Mack. The horse-piss people. You're friends with the Wellesley girls."

"Yes, ma'am."

"Those are nice girls. Well, speak up, what do you want? Shouldn't you be in school?"

"Sorry, ma'am. But I found this down by the creek." She held up the collar again, making sure that Olivier's nameplate was facing out. "It was caught in some branches. By the creek, where the water went down. I found it, and I thought... I just thought I ought to bring it to you, I thought you might want to have it."

And she stood there holding it out, but Ms Afton made no move to accept it from her. She wasn't even really looking at it, instead looking Casey appraisingly up and down, from her mud-caked boots to her tangled mess of hair. Then she stepped back and opened the door widely, saying, "Well, you'd better come in."

Casey took off her shoes, but she could hardly take off her sock, which was almost as wet and muddy, and she could hardly bear to look back to see if she left prints on Ms Afton's immaculate floor. The house inside was the neatest and the cleanest she'd ever seen. There was no clutter on the coffee table, no dirty dishes on the end tables waiting to be dealt with later; no piles of papers, mail, and bills on the table or buffet, not so much as a book out of place on the tall long shelves. Everything was dusted, polished, and perfectly clean. All the furniture was wood, dark and warm, even the legs and arms of the matching sofa and loveseat: curved and carved, the legs ending whimsically in the shape of talons, with four fat toes, three in front and one behind, splayed against the floor. There was only one exception: a comfortable-looking old armchair by the fireplace, wide and soft, its threadbare fabric covered in a fine layer of cat fur and here and there clawed right through to the straw-coloured stuffing underneath.

Casey sat on the end of the couch closest to that cat chair, as if hoping she might look less conspicuously out of place in its proximity. She perched on the very edge of the seat, deeply conscious of the smears of mud on her jeans and shirt and everywhere else, and she had no idea what to do with her hands.

A single picture hung on the wall, but it was enormous: a real painting, in tones of mostly grey and muted greens and browns, of a mountain stream tumbling down a slight precipice and foaming against the rocks beneath. Tall, sparse, and skinny pines grew on the slopes around it, stretching up above the frame, with shafts of sunlight angling down between them. But Casey was struck less by what the picture depicted than by the fact that she could see the uneven texture of the paint on its surface: she could make out the very shape of the brushstrokes, dried and preserved, and here and there beads of clumpy colour, and raised trails where the paint had dripped down out of place.

Ms Afton came from the kitchen carrying a tray with a pitcher of iced tea, two flowered tumblers, a pair of coasters, a damp rag, and a small plate of gingersnaps; and it was not until Casey had accepted a glass of tea and a cookie that she finally took Olivier's collar from her. Then she sat down too, taking a seat on the couch right next to Casey, so close their legs were almost touching: so close that Casey shrank inside herself, and had to battle down a momentary panicked urge to flee. On the stereo the piano piece had come to a tinkling and meandering end, and the radio announcer in his deep and soporific voice was telling some anecdote about Brahms and Schumann and some piece they had composed together with a friend.

"Now," said Ms Afton, taking the damp rag from the tray and beginning to carefully, methodically polish the collar. "Now tell me how you found this."

So Casey did, briefly at first, forced to repeat some parts more loudly even though the old lady was sitting so close to her. It didn't help, Casey thought, that Ms Afton hadn't turned down the stereo, which was now blaring out some urgent and plaintive violin piece. She took a bite of gingersnap: it was hard and extremely dry and burst in a spray of crumbs.

Ms Afton continued to ask her questions, pressing her for precise details: as where exactly along the river she had found it, how far above the receding water, and what sort of bush it had been snagged on; how Casey had come to notice it, and what she was doing down there by the river anyway, and whether anyone else had been around. And when she ran out of those sorts of questions to ask, she started asking Casey about herself: whether she liked school, if she had many friends, what life was like on her parents' farm, how she passed the time, what she wanted to be when she grew up. And all the time they talked, Ms Afton kept her face down and continued wiping and polishing the collar with that rag, though she'd long since made it as clean as it was going to get. Casey noticed that her hands and bony fingers were knotty, crabbed, and inclined to shake; they were lined with thick blue veins raised along the surface of her wrinkly skin like the trails of dripped colour on the painting; and Casey looked at Ms Afton's face and she could see a smear of tears coming down from the corner of her eye, and she thought how tired Ms Afton looked, how frail, and how her face was like a crumpled piece of paper. And when they were finally done, she had to sprint all the way down the hill and barely made it back to school in time to scramble on the bus before it pulled away; she didn't even have time to tell Nora where she'd been all day, and had to phone her when she got home.

The next day, a pair of RCMP officers dropped by the farm, just before lunch. Casey, who had spent the morning with her father out in the fields, watching the foals with their gangly legs as they skittered and played, was washing up in the bathroom when she heard Rusty and Mud burst into a sudden frenzy of cheerful barking as the car came up the drive. That was surprising enough, they never had unexpected visitors at the farm; and then she heard the siren go twice around, and she tossed down the hand towel and raced outside to see.

The police car had pulled into the drive behind her father's truck. Rusty was jumping and scratching at the passenger door playfully, while Mud was staying a little further away, moving back and forth in a rapid little dance and barking with frantic enthusiasm. One of the mounties had rolled down his window part way and was yelling at Casey's father, asking him to control those damn dogs so they could get out of the vehicle. Her father was trying to assure the men that the dogs were harmless and only wanted to play, but the officers didn't seem at all convinced, so he and Casey collared the dogs and dragged them to the house and shut them up in the mudroom. That lasted about two minutes, just long enough for the men to get out of their car and introduce themselves, before Casey's mother came outside to see what was going on and let the dogs back out with her. They came bursting out of the door on either side of her and surged towards the officers, tails wagging manically, eager to get a really good sniff of these strangers now that they had left their vehicle. One of the mounties stiffened and froze, the other actually leapt backwards, bumping up against the car, and Casey could have sworn she saw him make a feint towards his gun before she and her father got Rusty and Mud by the scruffs of their necks and forced them to sit.

"You never know with strange dogs," said Officer Garnett once they were safely inside. He sounded belligerent, embarrassed, and defensive, and he started to tell a story about a mountie they worked with who'd dropped by a farm not far from there just to ask a few routine questions and ended up having to get seven stitches and a whole battery of shots; and that farmer, too, had assured the officer his dogs were friendly and perfectly harmless.

"They say human bites are even worse," Maureen said cheerfully. "I once knew a young woman who got bit by a man on the arm. Turned all purple and swelled up like a football. She had to spend half a month in a hospital bed getting antibiotics through a tube."

"That's terrible," said Officer Powell. He was even larger than his partner: burly as a linebacker, with an incongruously high-pitched, squeaky voice. The two of them were too big for that little kitchen; they made it look like a child's play-set. No one sat down: the officers stood side by side between the table and the door; Casey's father stood at the far side of the table with his hands in his pockets, eyeing his lunch glumly: there were two plates of coleslaw, french fries, and bacon cheese and asparagus sandwiches on the table, for him and Casey, getting cold. Casey's mother took up her usual spot by the sink, and Casey herself stood next to the fridge, shrunk up against the counter and trying not to be noticed. "That's terrible," said Officer Powell. "Why'd the guy bite her, anyway?"

"Well, I *was* very pretty in those days," said Maureen. "I guess I just looked too delicious to resist. And I suppose I mustn't have minded too much, because we got married later that year, and here we are, still together."

Casey's father interrupted now to ask the officers if he could offer them coffee, or lemonade, or anything else they'd like.

"You folks go ahead and eat," said Garnett. "Don't mind us, we ate already. You go ahead and eat your lunch before it gets too cold, nothing worse than cold bacon."

"You're having us on," squeaked Powell. He had apparently been giving it serious consideration. "That never happened, you're having us on."

Casey's father, who was extremely hungry but felt too bashful to eat in front of the police, said desperately, "What can we do for you, officers? What brings you out here?" The bacon and melted cheese on the sandwiches were congealing, the toasted bread probably ossifying: too much longer and his lunch would be inedible, even reheated.

The officers exchanged furtive and embarrassed glances. "The fact is," Powell said, with elaborate reluctance, "well, I'm afraid that Ms Afton—you know Ms Afton, I suppose?"

"Never met the woman," said Casey's mother, and her father shook his head blankly; but Casey could feel herself turning red as she meekly said, "I know Ms Afton." She was squatting down now, looking as small as possible between the fridge and the cupboards, scratching Panger's neck as he pushed his body up against her. She was thinking, with a guilty conscience and something close to panic, of the round wooden coaster, old and scuffed, that she had slipped into her pocket and brought home with her from Ms Afton's house, and that had now joined her store of pilfered treasures. That the old lady would have actually called the mounties over a missing coaster, that the mounties wouldn't have just laughed and hung up on her—it seemed wildly implausible, yet here they were.

"Yes," said Powell. "Well, I'm afraid that Ms Afton has it stuck in her head that your young lady here is the one who took her cats, and probably killed them too."

Casey could feel her cheeks blaze with sudden heat, and everyone was looking at her: Powell with pity, Garnett with sly intent, her father with confused concern, her mother with frank amusement. Even Panger was looking up at her, and mriaowed accusingly; and the blood was pounding behind her ears and the tears were springing up to her eyes and it was all she could do to keep from running from the room, and her thin little body writhed and vibrated with the effort of restraint.

It was easy enough to prove that Casey had been safely at home on the farm the evening Olivier disappeared, and no possible way to get there. "Though I suppose she could have taken one of the mares," suggested her mother helpfully, "and galloped bareback into town to snatch this woman's cat."

Nor had Casey been in town the night Lady was taken from the family on Queen Street, or for several of the other disappearances either, though her mother generously offered to lie and claim that Casey had no alibi for any of it: "This might be the most attention you ever get in your life," she told her. "You might as well enjoy it while it lasts."

By Monday morning, everybody at school seemed to already know about Casey finding that collar and taking it to Ms Afton, and even all about the RCMP coming out to the farm. It was all anyone wanted to talk about, even the principal when she was sent to his office first thing, supposedly to get lectured about skipping school on Friday afternoon but really to get probed for gossip.

When Alma heard about Casey finding that collar in the river, left behind by the receding flood, she said, "What did I tell you?" with a kind of cryptic satisfaction. "You'll see, now that the river's going down, we won't hear any more foolishness about pets disappearing."

Nora couldn't remember her grandmother having said anything of the kind, and exactly how the two things might be related Alma couldn't or wouldn't say. "You'll see," she just repeated, "you mark my words." That night as Nora fell asleep she had a strange, unsettling vision of the river itself, swollen and insatiably hungry, calling out and hypnotizing the pets to break their chains, slip their collars, escape their homes, and come down to drown themselves.

THE FOLLOWING AUTUMN, when everyone was back in school and the Spring of Disappearing Pets was beginning to feel like a bad dream or the distant past, a new rumour about it started making the rounds: that a homeless man had moved in to the old Stone School and had been secretly living there all that spring, and that it was he who had been stealing people's pets, for the tragic and awful purpose of eating them to survive. He no doubt chose domestic animals over wild ones simply because they were easier to catch.

According to the story Nora heard, the man had gone to that school as a child, one of the last to graduate before it was finally closed down, and he had never gotten over the trauma of being ripped from his family as a young child, nor the abuse he had suffered in his years there: the beatings, humiliation, and molestation. In the decades since, he had drifted aimlessly around, working sporadically between ferocious bouts of drinking, in and out of prisons for petty crimes and misdemeanours, prisons that must have reminded him irresistibly of his school days; at last living on the streets, huffing glue and gasoline: anything to try and kill off those relentless black shadows of memory that were eating away at his soul. How or why he had drifted at last back to the now abandoned school where all his misery had begun, who could say? But come back he had, making a home of sorts in the old boiler room in the basement. He had pulled one of the old desks down there too: they found a torn and moldy textbook open on it, as if he had been reliving the days of his education.

According to the rumours, the bones and remains of at least two dozen cats and dogs were heaped in the old cold furnace, rotting and putrid, covered with so many black and gluttonous flies you could hear the buzzing halfway up the stairwell, and the smell was so foul and poisonous they could barely force themselves to approach. He had even made a clumsy attempt to skin several of the larger animals and stretch their hides, in a kind of botched and futile burst of atavism. They found the man too, or his body anyway. He'd been dead several days at least when they had discovered the corpse, his body swollen with grief, his face bloated and pocked and scarred with the long years of abuse, exposure, and hard living, yet with an expression in death strangely peaceful, almost beatific, like a sleeping child. His fingerprints allowed them to identify the man and piece together his sad history; he had no family left, no friends, not a person on the surface of the earth he belonged to, who knew him or who loved him.

That was the story that went around. Why the RCMP would have hushed it up, what possible reason there might have been for keeping it secret, no one could say; and even then, Nora felt pretty sure the whole thing was bullshit.

21

Casey buys a bike;
the girls spend time in the cemetery

CASEY ASKED HER MOTHER ONCE if *she* ever dreamed while she was sleeping, and Maureen said, "Of course I do, every night, I'm not a monster."

She told Casey a story about a woman she once knew, who dreamed every night that she had cut herself on something, some silly accident: a piece of broken glass, the lid from a tin can, that kind of thing. In her dreams, she said, this woman would just bleed and bleed and bleed, like a hemophiliac; and in her waking life she was starting to get pale, and short of breath, and she was tired all the time, until one day she collapsed at the grocery store. Just crumpled down in a heap on the floor and didn't move. They rushed her to the hospital, and the doctors said she had anemia due to excessive blood loss, and gave her an emergency transfusion.

Maureen said she also knew of another woman who dreamt that she got pregnant, and then when she was awake she had to get an abortion. Hard to blame her, Maureen admitted, though it would have been fascinating to know what the baby might have been like.

That year, Casey bought herself a bike. She had earned the money working for her father through the winter: scrubbing the rubber boots, scraping out the stalls. He paid her about a quarter of what he would pay a farmhand, though she worked probably twice as hard.

She bought the bike in the spring; Nora and Nora's father drove her down to Brandon and helped her pick out a really good one. Simon bought a new one for Nora too on that same trip, for she had long outgrown her old one, the same bike that Casey had learned to ride on.

Soon Casey could manage the ride from the farm into town with little effort at all; soon she could come and go as she pleased, whenever she pleased, and mostly she went.

In July, Nora went away to Alyssa's cottage again, this time staying for ten whole days, leaving Casey all alone. Now, Casey didn't resent this, or blame Nora for abandoning her, anything that Nora did was right in her eyes: but she couldn't help feeling aimless without her, bored, horribly lonely, trapped and unhappy.

So those ten days that Nora was gone, Casey spent mostly on her bike and on foot, alone, rambling about the back roads, following the creeks and streams and railway tracks, finding narrow paths through the bush, making herself familiar with the face of each individual tree. She had no plan, no thought at all beyond the persistent and overwhelming urge to go.

If Nora had been with her, they might have pretended that they were intrepid explorers in some undiscovered land, or a pair of desperate fugitives fleeing justice, or implacable trackers hunting down a pair of desperate fugitives, or plucky orphans lost in a haunted forest. But Nora wasn't with her, and she didn't pretend anything. She didn't talk to herself, either, no matter how lonely she might have felt: her mother liked to talk to herself, and she was determined not to do things her mother would do.

One morning she stole away from home early enough to watch the sun rise from the cemetery on the hill, splashing fistfuls of pastel and salmon pink across the stippled clouds, and the old Stone School all lit from behind and glowing like a hot coal. She lay on the ground, in the dew-cool grass, and the dew soaked through her pants and shirt, and she nearly fell back to sleep.

One evening, as she was slowly winding her way back home,

hot and tired and very hungry, walking her bike across a fallow and rock-strewn pasture, she got caught in a sudden rain shower that seemed to blow up out of nowhere, fat cold drops that came spattering down in gusts though the sky was hardly more than half-streaked with thin clouds and the sun never stopped shining. It had been a dry summer, dusty and hot, and Casey didn't even look for shelter, she laid her bike down and danced in the rain, holding her face up to the heavens. It lasted perhaps five minutes, and then it was over as abruptly as it had begun, but it left behind a delicious coolness and a shimmering quiet.

One day she stumbled upon a lake, a little hidden lake, not much bigger than a pond but immensely deep and perfectly clear, and the sunlight shimmered off the gently rippling surface. There were no beaches; the trees and grass all around it grew right up to the water's edge. It was so beautiful it snatched her breath away, it almost hurt it was so lovely to look at.

She could see no cabins or cottages anywhere, no boats or docks, no sign of human beings whatsoever. She listened intently, unmoving. No sound of distant traffic, no human sounds at all. Nothing but the faint rustling of the wind caressing the treetops, the lazy buzzing of a few drowsy flies. Under the midday sun, even the birds were silent. Reassured, Casey stripped down to her underwear and carefully stepped into the water. It was shockingly cold, and then it was deliciously cool. The rocks underfoot were both slick and jagged, and she had to step carefully, gingerly. It got deep quickly, and then about six feet out from shore, the bottom fell away abruptly, and the water was well over her head.

Casey was not as strong or natural a swimmer as Nora, but she was in no danger, she could keep her head above the surface without difficulty. And she could swim deftly underwater, eel-like.

She splashed around for a while, and then made her way back to shore. She sat on the grass at the edge of the water, and then she lay on her back on the grass at the edge of the water. She had to close her eyes against the bright of the sun, and it was still too bright, and she covered her face with her t-shirt, and she felt her body gratefully soaking up the heat of the sun. She daydreamed: how she would come back here with Nora, and it would be their own private lake. They could build a lean-to, and a firepit, and camp out, and it would be their own private cottage, and Nora would love it much better than Alyssa's cottage, and they would never tell anyone else about it. She daydreamed, and then she dozed.

When she woke, she was badly sunburnt: she felt baked, dehydrated, and slightly nauseous. Disoriented, too—unsure how long she had slept—several hours at least, judging by the sun. She went back into the water, tumbled in awkwardly and plunged underneath when the bottom fell away. She swam down and down. She could see perfectly the slime and undulating weeds along the bottom, the water was that clear. She saw a rock that seemed to have a face: two dimpled eyes, a puggish nose, a gawping hollow spot for an open mouth. The rock was about the size of a toddler's head. But it was too slick to grip and too heavy to lift, too firmly embedded in the lake bottom to even budge, and then she was running out of breath. As she turned her body to resurface, she lifted her head into a cloud of red, and as she swam upwards she saw that there were swirls and billows of red following her through the water: she had sliced open the pad of her foot on a rock or something and hadn't even realized it.

THAT WAS THE SUMMER that the girls became obsessed, briefly but passionately, with Isak Dinesen. It all started at Alyssa's cottage, for Alyssa's mother was just finishing *Out of Africa*. Her copy of the book had the picture from the movie poster on the cover, with Meryl Streep and Robert Redford in the long grass, lit with a nimbus of sunlight, and the Ngong Hills—presumably—in the background. Now, Nora had gone to see that movie, at the theatre out in Brandon, with her mother and her amma, and it had left a strong impression on her. She had found it sweepingly, swooningly romantic in a way she had been embarrassed to admit.

She asked Alyssa's mother if she might read the book while she was staying there, and Mrs Shaw said, "Of *course*, dear, you're welcome to try. I warn you, though, it isn't much like the movie, you might be a little disappointed. But you're welcome to try it."

Now, if Mrs Shaw hadn't said that, Nora might well *have* been disappointed, and might have quickly given up on it. It was certainly unlike the movie and unlike any book she'd read before. But she persisted with it out of pride and with Mrs Shaw's unintentionally condescending words in the back of her head. She read the book slowly, painstakingly, puzzling out the many unfamiliar words and vividly placing herself in the Baroness Blixen's shoes at all points. She pushed through until she came to the story of Kamante, which engrossed her entirely, and after that it wasn't any kind of effort any more.

If parts of the book bored or merely baffled her, there were enough and more than enough moments that moved, beguiled, excited or delighted her, or that she found intoxicating in their strangeness, and ultimately exhilarating: a way of looking at things, of understanding the world, that was completely new to her, and more foreign and exotic than pet storks and gazelles, plagues of grasshoppers and whips made of hippo hide: "My life, I will not let you go except you bless me, but then I will let you go."

Alyssa, perhaps a little jealous that Nora was spending half their time together with her nose in a book, decided that she would read it next and become obsessed with it too. Of course as soon as Nora got back to Whittle, she told Casey that she had to read it. They discovered that the town's library not only had two copies of *Africa*, but also another book by Dinesen called *Winter's Tales*. That book turned out to be rather different, a little easier to get into but satisfyingly strange in its own way.

Meanwhile, Alyssa's mother, happy to encourage her daughter's new enthusiasm, bought copies of the *Seven Gothic Tales* and the *Anecdotes of Destiny* the next time she went to town, and later picked up a strange novel called the *Angelic Avengers* that had yet a different name under the title, but that she assured them was just another of Karen Blixen's pseudonyms. All these books the friends passed eagerly from one to another, swallowing them whole, reading and rereading and then getting together to compare notes, preferences, and impressions.

By the time school started in the fall, the three friends had begun talking to one another in a kind of private, hermetic language of quotes and references. If one of them received a particularly good grade on a school assignment, or had been otherwise singled out for praise, the other two would ask her, "Did the son of the Sultan like the sauce of the pig? Did he eat it all?" Of anyone they took a liking to, they would say: "She is a Hottentot. But I want her." If ever bored, one of them might melodramatically declare, "If I do not soon get a little bit of fun, I shall die." Or she might solemnly inquire, apropos of almost anything, "How did they know which was the front and which was the back?" They spoke of brazen-serpenting, and rated people according to how good a brazen-serpent they would make. They addressed one another as "Honourable Lioness." They gave each other secret code names derived from the books: Alyssa was Lulu, Nora was Lucan, and so Casey of course had to be Zosine, though she didn't really think it suited her, except maybe for the hair. All of this was thoroughly alienating and irritating to everyone around them, which only magnified the amusement it gave them and increased their delight.

But it was Casey, in fact, who was the most devoted to the books, and the last of them to let go and move on to new and other interests. For when she had first read *Out of Africa*, starting it dutifully and not wanting to disappoint Nora, she had quickly discovered in Dinesen, not quite a kindred soul, but rather someone she had never imagined could actually exist in this world, but that she had obscurely felt was what the world exactly lacked. Not having seen the movie nor having ever seen a picture of the real Baroness, she was free to imagine her precisely like Nora, but as an adult. And then when she came to the chapter on "the Swaheli Numeral System," then it was as if Dinesen was speaking directly to her, signalling in a code that others couldn't or wouldn't understand, "I'm privy to the mysteries of the universe, you might glimpse some of them if you know how to decipher what I write."

IN THOSE DAYS Casey had decided to see how small she could make her handwriting, while still keeping it reasonably neat and legible—legible at least to her. Eventually she would get it down to thirty or more words a line, microscopic squiggles to every eye but hers, and then her friends would say, "How can you even read that?" and they really couldn't read it, but she could, usually, and that was tremendously gratifying. In the meantime, it gave her something to do, to pass the time in class, while still making it look as if she were studying, or doing her schoolwork. So she kept her pencils very sharp, which was good; but she also chewed her pencils, chewed them until flakes of paint and soggy fragments of wood would come off in her mouth, and coat her tongue and get caught in her teeth, and that was bad, and also disgusting.

Alyssa took to wearing her hair in pigtails again, which she hadn't done since third grade, and also to wearing her older brothers' t-shirts that she stole from their dresser drawers, and that would hang down almost to her knees, and this infuriated them. Nora sometimes brushed her long hair forward so that it covered her face completely, and then she could peer out at the world through a hazy golden curtain, and she would say teasingly to her friends, "You can't *seeeee* me," and they would roll their eyes and say, "Yes, Nora, you're invisible," or "Who's speaking? Where's that voice coming from?" and she would laugh with delight.

They spent New Year's Eve at Alyssa's place. Her brothers had all gone out to parties of their own, at other friends' houses, even Anthony. Alyssa's parents let them each have a half-glass of champagne when midnight struck. That night there were northern lights. It was after midnight. The girls were in Alyssa's room, half-settled for sleep and telling secrets, when Alyssa's father knocked on the door and told them they had to come and see. They wrapped themselves in blankets and huddled together on the back deck, their breath forming thick clouds of ice crystals. It was a cloudless sky, a new moon, and a still and frigid night. At first it was just a flicker of pale green here, a flare of pale green there, and then it was gone, so that you almost wondered if you'd really seen it. Then it was a shimmering, flickering pillar of light that unfolded outwards, and unfolded outward again, so that it became a curtain of light across the sky, billowing in a celestial wind: sometimes pale green, sometimes pale blue, sometimes a ghostly white that was also almost pink. And then it wasn't a curtain of light, but a waterfall of light pouring down the sky, and then it was shimmering and fading away, once again a flicker of light here, a flare of light there, spectral and elusive. It seemed to Casey that she could not only see it but hear it, too, a sort of faint delightful sound that was sometimes a humming, sometimes a fluttering sort of noise, and sometimes like the sound of water rushing over rocks, somewhere in the distance. Alyssa, who was always most sensitive to the cold, went inside first; Casey stayed out longer than anyone, even after the last flicker of light had long since disappeared. She lingered, wistfully, freezing cold but reluctant to leave, just in case it might start again.

Juliet wasn't with them for New Year's because Juliet's family had gone to Cuba for the Christmas holidays. It was true, too, that lately Juliet had been growing more distant from the three friends, was spending less and less time with them outside the classroom, stopped sharing in their secrets and their in-jokes. It had happened so gradually they had hardly noticed it at the time, even Alyssa, who had once been so close to her.

Then Casey was the first to turn fifteen. Alyssa's braces came off, and one time she came to school wearing pyjamas, and she was sent home and made to change into proper clothes, even though they were very nice pyjamas and perfectly clean, it's not like she had slept in them the night before, it was *so* unfair. Nora was finding it harder and harder to get to sleep at night, and even harder to wake up on time in the morning, and her mother was always giving her a hard time about stockpiling dirty cups, bowls, and plates in her bedroom, because even though she usually ate a good dinner she always seemed to get ravenously hungry around midnight, like a gremlin, and would sneak down to the kitchen for food that she could smuggle back up to her room, and her father said it was like living with a raccoon. She never ate breakfast any more but would stay in her room until the last possible moment before running out the door to get to school.

Juliet wore glasses now. In February she dyed her hair. She did it at Meredith Breame's house one afternoon when they were supposed to be working on a project about riverbeds and erosion. First Meredith helped bleach her hair, and then they dyed it green. It turned out a very bright, almost neon green close to her scalp and a sort of muddy greenish-brown everywhere else, but she was satisfied with it. They made an unholy mess in the bathroom, which made Meredith's parents angry, and Juliet's father was furious when he saw her hair. Whenever Juliet's father said something unkind to her, which he often did, or if her mother said something kind to her, which she sometimes did, then either way the tears would rush to Juliet's eyes and she would have to run to her room and slam the door until the storm had passed. At school once she burst into tears in the middle of history class, because after all history was nothing but centuries upon centuries of human beings being horrible, greedy, and cruel, it broke her heart to think about it, and she had to flee the classroom and run to the girls' washroom and lock herself in a stall to sob, and then Alyssa and Meredith both came to try and comfort her, and that was humiliating and made her cry even harder.

Nora had long since given up trying to play the guitar her father had bought her for her birthday once, but Casey often picked it up and fooled around with it when she was over, and after a while she could strum half a dozen songs or so—only simple ones, but still, pretty good for having never had a lesson. She could play the guitar but she couldn't and wouldn't sing, she refused to even try, so Nora would sing instead: Nora had a pleasant enough voice, though it was kind of thin, and she struggled to make herself heard over Casey's playing. Alyssa said they both sounded amazing and they ought to start a band, Juliet could play the piano and she could learn drums or something. Neither Nora nor Casey took her seriously, but they did have a lot of fun coming up with possible band names, like Ghost Foal, or Cinnamon Mouth, or Sultan's Son & the Sauce-Pigs. They would scribble these down on scraps of paper and surreptitiously pass them to one another in the middle of math class, or social studies or whatever, and then try hard not to giggle and get in trouble. Then Alyssa would design logos to go with the band names, because she was good at that sort of thing, and she would draw the logos on all three of their forearms in black pen over the lunch hour.

In June, when it was time for final exams, then Casey spent the whole week at Nora's house, supposedly so that they could study together. Each time Nora and Alyssa had a friendly competition to see who could be the first to finish their exam and turn in their papers, then wait outside smugly for the other and say, "Oh, what took you so long?" They were always the first two to finish, except once, the last exam, which was math. Then Casey finished before them, and it was she who got to wait outside the doors until they were done, and smile, and say, "What took you so long?"

It was early in the day and they had the whole day ahead of them. The sun was already hot in the cloudless sky and climbing higher. Alyssa had money, so they walked up to the Co-op and she bought them all bottles of iced tea and bags of chips. They felt giddy and also curiously deflated, for now they were done, not only with exams but done with that school. They had to go in for one half-day the next week to pick up their report cards and that was it, the next year they'd be starting high school in a new school. Now, the high school was in a building literally across the street and up half a block from their current school, and almost identical to look at, but it still seemed to them like a tremendous change lay ahead. "It's hard to believe," Alyssa said, and Nora said, "I know, right?"

They were just walking, without any direction or destination, unsure what to do with themselves. Then they found that they had wandered up the hill towards the Sally and Nora said, "Wanna go over to the cemetery?" and Alyssa said, "Is your Dad there today?" and Nora said, "Not on Thursdays, I think," and Alyssa said, "Sure, let's go to the cemetery."

The homes along this stretch of road were mostly drab little bungalows. They passed Ms Afton's green house, where the rusted old rooster on the roof creaked in the breeze and tall weeds had overtaken the yard, for the house had sat empty since Ms Afton had passed away that winter.

Ms Afton's headstone was along the south side of the cemetery, so that if you were looking at it, when you looked past it you saw the ground spilling down into the winding valley of the Whitetail, a lush green gash in the earth. Though she had herself requested something modest, the town had gotten together and raised the money for a dark marble slab, sleek and imposing, and even a piece of statuary: what was supposed to be an angel, holding its hands over its heart and gazing down serenely and sorrowfully on the grave; but because it would have been too expensive to get a life-sized one, it had ended up looking more like a chubby little cherub, and its hands were oddly placed, so that the girls decided it actually looked as if it were holding its stomach and staring down at an empty plate, thinking to itself, "I shouldn't have gone back for seconds."

Now that the girls had arrived at the cemetery they didn't know what to do. They wandered aimlessly among the headstones; they sat on the picnic table, their butts on the tabletop and their feet on the bench, looking out east across the river, finishing their drinks and chips. A blue jay, bright as a broken-off piece of sky, dropped from the branches of a nearby tree, pecked at a dribbled piece of potato chip in the grass, and then flapped back up into the tree, disappearing amid the thick leaves.

They talked about that weekend: Juliet's parents were going to be hosting a pool party for their whole class, a graduation party. It was going to start in the early afternoon and go on all night long, and the three friends had made a vow not to fall asleep the entire night and see the sun come up in the morning, and Alyssa would tell her parents she'd be crashing at Juliet's and Nora would tell her parents that she and Casey would be crashing at Alyssa's house, but really they wouldn't be crashing anywhere: that was the plan.

The heat of the sun soaked into the backs of their heads and necks, and the sun lit up the crumbling face of the old Stone School in the distance. It looked closer than usual, by some trick of the light or the clarity of the day, but also tremendously distant, for they knew that to get to it you had to go a long way around, almost fifteen kilometres north before crossing the Whitetail and then coming back south. There, while they were at Juliet's party that weekend, Alyssa's brother Anthony and the rest of the high school students would be having their own graduation party, the annual party at the old Stone School that was a dread and utter secret that everybody knew about and had always known about for the ten or fifteen years it had been taking place. Anthony had even invited them to go and said he'd drive them out, but though it was a little bit exciting to think about, and there would have been an undeniable prestige in going to a high school party before they were actually even in high school, they wouldn't have skipped Juliet's pool party for the world.

22

Casey explores the old Stone School;
she feels sorry for a neglected dog

In July, Nora went away to Alyssa's cottage for the last time, leaving Casey all alone. For the first few days that Nora was gone, Casey tried to find again that little lake she'd stumbled on the year before, but without any luck. She had thought she would remember which way to go, what direction to look, but then it turned out that she didn't have the slightest idea, it was tremendously disappointing.

Then one day she decided instead to bike out to the old Stone School and explore inside. More than that: she'd pack supplies and spend the night. She could pretend she was in one of those old shows, where someone has to spend the night in a haunted house in order to secure an inheritance. She thought of the stories that Alyssa's brother and others had told them about the old Stone School to try and scare them, Nora's older cousins too, Mark and Nat and Kat; and she thought about the more recent stories and rumours that had gone around after the Spring of Disappearing Pets. She didn't believe those stories and she didn't really believe in ghosts either, but she sort of hoped she'd see a ghost. It was going to be an adventure, the sort of thing she'd often fantasized about doing when she was younger, and that now she was actually old enough to do. She said to herself, reciting from memory, "You serious people mustn't be too hard on us human beings for how we choose to amuse ourselves when we are shut up as in a prison. If I do not soon get a little bit of fun, I shall die."

She spent a couple of days secretly preparing, stashing supplies in her school backpack, and it reminded her of when she was very young and used to steal things from the pantry to put in the old outhouse for her doll Polly. She knew that now she probably could have just told her parents what she was planning to do and they wouldn't have said anything, but doing it secretly was part of the fun. She thought, "Maybe I won't even tell Nora about it, it'll just be my secret," and she also thought, "I can't wait to tell Nora all about it."

She took her hoodie with her, tied around her waist, even though it was a hot and muggy day. She was planning to ball it up and use it as a pillow at night. The sun sent oblique shafts of light through the patchy clouds; her backpack was bulky, heavy, and uncomfortable, digging into her shoulders and the small of her back, and before long her shirt was drenched in sweat, but even so her heart was light.

She made a little detour off the highway, to a place she knew where the raspberries grew wild, and ate so many she felt faintly, satisfyingly nauseous. She watched a doe and her fawn browsing serenely on the leaves of a young aspen, maybe twenty yards away through the trees, and she drank more of her water than she knew she ought to, because she had to make it last, but she was just so thirsty she couldn't help it.

She got back on her bike and started north along the highway. It was mostly uphill—a gradual slope, almost imperceptible to the eye, but on her bike, under the hot sun with her heavy backpack, it felt like climbing a mountain. There wasn't much of a shoulder to the highway here, just a thin strip of dirt mixed with a little gravel, so when she heard the occasional car or truck approaching, she would pull over, get off her bike, and take a sip of water, happy to have a quick break anyway. One time a truck slowed down and pulled over, and it turned out to be Nora's uncle Matt, heading back to town, and he rolled down his window to say hello. Looking at her overstuffed backpack, he asked her jokingly if she was running away to join the circus or something, and asked if he could give her a lift anywhere. She had nothing against Matt particularly, she had always thought he was likeable enough, but it bothered her that she had been spotted by anyone who knew her, and it spoiled her mood for the next ten or fifteen minutes.

When she reached the bridge at last she got off her bike, and took off her backpack, and stashed them both in the shade of the bridge, and then she clambered carefully down the bank and removed her socks and shoes so that she could cool her feet in the stream as she sat on a rock and ate some lunch: a piece of cheese, an apple, and a peanut butter and honey sandwich that had gone slightly soggy where the honey had soaked into the bread. She ate slowly. It was still early—how early she didn't really know, she didn't have a watch, but the sun was nowhere near its zenith, and she hadn't planned to eat her lunch until she had reached the school—but she was starving. Above and behind her, she could hear the rattle and roar of a semi-trailer passing on the highway, raising a cloud of dust, and then the rumble gradually faded into the distance.

A light breeze was beginning to blow, cooling the sweat on her face; in the sky, a small cloud dimmed the sun for several sweet minutes. Just below the bridge, the shallow lazy stream picked up speed as it dropped a couple of feet, cascading over a jumble of slick rocks, taking shape, rushing and burbling, and the sound and sight of it soothed and cheered her. On the far bank of the creek and down a little ways, a dusty brown rabbit appeared in a rustle of grass, darted down towards the water, noticed Casey, and then darted back, disappearing again amid the tall seedy grass and purple loosestrife.

Back on her bike and across the bridge, she felt much better, she felt again that lighthearted sense of adventure she had started out with. Now she was in unfamiliar territory, she'd never before come this far in this direction. She turned right at the very first crossroads and started heading back south. Here it was all slightly downhill and the riding was easy, though the road was bumpy and rutted. The breeze was blowing from the west, just steady enough to keep her from overheating, and more and more clouds were drifting in to shelter her from the heat of the sun.

In the pleasure of the ride, it was some time before she began to feel vague misgivings and wonder if maybe she had turned south too soon and taken the wrong road. She could no longer see the Whitetail through the trees, though she knew it must be there; except for the occasional glimpse of a barn or a farmhouse through the trees, there was no sign of human life. No cars passed her on the narrow road. The wind was picking up, blowing from the south and the southwest now, making the leaves of the trees rustle loudly, and she could see a mass of black clouds on the horizon, distant but ominous. She couldn't make up her mind whether to turn and go back to the main road or keep going forward and hope for the best, and then she went around a bend and the road she was on abruptly ended in someone's driveway: so abruptly that when she came around the corner and a dog started barking at her, she tumbled off her bike, startled. For a brief terrifying moment she thought the dog was going to attack her, and she closed her eyes and braced herself to be bitten. Only after a few moments passed and the dog wasn't on top of her did she open her eyes and realize that it was chained up, barking frantically, half choking itself on its collar.

The dog was almost as big as Casey was, visibly a boy, with dirty big teeth and black speckled lips that flapped as he barked, spraying saliva; he had oddly thick and squat hind legs and a short, yellow coat, all patchy, matted, and filthy. He was obviously maltreated and neglected: she could see the outline of his ribs pressing against his sides, and brown and bloated ticks embedded in his flesh, and what looked like a nasty scab running along his left haunch. His chain was so short he could hardly go a dozen feet in any direction, and it was staked out right in the middle of the barren yard, with no shade or shelter anywhere in reach, and no sign of food or water either. The farmhouse behind him was clearly abandoned, the doors and windows nailed over with sheets of plywood. Behind the house, the rusted husk of a pickup truck sat on cinder blocks; past that was an old grey barn that had collapsed in on itself and looked as if it had been sitting there untouched for twenty years or more. But beyond that, and across maybe half a mile of overgrown field and up a hill, she could see at last the old Stone School.

Casey's hip and knee were bruised and scraped from her fall, and the palm of her right hand too was scraped and stinging, but she wasn't seriously hurt. Her bike chain had dropped off the crankset, but that only took a minute for her to fuss back into place, leaving her hands black with grease, and then her bike was fine. The dog had stopped barking as she did this and was now rapidly pacing from right to left and left to right, whimpering and occasionally growling. The wind was swirling up clouds of dust in the empty driveway, and those storm clouds in the distance were getting visibly closer.

Now Casey had to decide if she was going to bike all the way back to the main road, over, and then down again, or try to cut across the field: probably foolish, and she'd have to walk her bike the whole way, but at least she'd have her destination in sight the whole time and not have to worry about getting lost or taking another wrong road. But before she could decide about that, she knew she had to do something for that poor dog; she couldn't just leave him that way, it would be tantamount to murder.

Taking out a piece of the leftover ham she had packed for her dinner, she approached the animal cautiously, eyes narrowed, talking to it in gentle, reassuring tones, a calm and friendly voice, saying, "Hey guy, I've got something for you." His nostrils were pulsing frantically as he smelled the food. When she was close enough she tossed the ham gently towards him, and he snatched it right out of the air, snapping it up and wolfing it down, then looking at Casey expectantly, tail wagging tentatively.

She thought of a story her mother told her once, about a man who had gone blind, not gradually but suddenly, and he was very bitter about it. They gave him a guide dog, a seeing-eye dog, but instead of being grateful, he dug out the dog's eyes and used them to replace his own. Then he could see again, though of course he was now colour-blind. But now the dog was bitter and bent on revenge, and though it couldn't see the man, it had the scent of him, and tracked him ceaselessly by his smell, all across the country, and finally killed him in his sleep, tearing out his throat. In her mind, she had always pictured that dog as looking very much like this dog—except, of course, that this dog still had his eyes, that he was now using to stare at her imploringly.

She returned to her backpack and took the rest of the ham from its Tupperware container. It was her own dinner, and she was already feeling hungry again, but he clearly needed it even more than she would. She used the lid of the Tupperware as a plate for the pile of meat, and then poured some of her water into the container, and carefully carried both back to the dog, crouching down and placing them gently within his reach. As he gobbled up the food and lapped at the water, she scratched the dog's neck affectionately and—with a little thrill of danger and excitement—unclipped his choke collar from the chain, setting him free.

She hurried back to her bike while the dog was still eating and drinking, threw on her backpack, and hit the road. She thought she ought to get out of there quickly, before the dog realized he was loose, and just in case the dog's owner actually was around somewhere after all; and besides, she was going to have to hurry if she was going to make it to the old Stone School before the storm was on her.

Even though she was going uphill again, she had the wind at her back, pushing her along, and she went quickly; it was after she had gone further west and found the right road to turn down, a real paved road this time, then she was not only pedalling into the wind, but still going uphill. It felt like pedalling across a beach. Her shirt was drenched with sweat, and her eyes stung. The wind swept gusts of dust into the air in spinning clouds, or sometimes pelting her in the face, stinging into her eyes and getting into her mouth as she breathed heavily. She could see those storm clouds, looking massive now and darker than ever, steadily encroaching, making evening out of midday. The bottoms of the clouds looked as if they had been smeared down towards the ground, and here and there they were lit up by flickers of light, still distant enough to be silent. There were no signs of birds, animals, or other people anywhere. The temperature must have dropped five degrees or more in the last half hour.

The first drops of rain began to strike just as the old Stone School came into sight. She cut across the field, pushing her bike through the long stalky grass; and the seedy grass swayed, and the thistles were as high as her head, with their pretty purple flowers, bent sideways by the wind. She passed the remnants of what might once have been a barn but was now just a jumble of rotted timber and rusty nails, gobbled over by the grass and weeds—way back when, the school had been a real working farm, with the schoolchildren for labour and a few hundred acres of land. A fork of lightning split the sky, followed hard by a crack of thunder so loud it seemed to make her bones shake. Fat rapid splats of sudden rain came bursting across her face. And the crumbling brick building loomed before her.

It seemed smaller somehow than she had expected, having seen it always only from a distance, and more sad and shabby than sinister or ominous. The school consisted of three sections: a central building that was set a little further back but went higher up, four storeys high with a grandly peaked roof; and on either side, identical three-storey wings, flat-topped and boxy. In the weeds near the entrance an old piano bench lay on its back, legs sticking forlornly in the air, along with a scatter of broken bricks and splinters of wood and shards of glass.

A limestone archway framed the main entrance: down the left side of that archway was spray-painted the word BITTER, down the right side the words AS FUCK. The seven steps leading up to the main doors were made of crumbling cement. One of the doors hung precariously from its frame and seemed to be held in place by spiderwebs and sheer inertia; the other door was missing entirely, and the frame itself was all rotted and smashed.

She didn't really have much time to take it all in because the rain was coming down now with a vengeance, and though it felt pleasantly cool, even refreshing after that long hot sweaty ride, she had no change of clothes, and she didn't want everything in her backpack to get soaked through either. She left her bike at the bottom of the steps.

Inside it was dusty, and dank, and dark. The floors were thick with broken linoleum and all sorts of rubble: chunks of plaster, broken glass out of smashed light fixtures, rotted boards with rusty nails sticking out. Old radiators lay on their sides like fallen soldiers and a drinking fountain had been wrenched off its pedestal and viciously assaulted, and sat all dented and battered in the middle of the hall. Portions of the original stone structure, irregular-sized slabs of stone embedded in mortar, most about the size of two or three bricks laid together, had been preserved and built around. And here and there she thought she could see, along the walls, evidence of that long-ago fire, where the rocks had been scorched a sooty black—unless it was just some sort of mold.

The wide central corridor had two large classrooms off either side. Casey shone her flashlight into each of them, looking for a place to set up camp, but the floors in those rooms were every bit as covered with rubble as the floor in the corridor, if not more so. There were the remnants of smashed desks, and busted bricks, and broken chalkboards. One room was piled with torn and rotting textbooks, a great heap of them as high as a hay bale. Casey actually went in that room, thinking she would take a closer look at the books out of idle curiosity, but the smell chased her away. They absolutely reeked of urine, the stench was overwhelming.

The corridor came to an end at a wide and open stairwell. To the left of the stairwell, a door with a wooden cross affixed to the middle led to what had once been the chapel. Here the roof had been stove right in, leaving a gaping wound exposed to the stormy sky, the rain sluicing through in sheets, and beams and sodden plaster heaped across the scarred and busted pews, deep dirty puddles forming on the floor.

To the right of the stairwell was the door to the gymnasium. It was evidently there where people liked to come and party: there were the piles of old beer cans and liquor bottles overflowing with old cigarette butts, the empty chip bags and fast food wrappers, the used condoms and discarded pipes, the smell of stale old bodily fluids mingling with the must and the mold. Something scurried out of the corner of her eye and was gone; something flapped irritably in the exposed rafters high overhead. The rain was coming in here, too, not like in the chapel but drizzling steadily though a dozen spots in the ceiling, an intricate patter of drips striking the wood floor. The bench seat out of an old car had been propped against one wall to serve as a makeshift couch, and there was a hole in it with the stuffing all coming out where rodents had made a nest in it. An old zinc washtub was full of ashes and charred wood. The walls were covered with an intricate mural of obscene graffiti, some long-faded, some relatively fresh: calligraphic initials, and scrawled improbable penises, and dueling accusations of sexual deviancy, and terse boasts of sexual prolificacy, and crude drawings of sexual acts. Along the far wall there had evidently once been a stage: you could still see the scars on the wall and floor where it had been ripped down, and a fire exit hung above it, a wide grey metal door uselessly suspended four feet in the air.

Gradually, patiently, Casey explored the whole building. If Nora had been with her, they might have pretended that they saw strange shadows flitting past their peripheral vision, or heard sounds that might or might not have been footsteps or unearthly moaning, and unnerved one another, and generally worked themselves up into a pitch of delightful, delicious terror. But Nora wasn't with her, and Casey couldn't quite manage to spook herself, or feel really frightened. It was sad, and it smelled bad, but it wasn't scary at all.

The mess halls were on the main floors; the kitchens had been so thoroughly trashed and ransacked that it was difficult at first to tell what they once had been. Exposed pipes and wires stuck out of the walls, and the floors were so thick with debris that she didn't even go in.

She tried the basement next, and it was pitch black down there. She hadn't brought a strong enough flashlight; the darkness gobbled up her little weak beam of light like it was nothing. She could see enough to see that the floors were caked with thick years of undisturbed dust, and every step she took she got cobwebs across her face, and in her mouth and clinging to her hair. She could see what looked disconcertingly at first like a tree, a squat black tree with many thick limbs branching out in all directions; and then she got a little closer and of course it wasn't a tree, it didn't even really look like a tree at all, it was just a big old furnace. This, she remembered, was where the bones and remains of at least two dozen cats and dogs were supposedly heaped, according to the rumours that had gone around after all those pets had disappeared: and she was not surprised, but also relieved, to see that there had not been a shred of truth to any of it.

On the second and third floors there were more classrooms, in scarcely better shape than those below, but at least with no more heaps of urine-soaked books. The wide stairwell ended on the third floor, and a more narrow set of stairs led up to the fourth, to what must have once been a sort of apartment. There was even a private bathroom—the toilet had been smashed and the pieces tossed in the bathtub, and the tiles on the floor looked like someone had taken a hammer to them, and the vanity, sink, and mirror were missing completely, but a bathroom all the same. There were the remnants of a small kitchen that looked as if a bomb had gone off in it. In the back room, probably the bedroom, there was a larger than life-size purple spray painting of a naked and faceless woman squatting over an impossibly large, erect, and disembodied penis.

In the front room Casey discovered a piano, missing several of its keys and with a metal music stand stabbed through its guts. Here the wide picture window was not only smashed out but the window frame and a dozen or more bricks gone with it. Outside the storm was then at its height. She could see the trees in the distance bowing and twisting in the wind, and whenever a flash of lightning would sheet across the sky, it would illuminate the town in the valley down below, pretty as a postcard. And the wind and the rain came gusting and streaming in through the window and formed deep pools of water on the warped and buckled floor.

Back down on the second floor, she found her way into the side buildings, the wings. These had evidently been the dormitories, the girls' dormitory to the north and the boys' to the south, judging by the bathrooms. Mold grew in green and black patches all over, and there were holes punched in the walls to expose the lath, and parts of the ceiling had come entirely down. And Casey was disappointed to find that not a single bathroom in that whole building had a mirror remaining, not so much as a sliver: no hope that she might be able to conjure up a ghost or ghastly vision, like in those stories that everybody told. The sleeping areas were long, low rooms that might once have held ten or a dozen beds apiece. Here and there was still a bedframe left behind, rusted and bent, but she saw only a single mattress. It had been hauled into the bathroom and propped on its side against a busted urinal; it was slashed in several places and stank to high heaven, and was spattered over with motley stains, some yellow, some a light yellowish-brown, and a big one in the middle that was a dark reddish-brown in the shape of a starburst.

In one of the girls' bedrooms, up on the third floor, she found a section of floor still relatively intact and free of rubble, and here she sat down and ate what little food she had left for a dinner: the rest of the cheese; a handful of crackers, slightly stale; and a tin of peach slices. Her shoulders, legs, and backside ached from the day's bike ride; her clothes were still damp, from both rain and sweat, and felt clammy and uncomfortable. She drank the syrup from the tin of peach slices to satisfy her thirst. Outside, the rain had stopped. From the window she could see a scrape of deep blue sky in the distance, above the silhouette of Riding Mountain, and a fragment of rainbow, shimmering and iridescent. It was still light enough, she thought, to make it home before dark, so long as she left now. The idea of spending the night there no longer seemed fun, or appealingly frightening: it only sounded dreary, sad, uncomfortable and unpleasant. Zipping up her backpack, now appreciably lighter with no food or water left in it, she made her way quickly back downstairs.

When she told Nora all about it, a week or two later, she made it sound as if she really had spooked herself wandering through the empty rooms and corridors, even though nothing had actually happened, and that she had changed her mind about spending the night there because she really did get scared. It just made a more interesting story that way, and it made Nora laugh, and want to go herself, together with Casey.

But Casey never did tell Nora what happened when she left: how she had gone downstairs and stepped out into the early evening, gratefully inhaling the fresh air after being stuck so long in that dusty, musty, airless building—and there, at the bottom of the stairs, curled up on the ground beside her bicycle, was that yellow dog. In fact she never told Nora or anyone else about the yellow dog at all.

23

Lynn runs in the election;
Alma has trouble with her teeth

ONE DAY, LATE IN AUGUST, Casey went into the kitchen at Nora's house to get some cold drinks out of the fridge. Nora was outside, in the back yard; they had been outside all day, for it was a beautifully hot and sunny day, and who knew how many more of those they'd get that year. Tracy was over at April's house, Simon was at work, Lynn was at the library. Casey came in through the back door, loudly, laughing at something Nora was saying, and startled Alma in the kitchen. Alma was standing over by the sink, leaning back against the counter. She had a tooth, still wet and slightly bloody, in the palm of her hand, and was huddled over it, examining it closely.

Casey startled her when she came clamouring into the kitchen, and when she looked up at Casey, there was no recognition at all in her eyes. She looked confused, frightened, and angry; she berated Casey, yelling, "Who are you? What do you think you're doing, waltzing into someone else's house like this?" Her hand had closed into a fist around the tooth, and she was hiding it behind her back; her head was shaking tremulously. Casey was so astonished that she couldn't speak; tears sprang into her eyes, she felt as if she'd been slapped in the face. Without a word, she turned and ran back outside. Later, at the dinner table, Alma appeared to recognize or half-recognize her again, but still seemed confused and flustered, avoided speaking to her, and would only look at her surreptitiously, out of the side of her eyes, brows furrowed in consternation. The next day, things were more or less back to normal; neither of them ever spoke about what had happened to the other.

SUMMER WAS TURNING INTO AUTUMN while no one was paying attention. First the mosquitoes mostly disappeared, and then for a while it seemed like there were wasps everywhere. Morning came just a little bit later, and a little cooler; evening settled in just that little bit sooner. The air on sunny afternoons was dryer and crisper, with a bit of a nip in the breeze; the Whitetail flowed low and sluggishly, and a scatter of orange and yellow leaves were just beginning to appear amid the thick and overhanging green.

Everyone had so much on their minds. Tracy was turning thirteen, and Lynn kept saying, "Can you believe that both of our babies are teenagers now?" and Simon would shake his head and say, "Unbelievable. Can't believe it." And Nora would roll her eyes, and Tracy would look smug. Nora was starting high school, and Lynn would say, "Can you believe our baby girl is going to high school?" and Simon would say, "I can remember when she was so small I could just put her in my pocket and carry her around in my pocket. Now look at her." He had been making that same joke since she was four years old; when she was four years old, she might have found it funny. Now, if no one else was around, Nora would just roll her eyes, but sometimes they said these things in front of neighbours or other people, and then Nora would flush with embarrassment and irritation, turning her face to the side and slightly down, her lower lip jutting out in an unconscious pout, and Tracy would giggle ferociously, because even though she sometimes pouted too, at least it didn't make her look like their father.

Nora was a little bit nervous about starting high school, for all her teachers the past few years had often warned them how much harder it would be, so they'd better start paying attention now. Mostly she didn't believe them, but a little bit she did. And so she felt a bit nervous, but above all she was excited, because high school would mean, for the first time really since first grade, new faces. There were a few small towns nearby, smaller than Whittle even, that had no high schools of their own, only K-9, and had to bus their high schoolers to Whittle, places like Waabishkigwan, Oakstone, and Erick's Ditch.

On top of all that, there were the local elections coming up too, and coming quickly, and Lynn had little time or energy for noticing anything else, she was so wrapped up in that; and so at first none of them even noticed that Alma was becoming testy and withdrawn.

It was also true that Alma had been getting more testy and withdrawn in general for the past year anyway, so for a while it was difficult to notice the difference. For some time now she had been prone to forgetting simple things, and the names of things, and calling people by the wrong name, and mixing up Nora and Tracy, or calling either or both of them Lynn; and she would get easily tired, given to aches and pains, become irritable and quarrelsome. She had taken to frequently misplacing her belongings, such as her books or her reading glasses, and then would angrily accuse Simon or the girls of meddling with her things, sometimes even accusing them of doing it on purpose just to confuse her; and she had found reading her beloved mystery books increasingly difficult, not only because the print seemed to be getting inexplicably smaller, but because she would frequently forget the plot halfway through, or find the story getting confused in her mind with all the other books she'd read with the same detective, or by the same author, or even different but similar authors, so that what had formerly been one of her chief pleasures was rapidly becoming a distressing ordeal. All these small inexorable signs of aging made her feel fearful, fretful, anxious and resentful.

On Labour Day weekend, that last weekend before school began, they all went out to Casey's farm for a barbecue. They arrived around two o'clock, and the three girls promptly disappeared in the direction of the fields, Nora and Casey talking urgently, Tracy eager to see the horses again; Kenneth gave her a bag of fallen apples to toss to them. Rusty and Mud didn't run after the girls, as they would have in the old days, but rested listlessly near the lawn chairs. Maureen fed a great fire in the burn barrel that popped and crackled satisfyingly, and she charmed everyone with her usual stream of nonsense; nor did Lynn fail to notice her husband's admiring and surreptitious glances whenever Maureen stooped over the pile of wood to pick out more branches. Flies settled in the dozens on the legs and arms of anyone who sat still for a moment, crawling and curious, harmless but intensely irritating. The weather changed every fifteen minutes as low clouds scudded across the sky, covering and uncovering the sun, and the wind blew in gusts from one direction and then another. For five or ten minutes it even rained, though the sun was still exposed: just a few cold fat drops at first, and then suddenly slanting down vigorously, the wind in snatches blowing it sometimes almost sideways into their faces. It was over so quickly that by the time Kenneth had helped Alma out of her seat and over to the shelter of the garage, holding a jacket above her head, it had almost already stopped. Only Maureen, whose nipples were now clearly visible through the thinned and faded fabric of her sundress, had made no attempt to take cover, but stayed loyally by her fire, now more smoke than flame.

In the end they left early, for Alma—though she peevishly insisted that she was feeling perfectly fine—was looking shaky and frail, her eyelids drooping, her face pasty and slack, the skin sagging alarmingly, as if her face were in danger of sliding right off her skull. Maybe, they feared, she had caught a bad chill in that burst of rain.

IT HAD BEEN NOT LONG AFTER they'd all gone out to that wedding in Strathdale, back in July, that Lynn had decided she was going to run for a seat on the town council in the upcoming elections. The town had had the same mayor, and the same four councillors,

for quite a few years now, and there was an almost universal
feeling that it was time. Change was in the air, a kind of diffuse
and general dissatisfaction. It had been two and a half years
since that terrible spring of the disappearing pets, and while few
people brought it up directly, it was still very much at the back of
everyone's mind. It rankled; and though no one could say exactly
what the mayor and council should have or even could have done
about it at the time, almost everyone seemed to agree that it was
time for them to go. With the population of the town growing, a
fifth spot on council was being created. Of the incumbents, two
of the councillors had already announced their retirements; the
other two barely campaigned, and that with a kind of sheepish
resignation. Only the mayor, who had served a dozen years now,
was unwilling to give up without a fight, and everyone knew that
he was doomed. People now openly spoke disapprovingly about
what everyone had privately known and winked at for years, that
frankly he was almost never sober.

It was Matt, of all people, who had put the idea of running in
Lynn's head, that evening out in Strathdale, egging her on with
a shrewd mixture of suggestion, flattery, and cajoling. It probably
helped that she was a little tipsy at the time. Not only that, he
even promised her the moral and financial backing of both himself
personally and of Wellesley & Pettinger, Incorporated. This despite
the long history of quarrels and disagreements between them, and
even despite all the times that Lynn had vocally opposed, at town
meetings and in this or that committee, his company's various
developments and schemes, most recently and acrimoniously that
gas station and motel across the Yellowhead.

And so that autumn, their lives were briefly taken over
by the election. The votes would be cast on the Tuesday after
Thanksgiving. Nora, Tracy, and sometimes even Casey were
pressed into duty, trailing up and down the streets of the town
behind Lynn like a trio of faintly embarrassed goslings. Tracy's
accident formed the centrepiece of Lynn's campaign, as both a

cautionary embodiment of the perils of unchecked development, and a victim of the current town council's dithering ineffectiveness, their failure to put up traffic lights or at least a four-way stop at that intersection, despite the clear and steadily rising danger. And so Tracy would often be made to stand at her mother's side on this doorstep or that, and endure being squeezed affectionately and having her hair tousled as her mother retold, for the umpteenth time, how terrified she had been.

What roles Nora and Casey were supposed to play, why they were being dragged along too, was less clear. Just to stand behind Lynn, smile, and look decorative, they supposed. They wrote a campaign song for her, that they sang to the tune of "This Land Is Your Land" while Casey strummed the guitar:

> Lynn Wellesley *wants* you
> To vote *for* her,
> She'll repre*sent* you,
> Your happy *warr*ior:
> Lynn *Welles*ley will fight for you and me.
> From the Yellowhead *High*way
> To the ceme*tery*,
> From the Whitetail *Riv*er
> To the Community *Cen*tre,
> Lynn *Welles*ley will fight for you and me.

—but she forbade them to perform it in public, so that was no fun.

Lynn proved to be a natural politician, or at least a natural campaigner. Everyone knew her already, not only those who frequented the library, or sat with her on this or that board, or looked forward to the Christmas craft sale every December, or whose children went to school with hers, or who had gone to school with her themselves, or had had her mother as their teacher. Long years of assiduous gossiping had given her a knack for getting people to air their grievances, and she left everyone she spoke to satisfied that they had found a sympathetic ear, someone who really *listened*. Lynn's mother was much admired; her father was remembered, by those who did remember him, with sympathy and respect. And the Wellesley name carried weight. People who were in favour of the town continuing to expand and develop saw that she had the backing of Wellesley & Pettinger; people who were wary of expansion and development remembered that she had often publicly opposed Wellesley & Pettinger's plans and schemes. "Preserve" was the key word and central motif of all her campaign spiels, her pledge and promise to preserve all the qualities of their town and community that they loved. The joke among the family was that she ought to make it her official campaign slogan: "Lynn Wellesley: Not a Conservative, But a Preservative." And Lynn submitted to this teasing with uncharacteristic good-humour: she virtually purred. All in all, she was happier and more good-humoured during the time of her first political campaign than Nora could almost ever remember her being.

Soon it was October already. When Nora walked to school in the morning, the sun just above the horizon was right in her eyes, and the glare was awful, and it was cold enough that she had to wear a sweater in the morning, though by the time she walked back home in the afternoon it would often be too warm to wear it, and then it would just be a nuisance, to be crammed into her backpack or tied around her waist. Then for several days it rained steadily, just a dreary cold unceasing drizzle. The leaves that had already fallen to the pavement became slick with the drizzle, and treacherously slippery to step on; when dusk approached, the air would reverberate with the honks and squawks of geese overhead.

That year they had Thanksgiving dinner at Uncle Matt and Aunt Louise's house for the first time in a long time. Casey came too, of course; this time she was even invited. Louise had always had a soft spot for Casey and had always gone out of her way to try and make her feel part of the family.

The girls walked across town to Matt and Louise's house, leaving Nora's parents and grandmother to go in the car with a casserole dish of scalloped potatoes and a pair of Alma's famous pies, one pumpkin and one crabapple-saskatoon berry. The crabapples had come from Casey's farm.

They walked slowly, for there was no rush and much to discuss. It was a beautiful day, mild and blue and a riot of geese, the ground covered with a carpet of fallen leaves, coming down faster than people could rake them up. The leaves crunched beneath their feet, for it had been a dry week, and it made a very satisfying sound; the sun in the clear sky shed a tranquil warmth, and every gust of wind shook more leaves from the rustling treetops, and made the leaves dance and eddy along the street. The Tibbett kids, out in their yard, had raked up a great pile of leaves beside their front steps, and were taking turns leaping into them from the top of the stoop, hesitant and excited—for it must have seemed to them a great height, though it was hardly more than a few feet—their little arms and legs flailing as they leapt, squealing and laughing, and Tracy and Nora said, "Oh my God, they are *so* adorable," and Casey pretended to agree. But mostly as they walked they talked of Alyssa, who had been acting strange lately, at once manic and out of sorts, and Nora had much to say, and had been saying it all weekend. Casey had her own thoughts about it, but she kept them to herself: the fact was that ever since they had started high school, half the boys there were mooning around Nora, showing off for her or making cow's eyes at her, making her the centre of their attention and the object of their awkward infatuation, and Casey suspected that Alyssa was just feeling jealous, but she didn't want to say so to Nora, for she knew that it all made Nora intensely uncomfortable. Tracy, who was following the conversation with interest and sticking her oar in when she could, had a theory too: she suggested that Alyssa was probably on drugs.

Casey had only been to Matt and Louise's house a handful of times, and not at all for several years, but she remembered it clearly, with its wrap-around porch, ornate gables, and that small balcony on the second floor, above the porch, with the bright red door. The buff-coloured brick was covered by a thick layer of Virginia creeper that now, in autumn, had turned a deep vermilion. As they neared the house, they could see someone sitting on the porch, behind the screen, and hear their voices, pleasant and indistinct, drifting out across the lawn: Nora's cousins, Kat and Mark, sipping beer and smoking cigarettes. Kat had changed her hair since they'd seen her in the summer and was wearing it flapper-style with finger-curls; and she had new glasses too, to match her hair, two large circles with a thin gold frame, like the eyes of T. J. Eckleburg. She waved excitedly as they came up the sidewalk and called out to them so the whole street could hear; Mark waited until they were closer, nodding at them as they came up the steps and greeting them with a simple, "Ladies."

Inside the house, they were embraced by the warm enticing aroma of a slowly roasting turkey, of browning butter and weeping onions, of sage, celery, and rosemary. Lynn was talking of the election, of course, now only two days away—or rather, she was explaining to Louise that she had firmly decided *not* to talk about the election—that entire evening. "I'm not even going to think about it," she declared. After all, she went on, who hadn't made up their mind who to vote for by this point? It was all over but for counting the bodies, she'd done what she could, whatever happened on Tuesday she'd be at peace with the results. As she said to one of her neighbours the other night.... All this and more Lynn was pouring out to Louise in a loud, unnecessarily truculent voice, not pausing between sentences to let her sister-in-law get a word in edgewise; while Louise, who had stood up to go check on something on the stove, was now standing awkwardly halfway to the hall, held by her glittering eye, a sympathetic half-smile on her kindly face, only occasionally flitting her eyes anxiously in the direction of the kitchen.

Nora's father was there, and Matt, and their sister Bonnie, and Bonnie's husband Geoff, a wisp of a man with a perpetual, expectant half-smile on his face, as if he went through life in constant anticipation of a pleasant surprise that never quite arrived. Bonnie finished off what was left in her wine glass and got to her feet as the girls came into the room; perhaps she wanted to see if she was still taller than Nora. And she put an arm around her niece's shoulder and kissed her lightly on the side of the head. "Nora," she said, "you just look more beautiful every time I see you. I can't believe you're in high school already, it isn't possible!"

"I remember when she was so small," said Nora's father, "I could fit her in my pocket, and just carry her around in my pocket." Tracy looked at Casey, behind Nora's back, with a great big grin, and it was all Casey could do to keep from laughing out loud.

Louise had always felt vaguely guilty that they were just a small family in such a large house, a house that, when Matt was growing up in it, had been filled almost to overflowing. She would have happily given the old home more children if she could have—though not, perhaps, as many as Matt's parents had. Now especially, now that Mark and Nat were grown up, Nat moved away, Kat moved away—Kat who had, when she was a child, spent almost as much time in this house as her own, playing with her cousins—all grown up but not yet old enough to have children of their own, then it seemed to Louise that the house was especially lonely. Sometimes in the early mornings, lying in bed neither wholly asleep nor fully awake, it seemed to her that she could hear the ghosts of those early days stirring in the rooms below her, sounds that would start out quiet and intermittent, and gradually build: a cupboard door opening and closing, the flush of water from the taps, the subdued clatter of dishes in the kitchen; the happy conspiratorial chatter of young children, voices muffled and indistinct; cupboards and doors opening and closing, chairs scraping across the floor, occasional bursts of laughter. It was as if the house itself was having this dream of better days, of happy times gone by, an abundant and overflowing dream that spilled into Louise's head as she lay half-asleep. And Louise would try to prolong that half-asleep-and-dreaming state as long as possible, luxuriating in the music of it all, and thinking to herself that this was the essence and audible distillation of happiness itself; and she would always feel a deep and melancholy sense of loss when those voices faded and she was fully awake to a quiet, almost-empty home.

Louise asked the girls if she could get them anything to drink: ginger ale, or a coke, or lemonade maybe...?

"I could use another beer," said Mark, "if you're going anyway."

"Sure, I'll have a beer, too," said Tracy boldly.

"You certainly will not," said Lynn.

"Good try, kiddo," said Kat, patting her young cousin on the shoulder. "It was worth a shot, right?"

"Casey," said Louise, "why don't you come give me a hand in the kitchen?"

There was a large pot of salted water on the stovetop that was boiling furiously away. Louise turned off the heat and heaved a sigh. She said to Casey, "Now, Casey, I need your advice." When Lynn had asked what they could bring to contribute to the dinner, Louise had asked her to bring a pie, it wouldn't be a proper Thanksgiving without one of Alma's famous pies; but now Lynn had shown up, not only with two pies but with a giant pan of scalloped potatoes, too. In the meantime, Louise had all these potatoes that she had just been about to boil and mash—pointing to a colander in the sink, heaped high with peeled and cubed potatoes, enough to feed a small army. "I can't bear to let them just go to waste, but will Lynn be offended if I serve them as well?"

"Yes," said Casey promptly, for she knew Nora's mother well enough to know that. "She'll be horribly offended, she'll keep bringing it up for months, we'll never hear the end of it."

"Yes," agreed Louise sadly. "That's what I thought. Such a waste. I suppose I can put them in the fridge and cook them tomorrow, there's just so many. Well, we'd better get everyone their drinks..."

Alma, sitting in an armchair by the fireplace, shapeless as a heap of dirty laundry, had one hand groping in her mouth, absent-mindedly worrying a tooth. As Casey approached the old woman to hand her a glass of milk, Alma whipped her hand out of her mouth and hid it at her side, accepting the glass with the other hand, and glaring at Casey as she walked away with an almost palpable look of suspicion and dislike.

Matt, who was perched lightly on the arm of the larger couch, had been watching Casey, Alma, and their whole interaction, with a quizzical look on his face, eyebrows raised, half-puzzled and half-amused. He opened his mouth as if to say something, and then apparently thought better of it, but he did manage to catch Casey's eye as she walked by and gave her a reassuring smile. "I believe Nora is sitting out on the porch," he said kindly. And sure enough, she found Nora, Kat, and Tracy out there, Tracy sipping experimentally at Kat's beer and trying to suppress an expression of disgust.

Later, at dinner, Alma barely ate, pushing the food listlessly around the plate with a petulant look on her face, and her face was flushed and tremulous, and every time she took a sip of her milk, she winced and hissed. Her eyes darted furtively around the table, glancing from face to face with suspicion, confusion, or dismay.

Lynn sat on the other side of Alma, next to Geoff, who fussily cut his food into very small pieces before he ate it and dabbed at the corner of his mouth with a cloth napkin between every other bite. "I'll just be so relieved when this election's over," Lynn was saying to him. "Well, I had no idea how much *work* I was letting myself in for. It might even be a relief if I don't win," she said, with a forced and mendacious little laugh. "But I do think it sets a good example for my girls, and like I always say to them..."

Mark, meanwhile, was whispering something in Tracy's ear with a smirk, gesturing with a piece of dark meat speared on the end of his fork, and making her giggle ferociously; Kat and Nora, on the other side of the table, were talking about high school, what classes Nora was in and what she thought of the teachers, most of whom were the same as they had been when Katharine went to school there, and Kat had many varied and colourful opinions about them that Nora listened to eagerly, holding her chin slightly up and her shoulders down to accentuate the full length of her neck.

Casey glanced around the table: everyone was there, and everyone was happily engrossed in eating, or in conversation, or in both. Even Louise, who had spent the first ten or fifteen minutes of dinner standing up again as soon as she had sat down to go back to the kitchen and get something she had forgotten to put out on the table, or to ask this or that person anxiously if they needed this, that, or the other—even Louise had finally settled down now and was eating contentedly. Matt, beside her, was telling Bonnie and Simon about their Christmas plans: they had booked train tickets to go out to Montreal and visit Nat.

"Does Nat know you're coming," asked Simon, "or do you plan to surprise him?"

"Oh, he knows," said Matt. "Louise could never keep a secret from him, even if she wanted to. When they were little, I had to do all the Christmas shopping for the boys, I was afraid she'd tell them what their presents were. It was just lucky that she still believed in Santa Claus, so I didn't have to worry about her spoiling that for them."

"You're such a liar," said Louise, but her face was beaming and her voice full of tenderness and affection.

"You must be so excited about the trip," Bonnie said to her kindly. "You've never been to Montreal, have you?"

"I haven't," said Louise. "But I'm really just excited to see Nat."

"I'm more excited to ride the train again," said Matt. And then, catching Casey's eye, he raised his voice slightly—for she was further down the table—he raised his voice slightly and said, "Casey, have I ever told *you* my story about the train? God knows everyone else has heard it, but I don't think you have."

This was a long time ago, when their sons were both very young, and they took a family vacation to Toronto by train. Nat, in those days—he might have been four years old, or not quite four—Nat was obsessed with trains, as young boys often are; he could, and would, talk for hours about shunting and yawing, piston rods and coupling rods and Johnson bars... "We used to joke," said Matt, "that he was like a Jehovah's Witness, only instead of telling you all about God, he wanted to tell you the Good News about steam engines."

Nat was not quite four years old, so Mark must have been only one and a half. They boarded the train in Winnipeg at about ten o'clock at night; they had a sleeper car, two bunks. "Well past the boys' bedtime, of course. I remember Mark had already fallen asleep and we had to carry him with all our luggage, like a sack of potatoes, but Nat was so excited I thought his little head was going to explode."

In the morning, Matt was up very early, as he always was in those days. Louise and the children were still fast asleep, and would be for hours. It was so early that they had not yet started coffee service, so he sat quietly, watching the landscape slide by outside the window, thinking peaceful thoughts. And as he was sitting there, an elderly man came shuffling by. The man stopped and politely asked Matt if he knew which direction car 2-16 was. He had gotten up to use the washroom, he explained, and must have somehow gotten turned around, and now he couldn't find his berth. He seemed confused, or disoriented, and he had a fairly strong German accent—Mennonite, maybe. Matt had to explain that he and his family had boarded late the night before, after dark, and he didn't really know where anything was yet. He couldn't even remember the number of his own car, to be honest.

The man took notice then of the baby items that were piled by the table: the car seat, the diaper bag, the toys and picture books. "You have children, yes?"

"Two," Matt agreed.

He asked Matt how old they were, and whether they were boys or girls, and then he said, "Children are nice, it's nice to have children. The only problem with children is that they are all filthy." He put real emphasis on the word, there was real disgust in his voice: all children are *filthy*. And he went on to tell Matt how, when his own children were young, he would sit them on the toilet and not let them get off until they had done their *filthy* business, even if it took hours. No matter how they cried or complained, he would not let them stand up until their *filthy* business was finished. He then politely took his leave, and shuffled off in search of car 2-16, or whatever the number was.

The rest of that day, Matt kept an eye out for the old German man. He wanted to point him out to Louise. But he didn't see him anywhere. He didn't see him in the dining car, he didn't see him in the observation car; they went up and down the train all day and didn't see him anywhere. It hardly seemed possible: after all, when you're on a train, there's not very many places you can go. He started to joke with Louise that perhaps the old German man was a ghost—a restless spirit who was condemned to wander up and down the train from dusk to dawn, always searching for car 2-16 and never finding it, but pausing to dispense toilet-training advice to any strangers he encountered. It was only a joke. But the next morning, when Matt was again awake before the crack of dawn, and sitting at the window waiting for coffee service to begin, then that the same old German man came shuffling past. "Swear to God," said Matt. "I could hardly believe it." The old man didn't seem to remember him at all; he asked again if Matt knew which direction car 2-16 was, telling him the exact same story about getting up to use the washroom; and then he gave Matt the exact same lecture about how little children are all *filthy*, and how you must force them to sit on the toilet for hours until they were finished their *filthy* business, before finally shuffling off.

At this point in telling the story, Matt leaned well back in his chair and spread both his hands out wide as if to demonstrate that there was nothing up his sleeves. "Swear to God," he said.

"It's true," Louise said eagerly. "He told us the whole story as soon as we woke up."

So was the old German man a ghost after all? They had looked for him on the train again that morning, but once again, there had been no sign of him anywhere. Unfortunately they arrived in Toronto that same day and had to disembark, they didn't have a third night on the train. If it had happened three times in a row, then he would have been certain, but as it happened, he'd never really know for sure.

"What about on the trip back?" asked Tracy shrewdly.

"Sadly, it was a different train," said Matt. "Believe me, I checked. Now, what do *you* make of it?" he said, looking at Casey across the table.

"I don't know," said Casey. "Did you follow his advice about toilet training?"

"I didn't have the heart," said Matt. "Though there were certainly times I was tempted to," he admitted, looking meaningfully over at Mark.

"Hey," said Mark indignantly. "Don't even start."

Nora, thoughtfully—she had been listening with interest, not quite able to remember if she'd heard the story before or not—said, "Do you really think he could have been a ghost, or is that just a joke? I mean, do you even really believe in ghosts?"

"Well," he said. "I'll tell you. When I was your age, I didn't believe in ghosts at all. But now that I'm getting to be an old man, ghosts might be the only thing left I really do believe in."

THAT NIGHT, sleeping with her head next to Nora's, Casey had a horrible vivid dream: she dreamt that Alma's body had started to produce so many teeth they were coming out of her palms and her armpits, her stomach and her back all down the spine, cutting through her cheeks and coming out of the soles of her feet; and she had to help pull them out with a small black pair of pliers, and wash the wound with warm saltwater, kneeling on the floor.

When she woke up—it must have been five in the morning—it wasn't so much the dream that woke her, it was Pudge, mewling and scratching loudly at the side of the hide-a-bed. At first Casey tried to hush her and shoo her away, but instead Pudge jumped up on the bed beside her and began pawing at her chest through the blanket and mriaowing urgently in her face, as if something had upset her. Casey wondered if maybe Nora had forgotten to fill her food or water dish; anyway, she thought, she might as well get up and see what the problem was before the damn cat woke Nora, too.

Pudge jumped down from the bed, walked partway towards the basement stairs, then stopped and looked back at Casey, mriaowing again, to make sure that she was following. Up in the kitchen, Casey saw that there was plenty of food and water in Pudge's dishes already. But Pudge went right past those, not even looking at them, and then paused again at the entrance to the living room, glancing back once more. Casey noticed a low moaning come from the living room, and found Nora's grandmother sitting in her armchair, wearing her bathrobe open over a thin pink nightgown, head back and eyes closed but evidently awake, shifting uncomfortably in the soft half-light of dawn. The lower half of her face was swollen horribly, all splotchy and distended, her hands tremulous; her hair was matted and wet with sweat, despite the cool air pouring in the open window. She had her feet up on the ottoman, the knuckles protruding obscenely, the toes huddled and cramped, the nails yellow and horn-like. Pudge, at her feet, was pacing fretfully back and forth, her eyes locked on the old lady, mriaowing with concern. Alma's legs, sticking out from under her nightgown, were mottled and frail, the flesh sagging limply off the bone. She looked tremendously, tragically old, breathing deeply and slowly, the breath whistling between her teeth and rattling in her chest, and she was wincing and hissing in obvious pain; she started to bring her shaking hand up to her mouth, and then changed her mind, and lowered it to her lap, holding her breath as she shifted in her chair, then releasing it slowly with a low moan. A sickly odour was wafting off her body, a baby's smell, a smell of sour milk and thin seedy feces.

Casey, still unnoticed, slipped quietly out of the room and quickly back downstairs, and sat on the side of the hide-a-bed and shook her friend awake: "Nora," she was saying, "Nora, wake up. I think your amma's really sick, I think she might be dying."

24

Alma grows old;
Nora gets her first boyfriend

BACK WHEN THEY WERE STILL YOUNG, Nora's grandmother
sometimes used to feel nostalgic—not very often, but every now
and then—and she would reminisce about the days when she had
been a little girl, and the world was very different. She had grown
up in Winnipeg, the youngest of five, and the only girl—youngest
by eight years, for she had been a late and unforeseen addition
to the family. She had one old picture of herself, posing with her
family: her a plump, owlish infant in a little frock, being held by
a fretful, tired-looking mother; her father and brothers staring
into the camera all stiff, formal, and solemn, her father with a
square-cut beard coming down almost to his chest and deep-set
eyes that in the picture were obscured by shadow so that they
looked like black holes below a pair of hairy caterpillars.

One of her uncles owned a mortuary; her father, a carpenter by
trade, fashioned the coffins and drove the hearse. She could just
faintly remember the days when they still had a hearse drawn by
horses, and how once for a special treat her father had given her
an apple and urged her to offer it to one of the horses: how it had
sniffed cautiously at the fruit first, its enormous nostrils flaring,
and then hitched open its lips to expose its long teeth and took
it from her; and what she remembered was how terrified she had
been that it would take her hand with it, so maybe it wasn't such
a special treat after all. She'd had to promise faithfully not to tell
her mother they had let her near the horses, and to keep it a dread

secret. Her mother was a kind-hearted, worry-ridden woman, deeply religious, haunted by fears of sickness and death, always scrubbing everything in reach with the strongest soaps she could lay her hands on, Alma included. Her father, though he looked stern and sepulchral in that photograph, she remembered, on the contrary, as being good-humoured, good-natured, and easy-going, fond of a bad joke, a good smoke, and a glass or three of beer. And where her mother had considered Alma's teeth a source of constant worry, as something disgusting and slightly shameful, her father had been even proud of it, and liked to boast of it to his friends as something wonderful, a sign of luck and distinction, and he called Alma his good-luck charm, and liked to keep her close by him.

They had been fortunate, of course: even during the leanest years of the Depression, people still had to die, and the dead still had to be buried; and so though Alma's own family had never been particularly wealthy, they never suffered real poverty either. The funeral home was, she believed, still owned and managed by a third or fourth cousin of some description. But she herself had long since lost touch with her brothers and nieces and nephews and cousins: life had scattered them like dandelion seeds in a stiff wind.

For some reason she had always been convinced, or pretended to be convinced, that Casey was especially interested in these trips down memory lane. It was true that Casey felt almost flattered that Alma would single her out and speak to her about such things, in a cozy, confidential sort of way: "I know *they*'re not interested in an old lady's senile ramblings," she would say with a wink, "they" referring to her family in general and her granddaughters in particular. "But you don't mind humouring me, do you child?" She certainly didn't. After all, Casey had never had any grandparents of her own, or aunts or uncles or great-aunts or great-uncles or anything at all, Alma was the only thing like it in her life.

All that seemed long ago now. Towards the end, those last couple years of Alma's life, Casey spent less and less time at Nora's house, not because she didn't want to, but because no one was ever sure how Alma would react to having her around. When she did come over, then she and Nora would often sneak into Simon's greenhouse and hang out there. They were forbidden to go in the greenhouse, of course, but they'd been doing it for years anyway. They loved it in there, with the warm humid air and the riot of lush colours and scents, and the heady sensation that came from all that extra oxygen mixed with the thrill of illicit behaviour. When they were younger, it was almost the only place they could go that Tracy wouldn't try to tag along and make them include her in their games and their gossip, for Tracy always was a bit of a coward, too scared of their father to go in the greenhouse and too scared of her big sister to tattle on her. Nora and Casey would threaten her with vicious tortures if she ever told, and would promise faithfully to let her play with them later if she didn't. That was when they were young; now when they were fifteen, sixteen, seventeen years old, Nora and Casey would still sneak into the greenhouse, but then it was to hide from Alma and her violent, unpredictable moods, and sometimes also to take surreptitious nips from Simon's stash of liquor.

Alma's decline, which seemed at once abrupt and interminably slow, dominated the house. Her teeth were coming in faster than ever. She didn't read anymore, hardly ate, didn't cook or bake, didn't do anything but sit in that old armchair, hands groping in her mouth. She started keeping the teeth she pulled out—at first in an old jam jar, but later she would hide them around the house. She'd wrap each one up in a square of old newspaper with a piece of tape or elastic band around it, and hide the little packets in the clothes drawer, under couch cushions, tucked inside the heating vents or taped behind the pictures on the wall, behind the books on the shelves, under the carpet, even at the bottom of the flour canister and the back of the freezer; and if they discovered one, they had to be careful not to disturb it, for Alma would check on them frequently and fly into a rage if one was missing or even just moved out of place. She forgot so many things towards the end, sometimes even forgot who her daughter and granddaughters were, but she never seemed to forget where she'd hidden each and every precious tooth.

Everyone in the family dealt with it, or avoided dealing with it, in their own particular way. Simon drank, more than ever. Lynn, newly elected member of town council, threw herself into her new career, swollen with self-importance, and seemed in denial about her mother's state of mental health. Tracy spent half her life at her friend April's house and joined every club, team, and extra-curricular activity she could think of, from girl guides and church groups to the volleyball team, cross-country skiing, and the theatre club at school.

When Nora turned sixteen, her uncle Matt helped her get a part-time job waiting tables at the truck stop. At first it was for just a few hours every morning before school, to help with the breakfast rush. The Greyhound came through town twice a day, Monday to Friday: in the early morning heading east, to Winnipeg, and again in the evenings heading back west, bound for Saskatoon. In the old days the bus would only stop when someone was getting on or off, and then only for a moment; most days it would just rumble straight through. But after the new gas station and motel went up across the highway from the golf course, Matt and his partners made a deal with the Greyhound people and the town became a real scheduled stop: forty minutes in the morning for breakfast, and fifteen in the evening for people to stretch their legs, have a smoke, and hopefully spend some money in the convenience store.

The job was overwhelming in the beginning, but Nora soon got the hang of it; she even found she could be good at it, and that was gratifying. Waking up early was hard, especially in winter, but even that had a kind of satisfaction, a sort of daily minor victory. She learned to drink coffee. She learned to complain to her co-workers about the customers and the job, because complaining to one another about work was what her co-workers liked to do, but secretly she never stopped enjoying it. She got a little thrill when she heard the sound of the bus turn off the highway and rumble up towards the door. Sometimes it was five or ten minutes early, a mixed blessing: it meant they would have slightly longer for service, but they were never quite as ready. Sometimes the bus was running late, and they would feel a mounting anxiety and dread as every lost minute ticked by, each minute meaning they would be that much more rushed. And then twenty, thirty, or more people would come through the doors, all wanting and needing to be served breakfast at the same time, and quickly too. They were always tired, these travellers, many of them having been on the bus all night long: tired, stiff, huddled, and irritable, their clothes crumpled and stale, their faces smeared with sleeplessness and discomfort.

In the beginning Nora found it difficult to distinguish one customer from another, but soon she developed the knack of finding something distinctive in every face, or something about their person, the way they dressed, or wore their hair, or held their bodies, some particular surliness or air of grief, anything she could use to sort them out from the mass of others and remember their orders by. Nora quickly learned not to be *too* cheerful when she took most peoples' orders and delivered their food: she got the biggest tips when her smile and manner were something closer to coaxing and sympathetic, like a nurse. There was a real art, too, to making sure everyone got their food as quickly as possible, without ever appearing hurried: by the end of her first year there, she could do it better than anyone.

The forty minutes would fly by; then the clean-up afterwards was just as hectic, and then she would have to hurry to get to school on time. Only later in the day would she have the time and leisure to count her tips and idly imagine where each coin had travelled from: Yorkton, Saskatoon, Edmonton, maybe even as far away as Kamloops, Vancouver, or Victoria.

Soon enough she started picking up occasional shifts in the

evenings and on the weekends too, partly for the extra money—most of which she was saving up to move away for university—but also because she welcomed any excuse, in those days, to be away from her own home. Those shifts were always much quieter, especially in winter; sometimes they were interminably slow. Often Casey would come in and linger over a plate of fries for a couple of hours and keep her company; the year that Nora was dating Keith Lacoste, he would come and hang out, too, and she'd buy him a drink or a bit of food so he had an excuse to sit around, as well.

KEITH WAS NORA'S FIRST real boyfriend. Plenty of boys had asked her out before, including Alyssa's brother Anthony; she had even gone out on one or two awkward, desultory dates, but nothing had come of them. And so Nora had never yet had a boyfriend, or kissed a boy, or held a boy's hand even, not in that way. She didn't have it in her to take such things lightly, or to tell a boy she liked him if she wasn't in love with him, or to think of kissing a boy even without taking on full responsibility for his happiness forever after. Falling in love, she secretly believed, would feel catastrophic, something sudden and irreparable, like a fatal car accident.

Nora and Keith had come together over the May long weekend, at a party out behind the old Stone School. This was an annual thing, a longstanding tradition, the biggest party of the year. It was supposed to be a dread secret. Every year there were rumours that the RCMP had sworn to bust it up; they never actually had and probably never would, but that spurious hint of danger added to the fun.

Nora and Casey arrived just before sundown. It had been a warm day, but it was already starting to cool off quickly. They had to leave their bikes and hike in the last few hundred yards: only the people with pickup trucks could drive right up to the school, for what had once been the road had long since grown over with weeds and scrub brush. You could only really tell where the road had been by the deep, swampy ditches running along either side of it.

They cut across the field, pushing their bikes through the long stalky grass, the brittle burdock and tenacious thistles. The ground was muddy and uneven; there were still mounds and patches of snow in the shady places. Up ahead of them were half a dozen others, older kids, trudging across the field in a loose group: laughing, talking loudly, one walking backwards and gesturing animatedly as he talked, two of them lugging boxes of beer. Their voices, cheerful and indistinct, floated above the field. The one who was walking backwards suddenly disappeared from sight, falling abruptly into the long weeds: he must have tripped his heel in a gopher hole or something and gone down hard. His fall was met with shouts of laughter that startled a burst of sparrows out of the poplar trees.

With the sun behind their backs, low in the sky and lighting up the ruined face of the building, Nora thought it looked strangely beautiful. Scraggly, overgrown lilac bushes were growing almost up to the doors, weighed down with white and purple flowers, and their deep narcotic scent drifted out across the field.

The party was taking place out back, in the long shadow of the school, where it felt as if the sun had already set. Dozens of people were there already when Nora and Casey arrived: mostly kids they went to high school with, but a few older ones too, adults now who had graduated a year, or two, or more ago, but hadn't yet figured out how to move on.

Cheap plastic patio lanterns had been strung up by a row of coolers, shedding their weak and tinted light. Alyssa was there, standing in a loose group with her brother Anthony, Scott Vermette, Sam Anderssen, and that girl Shannon Laurence whose father used to be the mayor for more than a decade, but after he lost the last election he got drunk out of his face in the middle of the day, and he walked up the centre of 2nd Ave yelling insults, threats, and profanities, right up the steps of Town Hall, and then just pulled it out and starting pissing on the doors, with half the town out watching him, and he had to spend ten days in jail. Anthony spotted Nora and Casey right away, as they came around the side of the school, he waved and called them over and handed them a couple of beers.

The back of the school was in even worse shape than the front. All of the first floor windows, most of the second floor ones and even a few on the third and fourth floors were all smashed out. Plywood haphazardly covered one doorway and several windows, while others gaped wide. The walls and the plywood were all covered with obscene and vicious graffiti. There were calligraphic swear-words and scrawled childish swastikas and pentagrams, there was a giant penis painted in bright yellow and spewing yellow ejaculate, big disembodied tits, a dangling hanged stick man—also with a giant ejaculating penis. On one part of the wall, the bricks had been scarred and blackened by an old fire. There were sodden old cigarette butts everywhere on the ground, scattered about like seeds; the paving stones were all busted up and growing thick persistent weeds, and those weeds had leaves of broken glass and flowers of crumpled old beer cans.

Casey bummed a cigarette from Sam Anderssen; she had a few of her own, ones she had stolen from her father, in the pocket of her hoodie, but it was always better to smoke someone else's when she could, and save those for later. Then Sam lit one for himself, and Alyssa asked him for one too, and then Scott Vermette tried to get Alyssa to take one of *his* cigarettes instead, and Alyssa simpered happily, and Anthony told her she was stupid for smoking at all, and Alyssa said, "What are you going to do, tell Mommy and Daddy on me?" and Anthony said, "Fuck off."

Nearby, one guy was pretending he saw a ghostly face staring down at them from a third-storey window, and he acted as if he was scared. A few people laughed obligingly, half-heartedly, but more just groaned: somebody made that same damn joke every year.

The half-full moon hung just above the stand of crabapple trees, thick with wine-red blossoms just slightly lighter than their dark purple leaves. Casey saw Keith Lacoste emerge from the depths of those trees, carrying an armful of deadfall to help build the bonfire.

Shannon Laurence announced, abruptly, that she wanted to go inside the school and look around, go exploring. Who wanted to come with her? They ought to do it now before it got even darker, she said. She should have brought a flashlight, did anyone think to bring a flashlight? She wanted to go anyway, flashlight or not, who wanted to come with her? Shannon had either been drinking much faster than the others or had started much earlier: her speech was already a little blurred, her balance suspect.

Alyssa shuddered theatrically and said, "No *way*. It creeps me out just *think*ing about it." She looked balefully up at the blank busted windows looming above them, and shuddered again; she made her body small and her eyes big and huddled closer to Scott, as if for protection. That cigarette was burning peacefully away between her fingers, the smoke curling up around her; she had barely drawn two weak puffs off it, and then seemed to forget she had it.

"I *like* creepy," Shannon said, with an equally theatrical toss of her head. "I guess I'm just a freak that way."

Shannon tried to coax one or more of the boys to come with her, at first in a would-be flirtatious way, but none of them showed any interest; then she tried taunting them, she called them pussies and said they were chicken-shit but that didn't work either, they only laughed at her, unkindly. So finally she said, "Casey will come with me, won't you Case? You're not chicken-shit."

Back when they were children, from first grade to eighth, Shannon had been one of Casey's chief tormentors: an only child, cliquish, stout, prissy, and self-important, popular by virtue of relative wealth and her father's prominence, coddled and abetted by the teachers and other adults, and always slightly excited by her own capacity for cruelty. For years she had barely deigned to acknowledge Casey's existence except to tease and ostracize her, call her freak and try to make her cry. But adolescence had been unkind to Shannon, and not only because of her father's abrupt and very public fall from grace, nor just because her parents, as everybody in town humiliatingly knew, fought constantly these days, with all the savage and intimate nastiness that comes from pent-up years of tightly suppressed resentments. Now Shannon dressed always all in black, punctured her face with multiple piercings, shaved one side of her head and dyed the rest of her hair sometimes purple, sometimes green, and called her*self* a freak, with a kind of fragile bravado or sham defiance. She liked to dwell on death, decay, and other morbid topics, and to loudly proclaim that she had a darkness inside her heart; and in this new incarnation, she tended to act as if she and Casey were close old friends, two freaks together, with the apparent assumption that Casey would welcome it and feel grateful. And Casey knew that Shannon was ridiculous, but she never had the heart to despise her or to find her laughable or pathetic, though she quietly avoided her as much as she could without calling attention to the fact.

So Shannon said, "Casey will come with me, won't you Case?"

But Casey, at that moment, wasn't actually listening to her, didn't even hear her. She said, in an undertone and with a discreet gesture, pointing her chin in the general direction of the crabapple trees, she said, "Hey, Nora. Don't look now, but I think Keith over there is checking you out."

Nora turned and looked. The intense and childish crush that she had once harboured for Keith, back when she was twelve or thirteen years old, had long since dwindled to nothing, in fact she had nearly forgotten about it. Why he would suddenly take notice of her that night, after years of being around her with apparent indifference, she had no idea, but he was definitely staring directly and steadily at her. His back was to the trees and the half-full moon was directly above his head; the bonfire in front of him was just blazing into first life, and the young flames splashed handfuls of orange and yellow light across his lean, athletic body. He was frowning thoughtfully, as if the sight of Nora's face was stirring up some faint or vestigial memory that he was trying to catch grasp of. Their eyes met, and the impact was like a punch to her stomach. It was probably only five or ten seconds that they looked directly into one another's eyes, but it felt like a small forever, and as if they were standing only five feet apart, not forty. Keith's expression never changed or wavered at all, but Nora could feel her fair skin flushing bright red, and she felt gratified and embarrassed, self-conscious, weak, and triumphant, all at the same time. Then Tyler Klassen walked over to Keith and touched his arm, glancing over briefly to follow his friend's gaze, and the spell was broken. Tyler said something to Keith, probably asking him to go gather more wood for the fire, because Keith nodded briefly, turned, and disappeared back into the trees.

Later, they ended up sitting next to one another around the bonfire. By then Nora was quite drunk, slightly high, and intensely happy. She said she was cold, and he draped his jacket over her shoulders. Someone had brought a guitar: at Nora's boozy and loving insistence, Casey took a turn with it; she played "House of the Rising Sun" and Nora sang along. Keith told her that her voice was beautiful. Nora said she was still cold, and he put his arms around her, and she nestled up against him, watching the red and yellow flames of the bonfire lick and flicker and curl, and breathing in the mingled aroma of woodsmoke, skunkweed, and Keith's mild, not entirely unpleasant body odour.

After playing "House of the Rising Sun," Casey had politely passed the guitar back to the guy who'd brought it, pulled the hood of her black sweatshirt over her head, and hid her hands in the pockets. Her beer was empty: she wanted another one, but she didn't want to call attention to herself by standing up right away, she wanted to wait a few minutes until she could slip off unnoticed.

The bonfire popped and crackled. Tyler Klassen stood up and started tossing more wood onto it, swaying drunken and precarious above the surging flames; some people laughed, someone else told him to sit his drunk ass down. The guy who'd brought the guitar began playing "Rocky Raccoon." Casey watched Nora nestle closer up against Keith. She thought how beautiful Nora looked, her face lit from the outside by the caressing light of the fire, and lit from the inside by the glow of a manifest euphoria. And she thought how funny Keith looked, the way he was sitting exaggeratedly upright, as if trying to hide the fact that he was actually now shorter than Nora by a couple of inches.

Casey was just about ready to slip away from the circle when Landon Dueck sitting next to her passed her a joint, making her briefly conspicuous again. She didn't want to call attention to herself by turning it down, either, so she took a quick drag and passed it along. Now the guy with the guitar—his name was Duane Jensen but she couldn't remember it just then, only that it had something to do with a dog—Duane was playing "Copperhead Road" and some of the others were singing along. Landon was particularly off-key and enthusiastic, garbling the words of the verses and then practically shouting when it came to the chorus. Casey felt vertiginous, she didn't trust her legs, she was certain that if she tried to stand at that moment she would topple headfirst into the fire, so she sat very tight and still. She tried to imagine that her face had been erased, leaving only a blank space where her eyes, nose and mouth ought to be. Behind her, she could hear the rest of the party still going strong away from the bonfire: drunken laughter, happy shouts and angry ones, someone arguing, distant and distorted music blasting out of a cheap tape player perched on the hood of someone's truck. Above her, wispy fingers of cloud slid past the face of the half and waxing moon.

Standing just outside the circle of people around the fire was Anthony. At first he was little more than an indistinct dark shape, huddled against the darker dark of the crabapple trees at his back, but there was something Casey found vaguely disquieting about the detached, still, and silent way he was standing there. Casey had to focus her gaze on him for a minute or so before she was able to make out the features and expression on his face. She saw that he was staring fixedly and intently at Nora and Keith; she saw that he was staring at them with an expression of wounded petulance, of pained and sullen reproach. She thought that his head appeared to have swollen beyond its natural size, like an overinflated balloon: she imagined it gently detaching from his body and floating up into the sky, still growing in size, still glaring down on Nora and Keith from a great height.

Later that night, Anthony would give Casey her first real kiss, open mouth and all. She felt repulsed, yet at the same time strangely exultant, for she had no doubt that with his eyes closed he was imagining Nora. She tolerated his clumsy hand groping at her left breast, but when he tried to stick his tongue deep into her mouth, she bit it, hard enough to draw blood.

KEITH LACOSTE was no longer the sullen, moody, and restless boy he had been at fourteen; that seductive and misleading air of brooding romance and secret tragedy had passed along with the storms of puberty, leaving hardly a trace behind. He was now merely a good-looking, good-natured, easy-going young man with no particular ambition in life and with a previously unsuspected reserve of acute sentimentality.

Dating Nora inspired Keith to start drawing again; by the time she was back at school in September, he had already given her a dozen odd sketches in soft coloured pencil that she papered the walls of her bedroom with. They were all variations on the same basic theme: one small portion of her body in close-up—maybe her hand, or her eyes, or the back of her head to show her flowing hair, or the lower half of her face in profile—superimposed over a landscape, generally with a wild animal in the background, a wolf baying romantically at the moon, a jack rabbit alert in a field, a hawk with its wings spread wide against the sky.

He and his family lived in an old farmhouse on the far side of the highway, together with one old barn, two garages, and an acre or so of yard. An old camper sat on cinder blocks between the garages and served as a kind of guest house when the weather was good.

Since they had moved in, Keith's father, Albert, had partly refinished the basement, framing a pair of spare bedrooms and adding a half-bathroom at the back, sectioned off by an old shower curtain. The Lacostes used what had originally been the living room as the master bedroom, and Albert built an extension off the kitchen where the mudroom used to be, wide and long with room for a couple old couches and the television: it served as the living room during the day and a makeshift guest room at night. He had run out of drywall towards the end, leaving one and a half walls with the pink insulation still exposed behind plastic sheeting. He would occasionally make vague allusions to finishing it up properly someday, but nobody believed him. He had already moved on to his next project, a nice big deck off the back; when that was done, or almost done, the roof needed re-shingling and the outside of the house re-painting, and after that, Albert said, what he really wanted to do was gut the old barn and put it to some kind of use: just what he wasn't sure, but he thought he could make something out of it. Maybe turn it into a kind of indoor play structure for the little ones. His own kids were all grown up—Keith was the youngest of four—but there was never a shortage of grandchildren and other peoples' kids running around the place.

Albert Lacoste wasn't a tall man, but he managed to project the illusion of imposing size: he was burly, with a belly like a beach ball that he took a kind of fond paternal pride in, often patting or caressing it. That and his toothbrush moustache: short, coarse, and bristly, he claimed to have coaxed it into existence by sheer willpower and called it his favourite child. Keith said that his father had a temper, but Nora never saw it, she never saw him any way but laughing or trying to make others laugh. Young children loved to climb on him or hang off of him as if he were a jungle gym. His favourite joke was to repeat the last thing someone said as if it were a line in a blues by Muddy Waters or John Lee Hooker, improvising a verse around it, then make a wailing sound that was supposed to resemble the electric guitar: this could be irritating, but it could also be pretty funny. He would sometimes tease people mercilessly, especially his children, or mug and clown shamelessly, for he couldn't tolerate sadness or solemnity: long faces and serious conversations made him restless and uneasy; an open display of grief, emotional distress, or the least sign of tears would make him flee the room, quite literally. Then he would take refuge in the second garage, where he had all his tools set up, and a card table in the corner, and a beer fridge always stocked, and an old stereo to blast the same homemade mix-tape of electric blues over and over again. It was there in the second garage that he often had "business meetings" with Benji Pettinger, Uncle Matt, and sometimes Matt's son Mark, meetings that generally consisted of playing cards, smoking cigars, drinking, gossiping, and bullshitting. Nora saw more of her uncle Matt and cousin Mark that year that she dated Keith Lacoste than she probably had in the previous decade.

The house always seemed to have at least half a dozen young children in it; Keith's mother seemed to invariably have one baby or another on her hip or in her arms, whether it was one of her own grandchildren or the child of some niece, nephew, cousin, or one of her children's friends. Anyone from Waabishkigwan who had to travel down to Brandon or Winnipeg would stop and stay for at least a day or two on their way there and the way back. There were various elders and elderly relatives who would take up residence now and then as well; Nora never did manage to sort these out, or keep track of their comings and goings.

It was well-known that Keith's mother could make any baby stop crying almost instantly: she was a kind of universal mother. Then her half-closed eyes would crinkle joyfully at the corners, and her kind round face would beam with tender pleasure. She liked to bustle about and keep busy; she was usually on her feet, most often in the kitchen cooking or baking for the hordes of people who occupied her home, or puttering about the house tidying up after them. And she liked to complain that she never got a chance to sit down and put her poor sore feet up, but then when she did, she would quickly make an excuse to haul herself up again, pretending to have suddenly remembered something she needed to do, saying, "Oh my goodness," and waving her hands above her head and pretending to be flustered. She wasn't a large woman, just a little heavy-set, but she could move about with surprising quickness; she had long black hair, black and grey and fine and beautiful, that she usually wore in a long loose ponytail. She answered to any number of names: Pat, Trish, Trisha, Auntie, Mama, Mom, Naan, Nana, Gran. Her own husband would call her any and all of these, interchangeably and almost at random, occasionally throwing Ma'am into the mix when he wanted to tease her. Nora's Uncle Matt and Auntie Louise called her Trish or Trisha; most of Keith's friends—who, like all her children's friends, were in and out of the house constantly, coming and going as they pleased—most of them called her Auntie Pat or just plain Auntie; sometimes Keith would address her as Auntie Pat too: then she would cluck her tongue and pretend to be indignant, maybe shake a fist or wooden spoon at him laughingly.

Keith's oldest sister, Mindy, had the most kids. Around the time that Nora and Keith were first getting serious, she had just had another baby—her fourth, all boys, the oldest one only six. Mindy was so much like her mother, it was almost funny to see. Younger, of course, and a little less heavy, but otherwise almost identical, down to the way her half-closed eyes would crinkle at the corners when she was happy and the way she'd cluck her tongue or wave her hands above her head; even their voices could be hard to tell apart if you heard them from the other room. Both of them were inclined to be talkative at the best of times, but when you got them in the same room it was something else. They would spend hours and hours in that little kitchen together, both of them on their feet and bustling about the whole time, baking and cooking and passing the babies back and forth, and both of them talking non-stop, the words tumbling peaceably over top of one another, poring over the minutiae of the lives of everybody they knew in their warmhearted, gossipy way.

Mindy and her family lived up on the reserve, but they spent almost as much time at her parents' house as they did at home. Her husband Barry worked in the band office, right-hand man to Chief Willie Ouimette, who happened to also be his uncle. Now, Barry's uncle Willie Ouimette and Mindy's father Albert had been close friends when they were younger: survived the old Stone School together, were close like a couple of brothers as young men. They had worked side by side many times. Albert had helped Willie get elected to the band council back in the day and had worked on his campaign when he first ran for Chief. In those days Albert used to call him, affectionately, by old blues-man names: Blind Willie Ouimette, or Blind Lemon, or Boxcar Willie, or Broken Orange Ouimette, or the Rollin' Orange Peel. Later, after Mindy married Willie Ouimette's nephew Barry, then Albert started calling him Uncle Chief. "How's Uncle Chief?" he would ask his son-in-law, whenever he happened to stop by: "Still working his fingers to the bone?" or, "Say hello to Uncle Chief for me when you see him." More recently, ever since Chief Ouimette had had a new community centre built on the reserve, with a fancy new band office and a bingo hall and everything, then Albert had started referring to his old friend as the Bingo Caller, with a mild but definite undercurrent of hostility beneath the semblance of good-humoured ribbing. "How's the old Bingo Caller doing?" he would ask Barry. "Haven't heard from the old Bingo Caller in ages," he would say. "How's he holding up these days? Still calling a mean game of bingo? I-38! B-16! Blackout Bingo!" And Barry would smile uncertainly, never quite certain how to respond, and so preferring to say nothing at all.

The youngest of Keith's three sisters, Amber, had a new baby too, just a few months older than Mindy's. It was Amber's second child already: Nora couldn't imagine having two children by the time she was only twenty-one. No one ever referred to the father as anything but "that asshole," Nora never learned more than that about him.

Of Keith's three sisters it was Tina who Nora liked the most, though she saw her the least. Tina lived in Winnipeg and was going to law school. She was smart and cynical and imperturbable. She played poker with her father and his friends and beat them, too. She liked to joke that she was keeping a list of all the people she was going to sue as soon as she passed the bar and would threaten to put you on it if you pissed her off. She and Keith were great pals: they drank beer and played video games together, she called him Baby Brother and bossed him around, she lectured him and she loved him. Unlike her mother and older sister, Tina didn't have much interest in babies. She was fond enough of her niece and nephews and various young cousins, of course, but she couldn't take all the drool and poop; she liked the older kids best, the ones you could actually have a conversation or play games with. She couldn't or wouldn't cook, either. Whenever she came home for the weekend, Trisha would make a massive batch of bannock with cinnamon sugar, because that was Tina's favourite, and it would fill the house with its sweet hot smell, and it was the most amazing thing that Nora ever tasted. Up in Winnipeg, Tina would freely admit, she lived off ramen noodles, french fries, and those awful chef salads they sold at the university cafeteria, drowned in Thousand Island dressing. She wore little round glasses and oversized old sweatshirts and baggy faded blue jeans, her nape-length hair was wavy and always immaculately disheveled, and she was just so lovely to look at it made your heart giggle. Nora had such a crush on Tina that she half-seriously considered going to law school, too, after she graduated high school.

25

A party for Keith;
the trouble with owls

NEAR THE END OF SEPTEMBER, Keith's family threw a big party
to celebrate his eighteenth birthday. Keith and Nora had been
together then for four months and eleven days. The morning of
the party, Nora worked a shift at the truck stop. Casey met up
with her there and had a couple cups of coffee and a danish while
she waited for Nora to finish up her shift. Nora got changed in
the back, then together they slowly rode their bikes the short way
over to the Lacostes' place.

Nora had an overnight bag all packed: pyjamas, toothbrush
and toothpaste, clean clothes for the morning. The idea of buying
condoms had crossed her mind, but it being such a small town,
there was no way she could have gotten hold of some without word
getting back to her parents. Her parents didn't even know it was
Keith's birthday, she'd told them that she would be spending the
weekend at Casey's place. She didn't care if they believed her or
not: Nora and her parents were not getting along that summer,
they'd had another big fight just the night before, all yelling and
slamming doors and horrible things being said.

She hadn't told Keith about the overnight bag. She didn't
know yet what she was going to do, she might coward out and
leave with Casey, spend the night at her place after all. She and
Casey worked out a signal, a sort of code: at some point in the
evening, Nora would start talking about owls. If she said that she
had always loved owls, then she and Casey would leave together;

if she said that she had been terrified of owls when she was a kid, it meant that she was going to spend the night with Keith, and Casey could leave. The sheer silliness of this secret code made Nora giggle, and helped relieve some of her nervousness.

When they came wheeling up the drive, they found Albert and Barry getting the yard set up for the party: unfolding lawn chairs, putting up tiki torches. The sweet green smell of freshly cut grass stained the air. Mindy and Barry's two middle sons, shirtless as usual when the weather was fine, their proud and brown little bellies bulging out, were batting an orange balloon back and forth and shrieking happily when a gust of wind would push it out of their reach. One of them almost darted under the wheel of Nora's bike as she came slowly around the bend, and she had to swerve to one side, wobbling off into the grass and then leaping clear as the bike toppled over.

Albert complimented her on what he called her "graceful dismount." He said, "You just gotta stick the landing a little better. I give it an eight point five."

"I'm fine," said Nora. "Nobody got hurt. Thanks for asking, nice of you to be concerned."

He asked Nora if that's how she usually stopped the car when she was driving, too: "Just steer it off the side of the road and jump clear?"

Keith had been giving Nora driving lessons over the summer, she having failed dismally her first attempt at getting her license, back in the spring. Albert was always happy to let them use his beater for the lessons, a powder-blue Malibu with bald tires and a square of cardboard duct-taped over one of the back windows. But since those driving lessons consisted almost exclusively of going a short distance out of town, parking somewhere private, and then making out until their mouths were sore and their bodies ached with pent-up arousal, she was making very little progress. And Albert had taken to calling the Malibu "the Love Bucket," and made a running joke of Nora's poor driving skills.

There were card tables lined up against the side of the garage; Barry had spread checkered plastic tablecloths over top of them and was taping them in place, making a surprisingly fussy job of trying to have them lie flat and look nice. Nora had met Barry once or twice before, briefly: a smiling, quiet, stumpy man with an almost perfectly round head, who had apparently spent so many years unable to get a word in edgewise that he had forgotten what it was like to want to and was generally content to putter happily and silently in the background, making himself helpful.

In a homemade barbecue pit made of cinder blocks and a sawed-off metal barrel, the shoulder of a moose was slowly roasting over coals. Keith's great-grandfather was propped on a lawnchair in front of it, a walking stick across his lap, to guard the kids from tumbling against the barbecue pit accidentally. Albert introduced him to Nora and Casey: an adorable, toothless old man with skin the colour of an acorn and an intricately wrinkled face, who smiled beatifically at the girls like an infant passing gas.

Albert made a great show of raising the lid to check the meat. The shoulder was enormous, almost obscenely so, and completely covered in strips of blistered fatty bacon, and the bacon fat dripped down onto the hot coals and gave off a black, musky smoke; and mingled with the smell of the bacon and the smoke was a subtle aroma that made Casey think of freshly turned mud, or spring pussy willows in a wet ditch. Albert asked her if she'd ever eaten moose meat before. "Oh, you're in for a treat," he said, patting his belly.

When Casey had first been introduced to Albert, he had jumped to the conclusion that she was Indigenous, too. That was back at the height of summer, when Casey was always at her brownest. She had almost been tempted not to correct him; and after all, what did she really know about her father's family or where he came from? For all she knew it could even be true. Her father never spoke about himself, or where he came from; her mother never told her anything but nonsense.

"Oh, you're in for a treat," he said now, patting his belly, and making her lean over the shoulder and breathe in deeply. "This is going to change your life. It's like getting religion."

At the beginning of the month, Albert, Keith, and a pair of Keith's great-uncles had gone up north on a hunting trip. It was Keith's first time; he had never been interested in going before and wasn't really that keen to go this time but did it to humour his father. Albert himself hadn't gone in years but had suddenly decided that with his only son turning eighteen, it was an important rite of passage. They were gone six days.

Perhaps subconsciously, Nora had expected him to return subtly transformed, somehow: more manly, or wiser, or maybe a little taller. He came back instead with blisters on his hands and feet and complaining that it was cold up there and it had rained half the time and his body was stiff and sore all over. The moose had been killed by one of the uncles. Keith had fired a gun exactly once, scaring the hell out of a tree and leaving an ugly purple welt on his shoulder from the kickback. The best part of the trip was when his father left the tent one night to take a leak, and they heard a crashing sound and him all swearing like a drill sergeant, and he came back in the tent soaking wet and just covered in mud: he had lost his footing in the rain and the dark, drunk. That was funny. The hunting itself was boring, he told her: like fishing, it seemed to consist almost entirely of waiting quietly while nothing happened.

When they actually killed the moose, that had been exciting at first, and then Keith had burst out crying. He didn't tell Nora about that, how he had cried when he saw the animal dying and dead, its toppled massive body shuddering out its life and then lying still, emptied of *some*thing. Nor did he tell Nora about waking up to see the sun rise over the lake where they were camped and watching the surface of the water flicker and shimmer with purple and gold. One of his uncles told him that one time, years and years ago, he had gone up there on a hunting trip and happened across a man shooting at the lake. This man just stood on the very edge of the shore, pointing his rifle down at the water, and he'd fire. The bullet would hit the lake maybe ten or twelve feet from the shore, sending up a gout of water; then he'd reload the rifle carefully, train his sights on the lake, wait patiently for the water to become still, and fire again. He did this over and over and over again, never moving from the spot, always staring grimly down at the lake. Keith's uncle had watched him from a distance for a long time: he was desperately curious to know what this guy thought he was firing at, and why, but he was pretty hesitant to call attention to himself, to disturb or startle what was quite evidently a crazy person with a loaded gun. After watching him for what felt like hours, and it didn't seem like the guy was ever going to stop, he finally just crept away, and camped somewhere else that year.

Those hunting uncles—they were always together, like a matching set of salt and pepper shakers—had come up to town a few days before the party, bringing half the butchered moose meat with them, and spending pretty much all their time since then out on the golf course. Keith, Albert, and Barry had spent the day before out on the course with them, this being another rite of passage for Keith, and one he had been significantly more excited about. Albert was a pretty solid golfer, and Barry could hit the ball, but Keith had apparently been terrible, hacking chunky divots out of the green, taking great homicidal swings only to top the ball and watch it dribble a few weak feet from the tee, or when he did connect with it, watch it veer wildly into the rough; and he blamed it on still being sore from the hunting trip, and one of the blisters on his hand not totally healed; and his father, uncles, and brother-in-law ribbed him mercilessly.

Now Keith and Tina were in the living room, slumped comfortably on the old green couch, playing a video game. Both of them were still in their pyjamas, bare feet up on the coffee table; they were playing a racing game, and their bodies lurched from side to side as they navigated the twisty track, jostling against one another and cheerfully trash-talking. Mindy's oldest son and some other boy about the same age, who Nora had never seen before, were hopping up and down excitedly in front of the tv screen, cheering the racers on and blocking their view. Nora put her hand over Casey's hand and gave it a quick tight squeeze.

Steam and a babble of voices were coming out of the kitchen, as Trisha, Mindy, and a couple of the aunties were boiling potatoes, chopping cabbage for coleslaw and onions for frying, opening cans of baked beans, mixing cake batter, passing the babies back and forth and talking all over top of one another.

With one quick, long-legged motion, Nora hopped atop the coffee table and launched herself onto the couch, turning mid-air to land half on Keith's lap. His video game car spun out of control and off the side of the track, allowing Tina's car to speed past and sail across the finish line.

Keith gave out a squawk of dismay; Tina dropped her controller in her lap, threw both hands triumphantly in the air above her head, and hollered, "Yes! Yes! Undefeated!" She leaned forward with her hands still up to get high-fives from the little kids.

"Dammit," said Keith, "I was *that* close to winning."

"Sure you were, kiddo," said Tina condescendingly. "Whatever helps you sleep at night."

Nora laughingly pouting and delicately brushing Keith's fine black hair back from his forehead said, "I guess I'll just have to make it up to you." She leaned in for a kiss.

"Oh God," said Tina, "they're starting again." She heaved herself to her feet, holding the joystick out to the boys: "Who wants it next?" Both boys grabbed at it and started tussling over it like a pair of starving dogs over a single bone.

"Nice jammies," Nora said to Keith, running her palm across the soft plaid flannel. Like the video game, they were new, one of his birthday presents.

"Yeah, you like 'em?" said Keith, wiggling his long brown toes and waggling his eyebrows seductively.

"Very sexy," Nora whispered, hardly more than mouthing the words.

"Oh Jesus," said Tina. "I'm outta here." Only now, as she headed towards the kitchen door, did she notice Casey standing quietly in the corner. "Are they always like this?" she asked her; and Casey shrugged meekly and made a face that said, Yes, pretty much.

"I don't know how you stand it," said Tina, in that same tone of affectionately mocking banter; and then, on a strange and fleeting impulse, she reached out and touched Casey's upper arm, first stroking and then gently squeezing it, with the sort of awkward, consoling smile with which you might greet a newly bereaved acquaintance. The moment passed, quick as the shadow of an overhead bird; she said, "I probably oughtta go get dressed or something," and left the room.

While kissing Keith, Nora had deftly taken the joystick away from him and held it out to the boys. Now she stood up from off his lap and said, "You should get dressed, too. I heard there's going to be a party or something."

"Yeah," said Keith, expelling a long slow breath and shifting slightly in his seat. "I maybe oughtta just sit here for a minute or two first."

Nora, glancing down at his lap and then looking quickly away, both laughed and blushed. "Why don't I go say hi to your Mom?"

"Sounds good," said Keith, looking fixedly at the tv screen. Then turning his head slightly, smiling politely and waving one hand, he said, "Hey, Case."

"Hey, Keith. Happy birthday."

"Yeah, thanks. Thanks for coming."

"Thanks for inviting me."

"My pleasure," he said. He asked her if she had brought her guitar. He didn't know that it was actually Nora's guitar, having only ever seen Casey pick it up.

Casey shook her head.

"That's too bad," said Keith. "You shoulda oughtta brought it."

"Is Duane gonna be here?" asked Nora.

"The Dane?" said Keith. "Yeah, he's gonna be here. He told me he's coming for sure." Duane Jensen in elementary school had been given the nickname Duane the Great Dane; by high school it had been shortened simply to the Dane.

Nora gave Casey a meaningful glance, a quick pregnant smile. "*He*'ll have his guitar," she said. "He never goes anywhere without it."

"This," admitted Keith, "is true. That is an actual fact."

Nora lately, with a wholly unconscious, even oblivious cruelty—only because she herself was so giddily happy to be in love and wanted her friend to experience that same happiness for herself—Nora had lately been trying to coax Casey into finding a boyfriend, assuring her that this or that guy found her attractive, or that Keith had told her that one of his friends had told him that he would be into Casey if Casey was into him, and so on. Nora did it without thinking; she meant nothing but kindness by it. And Keith, too, was very keen to try and set Casey up with one of his friends, if only so that she might be less of an almost omnipresent third wheel. In particular they had convinced themselves that Casey and Duane would make a perfect couple, because they both played guitar and both liked wandering off into the woods.

After Keith got dressed, he and Nora and Casey played frisbee with some of the older kids until dinner. Already almost a dozen of Keith's family and friends were down from the reserve to celebrate his birthday; more kept arriving over the course of the afternoon, lining the driveway with their trucks and cars. One of the cousins from Waabishkigwan had brought a dog along, a dopey dishevelled collie who kept leaping and snapping at the frisbee, barking fiercely, and if he got his mouth on it he would pin it down with his paws and tear at it as if trying to kill it, and Keith would have to wrestle it away from him, and by the time dinner was ready, the frisbee was all slobbered and mangled and would only wobble unsteadily when you tried to throw it.

Nora's uncle Matt and Auntie Louise had come for dinner, and so had Mark. Matt gave Keith a real cuban cigar for his birthday; Mark gave him a little baggy with three rolled joints in it, passing it to him discreetly under the guise of a friendly handshake. Benji Pettinger was there too, a wiry little man with a rectangular moustache like a rusty razor blade stuck to his upper lip; and there was his son Trent Pettinger and Trent's wife, Marian. Trent had become mayor in the last election and carried himself now with a guarded, stiff, self-conscious assumption of dignity.

They ate outside, with paper plates on their laps and plastic cutlery. The moose meat was delicious, especially slathered in barbecue sauce and fried onions and piled on bannock. Keith stirred his up with his baked beans and ate it that way.

Tyler Klassen was there: he had squeezed a lawn chair in between Auntie Pat, as he called her, and Tina. The fabric of the chair stretched ominously when he sat on it, and his big chubby knees jutted comically high. There was enough food on his plate for three, and he shovelled it into his mouth with gross abandon, making vaguely orgasmic noises between mouthfuls. He had recently started trying to grow a beard, a wispy patchy blond fringe that was now collecting barbecue sauce, bannock crumbs, and scraps of meat.

"This is amazing shit, Auntie Pat," he said. "You're the best fucking cook in the world, you know that? When we get married," he said to Tina, "this is what we should serve at the wedding."

"Oh God," said Tina, putting her hand to her mouth in mock disgust. "I think I just puked in my mouth a little." This was an old, longstanding joke between them: Tyler always said that as soon as Tina had passed the bar, he was going to marry her and be her trophy husband. He'd make great arm candy, he always pointed out, and he would keep house for her while she jetted around the country suing important people, and she would keep him in the style to which he deserved to become accustomed; and Tina, whenever he started talking about it, which was pretty much every time he saw her, would always pretend to be physically ill.

"A whole fucking moose on a giant spit," he went on, ignoring her comment and pursuing his idea. "Keith'll go bag one for us, won't you Keith?"

He hollered that last part at Keith on the other side of the yard, but Keith didn't answer him: he was being monopolized by Marian Pettinger, who had given him a horoscope for his birthday, one that she had cast for him herself, and had been spending a good half hour now going over it with him and explaining the finer points.

Marian Pettinger was younger than her husband, still in her mid-thirties maybe, big-eyed and long-lipped, draped in a shawl and jangling with loose jewelry, long dangly earrings, three to each ear, and a dozen clacking bracelets to each forearm, and rings on every finger, and she stank of joss sticks and sandalwood. As she pored over the horoscope with Keith, talking about things like the significance of Saturn's transit to the Virgo-Libra cusp, she would occasionally touch his arm or laugh flirtatiously, and he would smile politely, and then she would glance with her big eyes over in Matt's direction, to see if he was noticing. Casey watched all this, and she watched Nora watching it and getting increasingly angry, her arms crossed and her long body slumped back in her lawn chair, pouting ferociously the whole time, picking at her food, hardly speaking.

After dinner, Nora helped out by carrying a garbage bag around and collecting the paper plates, used napkins, and plastic cutlery. Landon Dueck and Duane Jensen arrived together, and they and Keith and Tyler all mysteriously disappeared, coming back after ten or fifteen minutes with red and hooded eyes and a tendency to giggle.

As the sky started to darken and a mild chill set into the air, Albert lit the tiki torches and Barry and Tyler started the bonfire, arguing congenially about the best way to build it up. It was the most animated conversation that Nora had ever seen Barry engage in. Mindy brought out the birthday cake and lit the candles and Albert handed out sparklers to all the young kids, who jumped around waving them dangerously, watching the sparks leap up. He gave a sparkler to Casey too, having noticed her sitting meekly off to the side, not talking to anyone. She didn't want to take it, but he insisted, lighting it for her and practically dropping it in her lap.

Casey was notorious for leaving parties and other places abruptly, without saying goodbye to anyone, not even Nora; without even letting herself be seen to leave, just simply disappearing. She would have liked to disappear from this party now, but she couldn't; she had promised to stay until Nora started talking about owls: she was tethered, trapped, until Nora released her.

Out of the corner of her eye, she could see Duane approaching her, with his baggy canvas pants and that same green shirt with the thick and faded red cross printed on the front that he wore everywhere, his head dipping forward as if it was too heavy for his long scrawny neck to hold up. She felt her body stiffen like a wary bird, ready to burst into flight, and she held herself very still.

He sat beside her. He asked her if she was getting cold: he had a sweater in his truck if she wanted to borrow it. He seemed slightly self-conscious, something he had never been around her before, and of course she knew why. Since it was inconceivable to her that he could genuinely find her attractive on his own, she took it for granted that Keith and Nora had put the idea into his head, talked him around: he always did have a reputation for being highly suggestible.

He asked her if she wanted to borrow his sweater, and she said yes though she wasn't particularly chilly and didn't really want it, but she remembered Nora putting on Keith's jacket at that party behind the old Stone School, and so she knew that yes was what a normal girl would say.

He ambled off to get it. Nora was watching all this from across the yard, trying to catch Casey's eye and ask her in pantomime how it was going: thumbs up or thumbs down? Smile or frown? Casey smiled weakly, and made a wavering thumb-mostly-sideways-but-maybe-slightly up gesture, and dutifully waited for Duane to return.

Nora was sitting next to Auntie Louise. Since she had started getting serious with Keith, she had felt an extra closeness to Louise, or at least a desire to be closer to her. It seemed to her now that her Auntie was looking tired, worn-out, withdrawn. She had recently lost weight, and it didn't suit her. Nora asked her how Nathanael was doing out in Montreal—it was his last year at McGill, right? He'd be graduating in the spring, be a real dentist? Was he planning to move back then, set up practice closer to home? It always made Auntie Louise happy, Nora knew, to talk about Nat.

"Now did I tell you," Louise said, "that he's moved in with that girlfriend of his?"

"No," said Nora. "That's a little bit exciting. Are they going to get married? When is he going to bring her home so we can all meet her?"

"Your uncle thinks we ought to fly out at Christmas and surprise them," said Louise; and for a reason that Nora couldn't quite fathom, there was a deep and unmistakable melancholy in her voice when she said it; and she was looking in the direction of her husband with a sad and knowing smile. Matt was standing in a group with Albert, Mark, and the Pettingers, smoking a cigar and talking heatedly, making grandiose gestures. Nora thought how much younger he looked than his wife, though really only a few years separated them. The Wellesleys were known for aging slowly and gracefully, especially the men, and Matt most of all, so much like his father. Marian Pettinger had her arm around her own husband's waist and was leaning against him, but she never took her eyes off Matt. Nora, mistakenly, imagined that this was the cause for that sadness in her aunt's voice, and she felt a surge of sympathetic rage at her uncle. Later that night she said to Keith, seemingly out of nowhere and with a barely suppressed ferocity, "If you ever cheated on me I'd kill you."

Keith was startled and slightly frightened; he also felt vaguely guilty, supposing that there must have been something he had done or said to provoke it, though he couldn't for the life of him think what it could have been. But before he could protest his innocence, Nora had already repented her outburst, and she was kissing him and saying, "I know you'd never, I know you'd never."

It was late, then. The fat and harvest moon hung low above the horizon, tinted orange and impossibly large. Uncle Matt, Auntie Louise, and the Pettingers had long since gone home. Trisha and Mindy, having gone inside to put the children to bed, had fallen asleep themselves. Duane was playing guitar and singing quietly under his breath:

> Gonna drive my Pontiac
> Up to cemetery hill,
> My best girl in the back
> With a bottle and some pills.
>
> Gonna park beneath the stars
> And look down on this town,
> In the back seat of my car
> Gonna nail my baby down.

Earlier, at Albert's insistence, he had played through every blues song he knew—not many of them—while Albert sang along with great gusto, improvising verses when he couldn't remember all the words. Then Landon and Tyler made him play "Copperhead Road," and "Johnny 99," and "Lawyers, Guns & Money." Duane had tried to give the guitar to Casey to play a few songs, but she had refused, and not even Nora could make her change her mind.

Casey was very drunk by then, though you couldn't tell it to look at her. The sweater that Duane had leant her was enormous on her, it was a heavy wool and hand-knit, and it scratched and itched and she was terribly hot and sweating underneath it, though the night air was so cold now the tip of her nose felt sharp. Casey found that she was having difficulty making her eyes focus properly, so she tried staring intently at Duane's hands as he played: his long, skinny fingers made her think irresistibly of a spider's legs, moving over the strings like a spider scuttling back and forth across the surface of its web. He was playing and singing quietly to himself now, practising a new song he was still trying to learn, something called "Tam Lin." Casey thought that when he was like this, focused so gently and intently on his music, virtually oblivious to everyone around him, then she really could find him attractive, or see at least why others seemed to, which was good enough. When he laid the guitar down, she asked him if he had ever thought about giving guitar lessons.

He hadn't, he said; but then he added that he'd make an exception for her, if she really thought there were things that he could teach her. But she only said, "Yeah, maybe," in the blankest way imaginable, and turned away from the conversation. She turned to Nora. She said, "I need to go home before I pass out."

So Nora asked Duane if he could give Casey a lift. "The last time she biked home in the middle of the night, an owl swooped right down at her head and knocked her off the road."

"Really?" said Duane. "An owl? That's crazy, I've never heard of an owl doing something like that. That must have been one crazy damn owl."

"Owls are terrifying," said Nora. "I've always been terrified of owls."

"That really happen?" Duane asked Casey. "Seriously?"

Casey made a helpless gesture. "Terrifying," she said expressionlessly. "It was terrifying." And then, briefly channeling her mother, she added, "It was definitely trying to kill me. I think I saw it holding a little switchblade in its wing." She made a weak stabbing motion, as if brandishing a knife.

Duane laughed. "Sure, I'll give you a lift. We can throw your bike in the back of the truck."

"You'll have to tell me where I'm going," Duane said as he started the engine.

"Take the road north past the cemetery," said Casey. "I'll tell you when to turn."

He drove slowly, with the exaggerated caution of someone who knows he is far too drunk to be driving at all. They travelled mostly in silence; Duane once or twice attempted to start a conversation and was met with monosyllabic, monotone responses. And Casey did not look at him, either, not once, but stared blindly out the window at the black night and the occasional smear of a distant light. She had drawn her legs up onto the seat and sat with them coiled up to her chest, elbows on her knees.

She had him stop the truck at the side of the road near her driveway, she didn't want him to take the truck right up to the house. When he turned the engine off, then she did look at him. She thanked him for the lift, but she made no move to leave the cab, she just sat there, staring at him; and it seemed to him that her hazel eyes in the dark had a faint luminescence, like a cat's.

"I'll help you get your bike out of the back," he said, and then she uncoiled suddenly and leaned across and started kissing him: drunkenly, sloppily. For a second he was almost too startled to respond; and then, just as he began kissing her back with real enthusiasm, she abruptly broke it off and coiled back into her seat. And her eyes gleamed now with a cool but unmistakable satisfaction, and she said nothing.

"We used to call you Henry," he blurted out stupidly. "Back in junior high. Because you cut your hair so short, and one of the guys said you looked more like a dude than a girl, and another guy said you should be named Henry or something, and it just sort of stuck. But I never thought you—I mean, I always thought you were really pretty, even with no hair."

"You know, Casey *is* a boy's name, too," she pointed out. "I kinda have a boy's name already." She sounded, to Duane's immense relief, not offended but merely amused.

"Yeah. Sorry. I know, it's stupid."

She kissed him again, almost climbing across the cab and onto his lap. She took his hand and placed it on her left breast; when he put his tongue deep into her mouth, she resisted the urge to bite it off. She was sustained by the exultant thought of an almost mystical synchronicity, that she and Nora would each be losing their virginity on the same night—perhaps even, she imagined, at the exact same moment, a separate but simultaneous first instant of penetration. And she remembered a story her mother had told her once about identical twin sisters separated at birth, and how one of them—still just a child—had started spontaneously and inexplicably bleeding from between the legs at the exact same moment that her twin, in a distant city, was being raped.

She bumped her hip against the steering wheel and her head against the roof of the cab, he banged his elbow painfully against the door handle. He was aroused and confused, drunk, excited, and frightened; after a few minutes of scuffling, panting, and slobbering, as she began to ineptly and impatiently tug and fumble at his clothing, he stopped her, tried to manoeuvre her off his lap, he opened the cab door and they almost tumbled out into the road. And he left her standing with her bike at the end of her driveway, little and alone, with trepidatious assurances of affection and a promise to get together the next day. She never really forgave him.

26

Casey hates herself;
the girls dream of going away

IT WAS NOT WITH DUANE JENSEN, after all, but with Nora's uncle Matt, that Casey finally rid herself of her virginity. By then she had started to think that it was never going to happen at all, that there must be something wrong with her. Her eighteenth birthday had come and gone. Everyone she knew at school had done it, and was doing it; there wasn't much else for a teenager to do in that town. Even Tracy had already gone further with a boy than Casey had.

It happened, at last, on the night of Alma's funeral, when she was in a mood of nihilistic recklessness that she mistook, in the moment, for a detached and almost numinous clarity. She was also somewhat drunk.

This was the end of March, when the weather can be so shifty and unpredictable. In the morning it had been warm and dry, and she'd biked into town for the funeral with nothing more than a light jacket. It was the first funeral she'd ever been to. She hadn't seen Nora in days, had hardly even spoken to her on the phone, and was longing to be alone with her, but they never had the chance. Nora in those days was keeping her head down and keeping mostly to herself. She and Keith had broken up months back by then, when Nora had been feeling oppressed and depressed by the very smallness of the small town they were stuck in. She had told him she was tired of doing nothing but getting drunk and high with his buddies every weekend, and that had sounded in his ears like she was saying that she was getting tired of him.

HALF THE TOWN had turned out for the service. By the time Casey arrived, the pews were filled with people, and she couldn't see Nora or her family anywhere. There seemed to be nowhere for her to fit in, and she took a seat at the very back, along the aisle, close to the exit, feeling meek and out of place. Everyone was dressed in suits and fancy dresses, as if for a wedding; she was wearing jeans and a t-shirt.

It was Matt who spotted her, sitting alone back there, and came over to her, first crouching down and asking in a gentle voice how she was holding up. She shrugged, unsure how to answer; she knew that she ought to be feeling sad about Alma, but when she tried to think of Alma she only felt a sort of deep-seated numbness: another reason to believe that there must be something wrong with her. The only thing she really felt was that she missed Nora, and wanted to see Nora, and when she thought of Nora then, to her surprise, her eyes did get wet and her lip quivered, and Matt must have thought she was going to cry about Alma, and with his broad hand he gently covered her hand and said, "It's okay." She felt like a fraud. He insisted that she come up to the front with him and sit with the rest of the family.

The coffin was piled up with a wild profusion of exotic flowers, a crazy heap of colours. There was still no sign of Nora, Tracy, or their parents; it was Louise who explained to her that they were waiting in a back room and would come out just when the service was due to start. She was looking terribly ill, Louise was, tired to the bone: the skin on her face was taut and translucent, you could see the blood pulsing weakly past her temples, and her cracked lips were the colour of a dead dry leaf. She had lost all her hair to chemotherapy, and wore a black scarf to cover her skull. Just to say a few kind gentle sentences, and smile weakly, and lay a sympathetic hand on Casey's arm seemed to take as much strength as she could muster.

The service, when it finally started, droned on for what felt like forever. Nora's father cried throughout, to everyone's surprise and embarrassment: not gentle tears, either, but ugly, compulsive sobbing, at times almost blubbering. Drunk, obviously. Nora's mother sat next to him with her lips pursed tightly and her round body held rigid, clenched like a fist. Nora was looking more striking than ever in a plain black dress: pouting slightly, sullen, never looking at her parents or anybody else but holding her sister's hand and staring into the middle distance. The overcrowded church was airless and hot, thick with the stewing smell of flowers, perfume, and fresh sweat.

After the service was finally over, there was a reception in the church basement, crowded with old people eating finger sandwiches, drinking coffee, and chatting quietly with a kind of lightly suppressed cheerfulness. Here at last Casey thought she'd have her chance to be with Nora, but she was wrong, she couldn't get in more than one quick hug and a few stupid words, for Nora was locked up behind a glass wall of dutiful politeness, repeating the same handful of meaningless phrases as person after person shuffled up to express their condolences and trap her into awkward, stilted conversations. And Casey, feeling defeated and claustrophobic, tried to slip out unnoticed, but Matt must have spotted her, and caught up with her outside the church as she was unlocking her bike, and persuaded her not to leave, not yet.

The weather had changed while they were inside the church: the sky was dark, the air chilly, and the ground was slick with a thick, cold drizzle that was just starting to turn to fat wet snowflakes. Before long, Matt promised, they'd all be going back to Nora's house for another, smaller reception, just for family and close friends, and Casey ought to be there. He and Louise would drive her home safely when it was all over, they'd put her bike in the back of his truck, she didn't need to worry.

It must have been around seven in the evening that he came and found Casey again and asked if it was okay if they left right away, Louise wasn't feeling well. "I suppose I could take her home first and come back for you later," he suggested, but Casey was more than ready to leave.

Just before Christmas that year, Louise had had surgery to remove a malignant tumour from her colon, followed by a course of aggressive chemotherapy. The tumour had become quite large before she allowed it to be diagnosed: she had tried for a long time to hide or disguise the symptoms, the fact of her sickness, from herself as well as others. She didn't know what was happening to her body, but she found it particularly shameful; except for the weight loss and the blood-streaked shit, it reminded her in some ways of when she had been pregnant with Mark: the nausea and vomiting, the heartburn, the gas pains and the foul humiliating farts, the stomach cramps that were sometimes so intense she would have to steady herself against a wall or table, twisting and wincing and holding her breath.

For the sake of others, she had tried to maintain a dutiful façade of optimism before and after the surgery. She apologized too much, too often, to everyone around her; she knew it, but she couldn't seem to help herself. She thanked people excessively, almost oppressively, for any small kindness. The kindness of her husband and her sons in particular made her want to cry. Now, at the funeral, Louise felt especially ashamed of herself that she couldn't be stronger. It had required a tremendous effort just to be there and to appear as calm and as well as she possibly could so that she could try to be a comfort to the family, or at the very least not a burden or distraction. That effort cost her more than anyone could have possibly imagined. For throughout the service, she had been possessed by the strange, disconcerting conviction that she was witnessing her own funeral. Later, at the family gathering at Nora's house, she was still troubled by that same notion: that she was already dead, that she was a ghost spying on her own funeral. She knew that it was nonsense, and yet it was so persistent, it felt so real: then there was the frightening thought that perhaps she was losing her mind on top of it all. She began swaying on her feet, her eyes drifting in and out of focus, and the conversation she was trying to politely follow was becoming mere sound, a kind of sinister gibberish all around her. Feeling horribly selfish, weak, and defeated, she finally gave in to Matt, who had been quietly urging her to let him take her home for over an hour by then.

They took her home first, before driving Casey out to the farm. Matt asked Casey if she minded waiting a few minutes while he took Louise upstairs and helped her get settled. A few minutes ended up being more like fifteen or twenty. The house was quiet and dimly lit. When Matt came downstairs at last, instead of taking her home right away, he offered her a drink and a cigarette, and they sat and talked in hushed voices, sitting close so they could hear one another. He spoke to her, not like he was talking to a child, but to a friend, as one adult to another: that was flattering, and gratifying. It was then that Casey had what she thought was a moment of clarity, that she understood clearly not just how he was looking at her right now, but how he had often looked at her over the past year or two, letting his gaze linger on her with palpable desire, and she marvelled that she had never really perceived it before, when it ought to have been obvious all along. Of course she knew his reputation. Then she understood that they were going to make love, that it was finally, really going to happen; the idea presented itself to her, not as if she had any choice in the matter, not as if it required any kind of decision on her part, but as a fait accompli that she was, in the moment, more than willing to accept. The idea of doing it with him, doing it here and now, with his wife right upstairs so deathly sick and Alma's funeral still going on across town, seemed at once horrible and horribly exciting. It seemed a perversely fitting setting for her first time. And then, too, there was an obscure and satisfying thought that Nora would be disgusted and outraged if she knew—satisfying in the moment because, even though she knew it was utterly unfair, Casey was angry at Nora for hardly speaking to her all day. But Nora would never know; and if making love to Matt was, among other things, a way of lashing out at her friend, it would always be a secret one, Nora would never know. Just as it had happened that night in the truck with Duane, she uncoiled herself suddenly and stretched over and started kissing him, abruptly, aggressively; unlike Duane, he knew what to do, and didn't pull away.

The need to keep quiet led them to make muffled, poorly-suppressed panting noises. The couch started to squeak so they moved clumsily to the carpet. His hand between her legs was intensely, almost painfully pleasurable. He made no effort to be gentle; probably he had no idea it was her first time. Then instead of painfully pleasurable it was just painful, and she had a kind of panic attack when she felt him push inside her, and the weight of his body pressing on top of her, pinning her down; and it was all she could do not to cry out, and he covered her mouth with his mouth as if to swallow any sounds that might escape her, and she dug her teeth into his tongue. That seemed to even excite him, and with a feeling of tremendous relief and release she dug her heels into his legs and hammered at his back with her fists, free of restraint, and though it was still somewhat painful it was pleasurable again, and the more pleasure she felt the more freely she punched and kicked and scratched at him, all the while kissing and nipping at him aggressively, and he got more and more excited, and then it was over abruptly. The only thing that spoiled her sense of triumph and satisfaction was the immediate aftermath, the way he kept kissing her face tenderly, gasping for air, and whispering sentimentally in her ear about how wonderful she was: that was the part that really made her hate herself.

MATT MAY OR NOT have been Adelaide's father: it was a possibility, but only a possibility, one that Casey was always reluctant to admit even to herself, and that no one else ever really suspected; but all of that was more than a year away, anyway. For now, between that night, the night of Alma's funeral, and when Casey and Nora graduated high school and moved away to Winnipeg to go to university, Casey and Matt had sex a total of nine times.

Having said yes the first time, it didn't occur to her that she had any right to say no the next. She felt trapped and there was no one she could possibly talk to about it, no one to give her advice or even mere sympathy. Nora would have told her how to feel and what to do, but she couldn't possibly tell Nora. In fact she was terrified of Nora ever finding out, terrified of Nora even suspecting in the slightest, scared that it would damage their friendship irreparably, and then she would be completely lost, she'd have nothing to even live for.

Every time that Casey rode her bike to town or back, alone along the back dirt roads or the shoulder of the highway, she felt an oppressive dread that Matt's truck would pull up alongside her, or appear around the next bend ahead of her, and that he would open the cab door and cajole her to come with him. There was a furnished but untenanted apartment in one of the apartment blocks that he owned, and that he kept for himself, for these and similar occasions. He even gave her a key to it, and said she should think of it as hers from now on, and that she could come make use of it any time she wanted to, even if she only just needed to be alone.

Had he wanted to make use of her solely for sexual purposes, she wouldn't have minded, or at least that was what she told herself. The physical act itself was not only pleasurable, it provided the only outlet, the only sense of release and relief, however fleeting, that she could find in those days for her bruised and constricted state of mind, so that she ended up almost craving the very thing that was causing her so much misery. No, what made the whole situation intolerable, truly intolerable, was that Matt kept insisting that he had fallen desperately, deeply in love with her: an assertion so stupid and baffling it overwhelmed her with waves of helpless rage.

He would tell her how beautiful she was: how perfect her body, so slender and yet so strong, so sinuous and lithe; how lovely her delicate and feline face, how infinitely beautiful her deep, wide, hazel eyes, with their shifting and dazzling flecks of green and gold. And because Casey believed that none of those things were really true or sincere, she felt only humiliated by all his compliments, as if they were actually subtle and cunning insults.

He told her that she looked exactly as he had always imagined Joan of Arc; he said he liked to picture her wearing armour and holding a sword, beautiful, grim, and terrifying: "And if you said you wanted to cut my head off with that sword, I'd kneel down, bare my neck, and ask of thee thy blessing."

"I feel so young when I'm with you," he would say. "I feel so powerful. You make me feel so strong I could pull whole trees out of the ground with my bare hands." He liked to pretend that she was mysterious, enigmatic, and wise beyond her years. "What really goes on behind those beautiful eyes of yours, I wonder?" he would say, musingly, tenderly; or, repulsively, "I feel like there's so much that I have to learn from you, so much that you can teach me."

He spoke sometimes of sensing a sadness in her that reached far beyond her mere self, as if she were a direct conduit to all the ancient and compacted grief of the earth itself: he enjoyed giving her lyrical, incomprehensible compliments like that, as if she were not actually a person, just the personification of something.

He even spoke once or twice of wanting to marry her, to start a family with her, and then he would gently, lovingly caress her stomach as if she were already pregnant: that was terrifying. He admitted they would have to wait a little while after Louise passed away, of course, just out of respect—six months, maybe even a year, but then they could really be together. In those days it still seemed as if Louise was bound to die any day, she seemed so close to death already, no one expected her to make the recovery that she did.

And Matt in moments like those would boast to Casey of how much money he had, and of the life that he could give her. If she wanted, they could travel the world: see the mountains, see the oceans; anything her heart desired, anything at all. When Matt would say such things to her, almost always in the languid and, to him, pleasantly melancholic afterglow of love-making, he always seemed serenely confident that she would feel, that she *was* feeling, gratified, exalted, greedy, and smitten. He could somehow look straight at her and not see her at all, not see the way that her eyes would be glazed over with pained, dull, and sullen distress, unhappy and trapped; he could see only an adorable and adoring reflection of his own idiotic and overpowering infatuation.

The only thing that made the situation endurable at all for Casey was the certainty that it would soon be over, by necessity: soon she would be moving away, out of his reach, moving to Winnipeg with Nora to go to university. Everything was planned, everything was settled, everything was certain; and then she would be able to escape from this whole strange nightmare that she had somehow stumbled into.

27

Nora and Casey come home for Christmas;
on New Year's Eve there are northern lights

NORA AND CASEY ARRIVED BACK in Whittle on the twenty-first
of December. The bus was over an hour late. It had snowed heavily
that morning. Blowing snow poured back and forth above the
surface of the road, sinuous, swift, shifting, and treacherous; sometimes, along the side of the road, the wind would spin the snow
swirling up into the air like a dust devil, ghostly and luminescent.
And the clouds were torn to shreds in the sky above, and the sky
was spattered with bright cold stars, and the moon was squatting
above the trees, fat and bright, and the bare trees groveled in the
blasts of wind.

It was Tracy who met them at the bus station. She had taken
over Nora's job at the truck stop when Nora had moved to
Winnipeg; now they found her sitting at the counter with a plate
of mostly eaten lemon meringue pie, with Anthony Shaw on
one side of her and James Ritchie on the other, and one of them
must have been saying something pretty funny because she was
laughing raucously, her curly auburn hair bouncing crazily, and
the corners of her eyes were crinkled up delightfully and her whole
face glowed. And Anthony and James both were delighted to look
at her, and Tracy was delighted to be looked at. She seemed almost
disappointed that the bus had finally arrived.

Casey spent that first night at Nora's house. That familiar home,
with its pink and pockmarked stucco façade and a wreath in the
ship's-wheel window next to the front door, the same plastic wreath

with its tattered red bow that had hung in that same window every Christmas Casey had known them—the house itself looked smaller and dingier than she had seemed to remember it. In the corner the Christmas tree was up, covered with ornaments that Nora, Tracy, and Casey had made at school over the years: pipe-cleaner candy canes, gold-painted macaroni pasted to cardboard stars, angels made of toilet paper rolls. Hanging from the mantel of the bricked-up fireplace were all their stockings, including the one that Nora's grandmother had herself embroidered Casey's name on; atop the mantel sat the same old nativity scene, the familiar wooden barn with the plaster people and farm animals in pious tableau, including the headless Joseph, decapitated many years ago when being carelessly boxed away on New Year's Day.

Pudge lay curled up cozily on that faded yellow and red armchair where Alma used to always sit. When Nora came into the room, the cat lifted her head and looked up, at first lazily and as if barely interested, her eyes narrowed to slits, and then, recognizing an old friend, mriaowing to reproach her for being away so long and consenting to hop down from the chair and cross the room to greet her. She left behind her, on the seat, many months' worth of matted fur, forming a sort of white and tan blanket.

Nora's mother had prepared a big meal to celebrate their homecoming, and then had insisted on keeping it waiting, warmed over, until they finally arrived: an overdressed salad all soggy and wilting at the edges; carrots that had been boiled down to a sticky orange paste, served lukewarm; potatoes that had burned to the bottom of the roasting pan and were then scraped off; and a roast chicken, heavily dusted with decade-old sage, the skin tight and leathery as a bat's wing, the meat dry, flavourless, and difficult to chew.

Nora's father, who had spent the day ploughing driveways all over town, before being made to wait more than two hours for his dinner, was over-hungry, over-tired, and as petulant as a toddler. He had filled the time by downing glass after glass of eggnog, heavily laced with rum; he sat at the table in front of his conspicuously empty plate, his head sunk into his hunched-up shoulders, his face all blotchy and pouchy, his eyes glazed over, and his lower lip—covered with a film of yellowy-white eggnog—jutting out in a grotesque pout.

"Well," Lynn said, with a kind of breathy, self-deprecating laugh, "I was beginning to think you weren't coming, after all. Thought maybe you'd changed your mind and didn't bother to tell us."

She had put on even more weight since they had last seen her: she seemed not so much fat as inflated, or swollen like a boil, and Casey's eyes were constantly drawn to her forearm, fascinated and horrified by the way her thin silver watchband dug into the flesh of her fat wrist, she wore it so tight; and the skin on her arm was all taut and smooth, like a pink balloon.

Tracy, with irrepressible good cheer, loudly announced how awful the food was. "I'm sorry," she said, spitting a scrap of half-chewed chicken into her napkin. "I'm sorry, I can't swallow that." And she burst out laughing, as if it was the best joke she'd heard in a long while.

"It's not that bad," said Nora irritably, though it actually was.

"You want it, then?" said Tracy, holding the napkin out to her, and laughed again.

Their mother tried to pass it off by laughing, too, a forced and false laugh that was almost a whinny; but her face turned all mottled with red spots and her breast swelled and she was breathing heavily. "Well," she said, "that's what happens when some people are two hours late for dinner, I suppose…"

"Jesus Christ, Mom, it's not like we were driving the bus," said Nora. "You could've started without us."

"Oh, don't worry about me," said Lynn. "I just thought it would be nice to have a dinner with the family all together again. Silly, I know."

"Now tell me," said Simon abruptly, washing a mouthful of mushy carrots down with a sip of wine, "how are your parents doing?"

It took Casey a moment to realize that he was speaking to her. She had a piece of chicken in her mouth that she had been chewing for some time, without much progress; she took a drink of wine, too, and swallowed it painfully like an oversized pill. "They're fine," she said meekly.

"I'm glad to hear it," he said solemnly. "Be sure to give them our regards."

Lynn said to Nora, "Well, I suppose you must be looking forward to seeing all your *friends*, at least."

It was true that Nora had been looking forward to seeing all her old friends again, and catching up, especially Alyssa, who had moved to Toronto to go to university. Only, as it turned out, Alyssa wasn't coming home for Christmas that year, and Tracy almost vibrated in her chair with the excitement of telling them the gossip: Alyssa was staying in Toronto to spend Christmas with her *girlfriend*. They wouldn't believe this, but Alyssa had turned into a lesbian!

"Or I guess she always was one," Tracy corrected herself, laughing: "You know what I mean." She had found herself, or come out to herself or however you called it, when she'd gone away to university. "Anthony says he always suspected, that really he knew all along, but I think he's lying. Did *you* know?"

"I should hope not," said Lynn primly.

"What does that mean?" asked Nora, nettled.

"All *I'm* saying is I feel sorry for her parents. She seemed like such a nice girl, too. This is what comes from moving to a place like Toronto, there are all kinds of bad influences out there."

In the other room, the phone began to ring, and Tracy almost spilled her chair over backwards, leaping up from the table and darting off to answer it.

"Tell them you're eating dinner with your *family* and you can't talk now," Lynn called out to her.

Nora said, "How do you know it's for Tracy?"

"It's always for Tracy," said her father solemnly. "*Al*ways."

From the next room they could hear the sound of Tracy chattering brightly into the telephone, punctuated by yet another burst of laughter.

THIS WAS THE FIRST CHRISTMAS since Alma had passed away, the first Christmas without her. Away in Winnipeg, it had seemed to Nora that her grandmother had died a long, long time ago, another lifetime almost; but as soon as she stepped back into her old house, then it was as if her grandmother had died just the other day, and grief was a hard hot lump in the middle of her chest that made her angry.

The old woman's absence was present everywhere: in that faded yellow and red armchair that no one else had sat in since but that no one had the heart to suggest moving or throwing away; in the absence of Christmas baking, the gingerbread and shortbread cookies, the vinaterta and butter tarts, the heat from the always busy stove and the smells of cinnamon, cloves, cardamom, and molasses that used to suffuse the house all through the holidays; in the absence of her voice, prim, mild, and good-humoured, leading them in faintly embarrassing prayer around the dinner table, or fussing over her grandchildren's table manners, or chiding her son-in-law for drinking too much: all gone, and all so overwhelmingly vivid in its absence; and all that absence drove Nora, who had not yet learned how to grieve, into a frenzy of thin-skinned irritability that she felt helpless to control.

It was a bitterly cold night, the coldest yet that year. Fists of wind battered at Nora's bedroom windows, the cold leaked and seeped and slithered across her floor, the decrepit old space-heater buzzed and popped and sizzled ominously all night, and stank of burning dust.

THE NEXT MORNING, Nora borrowed her mother's Toyota and they drove out to Casey's farm. They had to leave the car at the side of the road and trudge in up the long and curving driveway that was choked with great drifts and sweeps of snow. The tall, skinny aspen stretched their thin bare branches up toward the pale blue sky, and the bright low sun dazzled off the snow and sliced into their eyes. Everything was quiet except for the scrunching of their boots in the snow. Three fist-sized shadows passed over their heads and flitted rapidly across the field as a trio of birds flew by above.

The old farmhouse had an air of sleepy dereliction, but for the thin white smoke that seeped from the chimney. Casey's parents had shovelled out wide and tidy footpaths from the house to the barn, the stables, and the chicken coop, but had left both their vehicles half-buried beneath the snow.

Letting themselves into the mudroom, they found Rumpel and Monk curled up together on an old blanket, heavy with the lethargy of boredom. Rumpel's full name was Rumpelstiltskin, so named for his disproportionately short, stumpy legs under his big, thick, barrel-like body, and for his oversized head, lumpy as a ten-pound bag of potatoes. Monk, all sleek and black, got his name because he never barked or growled, even under his breath, as though he had taken a solemn vow of silence. They were both excited to see Casey, and leapt up to welcome her home, their excited panting filling the little room, their nails scrabbling on the unfinished plywood floor, Monk pushing his head against Casey's ribs and snuffling and licking at her hand and wrist, Rumpel hopping on all fours in that funny way he had, his stumpy tail wagging manically, and he let out two low, booming barks of delight: *bouf, bouf.*

No person came to greet them. In the kitchen, a pot of her mother's onion soup was simmering patiently, giving off a dark, warm, almost malty aroma that brought memories of winter childhood surging up in Casey's mind. And Nora said, "They must be out in the barn or something." And Casey shrugged and said, "I guess." She dropped her duffel bag down by the table. She was about to offer to make some coffee, when they both noticed the sounds coming from deeper in the house: a distant wheezing noise, and something not unlike the panting of the dogs in the mudroom, and the occasional slapping sound, and creaking boards, and ghostly, muffled grunts and moans.

Nora made a face at Casey, dropping her jaw in exaggerated, pantomime horror, and mouthed the words: "Oh. My. God. Your parents are *fucking*."

Casey's body stiffened like a startled bird, ready to burst into flight. It was all she could do to keep from turning around and running blindly out of the house.

Now that they had noticed and identified the sound, it was unmistakable. Nora put one hand to her mouth to stifle a laugh. She was at once shocked and titillated. It was the middle of the day, it was eleven o'clock in the morning. "They *must* have heard us come in," she whispered in wonderment. They must have at least heard Rumpel barking, surely.

"Let's go say hello to the horses," whispered Casey, and Nora agreed. Standing there listening any longer would have been intolerable. As they were leaving the kitchen they could hear, overlapping the other sounds, a burst of staccato, strangulated, and ecstatic cries, and they closed the door quickly to cut off the noise.

THAT NIGHT, and every night over those Christmas holidays, Casey slept so well. She slept like the dead, alone in her cold little room, some nights for twelve or thirteen hours. The silence was almost perfect: the only sound would be the sound of the house itself breathing, the muffled rumble and wheeze of the furnace. The darkness was so dark it was almost palpable: thick and soft, it swaddled tightly around her, and she would tumble down deeply, almost immediately into lovely, dreamless sleep. In the mornings she would get out of bed stretching like a cat, luxuriating in the sensation of being well and truly rested.

She spent hours every day with her father in the stables, helping him tend to the mares in companionable silence, breathing in the warm wet air, heavy with the smell of straw and dung. She'd smoke a cigarette with him in the yard, hunched up against the cold, while the dogs snuffled at their legs, their noses white with frost. He seemed happy to have her around again, though she noticed sadly that he had lost the habit of eating in front of her, and could only pick at his food bashfully in her presence; and so she would tactfully absent herself at mealtimes, go take a bath, or check on the hens, or say she had something to do in her room, so that he would be able to eat.

In the evenings, she would sit near him and watch the hockey game, with the sound turned off, while her mother brushed out her hair. And Casey found that if she didn't look in her father's direction, then out of the corner of her eye she could see him smiling at her, fondly. She noticed too that when he watched the game, he squinted at the television set: his eyesight was certainly getting worse.

And Casey noticed that her mother had put on a little weight—not much, just barely enough to notice. It suited her, Casey thought: she looked healthier, more content. And there were a few strands of grey mingled in her magnificent red hair, and there were wrinkles on her face: not many and not deep but definitely there, crow's feet and bunny lines and crinkles at the corners of her mouth. Maybe they had been there for a while, and Casey had just never noticed them before; either way, it seemed to Casey that they suited her, too, they made her seem more human somehow.

CHRISTMAS DINNER was at Bonnie and Geoff's house that year. Matt and Louise were there, too, of course. Louise looked so much healthier than she had the year before. Her hair had started to grow back in, now completely white, and the colour had returned to her skin and the life had returned to her eyes. It was good to see, too, how Matt fussed over her fondly, and looked at her and spoke to her so lovingly, and even flirted with her a little, as if

they were a young couple again. Casey took note of it, and felt
relieved, and happy for Louise, and pleased with Matt: almost,
oddly, proud of him. Her eyes kept lingering on the two of them,
with pleasure, and when, later in the evening—by then she'd drunk
a great deal of wine—later in the evening when Matt managed
to get a few moments alone with her, she didn't feel the sense of
dread she had expected when she'd thought about this moment
over the past few days.

After a few conventional and desultory questions about her
life in Winnipeg, as if to feel out how she would respond to him,
Matt asked her quietly if she still had the key he had given her to
that apartment. She found herself saying, "I do. Did you want to
take it back from me?" in a flirtatious tone of voice, or as close to
flirtatious as she had ever come.

It had been six months since Casey had ended her affair with
Matt. Only of course she had never exactly ended it, she had never
managed to find the courage for that, she had just moved away
and let it end itself. In Winnipeg, it had seemed to Casey that
all of that had happened to her a long, long time ago, another
lifetime almost; but as soon as she was back in Whittle, and then
again when she saw him, then it was almost as if no time had
passed at all.

Except in her memory, by some strange alchemy, she could
hardly recall how miserable she had been at the time, how trapped
and unhappy she had felt, but now just vividly remembered, or
perhaps partly imagined, the excitement she had felt at doing
something secret and illicit, and the physical pleasure of the sex
itself. She told herself now what had probably only been partially
true then, that if Matt hadn't been idiotic enough to imagine that
he was falling in love with her and start babbling about a future
together, and if she hadn't been terrified of Nora finding out, she
wouldn't have had anything to feel unhappy about at all. Now, she
thought, things could be different: now with Louise getting well
and Casey herself living at a safe distance in Winnipeg, maybe

she and Matt could just have an occasional escapade with only the fun, and none of the intolerable parts.

ON NEW YEAR'S EVE there were northern lights. Casey spotted them first through her bedroom window, then went outside to watch them from the yard. It was a cloudless sky, a new moon, and a still and frigid night. At first it was just a flicker of pale green here, a flare of pale green there, and then they were gone, so that you almost wondered if you'd really seen them. Then it was a shimmering, flickering pillar of light that unfolded outwards, and unfolded outward again, so that it became a curtain of light across the sky, billowing in a celestial wind: sometimes pale green, sometimes pale blue, sometimes a ghostly white that was also almost pink. And then it wasn't a curtain of light, but a waterfall of light pouring down the sky, and then it was shimmering and fading away, once again a flicker of light here, a flare of light there, spectral and elusive.

Her father joined her to watch the northern lights in companionable silence. He lit them each a cigarette. The dogs snuffled and panted, circling restlessly on the hard-packed snow. And there was a flare of white light high above the horizon that seemed as if it was going to fade out, and then instead of fading it spread into a thin shimmering line that crossed the sky, and then a shudder ran across the length of the line from right to left, and it spilled out more light, green and blue and pink pale light that washed across the sky, like sheets of rain streaming down a windshield. And then it was like waves lapping gently at the edge of a lake, waves of light washing in and then gently pulling away. And for several glorious minutes it seemed to Casey that she could even *hear* those lights, a sound that wasn't quite humming, and wasn't quite singing, but was always perfectly in sync with the ebb and flow of the aurora. And then a black arm swept across the sky, sweeping the northern lights away, and then there was nothing but a blacker-than-blackness, embedded with stars.

epilogue

MATT MAY OR NOT HAVE BEEN Addy's father: it was a possibility, but only a possibility, one that Casey was always reluctant to admit even to herself, and that no one else ever really suspected.

Maybe it was meaningful that Casey's parents never tried to shame her, or berate her, or pity her, for getting pregnant at nineteen. Not only that, they never once asked her who Addy's father was, or even betrayed so much as the mildest curiosity. Kenneth would never, of course, Casey could have predicted that: with his mix of invincible shyness and delicacy, he must have found the mere idea of asking her excruciating. But Maureen didn't have a shy nor a delicate bone in her body. Not that Casey would have told her anything, but she might have appreciated the opportunity to refuse to answer, or maybe even concoct some outrageous and transparent lie. Perhaps it was precisely to deny Casey that satisfaction that Maureen showed no interest whatsoever in the identity of Addy's father; perhaps she thought she already knew; or perhaps, as Casey sadly suspected, she really just wasn't interested and couldn't be bothered to pretend that she cared.

She never could bear to sleep in the same bed, or even the same room, as her baby. This started as soon as they had come home from the hospital. Then they had no choice but to share a room, the apartment was far too small to do anything else. She didn't even own a crib or bassinet. Sleeping next to her infant daughter, Casey would have the most horrible nightmares.

These dreams were always essentially the same: she was always desperately, punishingly hungry, no matter how much she ate; and in her dreams she never did anything *but* eat. She was always on her hands and knees, on the floor of the apartment or out on the street, eating like a starving dog, gobbling and gulping: fancy cakes and hunks of bread, fat greasy hamburgers and fried chicken, oranges that she would eat peel and all and the juice would dribble down her face. She would attack the food with a compulsive and terrifying ferocity, breathing heavily through her nose as she'd use both hands to cram it into her mouth, tearing and gobbling, veins bulging in her forehead and neck, eyes straining white, only lifting her head now and then to take long deep swallows of air, arching her back. And no matter how much she ate, she only felt hungrier and hungrier. She felt as if she could swallow the whole world and still be hungry. Sometimes, if she ran out of food in her dreams, she would start eating anything she could get her hands on, no matter how disgusting: old coffee grounds and banana peels that she spilled out of the garbage can, strips of paper that she tore out of books, balls of used kleenex, the stuffing from a couch cushion that she tore open with her teeth. Or if she was outside, she would eat grass and dead leaves and handfuls of dirt and clumps of thistle that she scrabbled out of the ground, digging at the hard dirt until her fingers bled. She ate old cigarette butts out of the coffee can in the courtyard, scooping them out and cramming them greedily into her mouth, her face red and her whole body straining and shaking with the effort to chew and swallow them. And in the end she would even begin eating herself, tearing a chunk of flesh from her bicep and swallowing it whole, slippery and warm, then gnawing and sucking at the open wound: and though the pain was excruciating, yet in her dreams it would also be the best thing she had ever tasted in her life, salty and rusty and warm and delicious, and she never wanted to stop. After these nightmares, Casey would always wake more tired than when she'd gone to sleep, her sheets and blankets drenched with sweat and the incision in her stomach inflamed, seething and itching and angry and red, and she would feel filthy, disgusted, used, and ashamed. And Addy at her side would be sleeping sweetly, making solemn little sucking motions with her mouth.

MAUREEN TOLD HER about a woman she knew, or used to know, who after the trauma of giving birth—a long and difficult labour ending, like Casey's, in a caesarean section—after the trauma of giving birth, she fell into the curious delusion that her face had been surreptitiously and surgically replaced while she lay unconscious in the hospital, and that everyone was lying to her about it, including her doctor, her husband, her siblings, and her parents. For many months the delusion was so strong it was even violent: tears, tantrums, threats and accusations. Whether she ever fully recovered, by means of therapy, medication, and above all the simple passage of time, or whether she merely learned to dissemble, Maureen couldn't say for sure; what was very certain was that even years later, a shudder would ripple through her if she caught a glimpse, unprepared, of her face in a mirror.

Maureen had also heard tell of a woman who gave birth to twins, identical twins, happy healthy girls, almost six pounds each. The next day, still in hospital, the nurses brought her both babies to be breastfed; and after seeing that they had successfully latched on, left the woman alone to feed them in private. When they returned in half an hour, they found that the mother and one of her twins had fallen asleep, and were dozing beatifically; the other infant had been replaced by a doll, with a cloth soft body stitched into a pink onesie, and a hairless head molded out of slightly pliable plastic. The doll's mouth was formed into a permanent, slightly open pucker that the woman had fitted over her nipple; milk had pooled down the side of her body, and onto the bedsheets, and soaked into the doll's cloth body. When they tried to take the doll away, the woman screamed hysterically. No one ever found out what happened to the real baby, or who took it.

Casey herself was unable to breastfeed. Whether because of the c-section, the premature birth, or for some other unknown reason, she just couldn't seem to produce milk. It had been a difficult and dangerous labour. One of the twins inside of her had been already dead, the umbilical cord wrapped around her little neck, and the doctors figured she'd been dead for about an hour before they took her out. Casey named her Adelaide. And the other one was alive and well and born with a mess of sticky, sodden red hair and her green eyes already open, and Casey named her Madeline. At least, those were the names that Casey meant to give each of them, but when it came time to fill out the paperwork somehow she got mixed up, and she accidentally named the dead girl Madeline, and the living one Adelaide, and that was Addy.

Acknowledgments

My foreword is modeled closely on Shi Nai'an's foreword (if indeed he wrote it) to *Shui Hu Zhuan* (*The Water Margin*, trans. J.H. Jackson, Tuttle Publishing 2010). It also contains tips of the hat to Joseph Conrad (the preface to *Chance*) and Li Po's "Exile's Letter" in the Ezra Pound translation.

In chapters 22 & 23, the girls quote liberally (and not always precisely) from the writings of Isak Dinesen: "Did the son of the Sultan like the sauce of the pig?" is from *Out of Africa* (Penguin Books, 1982, p. 44), as are "She is a Hottentot. But I want her." (ibid, p. 255) and the references to brazen-serpenting, "Honourable Lioness," and Lulu.

"How did they know which was the front and which was the back?" refers to the story "The Monkey" in *Seven Gothic Tales* (Vintage Books, 1972, p. 131).

Lucan and Zosine are the central characters in that very peculiar novel *The Angelic Avengers*, published under the name Pierre Andrézel, from whence comes the quote (the exact wording of which Casey misremembers), "You serious people must not be too hard on human beings for what they choose to amuse themselves with when they are shut up as in a prison, and are not even allowed to say that they are prisoners. If I do not soon get a little bit of fun, I shall die." (Random House, 1946, p. 110).

Portions of this book were written while in residency at Deep Bay Cabin in Riding Mountain National Park, with the generous support of the Manitoba Arts Council. I would also like to thank Miriam Toews, for confusing me with David Scott, who might or might not have enjoyed this story if he was still around to read it, but I wish he was; the incredibly supportive and enthusiastic team at Great Plains Publications: Mel Marginet, Keith Cadieux, and my wonderful editor, Catharina de Bakker; and above all my family, Sarah, Agnes, and Henry, without whose patience, support, and senses of humour it would have been impossible to write, and without whose presence it would have been pointless.